PRAISE FOR CAROLYN HAINES

"A writer of exceptional talent."
—*Milwaukee Journal Sentinel* on *Them Bones*

"Southern storytelling is indeed a very special art form."
—*New York Times Book Review* on *The Darkling*

"Written with a languid sensuality, this rich and complex work features quirky, fully developed characters involved in an unpredictable story, with Mattie's long-awaited revenge providing a bittersweet but satisfying coda."
—*Publishers Weekly* on *Touched*

"So vivid, so energetic, so poignant that it seems to move on reels rather than pages."
—*Chicago Tribune* on *Touched*

"Like the heat of a Deep South summer, Ms. Haines's novel has an undeniable intensity; it's impossible to shake its brooding atmosphere."
—*New York Times Book Review* on *Touched*

THE BOOK OF
BELOVED

OTHER NOVELS
BY CAROLYN HAINES

Deception

Summer of the Redeemers

Touched

Judas Burning

Penumbra

Fever Moon

Revenant

Skin Dancer

Shop Talk

Greedy Bones

Bones Appétit

Bones of a Feather

Bonefire of the Vanities

Smarty Bones

Booty Bones

Bone to Be Wild

Rock-a-Bye Bones

Sarah Booth Delaney Mysteries

Them Bones

Buried Bones

Splintered Bones

Crossed Bones

Hallowed Bones

Bones to Pick

Ham Bones

Wishbones

Writing as R. B. Chesterton

The Darkling

The Seeker

A
PLUTO'S SNITCH MYSTERY

THE BOOK OF
BELOVED

USA TODAY BESTSELLING AUTHOR

CAROLYN HAINES

 THOMAS & MERCER

Published by Thomas & Mercer, Seattle

www.apub.com

Amazon, the Amazon logo, and Thomas & Mercer are trademarks of Amazon.com, Inc., or its affiliates.

ISBN-13: 9781503938069
ISBN-10: 1503938069

Cover design by M. S. Corley

Printed in the United States of America

For Eugene Walter, a ghost now himself.
He is always near as I feed the horses, chase the cats, or
stand beneath the tallow tree when the leaves quake
and the spirits are walking.
He gave me the seed of this story, and so much more.

"Now I know what a ghost is . . . Unfinished business, that's what."

—Salman Rushdie, *The Satanic Verses*

CHAPTER ONE

In Savannah, Georgia, two things could be counted on without question—the heat of summer and Alfred the mail carrier's regular arrival six days a week. I had come to anticipate his knock at four each afternoon, as regular as the milkman and the daily newspaper delivery. I looked forward to Alfred's arrival, not because I carried on a great correspondence with anyone, but because I needed regularity, routine. Death had taught me the power and stabilizing influence of routine. Alfred's arrival meant the world continued in an ordered fashion.

I opened the door and accepted the single letter he offered. "You're looking well, Miss Raissa. I suspect you're as happy to be out of the schoolroom as the students are."

"Yes, summer break is much appreciated. Remember to hold my mail beginning tomorrow. I'll stop by the post office when I return to let you know." Of course, everyone already knew about my pending travels. Savannah, for all its big-city attitude, was in many ways still a small town.

"Yes, ma'am. I'll take care of it. Mrs. Wheaton is going to Boston to visit her nephew, so I'm holding her mail, too. It seems her sister has been having a hard time of it." He made a sympathetic face. "Nerves, they say. Some form of female hysteria. Now you have a safe trip and a good visit."

The solid weight of the letter promised an Event, the kind with a capital *E*. My kindhearted uncle wanted to distract me from what he viewed as my overlong mourning. I'd been a widow now longer than I'd been a wife, and Uncle Brett felt it was his duty to drag me back to the land of the living. Still holding the vellum envelope addressed to me in a flowing hand, I walked out onto the porch of my small Savannah cottage.

The sweet scent of wisteria filled the peaceful air, and down the block a horse clopped. The day was concluding, and soon the shops would be closed, with the merchants at home dining with their families. Already the slower pace of summer had begun to creep over the lovely old city.

I sat in a wicker rocker without opening the envelope. Tomorrow I would travel alone for the first time since Alex had been killed in the Great War. It wasn't a step I was ready to take. To be jarred out of the familiar patterns of working and living made me anxious. And I knew I was still waiting. Even though time had passed, I hadn't fully accepted the fact that I'd never see my husband again. Taking up the reins of life meant that I'd accepted he was gone forever.

The unfairness of my husband's death—the slaughter of seventeen million people in the bloodiest conflict in history—coiled around me like a noose, strangling the pleasure from each day. Alex James had been twenty-seven, a lawyer with great dreams of fighting against injustice. I'd met him at a rally to demand the vote for women. He had been a dreamy-eyed activist with a megaphone and a passion for equality.

I'd been a bride and barely a wife before Alex joined the fight against Germany. After a too-brief honeymoon, he'd left for France. From that point, our marriage had consisted mostly of erratic letters, longings, promises, and hopes for the future. A future that never arrived. He'd died on a field of carnage that often invaded my dreams.

Pushing away the dangerous emotions, I broke the envelope's seal and pulled out a printed invitation.

As a celebration of the arrival of my niece, Raissa James, please join me for an evening of dancing on June 12, 1920. Extend your stay at Caoin House for the weekend and join in games of croquet, lawn tennis, and a hunting game with clever clues provided. Sincerely, Brett Airlie

Leave it to Uncle Brett to plan a party that lasted for a weekend. He was determined to show me that life still held joy and fun.

I considered canceling the trip to Mobile. I wasn't ready. I wasn't even certain that I could laugh and dance with strangers. Yet the summer stretched ahead of me with too much unoccupied time. When I was in the classroom, bringing the excitement and adventure of literature to my charges, or grading papers at home, the days passed. The loneliness remained at bay. Now the May Day festivities were over, and school was out for summer vacation. Even I had to admit I looked wan and unhealthy. A long-overdue visit with my high-spirited and popular uncle might help me break out of the coffin of my own depression.

My departure was set for nine the next morning on the Seaboard Air Line Railroad. The journey to Mobile would take three days, and I determined to once again find my adventurous nature and dispel the gloom. I was only twenty-four. I had many years ahead of me, and it was time I learned to step forward to meet them.

Tucking the invitation into my memory book, my hand strayed to the book's pages. I opened it to the photograph of Alex and me. It was the day of our wedding, and we stood on the courthouse lawn, where so many war brides had been photographed. The wedding had been a hurried affair, a civil ceremony, because I had no family in Savannah to invite and Alex's clan lived too far away in Boston to attend on such short notice.

My finger traced the smile on my face, and I could still feel the pressure of his arm around my shoulders, feel his whisper against my ear as he nuzzled my newly bobbed hair. He'd liked the short cut. Alex said it made me look formidable. He'd been so clever at making me laugh.

My fingers raked through the dark curls that stopped at my jaw. The school had not approved of my haircut, but the shortage of teachers made it impossible for them to send me away. New times were coming to America, and before the summer was over, women expected to have the right to vote in elections.

I put the memory book in the bulging trunk. To pass the remainder of the evening, I picked up a novel. I'd spent the past semester sharing the dark stories of Edgar Allan Poe and Nathaniel Hawthorne with my high school students. While many resisted the idea of "literature," they could not escape the thrill of a good ghost story—nor could I. My secret ambition, which I'd shared only with my husband and Uncle Brett, was to write and publish tales of ghosts and strange happenings.

I was now sampling Sheridan Le Fanu and Wilkie Collins, whose dark tales had kept me up late. The adventures of Sherlock Holmes was another favorite, and Sir Arthur Conan Doyle, the writer behind the London detective, was in the New Orleans area, speaking about spiritualism, a new study that piqued my interest.

If Uncle Brett was so inclined, I hoped we could make a trip to the wonderful city along the banks of the Mississippi and attend the lecture. Far, far at the back of my rational mind was the idea that perhaps, through a séance, I might have contact with Alex. It was a flight of fancy nurtured by the stories of Poe and others. If I could only know that my husband was safe and happy, that whatever horrors he'd suffered before he died had not marred his generous spirit, then I could release the past.

I'd followed Doyle's lectures on spiritualism closely, and I found consensus with his beliefs that reaching across the veil could be accomplished with the help of a true medium. Doyle worked with one particularly talented woman in New Orleans, Madam Petalungro. She'd acquired a following of devotees across America and throughout Europe. She could communicate with the dead.

If I convinced Uncle Brett to adventure to New Orleans with me, maybe I could book a session with her. Perhaps I could learn to communicate with the departed. In the past, such an idea would have terrified me, but many things had changed. The river of loss I'd endured had transformed me. I was no longer afraid.

CHAPTER TWO

Traveling through the South in early June made me believe in the powers of spring, a time of rebirth and bounty. For the first time in forever, I had no responsibilities, not even to myself. Meals were served in the club car by white-suited Negroes who worked hard to anticipate my every desire. As the train rumbled southward, I had time to read or watch the scenery pass by, an addictive vista that captured my eyes and imagination. Who lived in these small towns? What were the people like? What work did they do?

We passed through villages and then larger towns, the temperatures growing warmer. When the train stopped long enough at the different depots, I got off and gave myself a small tour of the area. More than once I spotted the same handsome young man, who always nodded politely and then disappeared in the crowds, only to reappear at the next stop. He was well dressed, with a strong chin and light eyes that seemed to hold laughter—and that followed me. An intriguing stranger appealed to my sense of adventure.

Horseless buggies were in every small hamlet, a fact that surprised me. The era of the horse was coming to a close. Let the mechanical vehicles haul the heavy lumber and churn through the mud in cold and rain. The life of a dray horse was not one to be envied.

We had a half-hour layover in Jacksonville, Florida, and I was eager to venture around the area. The sun seemed to limber up my stiff joints, and I found my step relaxing into a ground-covering stride. When Alex was alive, we loved to walk along the Savannah seawall. He teased me, saying the brisk Atlantic wind whipped color into my face. I told him the salty tang of the air made me think of pirates. For the past two years, I'd avoided the sea and had shut myself inside. Now, as I left Savannah and my sad memories behind, a smile found my lips more often.

When a gathering of young men at the station in Jacksonville stared after me, instead of feeling guilt or upset, I smiled at them. They had likely fought in the war and survived. Who was I to deny them a sunny day among the living? Before I knew it, the handsome man I'd noticed on several train platforms caught up with me. Hat in hand, he introduced himself as Robert Aultman.

"I'm traveling to Mobile, Alabama, on business," he said. "I hope you don't think I'm too forward, but we seem to be traveling in the same direction. I thought maybe we could chat and pass the time."

I thought to keep my destination to myself, but his open, sunny smile convinced me to lower my defenses. A conversational partner would pass the time. "My uncle, Brett Airlie, lives in Mobile."

"What a stroke of luck!" His enthusiasm was contagious. "I'm attending a party in Mobile at Mr. Airlie's country home. The fete is in honor of his niece."

I had to laugh. Were I in the middle of a Poe tale, this happenstance would have a darker coloring. Coincidence was denied by those who believed in the guiding hand of departed spirits. Believers would say that meeting Robert Aultman was my destiny.

"Well, Mr. Aultman, I'm Brett's niece, Raissa James."

He shook my hand with more heartiness than most men would. I liked that he failed to treat me like some delicate bit of bric-a-brac that would turn to dust if he touched it. "What a pleasant surprise," he said. "Your uncle is throwing quite a shindig in your honor, and I suspected something else entirely to be his motive."

"What motive did you assign?" I couldn't resist.

"I was positive the party was the prelude to marriage bids for some hefty, desperate, bovine niece who had just come on the marriage market."

His shocking words tickled my sense of humor. "That's the most unflattering thing I've ever heard."

"Well, you hardly need your uncle's help to capture a man's interest, so I was off the mark, but it was the first thing I thought of when I opened the invitation. A lot of women have been waiting for the war to end so the matchmaking can begin." The humor dimmed in his eyes. "So many men didn't return."

He spoke the truth, and it was a personal one for me. There would be a number of young girls who never married because their potential mates had been cut down in battle. And then there were those of us who were war widows.

"I'm sorry," he said. "You lost someone, didn't you?"

"My husband." I still wore my wedding band, and he noticed it at last.

"I lost my brother. I'm astounded at the ways I miss him." He looked into the distance for a brief moment, and I knew he struggled for control. "Aiden and I fought like territorial rats when we were little, and then we became friends. We started a shipping business together, and I saw him every day. I counted on his advice, his intelligence." He stepped away from me and inhaled. "I'm sorry. I'm sure you feel your loss keenly enough without sharing mine."

"It's odd, but it helps. A little." There were times when I felt myself encased in a glass room, unable to hear or speak to anyone who passed by. I was that alone and isolated in my grief. It did help to share those feelings with another.

The conductor blew his whistle to alert us to reboard the train. We'd been so busy chatting, we hadn't made it off the platform to explore the town.

"Join me in the club car for a lemonade, or perhaps something a bit more daring. I brought some rum as a gift for your uncle, but I have a bottle for personal use."

"It's against the—" I bit back the prudish words, envisioning the dour matrons who paraded in front of the city clerk's office in support of Prohibition. Alex and I had shared an occasional drink, and I could use the way it loosened the tension in my shoulders. "I'd love a drink."

"I'll meet you in the club car. Order two lemonades or, if you'd prefer a more exotic drink, get us two Coca-Colas, and we'll make our own fizzy giggle water."

He was trying to impress me, and I liked it. "I'll surprise you."

"You already have," he said as he jumped aboard the train and pulled me up before departing for his sleeper and the booze.

I arrived in Mobile the next day with a pounding headache and a desperate desire to get off the rocking train. Travis Wells, my uncle's burly groundskeeper, met me at the station in a Ford. The rise of the automobile had reached even sleepy Mobile. It didn't surprise me that my uncle would be in the vanguard of the automotive movement. He'd made his fortune designing steam engines for paddle-wheelers that ran up and down the rivers that fed the Tensaw Waterway and ultimately emptied into Mobile Bay. The money made from his inventions funded his purchase of Caoin House and the seven thousand surrounding acres.

I said my good-byes to Robert Aultman while Travis waited a discreet distance away, standing beside my trunk and other luggage.

"I'll see you at the party," Robert said, shaking my hand longer than was necessary. He whispered, "Go easy on the booze."

I'd had only three drinks over the course of a long evening, but it was at least one drink too many for me. "I learned that lesson, I think."

He leaned closer. "The hangover will pass. Drink a lot of water."

I groaned and turned away, unsure if I wanted to see him again. His laughter followed me as I moved toward the docks where Travis waited. In a moment I was in the midst of bustling stevedores and bargaining merchants. The war had brought industry and prosperity to Mobile. The shipyards boomed with orders for naval ships, and now that the war was over, the Mobile docks teemed with cargo from Central and South America, accessed by the newly completed Panama Canal.

A recent rainfall had left the station's parking area puddled with water. A miasma of exotic aromas—spices, fruits, cooking—floated on the breeze from the river. The melody of various accents and languages reminded me of the international scope of the port. The surroundings overwhelmed me.

Travis rescued me and escorted me to the waiting car. In a matter of moments, we were bumping out of the train station and onto a newly paved road that led through the heart of the port city.

When we passed Bienville Square, I asked Travis to let me select some chocolates for my uncle's party. The candy shop on the corner of Dauphin and Joachim was famous throughout the South for its confections, and I wanted to contribute something to my uncle's extravaganza. Travis obliged, and I hurried into the shop while he waited with the car. It was a tough decision, but I settled on a variety of chocolate-covered nuts and fruits and the pastel bridal mints that melted in one's mouth. I ordered two fountain drinks, one for me and one for Travis, to help with the heat on the drive home.

As I left the shop with my purchases, I stepped into the path of a young black man, really little more than a teenager. He hit me with enough force to knock the drinks into the air and my candy to the ground. Soda rained down on the two of us.

"My apologies, madam." He stood unmoving, too terrified to even blot the Coca-Cola from his face as it ran into his eyes and mouth.

"I'm not hurt," I assured him. "It was an accident."

A portly man in a rumpled suit came forward. "Look what you done, boy. You hit the lady and ruined her packages."

I picked up the candies where they'd fallen to the street, still in their wrappers. "Nothing is harmed," I said. "It was an unfortunate accident. I stepped into his path without looking."

"His path ain't on the sidewalk. No Negro should be on the side-walk. *They* walk in the street, especially when a lady is near."

Travis came to my side. He was at least six foot five, and his shoulders could easily fill a standard doorway. His ancestors had wielded the Scottish broadsword, and I'd seen him fell a tree as if it were a toothpick.

"It was an accident," Travis said. He offered me a handkerchief to wipe my dress. "Be about your business," he said to the youth.

"That boy needs to pay for what he broke," the stranger said. "I run a dry-goods store over yonder"—he pointed across the street—"and I know you can't let 'em get by with uppity conduct."

Travis took one step toward the man. He put a hand on the youth's shoulder. "Be off," he said. "Use more care." He waited until the teen-ager had run away, this time in the street, dodging horses and cars.

"You lettin' him off scot-free," the merchant complained.

"Thank you for your interest. I'm sure Mr. Airlie will appreciate your intercession when I tell him of it. May I have your name?"

The man looked at Travis, then me. "Not important." He crossed the street and kept walking.

"Are you hurt, Miss Raissa?" Travis asked when we were alone.

"Not in the least. If you'll hold my candy, I'll get us another soda for the ride home."

CHAPTER THREE

It took half an hour to make our way to my uncle's estate. Several miles of road had been paved, but it wasn't long before we were on the narrow, sandy track that led to Caoin House. To the east of my uncle's property, a vast swampland, the river delta area, stretched for miles. Travis said it was as treacherous as Okefenokee in Georgia or the Atchafalaya Basin in Louisiana.

There were other settlements beyond Caoin House, little hamlets with groceries and merchants, but Mobile was the county seat, the place of governance, and therefore of money. Caoin House, for all its beauty, was isolated. When he'd first moved to Caoin House, Uncle Brett had ridden to Mobile on horseback or in a carriage. His new Ford had obviously made life much easier for him.

As we struggled through the sand traps at five miles an hour, the heat wilted me. The sticky Coca-Cola made my blouse adhere to my skin. If Travis suffered from the heat, he didn't show it. He sometimes seemed more old-world God than mortal man. He'd been with Uncle Brett at Caoin House as long as I could remember. He was always friendly, but he never spoke out of turn, and his loyalty to Uncle Brett bordered on downright primitive.

At last we turned onto the crushed-oyster-shell drive that marked the entrance to the estate built by Eli Whitehead, a Civil War general. Caoin House had once been a cotton-producing plantation. Bathed in the alluvial soil from Chickasabogue Creek, the land was rich and fertile. Most of the vast acreage was in timber, a crop in high demand as the country had begun to grow and expand. Uncle Brett had built his own sawmill and exported thousands of board feet of pine timber down the railroad spur he'd also constructed. People said he could turn cow patties into money. He was a very wealthy man.

Yet the crudeness of making money had no place on the grounds of Caoin House. It was a vision of grace and loveliness. When we rounded a curve and came upon the front lawn, which stretched for at least twenty acres, I couldn't help the small intake of breath. Though I'd visited Caoin House as a young girl, the elegance touched me anew. Giant live oaks fluttered with Spanish moss. Trunks at least fifty feet in circumference supported limbs that stretched and angled, almost touching the ground and then rising again. Travis told me the lacy moss was a parasite, but it didn't harm the tree. Framed between the trunks and a tunnel of graceful limbs was the sixty-four-room antebellum home.

Caoin House was a three-story Italianate home that reminded me, from a distance, of a riverboat. The oaks offered the perfect frame for the house, but the views from the pecan orchard to the north and the formal gardens in the rear were also spectacular. Lush tropical plants to the south followed a path that ended two hundred yards later in a cypress slew. From the wilderness of the swamp to the formal rose gardens, Caoin House had a bit of everything a gardener could crave. Travis worked tirelessly, a true labor of love. On my last visit, I'd asked if he loved Caoin House or my uncle more. He'd said they both had their merits and their faults.

We motored to the front of the house, and Travis stopped. The lower floor of Caoin was used for storage, the laundry, and recreational activities. The main entrance was on the first floor, accessed by gracefully arched double steps that met at the porch. The stairs were designed prior to the Civil War, when women used the left staircase and men the right, because it was unseemly for a man to see a woman's ankles. Thank goodness things were changing for women. Once we obtained the vote, equality would come more swiftly.

I was halfway up the stairs when the heavy wooden door with a beveled-glass panel opened, and Uncle Brett stepped out. He was a tall, slender man with my same black curls, tamed by brilliantine and combed back from his forehead. His hazel gaze swept over me, taking in each detail. Gray shot through the hair at his temples, but it only made him more distinguished. Still, he'd aged rather more than I'd expected. His business had prospered, but Uncle Brett looked tired.

"Raissa! I've lured you to Mobile at last." He embraced me in a long hug. He was a neat man who always smelled of Florida Water. He had a ferocious humor and loved to tease me. "How many hearts did you break on the train ride down?"

"None." But I felt that I wasn't being completely honest. "But I did meet a young man you'd invited to the party."

He arched one eyebrow, something he did to make me laugh. "Oh? And you just happened to deduce this young man was invited to our party?"

"I had a conversation with him." As we entered the house, I told him about Robert Aultman and our meeting, leaving out any mention of rum.

"Robert is looking to buy two of my steamboats," Uncle Brett said. "Streamlining delivery of goods is the ticket for shippers. Faster, more reliable service. That's what people want, and that's what I can give him."

"Do you know Mr. Aultman well?" I hoped I didn't sound interested.

"Not personally, but his company is well thought of. I understand he's considering a move to Mobile." Uncle Brett glanced at me, his expression amused. "I wish you'd move here, Raissa. Keep me company in this big house. You wouldn't have to teach."

"But I love teaching." That was a mild exaggeration. I loved my independence, and I loved the moments when I captured a student's interest and generated a spark of passion for literature and reading.

"I believe you'd love running Caoin House, too. Perhaps you could explore your own writing. You've talked about it in your letters often enough. I think it would be jolly to have a scribbling woman in the family, especially one who wrote stories of the occult and supernatural."

I'd foolishly admitted my desire to write and my scouring of the Savannah library for books by authors of "sensational" stories. I had to laugh. "Uncle Brett, you've been reading Mr. Hawthorne's unhappy comments about women writers. I do believe his cud curdled in jealousy at the sales of some women authors." I was pleased that Uncle Brett remembered my dream to plunge into fiction and took me seriously enough to encourage me, even if his support was in the employ of moving me to Caoin House.

"As much as you love to read, Raissa, I'm sure if you turned your hand to writing, you'd have droves of followers. I have a pen name for you . . . Raissa Belladonna. And Caoin House is the perfect location to build your career. *Caoin* is an old Gaelic word that means 'lament.' The House of Lament. It has a ring to it—doesn't it? And, of course, everyone in these parts knows the house is haunted. So much tragedy. You could become an entrepreneur of the dark tale."

He wove a pleasant fantasy. "Thank you for your support, but I believe the teacher's paycheck is a lot more reliable."

He grew serious. "You wouldn't have to rely on a teacher's salary if you'd come to manage Caoin House. I would make sure you had a generous allowance and compensation for your talents."

I never doubted my uncle's generosity, but I also didn't want to find myself reliant on another person. "I'll give your offer every consideration."

"And I'll see if the dashing Mr. Aultman can also apply some pressure. Raissa, I know you needed to grieve the loss of Alex. I liked him immensely, and I know you were deeply in love. But you are almost twenty-five, and time stands still for no one. If you plan on children and a family, the passing years are a serious consideration. If you're content to remain a widow, take no heed of my intrusive questions."

My first reaction was a flush of anger, but that quickly evaporated. Uncle Brett was a businessman, and he'd often told me his success came from confronting the realities of a decision, both good and bad. He didn't mean to pry or even pressure. Biology was a fact.

"I will take your comments under advisement." Thank goodness I'd learned that phrase from the suffragettes in Savannah when they were confronted by angry men.

"Let's get your things to your room. I'm putting you in the peach bedroom on the front. There's a lovely balcony there, and it overlooks the oak grove. The sunrises are splendid."

I'd hoped for a room on the north side, facing the pecan orchard. For some reason Uncle Brett never used those rooms, even though they were the most elegant in the house. There was tragedy associated with them—some accident in the distant past—and it amused me a little that my uncle let such history affect his choices for my room. He might be easier to persuade to attend a séance than I'd anticipated.

Travis picked up my trunk and started up the stairs to the bedroom. I followed, until Uncle Brett grasped my wrist. "I'm glad you're here, Raissa. I look at you, and I see your mother. Evangeline would be proud of you. And your father, too."

"And I'm glad to be here with you, Uncle Brett. We're the last of the Airlie line."

"Perhaps not for long, my dear. Perhaps not for long."

He was still chuckling when I skipped up the stairs behind Travis. I was eager for a wash and some clean clothes. Coca-Cola and sweat made for an unpleasant eau de cologne.

When I entered the bedroom, which was wallpapered in a delicate peach with bouquets of wildflowers woven into the pattern, I found that Uncle Brett's housekeeper, Winona, had already drawn a warm bath. She waited for the arrival of my luggage to unpack me.

I went to her quickly and gave her a hug. Her arms closed around me briefly before she stepped away. Winona was not demonstrative, yet she was always where she was needed. My uncle teased her that she had the abilities of a bat to find her way to the epicenter of a domestic crisis without visual aids. *Stoic* was the perfect word to describe her, yet her glances at my uncle told me how much she cared for him.

"Miss Raissa, it's good to have you here. You were a child the last time you paid us a visit. Now you're a grown woman."

"I'm happy to be here. This visit is much needed. I only hope Uncle Brett doesn't party me to death or marry me off to the first eligible man who shows an interest."

Her smile was brief. "He wants children running through the house. Trust an old bachelor to want the very thing that will drive him to madness."

While most Mobile homes employed Negro servants, Uncle Brett had Winona and Travis—a woman with a mysterious past and a Scot from the Highlands. At least Travis sometimes talked about his upbringing. Winona brushed aside all questions. Uncle Brett said only that she'd suffered great tragedy and to keep my nose out of her business.

Her skin was a burnished oak, and her eyes a strange gold, ringed in green. She accepted the social status of servant, but she'd been educated somewhere other than Mobile. Her knowledge of medicinal plants and the local flora and fauna rivaled that of a professor, and the thick accent so familiar in the Deep South was absent. Although she never spoke of a husband, she had a son, Framon, who'd remained overseas after the war to further his studies.

Winona lifted the lid of my trunk.

"There's no need to unpack me. I can do that," I said, knowing she would continue until all my clothes were neatly folded in drawers or hanging in the chifforobe. Winona was never diverted from a task.

"Enjoy your bath. I'll lay out something comfortable for you to wear to dinner. Your uncle is casual unless he has guests, and I know he reserved the evening to spend with you."

"Uncle Brett wrote me that Framon was still in Paris pursuing his education."

"Yes, he is happier there, I think."

"Will he come home?" I remembered him vaguely from a visit to Caoin House with my parents. My mother had grown up in Mobile, but love and work had taken her to Savannah when she married my father. They'd both been fond of Framon, and I vividly remembered a picnic near the creek when I'd fancied myself in love with him. I was eight, and Framon had been a tall, gangly teenager who had no use for a tagalong girl.

"He's due for a visit this summer."

"I hope he comes while I'm here. I'd love to see him."

"I hope so, too." She removed several dresses from the trunk and hung them. There was no dissuading her from her tasks, so I stepped into the bathroom, eager for a long soak.

Dinner that evening was exactly as Winona predicted. Quiet, and a chance for Uncle Brett and me to catch up. When the last scrape of bread pudding had been eaten, Uncle Brett took my hand. "Get some rest because you're going to need it. We'll meet in the library in the morning and go over the plans for your welcome to Caoin House party. I've planned a humdinger this time."

CHAPTER FOUR

As my uncle laid out the party plans over breakfast, I told him he needed no help from me. The gala had been flawlessly organized. Menus were complete; liquor, though illegal, had been smuggled into the first floor; and the army of servants necessary to sustain a rollicking party for three days had been approved and hired. My help was merely icing on the cake. Raissa, what flowers should we place on the tables? Raissa, the croquet match is set for five o'clock. What refreshments would be best? Winona could have answered each question better than I, but my uncle wanted me to feel included. His manipulations worked brilliantly. My anticipation of the weekend grew with each detail determined.

Uncle Brett called me into the library, where Travis waited. "Travis will give you some driving lessons, and then I have a list of errands for you to run."

The idea of driving the car—by myself—was frightening but also thrilling. That my uncle trusted me gave me pleasure. "Of course." I'd never backed down from a challenge.

Uncle Brett handed me the key and turned to Travis. "Take her into the cow pasture. Be sure it's empty." He was only half teasing. "And while you're in the lesson business, Travis, if she wants to learn to shoot, there's a ladies' .410 with the other weapons. Guns are part of our life. She needs to know how to handle a weapon in case there's a livestock emergency."

"No guns for me," I said. "The car will be enough of an adventure."

Hours and several near accidents later, I'd mastered the Ford and was ready for the trip to town. Travis had done a thorough job of preparing me for every incident he could imagine, but he wore his worry clearly on his face as he waved me down the driveway. I drove with great care until I was out of sight of the house, and then I pressed the pedal with more assertion. The car sped down the shell drive, the wind whipping through my short hair. The sensation was more freedom than I'd ever tasted.

When I turned onto the road, though, I slowed. Travis had warned me more than once that the sand could grab the wheels of the car and send it careening into a tree or, worse, flip it over. While I loved the delicious sensation of speed, I would wait until I was on pavement.

In Mobile, I parked at the docks and shopped for the fruits Winona had listed. She'd put a special order in for crates of navel oranges that I had two stevedores load into the back of the car. Bananas and pineapples were exotics in abundance, their scent heightened by the hot sun until the air was so sweet it was almost intoxicating. I made the remainder of my purchases, storing everything in the car while I went for the next items on the list.

Bees hummed around the docks, and the smell of the water, with just a hint of salt, made me think of the adventure books I'd loved as a girl. Robert Louis Stevenson's *Treasure Island* and *Kidnapped* were also favorites of my younger students. *The Strange Case of Dr. Jekyll and Mr. Hyde* was a story I never tired thinking about. What dual impulses could be housed within one body—the possibilities were shocking and disturbing. My uncle had been correct in my aspirations. I spent far too much time fantasizing about writing such tales, exploring the darkness at the edge of a room or the image caught out of the corner of my eye.

My fanciful imagination had been a bane as a child. I'd seen and heard things no one else saw, and it had often angered my father. My mother, on the other hand, had been more sympathetic and assured me I'd outgrow such foolishness, because *she* had.

When I had the required items from the docks, I drove to the shops, where I purchased spices and the vegetables Travis and his helpers couldn't grow in the garden. My uncle had traveled extensively, and he enjoyed foods from many different countries. Shopping for the ingredients made my mouth water.

At last my chores were complete. The temptation of another Coca-Cola sent me down to the candy shop. This time I would sit at the counter and sip my drink while I made sure I hadn't overlooked anything Uncle Brett wanted. I'd also order some pralines for Winona. I'd discovered it was a favorite sweet of hers, and one, for some secret reason, she didn't make herself.

I slipped onto a stool at the counter and enjoyed the tart soda that fizzed over the ice. Sometimes the smallest thing could be such a pleasure.

"You're Brett Airlie's niece, aren't you?" The woman behind the counter had startling blue eyes and a smidgen of plumpness in her cheeks. She looked to be in her late twenties and moved with brisk efficiency.

"I am. Raissa James." I extended my hand and was pleased when she shook it with confidence.

"I'm Pretta Paul. I married the oldest of the candy-shop boys."

When I looked blank, she laughed. "The three Paul boys own the candy shop. That's why they call it the Three Pauls Candy Store. The store has been in business since before the Civil War. I married Hubert Paul, the oldest. My husband and your uncle are friends."

"I'm so sorry I didn't recognize the name. There are so many things I don't know."

She patted my arm. "Sometimes best not to get all tied up by history and facts that no one cares about anymore. But I know more about you than you do me. You live in Savannah and are here for a long-overdue visit with your uncle. And I know other things that might interest you."

Something in the way she said it tickled my curiosity. "Like what?"

She put a hand to her mouth as if something had slipped out, but instead of declining, she refreshed my soda, made one for herself, and came from behind the counter to sit beside me. "Ghost stories. I just love the tales about Caoin House. So deliciously creepy."

"I'm a fan of a good ghost story myself," I said, delighted to have met someone to share my interest. "So tell me a dark tale about Caoin House." The possibility of actually writing a bit of fiction centered on my uncle's beautiful home came back to me with a tingle in my gut that usually signaled I was onto something.

Pretta was about to talk when the bell over the door jangled and a very handsome man in business attire stepped into the shop. His suit had to have been tailored specially for him, and it fit his straight shoulders and narrow hips to perfection. Even though it was late afternoon on a hot and humid day, his white shirt remained crisp. He was a handsome, well-built man between my age and Uncle Brett's. His sharp blue gaze found me and held. The sunlight touched his brushed-back hair and the slight hint of a beard. He came straight toward me. "Raissa James! I thought I recognized Brett's car parked outside. I'll bet that devil sent you out to run errands for the party."

"He has." I took the hand he offered. To my consternation, Pretta rose and returned to her post behind the counter.

"What can I get for you, Mr. McKay?" she asked.

I knew him then. My uncle's lawyer, Carlton McKay, a man with great magnetism. I had no doubt he had the power to sway juries to his clients' benefit. I recalled several letters where Uncle Brett had mentioned the attorney's sharp mind and abilities.

"A Coca-Cola would be very refreshing, Pretta. How is Hubert doing? Not eating too much of the delicious candy you make, I hope."

"He's well, Mr. McKay. I'll tell him you asked." She put the soda in front of him in the place she'd vacated.

"Pretta, will you be a dear and prepare a ten-pound box of whatever confections you think would be appropriate for a weekend gala at Caoin House. I'll pick them up tomorrow."

And he had more than his share of charm, too. I stood. "It isn't necessary to bring a single thing. I swear, Uncle Brett has enough food to feed half of Mobile, and I'm sure he doesn't expect his guests to supplement the menu."

Carlton performed a gallant little half bow. "You can never have enough of Pretta Paul's confections."

Pretta blushed prettily, and I realized she had a tiny crush on the lawyer. I could see why. His air of confidence was as attractive as his appearance. Carlton McKay was a man who knew what he was doing in every arena he entered.

"Tell your uncle I'll be out tomorrow to lend a hand with setting up the croquet course and the tennis net. I also have to hide the clues for the hunting game on the property. You follow one clue to the next clue—exciting stuff, and one misstep and you've lost. It's based on ancient folk games that Travis mentioned to me, and it's going to require a degree of skill and deduction. I'm so glad Brett is hosting this party. We need to celebrate the end of the war and the beginning of prosperity. And the arrival of his beautiful niece."

I ignored his compliment, but the idea of a clue-hunting game immediately caught my fancy. "I'll be happy to help you with the clues and the details."

"I'll be at Caoin House in time to help with any last-minute preparations. Your uncle's parties are legendary." He turned to Pretta. "I'll write at least four clues especially for you, Pretta."

She laughed. "Be careful, Mr. Carlton, or Hubert will think you're flirting with his wife."

"Oh, posh. I am flirting with you." He drained his glass and set it back on the marble counter. "Ladies, good day."

It took a moment for his essence to clear the room. I turned back to Pretta. "So what about those ghost stories?"

She laughed. "On second thought, ask your uncle. Some of them are grisly, and I wouldn't want Mr. Brett angry with me for putting things into your head. I need to help John Henry in the kitchen. We have some pastries ready to fill and package."

Another customer entered, and I knew it was pointless to press. "It seems I'll see you this weekend at Uncle Brett's party. When you're at Caoin House, I want to hear the stories. Who knows, I may put them in a book."

"Now that would be a grand thing to do." She put my change on the counter and turned to help the three ladies who'd entered the shop. She called over her shoulder to the back area where the candy making took place. "John Henry, be sure and check the oven for the puff pastries."

I picked up my purchases and went to the car. If I didn't get home soon, Uncle Brett and Travis would both be worried about me.

At last, after a cold dinner of chicken salad and pickled condiments that Winona had put up from Travis's garden, I grabbed a book from the library and hurried to bed. It had been a long and tiring day. Driving the car had been exciting, but it had taken a toll in tension. My shoulders ached. I was eager for bed in the lovely room that gave me such a view of the moon peeking from behind the graceful branches of the oaks. The mild night was an invitation to leave the balcony doors open. Caoin House was isolated, and my balcony was without exterior access.

With Travis on alert, no one in his or her right mind would walk about the grounds without permission.

I settled under the sheet with a copy of *Ghost Stories of an Antiquary*, a new addition to my uncle's library, a first edition published in 1904. Uncle Brett was certainly an accomplished tempter, and I was very aware of his playful humor since the author, M. R. James, shared my last name. I loved nothing better than the ghost stories that were Mr. James's style.

"Oh, Whistle and I'll Come to You, My Lad" put me right at the old hotel and golf course that the author described. I could almost feel the dirt-crusted bronze whistle that the protagonist unearthed. When the narrator cleaned the whistle and blew it, I knew something terrible would happen. And, of course, it did. How my uncle would laugh at me if he could see me clutching the book, too afraid to get out of bed to shut the balcony door, where a gentle breeze fluttered the sheers.

As beautiful as my bedroom was in the daytime, it was spooky at night. The high ceilings and large dimensions offered layers of shadows and corners where wicked creatures might crouch. The branches of the oaks, swaying in the bright moonlight, cast moving images against the wall and floor. Caoin House was nothing like my small Savannah cottage, where there was no room for moon shadows to dance and caper. The one thing I knew for sure—I had the imagination necessary to follow in the footsteps of my namesake, M. R. James. My brain had already conjured up all sorts of dark entities waiting for a chance to leap out.

The wind picked up, and the sheers began to writhe like spirits dancing in torment. I forced my logical mind to assume control, and I got out of bed and ran to shut the balcony doors. The wind was unseasonably cold, and tomorrow, when I was involved in a heated game of lawn tennis, I would think of it with longing.

Struggling a bit, I pushed one side of the French doors closed and latched it into place. Movement on the lawn caught my attention as

I held the second door semishut. Someone walked among the trunks. Based on the breadth of his shoulders, it was a man. He wore a light-colored suit, but I couldn't see him clearly. At one point, he turned and looked toward me, and I swore he nodded slightly, but I couldn't be certain. In another moment, he stepped behind one of the massive trunks and was gone.

I latched the door and hurried back to bed. Tomorrow I would ask Uncle Brett. It could have been one of the workmen he'd hired, pacing off the ground to set up tents. Whoever it was, I had no sense of danger. He seemed at ease walking among the trees, almost as if he belonged there.

Burying myself in the covers, I was almost instantly asleep.

CHAPTER FIVE

The morning dawned clear and with lower humidity, a true blessing. June was still a month when spring could show up, delicate and filled with promise. More often it was summer that knocked at the door, complete with baking heat and a lack of breeze. The cooler temperatures were very welcome, and so was the lack of mosquitoes. While outbreaks of yellow jack happened less and less frequently and with less mortality, the mosquito-borne disease was a constant threat in the summer months.

The house was in full bustle when I made it downstairs to grab a slice of toast and a strip of bacon from the buffet. Winona served coffee, and I took my cup and saucer outside, where workmen were erecting three tents. One for food, one for alcohol, and one for the dance floor. Uncle Brett had an enviable record collection, and he loved to dance. So did I, although I was sadly out of practice.

As I wandered under the oaks, enjoying the clean smell of morning and the dew-soaked grass, a delivery truck arrived. A young boy took a bow-wrapped package to the door. Winona accepted it and took it inside. My uncle had purchased a gift for someone, perhaps a special woman. I suspected it was Isabelle Brown, a high-society lady friend he'd mentioned more and more often in his letters to me. I'd have to keep a sharp eye out to discover who had his affections.

Soon folks would be arriving. Uncle Brett expected at least thirty people to stay over. The logistics of accommodating all those people—cooking breakfast, providing lunch, drinks—I was surprised Winona didn't run screaming from the kitchen. But she seemed to enjoy the commotion as much as Uncle Brett did. Travis, too, stomped around the grounds, ordering crews of gardeners as they marked the winding trails through the property and decorated fountains and ponds. Hired hands set up floral bouquets in the tents and covered tables with white linen cloths.

I finished my coffee and returned to the house to dress for the day. As I entered my room, I was surprised to find the gift box, tied with a large red bow, on my bed. There was no card, and I opened the box with anticipation. It contained clothes, I was sure.

When I lifted the short set out of the tissues, I let out an exclamation. The blue-and-white set, complete with a sailor top, was exactly what I'd been longing for. Even though my contemporaries in Savannah would be shocked if I wore the outfit on the street, I didn't hesitate in putting it on. I completed the look with ankle socks and Mary Janes and tied a blue scarf around my head at a jaunty angle. Twirling before the mirror, I couldn't wait to thank Uncle Brett. By giving me the shorts, he had bestowed his permission for me to wear the daring outfit. I would be able to run and bat the tennis ball without the hindrance of a skirt. My bachelor uncle was quite the cat's whiskers in fashion, and I realized he'd had some help from a lady friend. I had no doubt I was going to like this Isabelle Brown.

Eager to track Brett down and hear all about his accomplice in fashion, I hurried downstairs. Uncle Brett was standing at the front door when he saw me, and his face told a story that slowed me to a standstill.

"You didn't buy the outfit, did you?" I asked.

"I've never seen it," he said. Recovering quickly, he added, "But it looks very fetching on you. Perfect for a summer lawn party."

I had to laugh. "You're a terrible liar. Are you scandalized?" I had fallen in love with the comfort of the shorts, and truth be told, they were no shorter than some of my skirts.

"The change is . . . unexpected." He arched an eyebrow. "The clothes were a gift?"

"Anonymous," I said, still not certain he wasn't pulling my leg.

He sighed. "I suspect Carlton McKay is behind it."

Suddenly the shorts felt very revealing. "Oh dear. I'll take them off immediately. I can't accept such a gift."

"Posh." Brett grabbed my elbow. "The man is incorrigible. I can't be certain if he's flirting with you or attempting to get my goat, but let's pay him back in his own coin. You wear the outfit and enjoy it, and we'll both pretend that I sent it."

My uncle was the king of mischief, and if Carlton thought to have a laugh at our expense, he would not get the pleasure.

"Are you certain?" I still felt a bit uneasy with the idea. Carlton had not only moved my wardrobe into the twentieth century; he'd guessed my size with great accuracy. And he'd judged my taste as well.

"Let's play him at his own game. Raissa, I want you to move here, and I want you to be free to be the woman you choose. Wear trousers and shorts. Crop your hair. Demand the vote. You are an Airlie, and you will not be a shrinking violet."

My emotions swelled, and I kissed Uncle Brett's cheek. "No one has ever believed in me like you do."

"Because we are two of a kind, my dear. Now, I see a carriage arriving. One of the old guard is here for the party. Go and greet them. If the shock of short pants doesn't kill them, escort them in here and I'll put a mimosa in their hand."

And the party was on.

Carlton arrived in blue-and-white-checked slacks, a blue bow tie, and a sporty cap. I was amused to see that he'd planned his outfit to match mine, but I never hinted that I knew the gift came from him. When he challenged me to a game of tennis, I eagerly accepted. While I didn't win, I put him through his paces, and when the game was over, we flopped into lawn chairs beneath the shade of the oaks.

"You're a very modern woman," he said, bouncing his racket on his knee.

"And ambitious." I said it without a smile.

He leveled a look at me and then burst into laughter. "You and your uncle are going to control the city."

"That's absolutely our devious plan."

He picked up two mimosas from a passing waiter and handed one to me. I almost refused, remembering the dreadful hangover from the rum on the train, but I'd helped Winona squeeze the juice from the wonderful navel oranges only last night. I couldn't pass up the chance to taste the efforts of our labors.

"A lady who can hold her liquor is a force to be reckoned with," he whispered, leaning forward.

It was another challenge, and I accepted with a smile and a big sip of the bubbly champagne mixed with the orange juice. "Delicious."

"Brett tells me you have an interest in writing and that you intend to record some of the ghost stories about Caoin House."

My uncle would stoop to the lowest level to win me over to his plan. "Dark tales of spirits and hauntings interest me."

"I know you're aware that Madelyn Petalungro, Sir Arthur Conan Doyle's very own spiritualist, will be giving a series of private readings in New Orleans next week."

"I do know. I'd hoped Uncle Brett would acquire tickets for us." I had a curious thought. "How did you know this?"

"Brett told me of your interest and asked me to arrange the tickets. My office often helps him with these little chores—wiring for tickets or booking travel and accommodations. It saves him a trip to town, and when Brett is working on an invention, he is making money. When he's making money, I'm making money."

"And everybody went to heaven," I added.

"You are quite the card." He tipped the bottom of my glass for me to drink more.

I obliged. "Is Isabelle the woman in my uncle's life? He knows far too much about fashion and women's issues to be the bachelor he's pretending to be."

"You're quite astute." Carlton nodded toward the tall dark-haired woman, who leaned against one of the trees.

"She's very nice." Uncle Brett had introduced us when she first arrived, but he'd failed to make their relationship crystal clear. I hoped to weasel information out of Carlton.

"Isabelle is one of your uncle's favorites. I believe in the last ten months, they've grown close."

"She's a beautiful woman." I wasn't certain how I felt. She was striking, with her olive complexion, dark hair, and large dark eyes. And soft-spoken. I wanted my uncle to be happy, and a solitary man was seldom happy. "Tell me about her. Has she ever married?"

"Widowed, like you," Carlton said. "Her husband was struck by a car. Terrible accident. It's been half a dozen years since it happened. Brett is the first man she's shown the least interest in."

My heart went out to her. I knew the loss of my beloved. Alex was never far from my thoughts.

"I'm sorry about your husband, Raissa. I heard he saved many men before he died."

I rose. I couldn't think about Alex's last moments, his rush to the tank and the bullets that tore into him. "Excuse me." I turned away and stumbled into someone. Strong hands captured my arms and caught me before I could fall.

"And you said you didn't drink a lot! Here you are, tippling again, and slightly tipsy if your balance is any indication."

"Robert!" I looked up at him and impulsively kissed him on the cheek. "I thought you'd changed your mind about coming."

"Caoin House is a bit farther in the country than I anticipated." He pointed to a departing carriage. "I had to find a ride."

"I would have driven into town to pick you up."

He stepped back and looked me up and down. "You are, indeed, the epitome of the modern woman. And here I thought you were merely a schoolmarm spending her free summer in the care of relatives."

He made me laugh, and I grabbed his hand and pulled him forward. "Carlton, this is Robert Aultman. He's doing business with Uncle Brett. Robert, this is Carlton McKay, esquire."

A spark passed between the two men, but I couldn't grasp the meaning. It was just a moment where some message was communicated between only them. The conversation continued pleasantly.

Carlton moved through life with the grace of a man born to privilege. Everything came easily to him. And if adversity dared to strike, he would survive and continue to hold his head high. Robert was younger, less at ease, more eager to please. I suspected beneath the cloak of a jester he hid a big heart.

After ten minutes of social talk, Carlton excused himself. "Your uncle has entangled himself in a game of croquet and been called out as a cheater." Carlton's lips twisted wryly. "I'd better step in."

"Uncle Brett always cheats at croquet," I told him. "Everyone here knows. It's a joke."

"And I must go and play my role as his defender." Carlton stood in a fluid motion. He was as graceful as a big cat. How was it that such a handsome, articulate man remained unwed?

Robert put a hand on his shoulder. "Mr. McKay, perhaps I could drop by your office next week. I'm opening a new business in Mobile, and I want to be sure I have all the paperwork properly filed."

"A new client is always a reason to celebrate. Now watch out for Raissa while I assume the mantle of the conniving but brilliant lawyer." He headed toward the croquet field, where Uncle Brett pretended to be insulted.

Robert reached for my hand and squeezed it. "You look amazing. You have the prettiest legs I've ever seen."

I flushed, self-conscious. "I would never have bought shorts, but I love them. To be able to run and play without a skirt flapping is . . . freedom." The word surprised me. I'd never really thought of freedom as a sensation. "In the summer heat, I know I'll enjoy them even more."

Robert's gaze slid from my eyes to my legs, and he whistled softly. He was an incorrigible flirt. "Show me the grounds. This is such a beautiful place."

Together we walked away from the tents, strolling through the lush grass beneath the shady oaks. I gave him a limited tour, including the story of Eli Whitehead and the construction of Caoin House for the most beautiful woman in the Confederacy.

"A very romantic story," Robert said. "This estate is the bee's knees."

"I should go and help Winona with the food. We're offering a buffet where people can pick and choose. Winona, my uncle's housekeeper and cook, is amazing. She can make the simplest thing, like chicken salad, into a feast. Last night I helped her pre—"

Robert pulled me behind one of the big oaks and leaned down to whisper in my ear. "I'm sure Winona is a paragon of virtues, but I'm far more interested in you." His lips grazed my earlobe.

"I don't even know you," I said, breathless.

"That's what I'm hoping to remedy." He ran his fingers through my short curls. "I really want to know you, Raissa." His palm gently cupped my cheek. "No, I really want to kiss you."

The mimosas had done their work to loosen my inhibitions. I wanted to kiss him. I'd barely been a bride before I was a widow. Alex had been dead for nearly two years, and at last I felt as if I was shrugging off the shroud of mourning. But when Robert leaned in for a kiss, I pushed him away. My dead husband still claimed my heart. "I'm not that kind of girl."

He instantly backed away. "I'm sorry, Raissa. My actions were too bold. I thought—"

"If I led you to believe I was ready to—"

"No. You haven't done anything wrong. I'm impetuous." He offered his arm to escort me back to the tents. "I believe that's a fox-trot. Why don't we see if I can remember how to dance?"

I planted my feet, forcing him to stop. "Robert, I'm sorry."

"For what? You love someone who died. You should never apologize for loving someone. My timing was off. If you can forgive my forward-ness, we can continue as friends, learning about each other. In time, maybe you'll develop deeper feelings for me."

"No promises, Robert."

"I'm not asking for a promise, only a chance."

"Chance is a gambler's friend." I sought to lighten the mood.

"And I am a gambler," Robert said, offering his arm to escort me back to the party. "But be warned, I always win."

The sounds of the party continued to the south of us. When I looked toward the tents, I found Uncle Brett and Carlton watching us. My uncle laughed and slapped Carlton on the back, and they retreated to the house together. No doubt my uncle was very, very pleased to find me wandering among the oaks with Robert. The handsome young man was yet another reason for me to stay at Caoin House. My uncle would be overjoyed if I found someone to love and could begin my married life anew.

CHAPTER SIX

Dancing was an activity I'd vastly underestimated. Alex and I had had little time to go to the Savannah blind tigers, or speakeasies where dancing was part of the evening. As a schoolteacher, I'd had to guard my reputation with great care, and many of the venues for dancing also served alcohol. Now I danced to make up for lost time.

To my surprise, I discovered I was at ease with the steps and a partner holding me. I found it deeply gratifying that both Robert and Carlton made sure I didn't miss a song. I lost count of the mimosas Carlton put in my hand. I simply gave myself to the music, allowing my partners to spin me, my bare feet skimming over the soft summer grass. Had it not been a private party on the grounds of my uncle's home, I fear I would have been a scandal. Something had loosened the ties of my social corset, and I decided life was too short to squander. The jaunty new dances like the Texas Tommy—which my partners executed with flair—were fun and left me short of breath. The fox-trot was wonderful and also quite physical, but the waltz was my favorite, and Carlton was the master of it.

As I drank and danced, a host of white-jacketed waiters served trays of drinks and kept the buffet table stacked with food. The night was filled with magic, and at least a hundred people chatted and laughed while the champagne and alcohol flowed freely and the phonograph spun the music into the cool night.

The clock struck midnight and continued to the wee hours, and still we danced. The champagne had given me a sparkling buzz that made the lights brighter and the conversation more entertaining. I was tipsy, but in a most enjoyable way. When Uncle Brett put on a record that was a slow waltz, I accepted Carlton's invitation.

The new style was a very close frame. Carlton danced with confidence, and he was a masterful lead. The lighted torches Uncle Brett had put throughout the oak grove were a swirl of golden light as I spun and almost floated on the beat of the music.

"You're a natural, Raissa."

"I love to dance. Must be inherited. Uncle Brett loves it, too." My uncle was dancing close with Isabelle, and they were no slackers at cutting a rug. To my chagrin, I realized I'd been so preoccupied with Robert and Carlton that I'd failed to find the time to really talk to Isabelle.

"It's been a wonderful party," Carlton said. "And you look fetching in those shorts."

I'd almost forgotten the prank Uncle Brett and I had cooked up. "Yes, my uncle has exquisite taste. I can't believe he purchased such modern attire for me, but I think I'll never wear a skirt again."

He laughed and whipped me around in a spin that made me giddy. "You're a naughty girl, Raissa."

"Not normally, but tonight, yes, I am naughty. Tomorrow I will likely pay, but for the moment I refuse any consequences."

The song ended, and he returned me to the table, where Robert waited. "Thank you for the dance, Raissa. I believe I'll turn in." Carlton finished the last swallow of his drink. "Good night, Robert. Tomorrow we must have a tennis match."

"You're on," Robert said, standing. When Carlton left, Robert sat back down.

"I believe the coach is turning into a pumpkin," I said. Uncle Brett had let the phonograph run down, and he was sitting at a table across from Isabelle. The look he gave her told me how much he cared for her. Tomorrow I would make it a point to seek her out and spend time with her. I didn't want my presence in the house to interfere with their romance. As I knew, time was too short to allow inconsequential things to stand in the way of love.

Robert and I walked to the front door, where one of the dozens of servants Uncle Brett had hired met him to show him to his room. I didn't know if Uncle Brett had picked the south wing—as far from my bedroom as possible—or if that was the luck of the draw, but it amused me. I had no intention of acting rashly with Robert. Some men thought that a widow or, heaven forbid, a divorcée, was prize plum pickings. I didn't intend to be one of those easy girls.

For a moment, as we said good night, I wondered if he would try to kiss me, but he didn't. His hand slid down my arm and caught my fingers for a quick squeeze, and then he followed the white-jacketed servant down the hallway.

When I got to my room, I changed into a nightgown and opened the balcony doors. The night was once again cool, such a blessing. I stepped onto the balcony, aware of the smell of tobacco. Someone was smoking a cigarette, and I went to the railing and looked down on the drive. Uncle Brett and Isabelle held hands. She smoked a cigarette in an elegant holder. They spoke softly, and I couldn't hear her words, but the tone was clear to me. She adored my uncle, and she was confiding in him.

I heard the words *niece*, and *pretty*, and *future*. She wanted to know if I was planning on living at Caoin House. Until that moment, I wasn't aware that I was actually considering my uncle's offer. I'd accepted my life as a Savannah schoolteacher and widow.

The luxury Caoin House offered was an existence far different from my mortgaged cottage, rigid work schedule, and stacks of student papers to grade each night. But it was Robert's presence in Mobile that tempted me. If I returned to Savannah, I could correspond with Robert and see him occasionally. But I would never know if real feelings might develop between us.

A soft breeze brought me the scent of gardenias as Brett put his arm around Isabelle and pulled her to him, pressing a kiss on her lips. It was hard for me to remember that he was not an old man, only in his forties. He had many years ahead of him and plenty of life left in him. I hoped that Isabelle was the woman he deserved.

Feeling a bit like a voyeur, watching my uncle woo his date, I turned to leave the balcony. My gaze swept the oak grove, and I froze. A man stood in the canopied oak trees, some fifty yards from the house. He was dark haired, and he wore what appeared to be a uniform, complete with knee-high boots. Cavalry? He had to be. He was definitely military, although the pale-gray uniform was nothing like the olive drab that Robert had worn.

When I'd seen him earlier, I'd assumed that he was a workman, but I knew, somehow, that wasn't true. He stood in the oak grove looking up at my window. Almost as if he knew I would come out to the balcony. I tried to convince myself that he was one of Uncle Brett's guests. There had been more than a hundred people at the party, and more would arrive tomorrow after church services for the Sunday games. In my heart, I knew better. There was something in his stance, the wide spread of his legs that claimed the ground he stood upon, and the fixed gaze at my window. This man was not at Caoin House for parties and celebrations. He had lost something here. I couldn't say what, but I knew he'd come to claim it.

And no one would stand in his way.

I gripped the wooden balustrade. The man took several steps toward me, moving into a ray of moonlight that illuminated the gold braid on his coat and the military insignia on the sleeves of his jacket. He ranked high in whatever army he served.

"Who are you?" I whispered.

Almost as if he heard me, he bowed low, and I saw the sword at his side, tied by a golden sash. He was such a young man, in his twenties. I knew him then, or at least the branch of his service. He was a Confederate. A man who'd fought for a defeated nation.

A dead man.

CHAPTER SEVEN

Rather than sleeping in, I woke early the next morning, still exhilarated from the events of the past night—the dancing and flirting, and especially the visitation from a ghost. I wondered if the vision had been brought on by the mimosas I'd sipped so liberally, or perhaps my subconscious was gifting me with an image to kick-start my writing. My Confederate visitor was an omen. I needed to write.

Winona was in the kitchen with coffee brewing, and I helped myself to a cup and hurried to the library, where I found pen and paper. If I wanted to write ghost stories, no more perfect opportunity would present itself. I'd seen a ghost. Now all I had to do was weave a story around the specter who haunted the oak grove. To that end, I couldn't wait for Pretta Paul to arrive. She'd sent word by one of the other guests that she'd been tied up in the candy store until late Saturday. She would arrive after church for the brunch Uncle Brett and Isabelle were organizing even as I put ink to paper.

It occurred to me that I should go and help them, but the memory of their closeness last evening argued that I should give them some privacy. To that end, I curled up in my uncle's plush wing chair and began to write a description of the ghost I'd seen.

What my eyes couldn't fathom, my imagination provided in great detail. Like a photograph in a tray of chemicals, my nocturnal visitor took on form and shadings. His dark eyes were melancholy, and his cheeks slightly sunken. He was hungry. But not for food. Hungry for life, for warmth, for the pleasures denied him as he drifted between the physical and spiritual worlds. Yet his uniform was impeccably maintained. He was a man who took pride in his service and his rank, which with a little research into the insignia on his lapel, I would soon know.

I'd noticed the three stars on the collar of his tunic, and the blue cuff below a gold scroll that somewhat resembled a fleur-de-lis. Or at least that was the best description I could give. Uncle Brett, who'd studied the Civil War for years, would be able to help me. He'd visited many of the battlefields and knew the history inside and out. Mobile Bay had played an important role in the war, and I always believed it was one of the things that drew him back to the city he'd left behind as a young man. He would know immediately the rank of my revenant.

With great care I drew the design as clearly as I could. It was peculiar how detailed my memory was, considering I'd only seen the phantom at a distance for a few minutes. But it was all in the service of my dark imagination, so I merely went with what I could remember.

When I had written my description and drawn what I could remember of the insignia, I put my tablet on the desktop and went to the kitchen for another cup of coffee. Soon the house would be awakening, and I would have duties as cohost. I would also see Robert. The thought of that shut off any hunger pangs.

Winona was bustling in the kitchen, and the smell of cooking bacon made me pause in the doorway. Long ago, my mother had fried bacon for my father's breakfast, and for mine. A wave of sadness hit me with a force I hadn't expected. My gentle schoolteacher father, whom I'd never heard raise his voice in anger, and my mother, more of a firebrand and fiercely protective of Father and me, had died in a boating accident when I was eighteen. Even though I was an independent woman already studying to become a teacher, the loss had left me stranded and very much alone. And then I'd met Alex. And I'd slowly rebuilt a life with the same rhythms that made me feel safe and secure.

I, too, cooked bacon for breakfast for my husband. And while I taught during the day, which meant I didn't prepare lunch, I had a hot supper ready when he came home in the evenings from his fledgling law practice. And those evenings had been so wonderful. We'd read, side by side, in the plush club chairs that were a wedding present from Uncle Brett. When we grew tired of our books, we'd shift to the floor in front of the fireplace and kiss away the cool evenings and the sad memories.

We'd laughed and dissected the books we loved. Alex teased me about my interest in the supernatural and sensational stories, but he'd listened like a schoolchild when I told him stories of the dead, risen from their moldy sepulchers, and premature burials.

"Miss Raissa, can I get you something?" Winona had come to stand in front of me, and in my memory-trance, I hadn't noticed.

"Another cup of coffee, please." I held out the cup and saucer. "I'll get dressed and come down to help."

"Everything is in hand." She filled the cup and returned it to me. "Mr. Brett and Ms. Isabelle are walking the grounds now. With Mr. Carlton. I believe they're planting clues for the game Mr. Carlton has concocted."

"Drat. I'd hoped to join them."

"They were headed to the family cemetery."

"Thank you, Winona. The first step is getting dressed." I hurried upstairs and went through my trunk for something cool and comfortable to wear. After the freedom of the shorts yesterday, everything would feel confining and hot. But it was Sunday, and a little decorum wouldn't hurt.

The trousers I chose were lightweight, but still not as cool as the shorts. I selected a sleeveless white-linen shirt and hurried back downstairs. Robert was in the kitchen, munching bacon and a biscuit at the kitchen table while he talked with Winona. Whatever he said made her laugh. It struck me that Winona was still young, maybe in her late forties. And she was pretty. Thick lashes framed her beautiful eyes. Servants were so often overlooked and treated as nonhuman. They were part of the furnishings, like running water and electricity. My uncle never took other humans for granted, and that attitude was one I'd also adopted. I wondered what Winona's dreams might be. Did she want to marry and set up her own household?

"Raissa!" Robert saw me in the doorway at last and stood. "These biscuits were made by angels last night while we slept. Winona is trying to take credit for them, but no mortal could create such light, melt-in-your-mouth delicacies."

Winona knew he was flattering her, but her smile was like a burst of sunshine. "He is a devil," she said. It was one of the most unguarded moments I'd ever shared with her.

"I'm well aware." I snatched a slice of bacon from his plate.

"The brunch will be served outside on the grounds in half an hour," Winona said.

"Can I help take out food or do anything?"

Consternation touched her features. "No, ma'am. That wouldn't be proper. You're the party honoree."

"Pox on proper. If I can help, I'd like to."

"Enjoy yourself and this gentleman. That's how you can help."

Robert took my elbow. "We should leave Winona to her cooking."

I wasn't quite ready to go. "Winona, have you ever heard of any ghosts on the grounds of Caoin House?"

She'd been lifting the lid on a pot, but it slipped from her hand and clattered loudly to the top of the stove. "Why would you want to know about ghosts?" Her response was almost as if I'd jumped out from behind a bush and frightened her.

"I've heard Caoin House is haunted. Even Uncle Brett said *caoin* is a Gaelic word that means 'lament' or 'grieve.'" I tried to pronounce it as he had: *qu-aine*.

"No ghosts around here. Your uncle keeps things too lively for ghosts. Talking of such things can bring on trouble."

Robert increased the pressure on my elbow. "You're making her uncomfortable," he whispered.

"Thanks, Winona." Robert was right, though I couldn't figure out why. "We'll track down Uncle Brett."

We left the coolness of the house and stepped into the June morning. Based on the heat that had already accumulated, the day would be much warmer than yesterday. Summer had overtaken spring. The seasons had changed in a matter of a few hours.

"I wonder why Winona was spooked by my question," I asked.

Robert guided me into the oaks and away from all the people working to put food on the long tables. Two dozen guests were already up, drinking coffee or starting the day with another round of beverages.

"A lot of people are superstitious about the dead." Robert grabbed my hands and spun me in a circle, as if we were children. The sun made starbursts against my closed eyelids.

"Raissa! Mr. Aultman!" Uncle Brett called out as he and Isabelle entered the oak grove. "Are you showing Mr. Aultman the grounds? Again?" He winked at me.

"We were actually looking for you," I said.

"I see."

"Leave them alone." Isabelle came toward me and held out her hand. "Men can try your patience, can't they? I don't believe I've met your friend."

"This is Robert Aultman," I said. "Robert, this is Isabelle Brown. Where's Carlton? Winona said he was with you. I told him I'd help him with the clues for the hunting game."

"He refuses all help." Uncle Brett pretended to be put out. "He told me he'd do this himself to be sure I didn't cheat. Imagine, saying that to a man in his own home."

"You do have a reputation for not following the rules, Uncle."

"You make me sound like a scoundrel." Uncle Brett was very pleased.

"If the shoe fits . . ." Isabelle laughed, and the sound was like a finely played woodwind.

Winona approached, and Uncle Brett stepped away to have a word. When he returned, he clapped his hands. "Brunch is served. Please help yourself. Don't overeat—we're having the championship croquet and horseshoe-tossing matches beginning at one o'clock."

Although I wasn't hungry, I couldn't resist Winona's crab omelet. Once I had my plate and was seated across from Robert at a small table, I found I couldn't eat. Robert, too, played with his food. We kept looking at each other and grinning like fools.

"We are not very subtle." I pushed my plate away.

"Blatant. That's the exact word." Robert's lip quirked for a moment. "You're a terrible influence on me. I'm normally all business. I should be talking with your uncle, working a deal, and all I do is sit here watching you not eat."

A breeze lifted my curls from my neck, and I wanted to escape the party. In another few hours, Robert would leave for town and perhaps more travels up the East Coast. Time was such a precious thing.

An automobile pulled up to the house, and Pretta Paul hopped out, followed by a tall man who wore glasses. Pretta's red swing skirt caught a breeze and puffed up, making her laugh. Her husband pretended to beat the skirt down in disapproval, but he was smiling. I waved her over and made introductions. "I'm going to spank the pants off Hubert at tennis," she vowed, making her husband snort.

"You're a frisky filly, but your aim needs work." Hubert put a hand on her shoulder.

Pretta rolled her eyes. "It's true his arms are almost long enough to put the horseshoe on the post."

"Help yourself to some food and join us," I suggested. I was dying to hear her ghost stories.

When they were seated, I asked Pretta about the tales involving Caoin House.

"I don't want to spook you," she said, her gaze shifting to her husband, who clearly disapproved of the turn the conversation had taken. "Let's not ruin a beautiful day with tales of the dead."

"I want to write ghost stories," I said. "Like Mr. Poe or Sheridan Le Fanu."

Hubert Paul cleared his throat. "I know you gals are modern and want to take the world by storm, but I'm not certain that's a profession for a lady."

I felt as if I'd been slapped, and I quickly put a hand on Robert's knee when he started forward as if he intended to challenge Hubert. "The world is opening up for women, Hubert. We'll have the chance to prove ourselves in professions once closed to us. But women have always been authors."

"I didn't mean any disrespect. It's just that ghost stories are . . . frightening. I wouldn't think a gentlewoman would want to frighten people."

I was relieved that his concern was for the content of my writing, not the writing itself. "Oh, but I do. I want to frighten people out of their socks and shoes!"

The moment passed, and our conversation turned to the coming Mardi Gras season. I decided to wait until I had Pretta alone to ask again about the tales. Sensing my desire, Robert led Hubert to the horseshoe stakes and engaged him in a game.

"So what ghosts lurk about Caoin House?" I asked Pretta.

She frowned. "Maybe I misspoke. All of the old houses have tales involving the departed. It's just foolishness. I should keep it to myself."

"Don't be silly. This might help me in my research for my own writing." When she still looked uncertain, I added, "I've already seen one spirit on the property." I leaned closer. "And a handsome one at that!"

"You have? Who was it?"

"I wish I knew," I said. "He was a Confederate officer. Cavalry, I think. I'll have to ask Uncle Brett about the uniform and insignia."

She bit her top lip with small, perfect teeth. "Hubert will be angry if I upset you." It was clear she wanted to talk.

"And I'll be angry if you don't." I hoped to jolly her into talking.

"It's so interesting you saw a Confederate soldier." Her eyes snapped with excitement.

"And why is that?" My uncle had cranked up the phonograph again, a war tune.

"Because Eli Whitehead, who built Caoin House, was a colonel in the Confederate cavalry. He brought in Vernon Lovett, the famous British architect, to draw up the house plans. It took Eli and a number of slaves over two years to finish the house."

"So you think I saw Eli lurking around, spying on who lives in his house and what we're up to?"

She shook her head. "It's a sad story. Are you sure you want to hear it?"

"Absolutely."

CHAPTER EIGHT

Around us the sounds of the party seemed to diminish as Pretta leaned forward and said, "Eli built Caoin House for his bride, Eva. It was said she was the most beautiful woman in the Confederacy, and that every man fell at her feet."

I loved stories where the woman's beauty had the power to slay. It was one of the elements of a terrific ghost story. Edgar Allan Poe's masterpiece was about "Ligeia," who was able to transcend death. And if the woman in the tale died tragically, all the better. "He must have loved her to build this house." I glanced over at Caoin House and gasped. A man stood on my balcony. A glint of sunlight reflected from the sword at his side.

"What?" Pretta turned, but after a moment gave me a blank look. "What did you see?"

"I thought someone was on the balcony. It must have been a shadow." If I spooked her, she'd never tell me the story of Eli and Eva. "Robert and Carlton are playing tennis. Let's go watch while you tell me about the most beautiful woman in the Confederacy."

She checked to be sure Hubert was fully engaged with his game of horseshoes, and we strolled beside the tents on the way to the tennis court. "Her portrait hangs in your uncle's morning room. I'm sure he'll show it to you if you ask. I've tried to convince him to hang it in the main parlor, but he won't. He says he doesn't want to taint the house with her sadness."

The hair on my neck tingled, as if a chill wind had blown against me, but there was no wind. "What happened to her?"

"During the last months of the Civil War, Mobile was occupied by Union troops. The residents were starving, and a group of women, led by Eva, marched on Union headquarters and demanded food. During the war, it was common for the womenfolk to manage the plantations. As the war dragged on, times became hard for Southern women. The men were on the front lines, and the slaves had fled."

I flagged down a waiter and picked up two glasses filled with planter's punch. The drink made good use of more orange juice, and I loved the exotic pineapple. Rum was one of the most accessible alcohols since it could be shipped straight into the Port of Mobile from Cuba, so we had an abundance of it.

"These are delicious," Pretta said. "Don't let me get drunk. I don't want to embarrass myself."

"No worries." I pointed to the court, where Robert rushed the net and returned a hard, fast shot. "So what about Eva and the hard times here in Mobile?"

"Mobile was embargoed by Union warships, and the supply of goods had been shut off. In the outlying areas, homes were raided by deserters of both armies, taking the food from the mouths of those who couldn't defend themselves. Those merely traveling through the region and headed for a new life took what they needed, because there was no work."

History revision painted the Rebel forces as all honorable men and boys fighting for the glory of a lost cause. I'd never really thought about how soldiers would steal from defenseless women, but it was a story as old as time. Rape and pillage. The Vikings, Hannibal, and Attila the Hun. My parents had given me an appreciation for the lessons of history.

"Anything of value, especially food, was stolen. Deserters, renegades, and stragglers were brutes who took whatever the war had left, and that wasn't much. Women and children were starving on the very land that had once brought such wealth."

Pretta was a good raconteur, but she painted a picture I didn't want to look at. Uncle Brett had told me some of the local history on prior visits, and my imagination could easily conjure up the horrors of that time period. The land around Caoin House still bore the scars. Not two miles away, the skeleton of Hornsby Plantation rose from the weed-choked ground. Broken and ragged columns seemed to guard a long-past dream, the last remnants of what had once been a grand plantation. As Union troops took over the area, the house had been burned to the ground. Honor Hornsby was left with nothing to feed her three children and no way to get into town for help. The four starved to death and were buried at the foot of a column that had once been a part of their home. Fifty years later, the wounds from both war and Reconstruction hadn't healed. In many ways, America was still a divided nation.

I'll never understand why people are willing to fight." My longing for Alex felt like a deep wound. "I want to believe that some good comes out of the loss of life, the destruction of property and history. But I don't. I really don't."

Pretta put a hand on my arm. "I know you lost your husband in the war. I was so glad Hubert came home. So many of my friends are widows. Their life is over before it even began. And some young women will never marry because there are no men for them to wed."

I swallowed my comments. "Please continue with your story." I had to dig out of the past.

Pretta's face, so often animated with good humor, drew into a frown. "Eli Whitehead was late joining the fight, but he did join in

1862. He said the Confederacy needed him, and he could no longer let others fight in his place. He left Eva at Caoin House with over seven hundred slaves. War had not yet touched lower Alabama, but that didn't last. Mobile suffered, like every other city."

"Did he ever get home?" The tennis match continued in my periphery, but my focus was on Pretta's tale.

"He was furloughed home in 1863, and their daughter, Elise, was conceived. He told everyone in town he was home to stay, but he was called back and eventually fought in the Battle of Franklin, just south of Nashville." She looked out over the lawn as if imagining the scene. "Ten thousand soldiers, mostly Confederates, died in that ill-conceived battle. As the Southern soldiers advanced across an open field, the casualties were so high the dead were held upright by the press of bodies. There wasn't room for the dead and wounded to fall down."

Uncle Brett had told me about many of the Civil War battles. War history was one of his hobbies. At the Battle of Franklin, General John Bell Hood ordered a frontal assault on barricaded Union forces tucked in the safety of entrenchments. The Union soldiers had repeater rifles; the Confederates had muskets. It was a slaughter.

Pretta was caught up in her story now, and though she ducked when a tennis ball swished by her head, she kept talking. "Somehow Eli managed to survive and was given permission for another brief visit to Mobile. That Tennessee battle scarred Eli for the rest of his life, but it was nothing compared to what he found when he got back to Caoin House. Eva had been brutally raped and murdered, and their little daughter, Elise, was found wandering about the house. Her baby footprints, coated in her mother's blood, were all over the first floor of the house. She'd been walking around her dead mother for at least two days before Eli arrived."

"How horrid." I tried to shut out the image of a poor baby unable to rouse her dead mother.

"Eli found the plantation abandoned. The slaves, now free, had left to find food. No one could say what had really happened to Eva, except that the murder was excessively brutal. Though law officials questioned a lot of people and tried to track down some of the slaves who'd fled Caoin House, there was never a trace of the killer. Eli almost lost his mind. He couldn't stand it, and he took Elise to Europe. They traveled for years."

"What happened to Eli?"

"Eventually he and Elise returned. He continued at Caoin House, buying more property. He had the ability to turn whatever he touched into money, a true Midas touch. While he had wealth in abundance, everything he loved he lost. He never remarried. He threw himself into this place, to bringing it back to life after the devastation of the war. Some say he worked to build a living monument to the only two women he loved. So that's what I know about your uncle's beautiful home. It has a tragic past."

"Tragedy is always good fodder for a ghost tale. Are there stories that Caoin House is haunted?"

Pretta nodded. "It's said that some can see Eva's ghost, wearing a lovely white gown and moving among the oak trees right here. Brett has hinted that he's seen Eva's ethereal spirit."

I had to laugh at the idea of my uncle seeing spirits. He was a wonderful storyteller and a well-known prankster. I had no doubt his talk of ghostly sightings had more to do with his sense of mischief than any real event. But my curiosity had taken another direction. "And Eli? Does he not haunt the grounds?" I had seen a Confederate soldier, not a female.

"The stories I've heard feature Eva, but it would seem sensible that Eli, too, would haunt the place he loved so much."

"Are there any pictures of him?" I asked.

Pretta frowned. "I don't know. I've never heard mention. He was black Irish, with dark hair and a dark complexion. That's what I've heard. Brett will know. Just ask him."

"Have you ever seen a ghost?" I asked.

"Heavens no." She mimed horror. "I would die of fright."

"There's a famous medium in New Orleans next week. Uncle and I are planning a trip over to attend a séance. I think I'll invite her back to Caoin House to see if we can bring Eva and Eli out of hiding. Perhaps we can give them some peace and send them on their way. It's sad that they would stay here, hoping for what?"

"Oh, Raissa, you are too brave. In fact, you are foolhardy. No one has any business messing with the dead."

I put a hand on her arm to calm her. "I won't mess with them—I promise. But if I could listen to them, or tell them something they needed to hear so that they could finish their earthly business and rest in peace, wouldn't that be a good thing?"

"I don't think a Christian should involve herself with matters of the dead. Leave this to the priests and ministers."

"An excellent idea. I'll invite one of each to attend."

Pretta turned to walk away, but she turned back. Her shock made me bite my lip to keep from laughing. "You can't be serious. That just isn't done. The people who consort with spirits and the dead—they're going to hell, you know."

"I want to write ghost stories. It's research. Surely a little risk of hellfire is worth a good story."

Pretta was even more upset. "Call it whatever you want, but society people will shun you. If you want to stay here in Mobile with your uncle, please don't do this, Raissa. Decent people won't have anything to do with you."

I couldn't laugh and hurt her feelings. She was sincere and attempting to be a good friend. "There's no need to worry. I won't become a social outcast—I promise." I hadn't indicated that I had considered my uncle's offer to stay, but I thought it was sweet of Pretta to be concerned for my social welfare. How awful to be a widow, a schoolmarm, *and* a social outcast.

"If you dabble in spiritualism, Raissa, you'll be worse off than a colored person. Quality people won't invite you into their homes."

I didn't answer because I wondered if her words held more truth than I wanted to hear. To me, this was a means to an end. I would learn things to use in my stories. And I couldn't be afraid to explore the supernatural world if I was going to write about it. Damn the social consequences. Uncle Brett would cast the deciding vote on my proposed adventure. Even if I couldn't invite the renowned medium to Mobile, I could attend one of her séances in New Orleans. My mind was made up about that.

"Raissa, I hope you aren't mad at me." Pretta tentatively touched my arm.

"Of course I'm not mad. You're trying to look out for me." I took her arms and led her back to the drink tent. She'd finished her punch and needed a fresh drink. Behind her was a clear view of the second-floor balcony outside my room, and standing there was the Confederate soldier. He put a finger to his lips, as if to hush me. His smile was conspiratorial. And then he was gone, his place marked only by the sheers of my bedroom blowing wildly out the window.

My expression gave me away, and Pretta turned to see what had caught my interest. "What is going on with those curtains?" she asked. "Someone must be in that room playing a prank."

"Highly possible," I said, though I couldn't keep a ripple of fear from slipping down my skin. I didn't mention that it was *my* bedroom. While I craved dancing with the dark side, I wasn't immune to the chills.

CHAPTER NINE

I had almost forgotten about Carlton's surprise when Uncle Brett used a megaphone to call us all under the main tent. Uncle turned the game over to Carlton, who divided us into teams of two, holding out the promise of a grand prize more wonderful than anything that could be found in *The Arabian Nights*. I would have preferred to slip away from the game with Robert, but we'd been put on separate teams. I was partnered with Isabelle, and I couldn't have picked better. Her knowledge of Mobile and Caoin House, combined with her fun-loving spirit, made for the perfect ally. Uncle teamed with Robert, so my new friend could use the time to advance his business schemes.

The boundaries for the game included all of Caoin House proper, the oak and pecan groves, the slave quarters behind the pecans, the family cemetery, and the fringes of the swamp. With each clue found, the team advanced to the next clue. The team that finished first would win.

The first clue told me instantly that Carlton had worked very hard to create a puzzle that could be solved, yet would take some hard thinking. Each team had a local person on it, to be sure that those from out of town were not totally at a disadvantage.

I read the first clue. "Brett spends his nights beside a woman of great beauty, the loveliest woman of the Confederacy." A bit racy, but that was Carlton's creative style.

"I know where the clue is," Isabelle whispered. "Wait until we can slip away."

While some gamers wanted to search Isabelle's pockets and shoes, I knew better. When the other players were preoccupied, Isabelle led the way to the house. We went to my uncle's morning room and stopped before the portrait of a woman who was not only beautiful but regal. Eva Whitehead. I'd not frequented my uncle's suite, so I studied the image of a woman whose beauty compelled. She wore a rose-colored silk gown that dropped off her shoulders, revealing an elegant neck and flawless chest. Beautiful and tragic.

The setting for the painting was not the traditional staircase or beside the mantel, but the oak grove. Although the trees were not so massive as they were now, sixty years later, I recognized one tree with a branch that swooped to the ground and came back up to create a perfectly flat surface. A large book rested on the limb, and Eva's left hand held the book in place. I couldn't make out the title, but it was bound in leather and appeared to be heavy.

She looked into the distance, and a hint of joy touched her features, as if some long-awaited guests were coming down the drive. Her pink lips were slightly parted. She looked so alive, I almost expected her to speak. No wonder Caoin House was reputed to be haunted by her. She was a woman who could defy death if she chose.

"If I were the jealous type, I'd have to banish this portrait from Brett's morning room," Isabelle said. "I wonder if she was this beautiful in real life, or if the painter enhanced her?"

Eva's dark eyes seemed to follow me as I stood on tiptoe to search behind the heavy frame. "She is truly beautiful, but she died a tragic death. Pretta just told me."

"Indeed." Isabelle came to help me lift the frame from the wall.

I felt behind it and finally discovered the slip of paper. I pulled it out and gave it to Isabelle to read as I readjusted the painting.

"In the long, sleepless watches of the night, a gentle face—the face of one long dead—looks at me from the wall, where round its head the night-lamp casts a halo of pale light." Isabelle frowned. "What does that mean?"

I knew the poem by Henry Wadsworth Longfellow. I'd taught it to my class, and had sometimes read it for comfort in the long days after I learned of Alex's death. "It's a poem about death. 'The Cross of Snow.'"

Isabelle stepped back from the portrait, distaste sliding over her face. "That's rather morbid—don't you think?"

Voices came to me. Another group of searchers were hard on our heels. "Shall I put the clue back?" I was tempted to take it and win the game by illicit means.

"We have to play fair." Isabelle's good humor was restored. "Put it back. Perhaps they won't be as literate as you are and will miss the reference. I would have."

I quickly replaced the clue, and we were at the doorway when John Mills, a banker from Birmingham, and Pretta came in.

"Did you find it?" Pretta asked. "It has to be Eva's portrait. I told you Eva was considered the most beautiful woman in the Confederacy."

I widened my eyes to perfect innocence. "I have no idea what you mean."

Pretta giggled. "I'm right behind you, Raissa. I won't let you win."

Isabelle and I hurried away, cutting through the dining room and a long hall that eventually led to a door that opened on the pecan orchard. When the coast was clear, we ran through the orchard and toward the woodland trail that led to the Whitehead family cemetery. In my visits to Caoin House, I'd never had occasion to seek out the burial plot of the Whitehead family. None of my kin was buried on the grounds.

My parents reposed in the First Episcopal Church of Savannah. Now, though, after hearing the tragic story of the Whitehead family, I was curious to see the place where Eva and Eli had been put to rest. Already I could think of a scene for my first story, "The Haunting of Beauty."

"Carlton must really want us to get some exercise," Isabelle said. "He's sitting under the tent drinking a cocktail while we're running through the woods, all for some unnamed prize which will more than likely be a joke."

"It isn't about the prize," I said, wiping the sheen of perspiration from my forehead. "It's the pride of the win."

She put her hands on her knees and bent down to catch her breath. "You are just like Brett," she said. "He adores winning."

I'd never thought of myself in that way before, but I liked it. I wanted to be the girl who came home with the blue ribbon, the prize. "Do you find that a negative quality in my uncle?"

My question made her stand up tall and examine me, but it didn't upset her. "I love your uncle. I believe, long ago, he lost a woman he truly loved, and now he is reluctant to test those waters again. Some hearts love too hard, and I believe he is like that. But I don't dislike his competitive streak. He wakes up each morning, raring to take on the day. So many people die and simply fail to crawl into a coffin. Your uncle is alive. Part of his joie de vivre comes from the win. How can I not love the quality that makes his eyes sparkle and brings forth that great laugh?"

Whatever else I could say about Isabelle, and I could say many complimentary things because I liked her, she loved Uncle Brett. "I hope you can share your life with him. I want you to know, should I move into Caoin House, I don't want to be a hindrance to your relationship."

Her laughter struck the tree trunks that surrounded us and bounced back. "You make your uncle happy. His happiness becomes mine. I'm glad you're here, and I sincerely hope you stay. Now let's find the next clue before Pretta catches up to us. She's very clever for a girl who pretends making candy all day long is the sum of her ambitions."

We started forward at a brisk walk, the sunlight filtering green around us. The song of a mockingbird followed us, making me think of Hansel and Gretel and the bread crumbs that would never lead them home. We hurried through the afternoon light to a wrought iron arch. "Whitehead Cemetery," in an elaborate scroll, was centered above the path. In smaller script was a verse: "Let those who enter rest in peace."

The cemetery was beautifully maintained, and it was much larger than I'd anticipated. The Whiteheads were not a big family, but there were grave markers for at least thirty people. Behind a screen of cedars, I saw wooden crosses that stretched into the woods. "Who are all those people?"

"Slaves," Isabelle said. "The mortality rate was high for the field-workers."

I couldn't think of anything to say. The numerous grave sites made slavery a reality. "Are there no stones or markings to tell their names?"

She shook her head. "Not for slaves or soldiers. In death we are all anonymous."

"Except for the ruling class." I hadn't meant the sentence to sound so judgmental, but there was no taking it back.

Isabelle wisely ignored it, and we walked into the cemetery shaded by live oaks, cedars, and sycamores, with their pale, mottled trunks that made me think of a snake shedding its skin.

"Where would Carlton hide the clue?" she asked.

"Eva's grave." Her portrait had sent us here. Besides, from the little I knew of Carlton, this sounded right. Eva had been the Queen of Caoin House. Her grave would appeal to his sense of drama. I surveyed the cemetery, aware of the beauty of this plot of ground where the dead slept, often covered with a slab of marble. The Episcopal cemetery in Savannah held the same moss-covered oaks, the same sense of time caught and held. Time meant nothing to the dead. For the living, time was either a weight or a sliver that evaded containment.

"Eva is buried over here," Isabelle said. She, too, had fallen into a pensive mood. "I came here once, with your uncle."

She led the way to a sarcophagus that bore a beautiful woman carved into the granite lid. I recognized Eva from her portrait. Though marble was a cold stone, the effigy of Eva was lifelike and alive. She wore a gown that flowed about her, and her curls spread across the marble as if arranged by the artist. "The work is incredible," I said.

"It is." Isabelle's hand traced the stone coils of Eva's hair. "The detail is exquisite. Coming here calms me. It's as if Eva merely slept."

Except for the white, unseeing eyes that stared skyward. To avoid those eyes, I focused my attention around the base of the grave, hoping to find a clue. The sun had slipped behind a cloud, and goose bumps danced on my skin.

"Are you cold?" Isabelle asked.

"No." I stood up, pondering my body's reaction to this tomb. "My mother would say someone walked over my grave." I rubbed my bare arms. "I just had a sense that something bad might happen. Foolishness."

We heard voices behind us, and I resumed my hunt. "We'd better hurry or we're going to lose our lead." My fingers worked the grass at the edge of the vault, pulling the thin carpet of runners back a little so I could look for the clue. At last I found something and brought it forth. The third clue.

"In the midst of vegetation, a mirror reflects the sun. Beware the lure of Narcissus. Look but do not touch." I read it aloud and returned it to the hiding place.

"What is Carlton going on about now?" Isabelle asked. She looked around the cemetery as if she expected someone to step out and reprimand us for being there. "Let's get out of here."

I shared her sentiment. "The clue directs us to that little pond on the way to the swamp. Let's hurry." We were almost to the lych-gate when I saw Travis. He came at a slow run, as he was a big man unused to moving with such speed. Instantly I knew he sought me, and for a reason that would hold pain.

"Travis!" I ran to meet him. "Is Uncle Brett okay?"

"He is. It's the young man, Robert. He's had an accident. You must come quickly; he's asking for you."

"What kind of accident?" Instead of speed, I was paralyzed. A red skein dropped behind my eyes. I saw nothing but pulsing veins. The red curtain fell away, and in my near-paralyzed trance state, I saw the blood. It ran in rivulets down the marble steps of Caoin House, inching ever toward the ground. So much blood. I knew the vision to be true.

Travis gripped my arms to keep me from falling to the ground. "Miss Isabelle. Help her."

"Raissa!" Isabelle patted my cheek. "Raissa."

I came back to the moment with the certainty that Robert was dead. "What happened?" I was unnaturally calm.

Travis could barely contain his agitation. "The young man took a fall. No one knows how. Miss Raissa, he's asking for you."

I sprinted toward the house, running like a creature pursued by the hounds of hell.

When at last I came out of the woods and raced across the pecan orchard, I saw the gathering of partygoers, once so festive, now standing in shock. I ran past them, failing to register the faces. No one attempted to stop me as I rushed toward the front steps of Caoin House, where my uncle, Carlton, and Winona were gathered. Uncle

Brett held Robert in his arms, the bright blood seeping away from them, inching and slowly spilling down the cascading steps. Just as in my vision.

"Robert!" I fell to my knees at his side.

The sound of my voice roused him, and he tried to lift a hand to me.

"Robert, don't go." I touched his face. I had no doubt he was dying. He lingered only for another moment. "Please, don't go." I grasped his shoulders as if I could force the life back into him. "Please, Robert: Stay with me."

Blood frothed at his lips, and he was gone.

CHAPTER TEN

The sequence of events that followed isn't exactly clear to me. Dr. Martin, Uncle Brett's personal physician, could do nothing. Robert was dead. Winona called the sheriff. Isabelle managed to coax me away from Robert's body and take me up to my room. Somewhere in the middle of it all, the guests departed and the servants dismantled the tents, tables, food, and drinks and hauled them all away.

My grief and shock were so acute, the doctor was sent up to attend to me. Though I struggled against it, potassium bromide was administered to calm me. I'd read about the effects of this treatment on patients, and I didn't want it, but the doctor prevailed. Finally, the image of Robert, his fine eyes boring into mine for one last moment before the life departed, slipped from my consciousness. Lethargy overtook me, and I slept.

When I awoke, the moon danced through the oak branches outside the French doors, which stood open. The night was pleasantly cool but far from cold. At first I had no recollection of the past day, but my reprieve didn't last long. Robert, a man I'd begun to develop feelings for, was dead from a fall, a freak accident.

But what was he doing, and how did he fall? My uncle's suite was on the main floor of the house. Robert's room in the south wing was also on the first floor and faced the cypress swamp, not the front of the house. It didn't make sense.

When I checked the clock in my room, I found it was only three in the morning. I couldn't go to my uncle and ask the questions that battered at my forehead like the wings of a moth against a streetlight. Answers would have to wait until tomorrow. My uncle was upset and tormented, too. If he'd fallen asleep, it would be wrong of me to wake him.

Although my spirit was raw, my body demanded food. I'd eaten nothing but a few bites of omelet and the bit of bacon I'd playfully snatched yesterday from Robert's breakfast plate. The medication had unsettled my stomach. Not even twenty-four hours earlier, he'd been alive and healthy, delighting in a biscuit and bacon. It was impossible that he was dead, and yet he was.

I thought to go down to the kitchen, but the lethargy came over me again, and I returned to bed. I felt as if I were falling, falling down a tunnel of wool darkness. I dreamed that someone called my name. "Raissa! Raissa, come down to me."

The balcony doors were open, and the voice called to me from the lawn outside. I went out into the night and looked upon the oak grove. The soldier stood, fifty yards from the house, in the middle of the trees. The dark oak branches, like the legs of giant spiders, stretched and bent. The moss gyrated in a soft breeze, and I thought of the tatters of a shroud.

"Who are you?" I called down to the soldier. Even though I spoke barely above a whisper, he could hear me.

"Raissa, come down to me."

I moved as if my will had been stripped from me. Back into the bedroom, down the hall, down the cantilevered spiral staircase that seemed to hang suspended. At last I was at the front door. After turning the lock, I stepped into the night. I would find this soldier and name him, once and for all. I would learn why he called to me.

I crossed the drive and stepped into the dew-soaked grass, so cool beneath my bare feet. A wind caught the fabric of my cotton gown and blew it against my body, outlining my form in a rather indecent way. I didn't care. My only goal was to meet with the soldier. He didn't walk, but he drifted closer to me. I heard the clank of his sword against his polished black boots.

"Who are you?" I stopped beside the limb where Eva Whitehead had stood for her portrait.

"I've waited for you," he said. "Come with me." His voice was deep, with the hint of an accent that was more Mississippi or rural Alabama than society Mobile.

"Who are you?" He was not three feet away. His face, gaunt and handsome, held mysteries. Three stars gleamed on the collar of his tunic. His cavalry hat was held in one hand. The other hand extended to me, imploring.

"What do you want?" A glimmer of warning traced up my back. "Who are you? Tell me or get out."

He began to fade away. From transparent he dissolved into nothing.

I came to my senses on the floor of my bedroom, head pounding. At first I couldn't remember where I was, or why the furnishings of the room were so elegant. I looked out the open balcony doors into a night graced with the soft shadows of a full moon. I was at Caoin House. The whole dreadful day came back to me. The doctor had given me a drug to calm my emotional turmoil, and the sedative had resulted in the strangest dream. I'd spoken with the Confederate soldier, a man who was long dead.

The clock in my room showed three thirty. Soon it would be daylight. But not soon enough. I forced myself from the floor and into the bed. I'd thought I'd never sleep, but the bliss of unconsciousness came over me instantly. I escaped into a gray landscape of fog and the echo of hounds on the trail of prey.

"Raissa, wake up." The soft voice called to me as someone shook my shoulder. "Raissa, are you okay? Wake up."

I opened my eyes to bright sunlight and a worried Isabelle leaning over the bed. I tried to swallow, but my mouth was so dry, I coughed instead.

"Here." Isabelle helped me sit up and put a cup of strong black coffee in my hand.

"What time is it?" I asked.

"It's nearly noon. The sedative knocked you out." She sat on the side of the bed and offered a bite of scrambled egg to me. "Eat this. You need to put something in your stomach or the medicine will make you queasy."

The thought of eggs made me want to retch, but I ate a bite. And another of toast. With each mouthful, I felt more like myself. "I had terrible dreams." Truthfully, I couldn't discern between the horrible dreams and the even more awful reality.

"It's a side effect of the bromide," she said. "Nasty stuff, but you were so upset. Brett was terrified that your mind would snap. For such a young woman, you've suffered many losses." She looked away for a moment to compose herself. "I'm so very sorry, Raissa."

"Where is . . . he? Robert." There were so many questions to ask. His body had been removed, but where had they taken him?

"The doctor took him to the hospital in Mobile. Brett has been trying to notify his next of kin, but we can't seem to find a living relative. He was such a young man—surely he has parents or siblings or cousins. Did he mention anything to you?"

I hadn't thought to ask Robert about his family, possibly because I had none of my own to share. The interest we'd nurtured hadn't moved beyond the immediate. It was a blow to realize I knew nothing about Robert, except for the wartime loss of a beloved brother. I had no answers regarding his next of kin or even his permanent residence. "I didn't ask. There wasn't time to . . ." I swallowed back the emotion. "It's ridiculous to feel so bereft when he was a stranger to me."

Isabelle patted my hand. "I don't know what's hardest, losing someone you've loved for a long time or young love cut short. And I know you weren't in love, but the attraction was plain for all to see. I'm so sorry you're hurting." She brushed my hair back from my face. "If you feel up to it, your uncle needs you. He's very upset, and he's worried about you. Seeing you up and about will do him a world of good."

Though I wanted to burrow into the pillows and coverlet, I could not fail Uncle Brett. "Yes. I'll get dressed and come downstairs." I tossed back the covers and stopped. The sheets were streaked with mud and grass. Isabelle looked at them, and I looked at her.

"What happened?" she asked.

Pieces of grass still clung to my feet and ankles. "I dreamt I went out onto the lawn to meet a Confederate soldier. But . . ." My mind was still foggy from the bromide. It wasn't possible that I'd *actually* gone out onto the lawn. Yet my dirty feet told another story.

"Tell me about this soldier," Isabelle said.

"He's not real." I had to explain this properly or Isabelle would think I'd lost my mind. "He's a cavalry officer. I believe it's Eli Whitehead."

"Eli's dead. He's buried in the family cemetery." Worry drew her brows together. "You were sleepwalking, Raissa. It's another of the side effects of the bromide." Her tone changed. "I told the doctor not to give you a full dose. And you should know, the effects linger for several days up to two weeks." She grasped my hands in a gentle grip. "Potassium bromide can lead to hallucinations and a trancelike state. I should have stayed here with you to keep you safe."

"Other than dirtying the sheets, I'm not hurt." I didn't want her to think that I had a weak mind. "I'm fine, Isabelle. Really. I had a dream and saw a ghost." I almost mentioned that I'd seen the soldier long before I took the medicine, but for some reason I didn't. Isabelle was too upset, and I didn't intend to worry her more. "Let me freshen up, and I'll be down. Please tell Uncle Brett that I'm in no danger."

"I'll tell Winona to send a girl to change the sheets." Isabelle rose. "We'll get through this, Raissa."

"Yes, we will." My resolve to travel to New Orleans to meet with the famed medium had grown stronger. If I could see and speak with a Civil War ghost with whom I had no connection, then why not Robert? Or Alex? Or my parents? There were many on the side of the dead with whom I wanted a word.

I hurried through my toilette and dressed in a skirt and simple blouse. Uncle Brett was standing in the foyer, and the relief on his face made me wish I'd not slept half the day away.

"Raissa, how are you?"

I kissed his cheek. "I'm okay. I have questions."

"I thought you might," he said, taking my elbow. "Isabelle, would you ask Winona to send coffee and something light to the library?"

"Of course." She left us and went to the kitchen.

"Shouldn't Isabelle be with us?" I asked. It seemed unkind to exclude her.

"There are things I wish to tell you and only you," he said. The skin under his eyes tightened. "You are heir to Caoin House, Raissa. My only blood. Should anything happen to me, you will inherit. It's time to settle some things between us. Robert's tragic death has brought that point home."

CHAPTER ELEVEN

Winona served coffee and a bowl of fresh strawberries. I'd told her earlier how much I loved the summer crop of berries. Worry was etched on her face, and her gaze lingered on Uncle Brett. She was far too discreet to show her emotion publicly, but she was worried about him. I thanked her for her kindness, and she left with only one backward glance at Uncle Brett.

"Ask your questions," he said. This was a side of him I didn't see often, the businessman who dealt with unpleasantness head-on. "Ask and I'll answer honestly."

"How did Robert fall?" I kept my voice steady by great effort. If Uncle Brett could be open and direct, I could be sensible and strong.

"No one can figure out what he was doing on the roof. Carlton and I went up there and found a handkerchief with his initials. Perhaps he went for a better view of the hunting teams. All I know is that he was beside me one minute, and then he was gone. I had no idea what had happened to him. I wasn't much inclined to continue the hunt without my partner, so I went to talk to Carlton in the beverage tent. I don't know if we'll ever understand what motivated Robert to climb onto the roof."

I didn't react, but I found that possibility unacceptable. I would learn what drew Robert to his place of death. As soon as I was out from under the watchful gaze of Uncle and Isabelle, I would go to the roof myself.

"You were teamed with Robert," I said. "Did he say anything?"

"Only that he was disappointed not to be teamed with you." Brett's words were tinged with sadness. "He was enchanted by you, Raissa." He patted my hand. "I liked him. In time, he might have been the son I never had, and you the daughter."

In his own way, Uncle Brett had lost as much as I. It struck me how lonely Uncle Brett must be. I changed the subject. "Who was Robert involved in business with?" I realized when I asked the question that I sought motive for a murder—not an accidental fall. Uncle Brett realized it, too.

"Next you'll ask which of the guests was unaccounted for."

"That was my next question." The certainty that I was on the right track made my lungs contract ever so slightly.

"As far as I understood, Robert was starting his own business in Mobile. And I have no idea where half the guests were. They were all over the property hunting for clues." He sighed. "You suspect foul play?"

"I don't know, but I'm not ruling it out. Robert was fit and athletic. It makes no sense that he was on the roof, and it makes even less sense that he somehow managed to fall."

"Your observations greatly trouble me." Brett pushed his cup and saucer back from the edge of the table and stood. "There are things about Caoin House you should know."

"I know the house is haunted." I dared a lot, asking my uncle to believe in my visions.

"You've seen her?" Brett asked, his healthy color fading into pale. "Thank God. I thought I was the only one who saw her."

"Her?"

"Eva Whitehead. She haunts the house and the grounds. It's why I had the sarcophagus built for her. I wanted her to find rest, and the priest told me that building a final resting place for her might work, but it didn't. She beckons me outside. There are nights I've awakened at the gate to the family cemetery. I feared I was going mad."

"And no one else has ever seen her?"

"As if they'd come out and say, 'Oh, by the by, Brett, old boy, you have a ghost sporting about the house.'" He frowned. "What is it?"

"The ghost I saw wasn't female. He was a Civil War officer. Three gold stars on his tunic collar."

"A colonel. Eli Whitehead was a colonel."

We stared at each other, both thinking the same thing but unwilling to express it. The original owners of Caoin House were still here, and something was holding them to this property. I found the notebook and pen I'd left on one of the library tables and sat down to make notes. "Tell me about Eva," I said.

The woman my uncle described could have stepped right out of the portrait in his morning room, except her time among the shades had darkened her beauty. While she was as alluring as ever, my uncle also feared her.

"She insinuates herself into my dreams," he said, now pacing in front of the cold fireplace. "She begs me to go with her to the cemetery." He inhaled and swallowed. "I fear her desires are degenerate."

"She died during a terrible assault," I said, feeling my way into my own thoughts. "Perhaps her behavior is residual."

"As if she's still angry and wanting to punish the men who harmed her?"

I had only the tales of Poe, Le Fanu, and others of that ilk to go on. "Maybe. I don't know. The man I saw seems only sad and lonely."

"These are not healthy imaginings," Brett said. "I have changed my mind about you staying here. Evangeline was right. It would be best if you returned to Savannah."

"My mother . . ."

"During a visit, something upset her. You were a child, but you were hysterical. She never returned here. And I think you should leave."

"No. I won't do it." I'd never openly defied my uncle—or any other figure of authority.

"Raissa, this house is dangerous."

"No, I won't leave you. If you wish to come to Savannah, I'll accompany you. We can put the house and grounds on the market. You can build and sell your steamboat contraptions as easily in Savannah as here."

Pain shifted across his face. "I can't leave here."

"Then I can't either. We're in this together."

"I admire your courage, but this house isn't safe."

"Then we'll get to the bottom of what's wrong here." I rose and faced Uncle Brett. "I want to write. I want to be a serious author, to tell stories. Ghost stories." I inhaled so that my voice wouldn't shake. "I have a gift. I can see them. And I want to write about them. To discover why they remain trapped here."

"And you think you can do this? You think you *want* to do this?"

"I want to try."

"Then I'll support you, though I simply can't imagine sitting alone and making up a tale."

The relief was immense. Uncle Brett hadn't laughed or scoffed at me. "Oh, I won't be alone," I reminded him. "Now tell me about Caoin House."

CHAPTER TWELVE

Pretta had related the bones of the story. Uncle Brett fleshed them out. It wasn't surprising that my timid friend left the more gruesome details of Eva's death out of her version. Uncle Brett spared me none of the gore. He had his reasons, as I was to learn by the end of the conversation.

"I don't believe Eva died at the hand of some deserter Union soldier," he said.

"What do you think happened?"

"I don't know, but there's more to the story. I found some letters." His face reflected his serious thoughts. "I haven't told anyone about these letters, not even Isabelle."

"What kind of letters?" My uncle acted as if he'd uncovered correspondence between President Wilson and the kaiser making illicit plans to take over the world.

"Love letters."

I didn't laugh, but I wanted to. "Whose love letters?" I'd read my fair share of love letters regarded in literary circles as the ultimate declaration of romantic love. I couldn't think of a single example that warranted such dark concern.

Brett went to one of the built-in teak shelves of the library and removed all the books. Using a letter opener from his desk, he manipulated the back panel, which sprang free and revealed a shallow hiding place. "Many of the homes of the wealthy have small hidey-holes in different places around the house. During the Civil War, the women stashed the household silver, valuables, papers of slaves, things of that nature, when they anticipated the Union troops were headed their way."

Uncle Brett reached into the depression and brought forth a bundle of letters tied with a green silk ribbon. "There are no names, but it's evident to me by the dates that Eva is the recipient. The author is a mystery."

I reached for the letters, but he withdrew them. "When I bought Caoin House, someone had ransacked the property. The former owner, Charles Wickerton, told me he'd been robbed three times in the years he owned the house. Nothing of value was taken—none of his silver or his wife's jewels. But someone systematically combed portions of the house, searching for something. He had no idea what."

"You think it was these letters?" Now I was eager to read them. What love letters from sixty years ago could generate such interest in modern times?

"I don't know. But twice in the past six months, when I was out of town, I've had someone break in and tear through the house. They were obviously searching for something, and they went through cabinets, strongboxes, drawers, cupboards. They completely ignored the silver and other items of great value. The paintings here are worth a fortune and could easily be sold to private buyers."

Two things struck me. The robber had to know when Uncle Brett would be gone, and it seemed apparent that whatever he was searching for, he hadn't found. He kept returning.

"May I see the letters?" I asked.

He handed them over. "I've read them all. Though they are remarkably literate and speak of a great passion, there's nothing in them worth stealing. As I said, the female is Eva, but the other correspondent, obviously a man, is not her husband. Or my presumption is that Eli didn't write the letters. You can judge for yourself."

The slightest chill traced over me. I opened the first letter, which was written in a strong, sloping hand that I associated with a male. It was dated December 3, 1864.

My Beloved,

The gray days of November are upon us, and I worry that you and the child are without the necessities. In the city, everything is scarce, but food can be found for those with the coin to pay for it. I know the grounds of Caoin House can produce abundant food for you, but I also realize there is no reliable workforce to help harvest what has been planted. The legal bonds of ownership no longer bind the slaves to their masters, and you know I believe this is just and right. Nonetheless, I hope that some of the more loyal slaves will stay to help you.

I will come to you Friday, as planned. After our reunion, I will work the garden in the hopes cold weather won't arrive and kill the meager plants that remain. You are not a woman who should have to survive on turnips and potatoes, so I will do my best to bring two laying hens when I come.

I read your last letter with great sadness. You have lost hope that we will ever be together. The war drags on, and news from the front is never good these days for the plantation owners. The inescapable fact is that the South is losing. For you, it is the loss of a dream, a way of life filled with grace and plenty. Though my feelings are vastly different, I hurt for you. I would never wish for you to shed a tear at the loss of any element of your life, save the one you no longer want. Your husband.

In my rounds of the society homes, I hear that Eli, at the side of General Nathan Bedford Forrest, led a charge with General Hood. The casualties were high, and some homes in Mobile wear the black ribbons of death that even I have come to dread. I will offer a full report of what I glean when I see you.

Master Granton has confirmed my time with you Friday evening. He is allowing me to ride one of his horses. He guards the horses jealously, but he loves money even more. Just know that each night I dream of your stormy eyes, fringed in black lashes, the peach tint of your skin against the sheets, and the softness of your lips. I have never known a woman of such beauty. While I have little to offer you, I put before you everything I have and everything I am.

I dream only of you and our hours together.

I cleared my throat and put the letter away, feeling as if I'd spied on the most intimate of moments. In my imagination, I saw the woman in the portrait in Uncle Brett's morning room, Eva Whitehead, as she opened this note and read words that could possibly wreck her world, if anyone had intercepted the letter. "You're correct about one thing. Clearly this wasn't penned by her husband." I scanned the note again. "This would have been very dangerous to Eva. I can't believe she didn't burn it." I looked at the stack of letters, probably twenty or more, in two different scripts.

"There was so little of beauty or hope to hold on to during the war," Uncle Brett said. "The entire social structure of the South was crumbling. You know I oppose slavery in every form. It's unfortunate that the underpinning of one of the most gracious and elegant cultures was built upon the trade of human flesh. What I'm saying is that I understand why Eva kept the letters, thinking them safe forever in this cubbyhole. She would have something to turn to in those darkest of times when the world as she'd always known it was gone."

"If the notes are not from her husband, she would have been ruined if he'd found them." I liked to think myself brave, but to flaunt infidelity would take more courage than I possessed. While men were forgiven the weakness of the flesh, women were not. Harlot, strumpet, whore, Jezebel—I knew the words that would have been applied.

"She courted ruin, for sure," he said. "From what I've read about Eli, he was a prideful man. To be made a cuckold while away on the battlefield . . ." Uncle Brett shook his head. "It is possible he killed her. Everyone from judges to law officers would have turned the other way, thinking it was her just punishment."

"But to leave his child beside the dead body of her mother—no father could do that."

"People are changed by war, Raissa. Seldom in a good way."

I knew it only too well. Another thought came to me. "If the ghost I saw is Eli, and you have seen Eva's ghost here . . ." I didn't finish the sentence because the idea that a jealous ghost had harmed Robert sounded insane. "The soldier ghost seemed more lonely than angry. But from all I've read, ghosts can be very devious."

"We'll discuss this more at a later time. I think we'd better open the library door. Isabelle is patient, but even a saint has limits."

"Thank you for sharing the letters. And your concerns."

"I'm going to return them to the alcove, but you know where they are. I hope you'll find time to read them. They might inform one of your ghost stories."

I rushed to him and hugged him. "You are the best uncle ever."

"Raissa, be careful here at Caoin House. Perhaps I'm shaken by Robert's death, but I am not satisfied that he fell, and I'll never believe that he jumped."

Those last words caught me by surprise. "People are saying he jumped?"

"Accident, suicide, murder. There are only three options for the death of a young, healthy man."

"I'll find out what happened to him, Uncle Brett. I will. And I'll figure out the ghosts here, too. I'll be like Sir Arthur Conan Doyle's detective, Sherlock Holmes."

Uncle Brett smiled. "Just remember, when you poke under rocks, you might turn up a snake."

"Then I will capture it." I put more enthusiasm into the words than I felt.

"I love this house and this city, but I love you more. Mobile is a place that refuses to acknowledge the South lost the war. The colored people are kept in line by harsh means. I know you share my view of slavery, but it's best to keep your political opinions to yourself."

"But I feel strongly—"

"I'm proud that Evangeline and Frank raised a daughter with an independent mind, but Mobile is a provincial town. Women are not as free as they are in Savannah, especially not women of your class."

I wanted to argue that Mobile was exactly the place that needed more outspoken women, but I had to consider my uncle's place in society. He enjoyed the comforts of acceptance into the highest ranks, and I would be the beneficiary of his standing. To behave in a way that put him at odds was unfair. "I promise you, Uncle, that I will govern my tongue, and I won't let my guard down."

CHAPTER THIRTEEN

Uncle Brett kept me busy with fabricated trips to town, dinner parties at local restaurants, and even a pajama party with Isabelle. She was a delightful companion, and I liked her more each time I saw her.

Several days passed before I had a chance to go to the rooftop. I told no one of my plan. I wanted time to go alone, to examine the area with the methods I'd learned from reading the adventures of Sherlock Holmes. The tiniest details were important, if one only knew how to find and then interpret them. By putting myself in the shoes of the famous fictional investigator, I could push my emotions away. Literature had always been the best place I knew to hide from pain.

The afternoon was hot, and as I searched for the means to gain access to the roof, I became more and more certain that Robert had not gone to the roof alone. How would he have found the way? All the help denied that he'd asked directions of them. Nor had any seen him wandering about the house.

A narrow stairway off the back servants' stairs led through the attic to a trapdoor that had to be pushed up and moved to get to the roof. For a moment I thought the weight of the door would defeat me, but I managed to push the hatchlike contraption aside enough to slip through.

If Robert had gone up to the roof and jumped, then who had replaced the cover? It became more and more clear that he had not been alone. So who had been with him? The physical evidence told me there was a witness to Robert's death. If not a witness, then a participant.

The idea that a murderer might have been lurking in Caoin House troubled me as I pushed my body through the opening and onto the roof. The sun was bright, hot, and very welcome after my chilling thoughts. Before me lay a gabled slate roof with a manageable slope. Looking for any clue out of the ordinary, I made my way across the tiles toward the front of the house, slipping only twice. Traversing the roof was no easy feat. Why had Robert come up here? It didn't make any sense at all.

At last I found myself at the ornamental pediment where, based on the position of Robert's broken body, we believed he had stood before he fell. I was strangely reluctant to search the area. After all the trouble I'd gone to so that I could get onto the roof, I wasn't about to lose my nerve. I owed this to Robert. A light breeze traced down my neck, and I felt certain it was him, letting me know he was with me, urging me to continue.

For a moment I gazed about the grounds of Caoin House. The rooftop gave an incredible view of the oaks and the shell drive that had seemed so welcoming when I'd first arrived. To the south, Travis worked in the rose garden, pruning the thorny branches of the plants that produced the heavy-headed blooms that filled the front parlor of the house with such rich fragrance. Several of the colored men Travis had hired were putting the front lawn back in pristine shape after the party.

A breeze lifted the skirt of my dress, fanning it behind me. Was Robert on the rooftop with me? I couldn't say for a fact, though I sensed him. If he was, I hoped he approved of my attempts to find out what had really happened. I believed he would. He would want justice. And to find that justice, I had to push myself, step by step, toward the edge of the roof.

When I stood looking down at the ground, I couldn't stop myself from remembering the pool of blood that had accumulated beneath my uncle and Robert, slowly spreading down the front steps. Winona had spent two days scrubbing the stain from the bricks. No trace of the tragedy could be found, yet I could call it to mind in an instant.

Sun glinted on metal far in the distance, and I looked down the drive to see Carlton's dark-blue Meisenhelder Roadster coming toward Caoin House. I hadn't heard from Carlton since the party, but I knew he'd communicated with Uncle Brett and assisted with the legal complications surrounding a death on the property.

Watching the car draw closer, I realized I looked forward to his visit. Just yesterday my uncle told me that Carlton had found Robert's family and had let them know what had happened. As it turned out, he had parents and a sister who were devastated by his freakish death. Carlton had explained the circumstances in such a way that the Aultmans had been satisfied that the death was accidental. Carlton had proven to be a good and caring friend. His visit would take Uncle Brett's mind off the things that troubled him.

With Carlton's arrival, Uncle Brett would be looking for me. He relied on me to serve as his hostess when Isabelle was absent. But I needed to examine the area. If I intended to align myself with the great detective Sherlock Holmes, I had to detect. And quickly.

I examined the rooftop. There was no sign of a scuffle or anything that I could find. The slates were in good repair, and the lead drainpipes that filled the household cisterns were mostly clear of all debris. My efforts were in vain. Uncle Brett and Carlton had already searched the area. I'd been foolish to think I might find something they'd overlooked. I was leaving when my shoe caught the edge of a slate shingle. The stumble nearly sent me to my knees, but I caught my balance. When I looked back to make sure the roof wasn't damaged, something winked, bright and shiny in the sunlight. My clumsiness had dislodged a tiny pearl-white button hanging from a tag of cloth. I picked it up and examined it. It had been pulled loose, and the fragment of material appeared to have come from a man's white cotton shirt.

I put the button in my pocket, retraced my steps, and within a few minutes I was back inside the cool halls of Caoin House.

Uncle Brett and Carlton already had bourbons in their hands when I made it down to the library, flushed by the heat of the roof. I did my best to cover the evidence of my adventure because I didn't want Uncle Brett or Carlton worried about my actions. While I hadn't solved the mystery of Robert's death, I'd learned one thing for sure—Robert had walked out onto the roof of his own volition—it would have taken a preternaturally strong man to force him across the sloping slate tiles, which were slick and untrustworthy. So he had gone under his own power, but why? I didn't believe his death had been an accident. The button and scrap of cloth told a story of struggle.

"Raissa," Carlton said as he came toward me. He took my hand and squeezed it. "How are you?"

"I'm thirsty. I think I'll join you two." I poured a bourbon for myself. "Has Sheriff Thompson closed the investigation into Robert's death? Uncle Brett and I have been so concerned."

"He has," Carlton said. "The coroner's jury studied the evidence presented, and it was ruled accidental. Your uncle is in no way held responsible. Whatever Robert was doing on the roof, it's clear he tripped and somehow accidentally fell."

"That's a relief." I went to Uncle Brett and gave him a one-armed hug. "There's no logical explanation as to why Robert was on the roof, but I'm just glad the ruling wasn't suicide. That would have damaged his family."

"Yes," Uncle Brett said. "A tragic accident."

"Let's put that sad incident behind us. Raissa, why don't you drive into town tomorrow?" Carlton asked. He reached into his coat pocket and brought out a telegram. "You and Brett come and have lunch with me. Afterward, make him take you shopping for a new outfit. I've arranged tickets for Brett, Isabelle, you, and me to attend a séance with Madam Petalungro in New Orleans next week." He handed the telegram to Brett but spoke to me. "If you're going to write ghost stories, you'll need material."

"Thank you!" I hadn't forgotten the proposed séance with Arthur Conan Doyle's medium in New Orleans, but I hadn't wanted to push Uncle Brett. So much had happened at Caoin House. Thank goodness Carlton hadn't forgotten. I could have hugged him.

Carlton was busy with his plans. "I've arranged tickets on the train to New Orleans, and I've secured rooms at the Hotel Monteleone for all of us. This will be an adventure." He patted Uncle Brett's back. "We need to get out of Caoin House and forget the misfortune that occurred. Or at least put it aside for a time."

"Thank you, Carlton." I was indeed grateful. This was exactly what Uncle Brett needed, and it would also be good for me.

"Brett, I hope I haven't overstepped, but we're booked to leave Saturday morning. The séance is Saturday evening, and we'll return to Mobile Sunday. It isn't a long journey, but enough to give you both a brief respite from worry."

"It's a wonderful idea, Carlton." A bit of life had returned to Uncle Brett's eyes as he spoke. "I'd forgotten about Raissa's interest in attending the séance. Thank you for taking care of it."

"My pleasure," Carlton said. "So it's decided. Raissa, I understand your curiosity, but what is it you hope to gain, Brett?"

My uncle swallowed the last of his drink before he answered. "Peace at Caoin House. You'll scoff at me, Carlton, but there are unhappy spirits here. Perhaps even dangerous."

CHAPTER FOURTEEN

The train ride with Carlton, Isabelle, and my uncle was a far different trip from my mostly solitary journey down from Savannah. In the rare moments I had alone, the memory of Robert sat beside me. I hardly knew him, but I felt the loss of what could have been.

Carlton kept the conversation lively and the alcohol flowing abundantly. For a country that had passed an amendment to prohibit drinking, there was an amazing number of flasks and discreet bottles of gin, rum, and bourbon about in the club car.

I learned from my uncle that the Gulf, Mobile, and Northern rail line had originally been built by a cadre of wealthy Northern timbermen. The railway's specific purpose was to move timber from the vast stretches of pine and hardwood in Alabama, Mississippi, and Louisiana to Northern cities experiencing a housing boom. The end of World War I was bringing prosperity to many Americans who could now afford homes.

Rail passengers were an afterthought, but the wealthy investors smartly realized if the train was chugging the timber to New Orleans and locations north, adding a few passengers would cost very little and bring even more profits.

When we'd rocked halfway to New Orleans, Isabelle and I struck out to find a water closet, since the one in the club car was out of service. I'd never cared for changing cars, even though it was perfectly safe. Something about that step from one moving carriage to the next unnerved me. I hated looking down at the tracks disappearing beneath the train. The sight mesmerized me, and I had the sense that I was being pulled under the train. Uncle Brett would have laughed at my foolishness. To prove to myself I wasn't a mouse, I pushed open the door and held it for Isabelle. She stepped ahead of me and hesitated. With a laugh, she took the step—and stumbled. For one incredible moment she hung in midair, between the two cars. Below us the cross ties rushed past. My reaction was involuntary. I lunged forward and grabbed her waist. The force of the moving train, her weight, my lack of solid footing—I, too, lost my balance, and, though we both fought against the gravitational pull, we slid toward the gap between the cars.

My life didn't rush before me. Instead, I could only think, *What a terrible mistake*. I was going to be crushed beneath the train because of a stumble. *Irony* was the word that came to mind.

At the last moment strong arms circled my torso, and I was pulled backward with great force. I held on to Isabelle as we were both literally hurled through the air.

We slammed backward into the car we'd been attempting to leave; all of us tumbled in a heap. I landed on top of our rescuer, and Isabelle on top of me. It took several moments to get over the paralysis that came from fear and to sort out our legs and bodies. I managed to slide Isabelle aside and move off our benefactor so he could breathe.

"Ladies, are you okay?"

I turned to thank him, only to find that it was Carlton. "A narrow escape," I said, trying not to imagine Isabelle dismembered beneath the wheels of the train. While my vivid imagination would work in my favor as a writer of ghost tales, it was not helpful in everyday life.

Isabelle, too, had glimpsed her dire end. "Raissa, you risked your life to keep me from falling, and thank God you came along, Carlton. We both could have died." She inhaled, visibly shaken. "I didn't stumble—I was pushed. Someone put a hand on my back and shoved me so that I lost my footing."

"Pushed?" Carlton asked. "By whom? I was coming down the aisle of the car and could see you through the door window. Raissa was beside you, to the left. No one else was there."

Isabelle looked as if she might cry. "I don't care what it looked like. Someone pushed me."

"All that matters is that Carlton saved us." I'd found my feet, but my legs suddenly jellied beneath me, and I searched for a place to sit down.

Carlton assisted me to a seat and sat beside me after he'd helped Isabelle to one of the leather benches. "Ladies, you took at least five years off my life. What a scare."

"I'm telling you, I was pushed," Isabelle said, two tears tracking down her cheeks. "I'm not careless."

"Sometimes the train rocks hard to the left or right, and in the process of rebalancing, it can make the couplings snatch." Carlton leaned over so that he could lift Isabelle's chin and gaze into her face. "You're not hurt, are you? Brett would never forgive me for orchestrating this trip if anything happened to either of you."

"Shaken but unharmed." She drew her shoulders back and repinned some curls that had come loose.

"And you, Raissa?" Carlton performed the same maneuver on me.

"I'm fine."

"Good, then. Shall I help you ladies into the next car?"

I wanted to say no, but my pride stopped me. "Of course. I'll go first." I stood and approached the door. Every cell in my body cried for me to turn back, but I pushed open the barrier. The clackety-clack of the railcars speeding over the metal made my stomach tighten.

"Let me go first and help." Carlton stepped across the gap as if it were a minor puddle. When he was on the far side, he handed me across the dizzying tracks. Within a few seconds, I was in the next car.

"I'll help Isabelle," he said, leaving me with some privacy.

I proceeded to the water closet—a tiny enclosure with a toilet and sink. With barely enough room to turn around, I splashed cool water on my face to tamp down the heat that fear and anxiety had produced. I had to calm myself and think of the positive. I'd been party to an accident averted, a tragedy that never happened. We could thank our lucky stars that both Carlton and I had such quick reactions.

At last my skin cooled and I stepped out of the WC. For the first time I noticed the occupants of this car, almost a duplicate of the one we rode in. The half-dozen passengers dozed. Except for one. An elderly woman sat facing me, her gaze uncomfortably intense. I glanced at her in a sidelong manner so as not to appear rude. I didn't recognize her, but judging from her unabashed interest, it seemed she might know me.

I started down the aisle. When I came to her, she lifted one spotted hand from her lap and clutched at the skirt of my summer dress. In a deep monotone, she said, "Take care, Raissa. Robert says to tell you all is not as it seems."

The words were as effective as a blow, and I sidestepped, almost falling into the lap of a sleeping businessman. "Excuse me," I said, mortified at my clumsiness. But the shock of the woman's tone and the fact that she used my name had caught me by surprise.

"Are you hurt?" the businessman asked, polite but disgruntled that I'd shortened his nap.

"No, it's just that she—" I turned to the woman across the aisle, but the seat was empty. "Did you see the woman there? Older, blue-and-white-dot dress." I'd seen her clear as a bell.

The man shook his head. "No one's been in that seat since Mobile. Is this a joke of some kind?"

"No, sir," I assured him. "She spoke to me . . ." But there was no point arguing about what I'd seen and heard. No one else on the train would know the woman. Or whatever she'd been. I could have sworn she was real, but she wasn't. She wasn't real, and she wasn't human. She'd brought a message from the other side and then vanished.

A harsh possibility entered my mind. Isabelle claimed she'd been pushed as she stepped from car to car. She'd nearly fallen to her death. It made me question how Robert had come to fall from the roof. Had he been pushed by a person or an entity?

The door of the train car opened, and Carlton entered with Isabelle. Her face was white with fear, and she gripped his arm tightly, but she forced a smile as she drew near.

"Raissa?" Carlton took my elbow gently. "Are you okay? You look pale."

"I'm fine, just unsettled." I wasn't ready to share my strange experience with anyone. "I guess I'm still dizzy from nearly falling under the train."

"That was enough to take the starch out of anyone's petticoats." He looked at the seat where the woman had been sitting, and for a moment I wondered if he'd seen her—could possibly still see her. But no, he motioned me to a seat near the door.

"When Isabelle has refreshed herself, we'll go back to the club car." He faced me. "Only another forty minutes or so and we'll be at the station in New Orleans. Tell me what you hope to learn tonight at the séance."

"If Madam Petalungro is as talented as I've come to believe, I hope to witness her communicating with the dead. Maybe she'll have a message for me." After the vision of the elderly woman and her warning, I wasn't certain I was up for more communicating with the departed. Perhaps the whole adventure had been a mistake.

"Any dead in particular?"

The question caught me by surprise. Of course I hoped to speak with Alex, and Robert, too. "My parents, first and foremost. Then my husband. And Robert, if he's available. I read somewhere, perhaps in a fictional tale, that sometimes it takes the dead a while to be able to return and communicate. It's an adjustment period for them as well as those who are left behind mourning their loss."

"Do you think it's healthy to focus so much on those who've died? Life is for the living, as they say."

His attitude was more curious than judgmental, and I found it a relief to have a frank discussion of the subject. "I think we all have questions about those who've died, and sometimes, a bit of communication may give closure."

"If you could say one thing to your parents, what would it be?"

"You have the gift of asking good questions, Carlton. No wonder you're a successful lawyer."

"And you're adept at dodging the question." He smiled. "I'm just curious. I lost a brother to drowning when we were both at law school in Tuscaloosa. If I could speak with him, I'd ask him if he forgave me."

"Forgave you?"

"I was supposed to go with Craig to the river that weekend. Instead, I went home with a young woman I met at the university. We'd fallen in love, and I was taking the serious step of meeting her family. If they approved of me, I planned to ask her to marry. After Craig . . . I lost her, too." He looked out the window, and for a moment I saw the young man who'd lost his brother and his intended. We had more in common than I'd ever expected. "I always felt if I'd been with Craig, I could have saved him."

I touched his cheek lightly to encourage him to look into my eyes. "I don't know the circumstances, but though you're very good at rescuing ladies from falling under trains, I'm not certain you can save everyone from misfortune. That's a lot to put on your shoulders."

"In the small hours of the morning when the world is quiet, you don't suffer from guilt? You're alive, and they're not."

Carlton's questions were acute and dead-on. I forced myself to meet his gaze. "I should have been a better correspondent with my husband. I should have told him how I loved him. I'm ashamed that I let shyness hold me back." I thought of the letters Uncle Brett had shown me, the passion on the page that the writer had shared for Eva. I had loved my husband, but I'd been young and reserved. I should have given him more to hold on to. To die with.

"Your honesty only makes me admire you more," Carlton said. "You're good for Brett, and I'm glad you're in Mobile. I hope you stay."

"I can't simply put up in Caoin House and rely on Uncle Brett to support me."

Carlton laughed, and the mood of our conversation was instantly lightened. "He can easily do that, you know. I doubt you'll eat more than, say, ten pounds of food a day. I'll kick in on the clothing fund if it makes you feel better. You're bold enough to wear the modern styles, and it's good to have someone in Mobile break new ground for women. I fear our Southern cities are far behind our Northern cousins."

"You're an awful man!" But he made me laugh, and I'd come to value laughter above almost any other attribute.

Isabelle joined us. "I'm glad to see you've both recovered from the scare of my misstep." She was still a bit pale, but her color was returning. "Let's not mention this to Brett. He has enough on his mind."

I nodded agreement. "Let's enjoy the evening. I'm looking forward to the Hotel Monteleone. It's been written up in several magazines that I follow. The photographs are sumptuous."

"I did a little poking about regarding Madam Madelyn Petalungro." Isabelle crooked her arm for me to take, an indication she was ready to brave the return journey.

"As did I," I said. "What she does is terribly exciting. She can actually speak with the spirits and get answers from the dead. Reports about her séances are remarkable. Sometimes tables lift, or bells ring. A story in the *Times-Picayune* newspaper said she works with a very handsome assistant."

"Someone is eager," Carlton said drily.

"Let's rejoin Brett before he worries." Isabelle took a breath and straightened her shoulders. "We'll have time for one more drink before New Orleans. Raissa, you can tell us everything you learned about our famous medium."

CHAPTER FIFTEEN

Isabelle had given me her sources at the *Mobile Commercial Register* to find out Madelyn Petalungro's history, and it was indeed very strange and thrilling. She'd been born into a Romany family in Meridian, Mississippi, the youngest daughter in a long line of women who often inherited the ability to see beyond the veil that separated the living from the dead. "This trait is one of the most valued in the gypsy culture," I quoted from the article I'd partially memorized. "Even as a child, Madam's talent was bigger than any her family had ever seen."

"Hold the train!" Uncle Brett said. "Isabelle looks a tad pale. We need a drink to continue this conversation."

When the Negro waiter brought setups of Coca-Colas, Uncle Brett added the rum and signaled me to carry on.

Madam's pedigree was impressive. Her great-grandmother had married into the royal Gypsy bloodline, and Madam grew up with special privilege—private schools, instruction in languages and ancient history, and, finally, she had been sent to Europe to complete her education. She was fluent in six languages. By the time she turned nineteen, she'd toured the major cities of the civilized world.

I grew more excited as I revealed each detail. "Thank you for coming with me, Uncle Brett and Isabelle. And, Carlton, thank you for getting the tickets."

"Oh, I called my friend Ramona who lives in New Orleans," Isabelle said. "Madam's life has been a scandal," Isabelle said. "She's had a multitude of lovers. She's had three children and never been married, and, according to the newspaper, she's amassed a fortune."

"Fascinating," Carlton said in a tone that could either be sarcastic or sincere. "She's certainly led a life outside the boundaries of polite society. But can she really speak to the dead?"

"Sir Arthur Conan Doyle doesn't doubt her, and he's a brilliant man." I spoke with passionate conviction.

"Yes, he writes about a fictional detective." Carlton took the sting away with a grin. "We all know he doesn't make things up."

I laughed out loud at Carlton's wickedness, but I wouldn't be diverted. "The first time Madam saw a spirit, she was six years old. It was at her grandfather's funeral, and while his body was in the coffin, she saw him standing beside it, very pleased with all of his friends and relatives who came to honor him in death."

Isabelle inched closer to Uncle Brett, as if she were afraid. "I think if I saw a ghost I would die of fright on the spot."

"Was she able to speak with the ghost?" Uncle Brett asked. "Could he tell her what it was like, being dead?"

"The articles didn't go into a lot of detail, but they said she was able to bring messages from the dead to the living. She uses names, and she often knows things she'd have no way of knowing. She's a confidante of the queen, and there was a long article where she assisted England's war efforts with information passed from the grave of deceased soldiers." I had almost depleted my information.

"Most churches frown on this activity," Carlton said. "I've never been religious, but some people think the medium is communicating with the minions of Satan. That demons take on the visage of the dead in an effort to lure innocent souls into their grip."

"Do you believe that?" Isabelle was stricken.

"I wouldn't have suggested this trip had I thought we were at risk of losing our immortal souls." His grin was rakish. "But if we are going to play in the zone between the living and the dead, I thought it prudent that we all know the score."

"You're just trying to agitate Isabelle," I said. "In one article I read, Madam was able to bring comfort to several families. She spoke with some departed children who convinced their grieving parents they were safe and happy. I would think that would be viewed as a good thing by the church, or anyone else who has an ounce of compassion."

"A very pretty story that I could make up on the spot," Carlton said.

"But she provided personal details, specific information."

"I hate to destroy the fun," Carlton said, "but I have done a bit of research, too. While I think this trip will be helpful to our budding authoress, remember that personal information on those attending a séance can be supplied by a confederate or assistant. Or the person who is being read is a shill. Like the old faith healers who would make the crippled walk and the blind see—they were never crippled or blind, so their miracle healing was a sham."

"Now, Carlton, this adventure was your idea. Don't tell me you're going to put a damper on the whole experience before we even begin?" Brett was a tad annoyed.

"View this like going to a theatrical production. It should be fun, but if you take it seriously, it's only going to lead to disappointment." Carlton was enjoying his role as devil's advocate. "We've all lost people we love. I don't for a minute believe some Gypsy can bring them out of the grave and talk to them. I like a good show, but I don't want anyone, especially not my friends, getting caught up by a charlatan."

94

Isabelle laughed. "Ramona said the medium addressed those who doubt her in a newspaper interview. She dared them to attend a séance and then say she was a fraud."

Carlton finished his drink in one long swallow. "I'm eager to see what she has to offer."

"What would you say if I told you I'd seen a ghost?" Uncle Brett asked.

The question caught Carlton by surprise, but he had a ready answer. "I'd say you're pulling my leg. I know you go on about unhappy spirits, but to say you've actually seen a ghost is a step further."

"What *are* you saying?" Isabelle said. "What ghost? Did you see one at Caoin House? I've often had the sense that someone has been watching me."

I had the strongest desire to tell my uncle to stop, but it wasn't appropriate, so I didn't speak up. There was no reason he shouldn't share this information with Isabelle and Carlton, but it felt wrong.

"I've seen the ghost of Eva Whitehead." Uncle Brett was pleased with the sensation he caused. Isabelle drew in a sharp breath, and Carlton looked worried.

"That kind of talk will get you a stay in the loony bin, old man," Carlton said, passing it off as a joke. "Be careful or you'll be having the electric cure."

"That's a terrible thing to say." I rushed to Brett's defense. The horror tales of convulsive therapy used on those with mental problems made my heart pound. The treatment often failed to bring any results except a loss of memory and sometimes destruction of the personality.

"Why is talk of seeing spirits a sign of mental illness?" Brett asked. The reasonable tone of his voice told me Carlton had fallen into his trap. Uncle Brett had set the lawyer up. He was eager for a debate of the topic. "Those who practice religion believe the soul lives on. Why is it so unreasonable to think that perhaps some spirits remain earthbound?"

"And why would they?" Carlton countered. He'd entered into the discussion with enthusiasm. I finally understood that this was part of their relationship—one of the things that made them such fast friends. They enjoyed the art of argument. Isabelle confirmed this.

"They'll be at this for hours," she said, stifling a yawn to show her boredom.

Uncle Brett gave her a smile and whispered loud enough for all of us to hear, "Bear with me, my dear. Carlton has taken a losing position, and I'll best him in a few sentences." He returned his full attention to the lawyer. "Because in the instance of Eva Whitehead, she has something to tell me."

"And what might that be?" Carlton asked, his tone definitely patronizing.

"She's going to show me something," Brett said. "Something important. Something that's remained hidden at Caoin House for decades."

"I know—it's the silver, tucked away from the Union forces who came to raid the home. Seems to me it would have been a smarter move to give up the silver and jewels and retain her life," Carlton said.

"I don't know what she'll tell me, but I'm hoping the medium brings me a message that I can understand. I've discovered that ghosts talk in riddles, and so far I'm not up to interpreting."

Carlton's assurance wavered. "You're winding me up—aren't you, Brett?"

My uncle only smiled. "We'll find out soon enough, Carlton. Soon enough. Now, I believe we're at the station."

As we stepped out onto the still, humid New Orleans train platform, I felt as if I'd entered a world where strange was the norm, and all I'd grown up with was trapped in a different time.

A small Negro band played music to greet travelers to the City That Care Forgot. The Dixieland rhythm worked on my feet, inviting them to cut a rug right in public, but I held myself in check. Isabelle, too, looked enchanted by our destination. The pallor of her near accident had been replaced with a healthy flush, and she held on to my uncle's arm with affection and pleasure. Carlton offered me his left arm as a porter picked up our bags and took them to the taxi stand.

"Is it too far to walk to the hotel?" I asked Carlton.

"Let's ride, stow our bags, and I'll take you for a walk in the French Quarter."

I hadn't researched New Orleans, but I knew some of the history— the region's reputation for free and easy living, eccentric residents, drunken tourists, and foreigners from the boats that delivered goods and passengers to one of the nation's busiest ports. New Orleans was an exotic blend of history, decay, modern attitude, large churches, and an easy familiarity with sin. The very air seemed charged with a sexual tension far different from anything I'd found in Savannah or Mobile. New Orleans was a naughty femme fatale who cleverly revealed a glimpse of a breast or the feel of a firm thigh.

As we passed through the narrow streets of the French Quarter, I caught the intoxicating odor of freedom. Sexual, racial, gender, musical, even freedom of thought. On a street corner a young boy tap-danced for a crowd of tourists, and I took note of his honey-colored skin, which looked as if the glow of the afternoon sun was trapped just beneath the surface of his cheeks. The races had been mixing in New Orleans for decades, and the city accommodated the golden children with ease. Things were very different in Mobile, where the color line was rigid, and "pure" pedigrees were highly regarded. A hint of Negro blood, proven or not, would shunt a person into a subclass. Children from liaisons between plantation owners and slaves had still been slaves and were treated as such, often sold and never acknowledged.

In New Orleans, the color line shifted and blurred, and I found that I liked it. My parents, like Uncle Brett, had loathed the cruel treatment of colored people and held organizations like the Ku Klux Klan in contempt. But New Orleans wasn't the place, nor was this the time, to worry overmuch about things I couldn't change. I'd come for fun and adventure after too much tragedy.

I inhaled the scent of fresh baked bread and reveled in the tantalizing spices of cooking gumbo. When we came to the Hotel Monteleone, I sighed with pleasure.

The hotel reminded me of photographs of French palaces. My room was appointed with lovely antiques, and I put my clothes away in the chifforobe, leaving out the new dress I'd bought for the séance. A wiser woman would have taken a nap so as to be refreshed for the evening, but I couldn't resist a walk with Carlton. He'd visited the city many times and would be an able guide.

A knock at the door let me know he'd come for me, and I hurried into the afternoon, eager for fun and adventure. Our destination was Jackson Square.

The square, which contained a statue of Andrew Jackson on horseback, was a shady park surrounded by fascinating shops. Against the wrought iron railing of the park, artists had set up their easels to paint while tourists gawked. We lingered, watching the paintings take shape in pastels, watercolors, and oils. The smell of caramel, made with sugar harvested from the nearby cane fields, came thick and sweet from a praline shop. Carlton split one of the delicious candies with me.

"Perhaps one day, one of these artists will be famous. Just think—if you bought a painting here for a song, only to discover in thirty years that you'd purchased an early work of a master, you'd be considered a great judge of art."

"I'd be far more apt to pick a literary success than an artist," I said. "I love watching them work, but I'm no judge of painting or charcoal."

"Brett has a grand eye. We've frequently come to New Orleans and visited art galleries where he'd tell me which painting to buy. Invariably, the artwork has dramatically increased in value. He never buys because Caoin House came complete with so many wonderful paintings. The portraits are amazing."

"Yes, especially Eva." I hesitated but then continued. "Uncle Brett is strange, very private, about that portrait. I'm surprised he wasn't upset that you used it for one of the scavenger clues."

"He wasn't thrilled."

And Carlton's attitude told me he wasn't apologetic about upsetting Uncle Brett. "He should relocate that canvas to one of the front parlors. The trees, the gown, it's as if she might step out of the frame."

"Apparently, if your uncle is to be believed, she has done just that." He looked at me closely. "Brett's a great one to tease, so I don't know whether to take him seriously about the ghost or not."

Carlton was hitting too close to a subject I didn't feel free to discuss. I pointed to a watercolorist. "That looks exactly like Saint Louis Cathedral with all of the crowds passing by." I didn't want to talk about ghosts. I had my own vision, and I wasn't ready to share the fact that Eli Whitehead had presented to me.

"Dodging the question, Raissa?"

"Attempting to be discreet. Not something I'm accused of very often. Let my uncle tell you what he wants you to know." I took his arm and strolled along the square. "I love watching the painters work, but I'm drawn to the fortune-tellers."

A number of Gypsies, real or pretend, had set up small tables covered with brightly colored scarves. Some wore large earrings and head coverings. Signs declaring a reader as a real Gypsy or Irish traveler were propped beside various fortune-tellers. Some read palms, and others offered to read my aura.

"It's a waste of your money," Carlton said.

"No, it's a waste of Uncle Brett's money," I corrected with a grin. "And as you noted, he has plenty, so he won't miss a quarter." I selected a dark-haired woman in her middle years who wore a scarlet scarf tied below her right ear. Her golden-brown eyes assessed me as I walked to her table and asked if she would give me a card reading.

"You will learn," she said, "but your companion is a skeptic. His lessons come hard."

"I'm Raissa James, and this is Carlton McKay. He's a lawyer," I said. "All lessons come hard to a man of the law."

She stared at Carlton longer than was polite before she agreed to take my money and lay out the cards. "I would prefer to read for you in private," she said.

Carlton gave her a stiff little bow. "I'll retreat to the speakeasy on the corner," he said to me. "Retrieve me when you have need of me again."

"Carlton—" I almost went after him, but I didn't.

"He won't go far," the Gypsy said. "He's interested in you, though he hides it well enough."

"We're friends."

"And he hopes for more than friendship."

Carlton was my uncle's confidant. He was at least a dozen years older, and while he was handsome, charming, and interesting, I'd not allowed my thoughts to shift toward a romantic interest.

"Cut the cards," she instructed. When I did, she began to lay them out on the purple scarf that covered her table. The cards were strangely beautiful, but I had no understanding of what they meant. I'd never before seen a tarot deck.

When ten cards had been put out in a complex spread, she sat quietly, staring at them. "You have a gift, Miss James. You're an artist."

"A writer. Or at least I hope to be."

"Success will come to you." She tapped a card that showed two dogs baying at the moon. "You see things that others do not. Sometimes disturbing things." She pointed to a card at the top of the spread. The wicked-looking image of a man's body topped with a horned goat head made me shift in my chair.

Diablo," she said. "The devil. There is danger around you. And loss. You have lost many dear ones. I fear there will be another loss. The past is more alive than it should be." She turned over two more cards. "The solution lies in revealing the past."

"How?"

The question was barely out of my mouth when a huge black dog crashed into the table, lunging for the Gypsy's throat. Cards and saliva from the beast's mouth flew into the air. The Gypsy screamed and fell back, the snapping jaws missing her by inches.

"Brutus! Brutus!" a woman cried somewhere behind him.

I grabbed the dog's collar and tugged against his ninety pounds. I didn't divert him, but I knocked him off balance long enough for the Gypsy to scrabble backward. The dog quickly regained his footing and lunged for the Gypsy's throat again.

My grip on his collar failed, and he surged forward, knocking the table away. Out of nowhere an umbrella thwacked down harshly on the dog's snout.

"Back!" the gentleman brandishing the umbrella yelled. He struck the dog again, and it dropped to all fours, suddenly calm and wagging his tail. At the same time his owner arrived and snapped a leash to his collar.

"Are you okay?" she asked us. "I'm so sorry. He got away from me. Are you okay?"

I helped the gypsy to her feet. "Are you hurt?"

She didn't answer. She threw a terrified glance at me. *"Diablo!"* she said and crossed herself before she fled into the crowd.

I pivoted and hurried across the square to the speakeasy into which Carlton had disappeared. As soon as I found him, I asked to return to the hotel.

CHAPTER SIXTEEN

By the time we joined Uncle Brett in the hotel lobby, I had mostly recovered from the strange attack by the dog, which I didn't mention to Carlton. The Gypsy was unharmed, and the dog's owner had hustled away before the police could be called. I'd been left with a pounding heart, a warning, and a word. *Diablo.* The devil. I determined to put the incident out of my head. If I intended to write ghost stories, I couldn't run around like a scared ninny. Carlton took my arm, and we walked the few blocks to our destination.

The séance was held in the Benoit house, a three-story Victorian that blazed with light as we arrived. A butler showed us into a parlor where a round table had been placed with nine chairs. We would be joined by four people we didn't know for the session.

Madam entered the room on the arm of the most handsome man I'd ever seen. He wore a tuxedo cut to emphasize his broad shoulders, narrow hips, and lean build, though he was far from slight. Sophistication seemed to be his signature, and while he wasn't comic, he put me in mind of the French comedian Max Linder. His well-groomed hair caught the light from the chandelier, and I thought of the glossy feathers of a raven. His neat moustache offset lips that were thin and sensual.

My guess was European. None of the American men I knew cut such a polished figure.

"What a pretty boy," Carlton said under his breath.

I didn't understand his sarcastic remark or snide attitude. "He is very handsome," I said. "The reports I read are true. And he can communicate with spirits."

Uncle Brett chuckled, and Isabelle raised her eyebrows in question. She shook her head, indicating she was as much at a loss as I was. In a moment the butler served a fruity red wine and showed us to our seats. The four additional guests were three women in their fifties and one young teenage boy. They were all either friends or relatives, but I couldn't figure out the connection exactly.

When everyone had gathered in the parlor, Madam said, "I'd like to introduce my protégé. This is Reginald Proctor. He's a talented medium in his own right who's come to study with me. Tonight he'll be my assistant."

I wondered what the duties of an assistant to a medium might entail, but I didn't ask. It seemed he made sure of Madam's comfort, supplying her with things before she even had to ask. Perhaps he was psychic. The thought made me smile.

Reginald took that as an invitation to join me at the sideboard, where an array of light snacks and iced tea had been set out. "You must be Raissa James, the woman whose interest in spirit communication brought you and your friends on a journey to New Orleans," he said.

"How did you know that?" I was thrilled. "Are you psychic? Did a spirit tell you?" I didn't say it aloud, but I desperately wanted it to be Alex.

Amusement made him even more handsome. "I studied the guest list so I could provide Madam with biographical information if she needs it. But I will seek psychic information." He touched his forehead and closed his eyes as if he were receiving a message from the

Great Beyond. "You're a schoolteacher visiting your uncle in the wilds of Alabama. *And* you're an aspiring writer."

"You discerned all of that by talking to a spirit?"

"But of course."

"Don't hand me that line." He was too charming for his own good. And such fun.

"You injure me, madam." He put his hand over his heart.

"How did you find out I wanted to write?" I so wanted it to be Alex telling my secrets; it would mean Alex was near, and that I might one day speak with him myself if I learned how.

Reginald's easy charm slipped away with his smile. "You're hoping I obtained the information from a departed person who knows you. One you miss."

The tears collected in my eyes, and I fought for self-control.

"There was nothing supernatural involved—I swear to you. I asked some questions of Mr. McKay when he booked the tickets. That's all. A little snooping and snitching. Nothing supernatural. I'm sorry. I've opened a wound."

I felt like a total fool, and I struggled to regain control. "So you are Madam's Watson." I picked up a dainty cucumber sandwich and took a bite. It tasted like paste.

"The answer is yes. I perform the duties of Watson as I study her methods."

"If Sherlock had been able to communicate with the dead, he would be able to solve any mystery. Perhaps you should sell your skills as a snitch."

"One day I hope to be Sherlock and have my own Watson. Part of any séance, if the medium is a serious professional, is a bit of background on those attending. It focuses the energies in the room and provides Madam with a framework for each individual event. Spirits communicate in symbols most often. It helps to know something about the attendees so Madam can interpret the meaning of what she sees and hears."

"Can you show me how to communicate with the dead?"

"You have to be a sensitive. It isn't—"

"I've seen a ghost at Caoin House, and so has my uncle."

"You have?"

"A Confederate soldier and the most beautiful woman in the South."

He brushed the right corner of his mustache. "I'd love to visit Caoin House, then. Explore the spirits there. Tell me about your writing." Heavier fare was also available, and Reginald chose a ham slice on rye bread. He took a bite, showing strong, white teeth.

"An aspirer," I said. "But I am young and have years to practice my skills."

"You don't strike me as someone who takes years to find success at whatever you aim at. I expect to see your name on the spine of a book shortly." The awkward, emotional moment had passed.

"Your confidence in me is extraordinary, and totally unsupported." He was overflowing with flattery, but I liked him.

"I'd wager a month's wages that you'll publish a short story within the next few months."

"Now that would be an accomplishment since I haven't finished writing one."

He laughed out loud and drew the curious gazes of everyone else in the room. My uncle and Carlton were pouring glasses of tea with unhappy faces—of course they preferred bourbon, but with the exception of the first glass of wine, alcohol wasn't allowed until the conclusion of the séance. Isabelle caught my eye and pretended to drink and stagger, making me laugh.

Reginald ignored everyone else, his attention totally on me. "By Wednesday you'll have a story in the mail to the *Saturday Evening Post*.

I'll be telling my friends, 'Oh, that beautiful young female writer Raissa James. I had drinks with her in New Orleans.'"

"I'm not going to write under my real name." I was surprised I told him of my secret plans.

"Initials!" He was thrilled. "So that people assume you're a man. Perfection."

I hadn't really thought beyond taking a pseudonym, but the idea of initials instantly appealed to me. "Yes, I. B. Deadly."

"You are the zebra's stripes," he said. "I like you. You've got spirit. You might be a flapper, though you're dressed as more of a conservative society lady."

"Beaded dresses are de rigueur for those hoping for communication with the dead. The spirits have their clanking chains and ghostly moans. I have my clacking beads and rustling silk." I was surprised by my own high spirits.

"You are delicious," he said, "and now I have to attend to my duties."

I engaged the newcomers in casual conversation, learning their reasons for attending the séance. Reginald stood at Madam's side as she chatted casually, asking a few general questions of everyone in the room, telling a story or two about her youth in Paris and her family's heritage. She was a striking woman dressed completely in black. Judging by her proper posture and appearance, she might easily be a society woman found in any New Orleans parlor. I'd hoped for something more exotic, more . . . dangerous.

At last we took our places. I sat between Emily Rainfield and her nephew, Tyler, who'd lost his mother eight months earlier in a flu epidemic. The other two ladies were family friends who'd accompanied Emily and Tyler on the trip down the Mississippi River from Memphis. They radiated discomfort.

I made an attempt to talk to the teenager, but he replied only in monosyllables. I felt his grief and wondered if this attempt to contact his mother was such a good idea.

At last, Madam took charge of the evening. The lights were dimmed and candles lit. She briefly described the ways in which spirits might communicate, from knocking to thumping to even materialization.

She warned us that if a spirit possessed her body, we should remain seated and calm and not interrupt. "There is no danger if a spirit uses my body to communicate unless you overreact and disrupt the natural sequence of events. The spirit will leave of its own accord, so do not attempt to intervene."

We all joined hands, and I squeezed Tyler's clammy fingers. As much as I wanted to speak with my parents, Alex, and Robert, I hoped if a spirit came through, it would be for the boy. I knew nothing of his circumstances, but I felt his desperation. He needed to hear that his mother was safe and happy.

Across the table, Carlton winked at me, and I thought of the fortune-teller's assessment that he wanted more than friendship from me. I wasn't certain she'd read Carlton accurately. I enjoyed his company, but on what level? A question I couldn't—and didn't want to—answer.

Madam spoke a Latin incantation and then inhaled deeply several times. In midbreath, she went rigid. Her left hand broke free of Uncle Brett's and began moving in circles on the table.

Reginald jumped to his feet, went to the sideboard, and grabbed a sheaf of plain white paper and a packet of pencils. He captured her left hand, inserted a pencil, and aimed her hand at the paper. Without missing a movement, Madam began to draw large circles on the page.

I chanced a look at her eyes, which stared directly ahead without any seeming comprehension of what was in front of her. Her hand moved as if it belonged to someone else. The hair on my arms began to stand on end.

Madam jerked, and the pencil snapped in her hand. Reginald removed the jagged stub immediately, and a good thing, as her hands became very animated before they stilled beneath his. A low moan escaped from her throat.

"Come with me," she said, but it wasn't her voice. It was deep, a male voice that sent shivers through me. I knew the voice. I'd heard it before, coming from the front lawn of Caoin House. I was so shocked that I felt paralyzed.

"We can be together forever." Madam's body was rigid, and her eyes were rolled completely back in her head. "Come with me. I'm so cold."

I swallowed a sob. I wasn't afraid, but I was overwhelmed with sadness, a sense of loss so deep that my heart wanted to quit. The words could have come from Alex or Robert, both buried in the damp soil. Or my parents. But it came from Eli, and while I wished to help him, I had no desire to go with him or follow him anywhere, especially not to the grave.

"Who is with us, Madam?" Reginald asked.

"Betrayal."

The hoarse voice that spoke gave the word added dread. "Who is betrayed?" I asked softly.

The laugh that came from Madam made my skin bump and dance. "Give us revenge."

The two women from Memphis who'd accompanied their friend started to push back their chairs, but Reginald stopped them with a command. "Be still," he said in a tone that brooked no disobedience. "When she's in a trance, you have to be still. If you don't, she could be harmed."

That quelled their cowardly retreat, but their faces showed their unhappiness and fear.

"Madam, who is with you?" Reginald asked.

Madam's normal voice had returned, and she said, "He's come from far away, a place of neither land nor water." She nodded, her blind eyes seeking around the table until they rested on me. "He comes for you."

Across the table, Carlton started to rise, but I shook my head.

"Mrs. James," Madam said, "he is for you. Heed his words."

"I will," I said, proud of the solid sound of my voice. "Tell me his truth."

"The past rules your present. The hidden rules his actions." She sighed, and her head dropped forward. A death rattle came from her chest, but Reginald signaled us all to remain seated. At last she lifted her head, and her voice was feminine, light, and filled with warmth.

"Tyler, let your grief pass like a cloud across the sun. I am with you. I will never leave you. Remember when we said our prayers. You always asked for a bicycle, and I told you you'd get your wish. And you did. Your wishes will always be granted. Hold that knowledge. I am with you always."

The young boy sobbed once and covered his face.

Madam slumped sideways in her chair, and Reginald calmly got up and caught her before she slipped to the floor. He lifted her in his arms with such ease, as if she weighed nothing. Without a word to anyone, he left the room.

The aunt comforted her nephew, and the other two ladies stood so quickly they almost overturned their chairs. Their transition from parlor to door took only seconds. "We'll meet you at the hotel," one said before they let themselves out.

Carlton went to the decanters filled with liquor on the sideboard and poured four drinks. The séance was over—the prohibition against strong liquor was no longer in play. He looked at the woman who still held her nephew. When she nodded, he poured a fifth for her.

"Should we leave?" Isabelle asked. "I don't think Madam is well."

"Please, finish your drink." Reginald had returned to the room so silently that we'd failed to notice. "When a very powerful entity takes over, Madam is sometimes overwhelmed. She'll be fine tomorrow. She sends her apologies that she couldn't continue."

"I'm sorry she's not feeling well, but it is a little disappointing." Uncle Brett sipped his whiskey. "Perhaps tomorrow we could return. I have some questions."

Reginald frowned. "Madam won't consider your request. I'm sorry. You brought an entity with you that she fears."

I thought of Isabelle's near death on the train. She'd said someone pushed her, yet no one was near. "Does Madam know who the spirit is?"

"She said the entity was cloaked. It *seethed* with power. Her word. She will not risk another encounter. I'm sorry. I've been authorized to refund your money."

"That won't be necessary," Uncle Brett said. "It was an exciting evening. I'm sure Raissa will benefit when she sets about writing her stories." He finished his drink. "We should be off."

Reginald glanced at me before he spoke. "I could pay a visit to Caoin House myself. Perhaps I could divine the answers you seek."

"And you have the same abilities as our medium?" Carlton asked in a tart tone. "You look more Hollywood than Gypsy."

"My ancestry is Irish Italian, both cultures which respect the ability to communicate with the dead." He smiled. "I would offer my services at no charge, of course."

"A capital idea!" Uncle Brett's disappointment had vanished like fog beneath a summer sun. "Why don't you ride back on the train with us tomorrow?"

"Brett—" Carlton began.

"Nonsense, Carlton. Reginald will make an excellent traveling companion, and we'll get to the bottom of Raissa's peculiar haunting and some issues at Caoin House that I'd like probed."

"Do not let this . . . four-flusher into your life." Carlton's steely eyes held a dare that Reginald met with a glare of his own.

"What are you afraid I'll find?" Reginald asked.

I thought for a moment Carlton might punch him. I couldn't understand the animosity between the two.

"Gentlemen." Isabelle stepped between them with perfect ease. "I think this is a wonderful idea. Brett will get his answers, and we'll have the pleasure of Reginald's company for another few days. Carlton, I know you don't believe in anyone's ability to speak with the departed, but loosen up a little and enjoy the fun." She put a hand on his arm.

Her gentle words calmed the moment, but I could tell by the way Carlton turned away that his dislike of Reginald had only intensified. I went after him to smooth the waters, leaving Reginald to finalize arrangements with Uncle Brett and Isabelle.

"Don't be upset with Uncle Brett," I said when I had Carlton alone in a corner of the room where we could speak softly. "He doesn't really take this seriously."

"And what about yourself? Are you going to be led around by the nose by a fag?"

The word caught me up short. "What?"

"Reginald is a nancy-boy. Surely you can see it."

Anger hit me quick and hard. "Why should that matter to me? I want him to talk with the ghosts at Caoin House. I'm not interested in dating him."

"You're determined to do this?"

"Uncle Brett has issued the invitation. Caoin House is his to offer if he chooses. That's something we both need to remember." I pivoted on my heel and went over to Emily Rainfield and Tyler. They'd both recovered their composure. In a moment Reginald joined us.

"Please thank Madam for us," Mrs. Rainfield said. "She's given Tyler some comfort."

"Yes, I was glad to hear that my mother is happy and watching over me." The boy's solemn expression had lightened, and even his freckles seemed more vivid and happy.

"Indeed, she is," Reginald said. "They never truly abandon you. She will be with you as long as you need her."

"And then what?" Tyler asked. "Where will she go?"

Reginald considered for a moment. "Into a new life. She will return to live again. And there are those who believe that you'll return, also, that souls are reincarnated in clusters or groups, though the next time around you might be her father or brother. Or sister." He grinned as he put a hand on Tyler's shoulder. "The thing is, we don't remember our past lives, for the most part."

"But I'll return with her?" Tyler's face showed all his hope. The boy missed his mother with the intensity of youth.

"I believe that to be true," Reginald said with great gentleness. "From my communication with the spirits who linger here—those who have a reason to remain, like your mother is here to care for you, certain souls are bound together. Forever."

While his words to Tyler were said with kindness and compassion, a chill traced through me as I thought of the Civil War ghost who called my name and lured me to follow him. Why was Eli lingering at Caoin House and visible only to me? What could I possibly have in common with Eli Whitehead, a pillar of antebellum society, a soldier, a man of great wealth? Had he been the entity at the séance that uttered the word *revenge*? Revenge for what?

"Please thank Madam for us," Emily Rainfield said. "Tyler and I will be going."

"May I call a taxi for you?" Reginald asked.

"It's a short walk, and I believe the night air will do us both a lot of good. There are some things about his mother I wish to share with Tyler. She was my sister, and I loved her greatly, but she was far from a saint. Tyler needs to understand that she was a spirited young woman before she was his mother."

"He does, indeed," Reginald said as he walked to the front door with them. When the door closed, he signaled me into an alcove beneath the grand staircase. "Your friend is clear in his desire that I not return with you to Caoin House. I don't want to start trouble. Should I make up an excuse for your uncle and decline?"

"My uncle has invited you, and it isn't Carlton's place to monitor Uncle Brett's social activity. Carlton is a good friend, but he has no right to attempt to control my uncle's guests."

"And you? What would you prefer?" Reginald's gray-green eyes searched my face. "You know my tastes differ from . . . other men. Will that be an issue?"

"No." I'd never given it much thought, but my answer came easily enough.

"Then I'll be happy to be your uncle's guest for a few days. Perhaps I can discover something at Caoin House that answers both of your questions." He shrugged. "And perhaps not."

I looked into the main parlor, where Isabelle and Brett were chatting away. Carlton was examining a painting of a New Orleans street. "We should go. I hope Madam feels better. We're scheduled to depart tomorrow at noon. We'll meet you at the train station. Bring enough things to remain for at least a week. I suspect my uncle will want to host some parties." I smiled. "He works hard, but he also likes to play."

"Until tomorrow." Reginald picked up my hand and kissed the back of my fingers with unfettered sensuality—all while he eyed Carlton. No matter who or what he liked, he was a charming devil, and he had no qualms about going nose to nose with the lawyer.

CHAPTER SEVENTEEN

We breakfasted in the hotel the next morning, and Uncle Brett and Carlton left "the girls" while they completed some errands. Isabelle and I retained an air of perfect decorum until the men walked out the hotel door. We grabbed each other's hands and ran to the street. We were on our own in the City That Care Forgot, a den of sex, liquor, and bad behavior.

To my utter delight, Reginald leaned against a street sign smoking a cigarette at the corner. "Ladies, do you need a guide?"

"Oh, yes, we do, but you can't tell Brett and Carlton. We want to explore."

"I'm your man," he said. "You'd be perfectly safe, but it's better to have a male companion. Let's walk."

Reginald's knowledge of the French Quarter and his clever wit and charm made the hour pass, and too soon it was time to collect the men and the luggage and catch the train home.

"I took the liberty of leaving my bags at the station," Reginald explained. "So we're off."

Uncle Brett and Carlton joined us not long before the train arrived. Carlton was distant with Reginald on the trip home, but everyone ignored it. The medium entertained us with stories of Madam's varied clients. When I asked about Arthur Conan Doyle, Reginald kept us laughing as the tall pines marched past the train window like sad sentinels.

Always good-natured, and with an astute ability to sense the emotions of those in our little group, Reginald fit in as if we'd known him all our lives. Even Carlton occasionally loosened up. By the time we pulled up at the Mobile station and found Travis waiting to retrieve us, I felt a warm friendship growing between us.

On the ride home, I sat between Reginald and Carlton. Reginald took in the port and the bustle of Mobile, but it was a small city compared with New Orleans. It wasn't until we turned down the drive to Caoin House that Reginald leaned forward and spoke.

> *"A moon ago he died. A moon ago died the dutiful son.*
> *A moon ago died the faithful husband. A moon ago died*
> *the brave, the friend.*
>
> *His ghost is cold.*
>
> *His ghost is naked.*
>
> *Let the ghost of the brave be carried away."*

"A bit morbid, don't you think?" Carlton asked.

"It's part of a poem about a Meskwaki ritual called 'Carrying the Ghost.' For some reason the words came to me when I looked at the light filtering through those trees."

Reginald had gone slightly pale, and I wondered if he'd seen something. "Who or what are the Meskwaki?" I asked.

"Native American tribe. I spent some time in Canada and learned their traditions. They ended up on reservations in the States, but they had a ceremony to release the ghosts of warriors. The tribe sent them on the ghost road, a long journey. They were warned not to return down the road. Not to come back."

Though the day was sunny and the car hot as we passed beneath the oaks, I felt a chill.

When the car stopped, Reginald helped Isabelle out, and Carlton offered me his hand. Winona met us at the doorway. "Come inside. I'm sure you're famished from your travels. I've made tomato aspic for you, something light and cool after your travels."

And we were swept into the rhythm of Caoin House as if we'd never been away. Reginald was pulled along with us. In no time he'd won Winona and Travis over with his easy conversation about plants and cooking. Reginald knew a little about a lot of things, and it made him facile and at ease.

"If you'll excuse me," Carlton said, standing, "I think a nap is in order. Tomorrow I have to return to town and work, but tonight I'm eager to see what Reginald can discover about Caoin House. I want to be rested and on my toes in case a savage spirit decides to gust through the house."

Instead of taking offense, Reginald laughed. "I'd like some time to explore the property before I host a séance," he said.

"Anything to delay." Carlton spoke under his breath, but I heard him. I turned away and spoke to Reginald.

"That makes perfect sense. You should explore the house and grounds. I'm very eager to see if you witness the same presences that Uncle Brett and I have seen."

"Tomorrow, when I'm rested, I'll give it my best shot. As for now, I think I'd like to talk a walk about the property. The aspic was delicious, Winona. As good as any I've had in Quebec, where the French consider it their invention."

Uncle Brett and Isabelle decided to accompany Reginald, and soon I was left alone. A nap called to me, too, but I had other things to do.

Winona refused my help to clean up the dishes, but she had questions about our adventure.

"How was the séance?" she asked.

I'd come up with a plot and a title for my story, "The Unexpected Visitor." Since I was stuck at a description of one of the characters, I welcomed Winona's curiosity.

"It was very exciting. Madam Petalungro communicated with several spirits. One from Caoin House distressed her so that she had to stop."

"Oh my." Winona stilled. "Please, tell me if I'm interrupting you."

"Not at all, and I'm happy to spill the beans, but only if we can have a cup of tea."

"That would be the best plan, so I can get your uncle's favorite pot roast in the oven while I listen."

Instead of the truth, I decided to try a fictional version—the nub of my idea for my first ghost story. When we had the steaming tea in front of us, I told her about our adventure at the séance, dramatizing the deep voice that had come from Madam and adding a few details, such as the fact that Eli haunted Caoin House to avenge the brutal death of his beautiful wife, Eva. As I spun the tale, I watched Winona's reaction, mentally marking areas where my tale needed revision.

"So what will happen to Mr. Eli now?"

I was pleased that she was caught up in the story enough to care. "According to Madam, ghosts linger for a reason. To protect someone or something, to reveal something, or for revenge."

"I don't believe in ghostly revenge." Winona chopped an onion with such force a piece flew across the room.

"Haven't you ever felt anything here? I'd love to hear your stories so I can write about them."

Winona faced me. "My son used to tell me there were spirits here. Unhappy spirits. But he's in Paris now. When he comes home, I'll ask him to tell you some of his stories." She gathered the carrots she'd washed and left to drain at the sink. "Now I have to finish preparing for dinner or your uncle will be serving raw beef with his cold potatoes and corn bread."

"If you think of any old stories, please tell me."

"Of course." She paused in her chopping. "I'm glad you're here, Miss Raissa. Your uncle is so much happier. He's at ease in a way he hasn't been for a long time."

"I love being here. I don't want to be a burden or take advantage. I want to do my share."

"Oh, when he gets in the mood to throw a party, he'll have you hopping, just like he does the rest of us. Even Miss Isabelle runs around with her tongue hanging out."

The thought of my uncle organizing and marshaling all of us to bring off a party made me smile, and I was delighted to see the wall of reserve Winona erected crack a little. She was talking to me as if we could be friends. "I heard Uncle Brett used to have the White Ball each year. Do you think he might again?" The White Ball was a winter extravaganza that marked the conclusion of the year and led into the Mardi Gras season, when all the secret societies held balls and parades. The secret organizations formed the echelons of Mobile's power structure.

"He might. I guess only time will tell."

I left her to the kitchen work and hurried upstairs. When I opened the door of my bedroom, the first thing I saw was a brand-new green typewriter sitting on an elegant little teak desk that had been placed beside the French doors. I rushed forward, squealing with pleasure at the wonderful green color, so much more fun than the traditional black I'd seen in offices. My fingertips slid over the keys. I'd taken secretarial courses along with my teaching instruction when Alex was first called overseas, mostly to occupy my mind, but also in the thought I'd take on a part-time job so we could save to buy our own house. I ended up working full-time as a teacher, but I could still type at a respectable speed.

A stack of plain white paper had been left beside the machine, and I sat down in the straight-backed chair. I opened the French doors and looked out upon the oak grove for a long moment as I visualized the opening of my story. My fingers found the keys, and I began to type. "The Unexpected Visit." It looked so official, so solid and real. Without another thought, I entered the world of my story and began to write.

When a knock came at my bedroom door, I almost leaped from my chair. My heart pounded madly—I'd been in the middle of introducing my fictional ghost, the very handsome and seductive Captain Eli.

"Raissa, are you okay?" Carlton asked.

"You'll laugh at me," I said as I composed myself and opened the door. "I was writing a story, and you startled me." I could feel the flush in my cheeks and neck.

"Then you like the typewriter?"

I looked from him to the Corona and finally grasped the situation. "You?"

His grin erased time and care from his face. "Every self-respecting writer needs a typing machine. My secretary recommended the portable Corona, but if it doesn't suit you, I—"

"No! I love it. Thank you, Carlton." I threw my arms around his neck and hugged him. It wasn't simply the gift of the machine; it was his belief in me. "Thank you."

He kissed my cheek and stepped back. "I have to say, it never occurred to me that a writing machine could produce such an enthusiastic thank-you. The secretaries are never so thrilled when I purchase new office supplies."

I caught his hand and drew him toward my desk. "I'm debating whether I can accept such an expensive gift. I'd assumed it came from Uncle Brett."

"We conspired together, and before you think I'm lavishing gifts on you, keep in mind that I work for your uncle and I'll simply charge him an arm and a leg on his next legal bill. In a way, he is gifting you with the machine."

"Now that's a crooked mile. And the desk?"

"Brett arranged to have that delivered while we were in New Orleans. You need a place to work, and while the library is wonderful, we both thought you might prefer a more private nook. The creative process and all."

I led him out to the balcony. "This is the most wonderful place. I can just imagine the ghost of Eva Whitehead down in the oak grove, waiting for her revenge." That was the story I'd chosen to write.

"Revenge? Against the soldiers who killed her?"

I didn't want to give away the surprise of my tale, so I merely smiled in what I hoped was a mysterious way. "You'll have to wait until I finish writing."

He shook his head. "As your benefactor, I don't even get a peek?"

"Nope."

"Can I at least take a look at what you've written?" He reached for the typed pages beside the Corona.

I snatched them away and held them behind my back. "Not until I finish. Then you'll be the first to read my story."

He stepped closer, reaching behind me as if he meant to grab the pages. Instead, his hands supported my back. "I want to apologize for the way I behaved about Reginald. He's a likable fellow. I made an ass of myself in New Orleans. I don't care about his romantic life."

His apology caught me completely off guard. "Why did he upset you so much?"

"I have feelings for you, Raissa. I shouldn't, I'm aware of that, but it doesn't stop me. Brett is one of my best friends, and you are his niece. I've heard stories about you for years. Brett adores you." He swallowed. "I hadn't realized how much Brett's stories had influenced my thoughts about you. Your obvious interest in Reginald struck a nerve."

"Reginald is my friend. As are you, Carlton. You're getting the cart way ahead of the horse."

Carlton's dimple came into play. "Jealousy is not a flattering trait."

"You were jealous, even knowing he's gay?"

"Emotions aren't rational. I make my living from people who can't separate emotion from fact. When I saw how taken you were with him, it just tapped into my . . ." His mouth quirked up on the left. "My jealousy."

"Even knowing it wasn't romantic interest?"

"Time is the only thing we have of value. If you're more interested in spending time with Reginald than with me, it doesn't really matter what you're doing—does it?"

His directness surprised me. Carlton bent words in a courtroom to serve his clients. This straight talk cautioned me that he was serious. "I see your point. I didn't intend to make you uncomfortable."

"Jealous. You can say it. The more I'm around you, the more I see qualities I admire. You're smart and willing to work for a dream. So many of the women I meet in Mobile want to be flappers or clamor for the vote and to be equal, but they're only talk. You actually do what's necessary to be an equal partner. You're curious and open to the world around you, whether it's ghosts or gays or aunts with a hurting child. I admired your kindness to the young boy at the séance."

"Thank you, Carlton." I needed time to digest his revelations.

"I don't expect you to return my feelings. Not so close upon the heels of your recent losses. My timing is wrong, and I'm generally an expert at timing. It's just that you're such an extraordinary woman, I wanted you to know my feelings before other men lined up to claim you."

I had to laugh. "I hardly think there's a worry."

"You have no idea how men follow you with their gaze. Walking around Jackson Square, every man you passed took a second look. It's the way you carry yourself, the expression of openness on your face. Your extraordinary beauty."

Heat flushed my cheeks, and at last Carlton turned away with a chuckle. "I've embarrassed you. Enough of my proclamations. Let's make a bargain. I won't press you or tire you with constant attention, but you have to make time for me, on occasion."

"That's not a chore, Carlton. I enjoy your company." And I did. Did I have romantic feelings for him? I couldn't say. I was attracted, but that was a far cry from the more serious emotion of caring. My feelings had been whiplashed by death. I felt numb, but that was normal and would eventually wear off. Then I would know my true feelings for Carlton.

"Let's go down to dinner. Brett sent me to retrieve you, and here I've kept you much longer than I intended." He offered his arm, and together we descended the stairs.

"Thank you for the typewriter." I intended to speak to Uncle Brett and be sure it was appropriate to keep the machine, though it would take a team of mules to pull it away from me now.

"I expect to see your name in print in the very near future. That will give me the utmost satisfaction."

"You're a rare man, Carlton McKay." I'd never known a male who honestly supported a woman's desire to have a career. Not a job, but a career. I accepted his arm as he led me from my room and to the stairs.

CHAPTER EIGHTEEN

Dinner was a merry affair, and Carlton and Isabelle left shortly thereafter. Uncle Brett retired to the library to read, and I went outside with Reginald for a smoke. I'd been dying to grill the handsome medium about the spirits at Caoin House. With his help, I hoped to discover the reason Eli and Eva haunted my uncle's home. And, possibly, what had happened to Robert. The button torn from a shirtfront was still in my dresser drawer.

If there had been some altercation on the roof of Caoin House, it was with a mortal, not a ghost. Ghosts might frighten someone over the edge of a roof, but they could not wrest a button from cotton fabric.

At least my understanding of ghosts was that they had limited corporeal powers. Banging a few shutters, tinkling glass, a blast of energy bumping open a door. This was the limit.

Two things challenged my beliefs. The push Isabelle had received, which nearly killed her, and Robert's death. I refused to let Robert's death go. I could find no one unaccounted for at the time of his fall. Carlton and Uncle Brett had helped me establish alibis for all the partygoers.

Reginald and I sat on the curving stairs that led to the front porch, and he lit my cigarette for me. I didn't smoke often, so I had to work at barely inhaling or otherwise I'd have a coughing fit—not the image of sophistication I wanted to convey.

"Your uncle is eager to hold the séance." Reginald looked worried.

"He's a bit too eager. Just tell him you need time to explore the spirits here. That's not unreasonable." It amused me that Uncle Brett was so excited. I knew his concerns about Eva's ghost, but Reginald needed to be grounded. "I've read that mediums work best in familiar terrain."

"How about a little history of the house? I'd hoped to talk to you earlier, but Carlton kept me busy."

"I know. Carlton's . . . peculiar sometimes." An owl who-who-hooted in the oak trees as I told Reginald what I knew of the house. How it had been built for Eva Whitehead by the elegant and chivalrous Eli Whitehead. How she'd died at the hands of deserters at the very end of the Civil War while her husband fought in Tennessee for the lost cause of the South, and how her daughter had been left with Eva's decomposing body.

Reginald lit another cigarette from the butt of the one he held. "Many old homes are steeped in tragedy, but Caoin House seems to have had a double serving of it."

"Yes. That's true."

"I heard you, too, have lost people close to you."

"A husband, my parents, most recently a new friend. I'd hoped to talk to one of them at the séance."

"The entity that came to Madam was a very strong presence. Do you know who it is?"

"Uncle Brett sees a woman. We believe it's Eva. I've seen a soldier on the grounds. I presume it's her husband, Eli."

"Carlton mentioned that I should be careful here, but it seems more to the point that you should use caution. Ghosts that try to connect emotionally with the living can be . . . tricky."

"Tricky?" He'd obviously wanted to use another word.

"There are barriers that shouldn't be crossed, Raissa. If you feel this spirit's yearning for you, that's a danger zone outside my expertise. Perhaps we should cancel the séance and I should return to New Orleans."

"No!" I still hoped to connect with Alex or Robert or both. A word with my mother and father would also be greatly appreciated. It had occurred to me that if I could see the ghosts of Caoin House, and Uncle Brett could, too, perhaps my mother had the same ability. She might be able to help me—plus, it was something I wanted to know. "We really have to have the séance."

"Raissa, I'm an apprentice."

"But you see the spirits. We can at least try. If it gets too scary, we'll simply stop."

"What if I'm overpowered? The entity that came through in New Orleans was very strong. Madam was thrown for a loop." He lit another cigarette. "I don't like this. There are spirits that have their own agenda."

I proposed another scenario. "What if the spirits here want to help us learn the truth about the past? Maybe Robert will tell what really happened on the roof."

"Either way, it could be dangerous."

"Is it honestly risky for you to do this? Will you be in danger?"

He considered. "Madam was exhausted when he came through her. She told me she had to struggle not to lose herself. Even she was afraid of his power. When I took her upstairs to her room, she asked me to follow through for her, but she also said she was worried about you and the others. She had a sense that something bad was going to happen."

I sat up straighter so I could think better. My mother had often told me that a straight spine allowed the brain to function. "You should tell this to my uncle. He'll understand that you don't want to continue with plans for the séance." The warning of the tarot reader in Jackson Square lingered with me. She'd cautioned me that the loss of another I loved could happen. I didn't want Uncle Brett endangered by my curiosity.

Reginald sighed. "If I'm going to be a coward, I shouldn't have come in the first place. No, we should go through with this."

"What are the real dangers?"

"There have been cases of permanent possession. Where the medium was unable to reclaim his or her body."

"That's serious. You could become possessed." The owl hooted only twenty feet from where we sat. The sound, up close, was far more ominous.

Out of the corner of my eye, I caught a glint of moonlight on something shiny. The soldier stepped out from behind the trunk of the nearest tree. An air of melancholy clung to him, and he beckoned to me. In the moonlight he was pale, his dark hair curling slightly on his brow. He beckoned again, and, although his lips didn't move, I heard him calling my name.

"Raissa, come to me."

My ribs seemed to squeeze down on my lungs, imprisoning them in a corset of bone so that I couldn't get a deep breath. Even sitting with Reginald, the ghost compelled me to him.

"Raissa!" Reginald grasped my shoulders and shook me. "Is he here?"

"There, beside the first oak."

He turned and stared.

"Can you see him?"

Reginald faced me again. "No, I don't see anything."

I looked beyond Reginald. In the dancing oak shadows, Eli beckoned me, and I rose and started down the steps. When I got to the bottom, I felt someone grab me.

"Wake up!" Reginald's hand met my cheek with a sharp crack.

I let out a startled yelp and whirled on him. "Who do you think—"

He was looking past me at something near the trees. "What do you see? What's out there?"

"It's him. Eli. The Confederate ghost. Can't you see him?"

"Raissa, listen to me because I may never have the courage to say this again. I'm not a medium. I don't have any talent at seeing the dead or communicating with them. My talent is theater. I'm very good at playing a part. I told Madam this was a bad idea."

Eli had stepped behind the trunk of an oak, but he was still there; I could sense him. And the man in front of me was a fraud. "Why did you come here?" I wasn't angry. I was disappointed.

"I was tired of being Madam's lapdog."

"So you thought you'd come to Caoin House and be . . . what? The butler?" My unkind remark hit home. Reginald flushed.

"I deserved that. To be honest, when the spirit was so strong with Madam, I hoped that by coming here, with you, I might learn *how* to see them. She said the entity that came with you was the strongest she'd ever seen. I want to have that gift, Raissa. I want it desperately, but wanting isn't enough. You were born a sensitive, like Madam. The gypsies would say you were born with a caul covering your face, which allows you to see beyond the veil of life. It is a gift but also a curse. You must be careful. Most spirits are here for reasons of love, or they may simply be lost. But there are those who died in moments of darkness who are motivated by evil."

The compulsion to go to the oak grove had passed, but I was in no mood to go to my room alone. I climbed the stairs and returned to my perch on the top step. "I'm exhausted. Let's leave this until tomorrow."

"I will pack and be gone before breakfast."

"There's no rush, Reginald. You're here. While you can't see the spirits, you do know more about how they work than I do. Eli and Eva are here for a reason. Perhaps you can help me discover what it is."

He brightened. "I can do that. I pay attention, and because I do, I see things others don't. Not spirits, but the reactions people have to information or circumstances. For example, the lawyer was highly agitated when Madam connected with the male ghost. A curious reaction for a nonbeliever." He offered another cigarette. "Sit with me a moment. Before I decide what I should do, I need some information. Tell me about the ghosts, and about Carlton McKay. What's his role in all of this?"

"He's my uncle's overprotective lawyer." Carlton's reaction to Reginald related to his feelings for me. I didn't really want the cigarette, so I crushed it out and leaned back. A breeze tickled the nape of my neck. The sense that we were being watched came over me. Instead of yielding to the chills of my imagination, I forced my mind to the mundane. I thought of the portrait of Eva. How did those women survive the summers in corsets, petticoats, and long, heavy dresses? Even with a breeze, the humidity made me feel sticky. "Carlton isn't an issue. Don't worry about him."

"Carlton has made his peace with me being here temporarily, but I'm not sure he approves of me. When he finds out I'm . . . that I can't really see spirits, he's not going to be kind."

Reginald might not see spirits, but he could see the future where Carlton was concerned. "Let me worry about him. Carlton comes across strong, but he can be reasonable." I took a breath. "My friend Robert died here at Caoin House recently."

If Reginald had been uneasy before, now he was positively bugged. "I understood he was a young man . . ." He tapered to silence as the full implications hit him. "How did he die?"

"In a fall from the roof." I didn't mention that he'd died not ten feet from where we sat, but Reginald *was* intuitive. He followed my glance.

"Was he pushed off the roof?"

"Can a ghost pop a button off a new shirt?"

"You found evidence of a struggle?" Reginald lit another cigarette. Neither one of us was likely to sleep well after this conversation.

"There was no evidence of a scuffle on the roof, but the tiles are slate and slippery. From afar, the roof looks flat, but it's gabled. There's access from the attic. But there was no reason for Robert to be on the roof. The coroner ruled it an accidental death, which is better than what I feared it would be—suicide. But I don't believe Robert fell. I don't even know why he was up there. We were in the middle of a hunting game with clues, but no clues led to the roof."

"Who was he partnered with?" Reginald asked.

"My uncle. Brett hardly knew him but was looking forward to doing business with Robert. And I think he was very pleased to see me interested in having some fun."

"Would it be okay if I spoke with your uncle about this? He is more likely to tell me things that he wouldn't tell you."

It had never occurred to me that Uncle Brett would withhold information because of my gender or his tender feelings for me, but Reginald was correct. "Yes. Feel free to speak with him."

"The soldier that came through to Madam. He said something was hidden—do you have any idea what it might be?"

I thought of the burglaries in Caoin House. "Someone has broken in here numerous times, even before Uncle Brett bought the property. They are searching for something, but we have no idea what. If Uncle Brett had an inkling, I'm sure he'd tell me."

"Something here that dates back to the death of Eva, perhaps." Reginald was musing out loud. "Whatever it is must be tied to that moment in time that connects both spirits to this house."

I recognized the wisdom in his words. "I think you've hit on it. But what? There are some love letters—"

"To Eva?"

"Yes."

"They were from someone else. Her lover, I believe."

"A lover?" Reginald's interest piqued. "Rather a scandal back in the 1860s for the paragon of virtue known as the Southern woman to commit adultery."

"People are people. I'm sure women took lovers even back then."

"That's a thoroughly modern view, Raissa. I'm not so certain others would approach it with the same blasé attitude. A Southern plantation wife who took a lover would be a huge scandal. Even today. There was a standard—"

"For the women. That code of conduct didn't apply to the men." My tone was rather heated. "Sorry, the whole double standard hacks me off."

"It's the bloodline, Raissa. An unfaithful wife can destroy the bloodline of a family. The heir isn't truly the heir, if you get my drift."

The debate over equality had calmed my nerves after seeing the ghost in the oak grove. The heat of my passion had driven all revenants away, and that was a good thing to know. "If a husband treats his wife well, then she wouldn't stray." I'd had it with the woman carrying the blame for the same action men took whenever they chose. Hawthorne's *The Scarlet Letter*, which put all blame on poor Hester Prynne, made me livid. I didn't like to teach it. "A man can father a child out of wedlock and then walk away from his responsibility. How is that right?"

"I'm not defending the wayward louse, but it's the woman who pays the price because the evidence is so . . . evident."

I couldn't argue with the facts, though it galled me to button my lip. "So you think Eva strayed, and what? Her ghost protects the letters and keeps Eli out of the house, so he lurks around the oak trees?"

He gave me a sidelong look. "You make it sound preposterous, but it isn't. I've seen cases like this before with Madam. Eva can't let go of Caoin House because she doesn't want Eli to find the letters. He can't let go because he still loves her."

"So why is he trying to draw me into the oaks with him?"

"Payback to Eva."

"Well, that's certainly unflattering." But a very male response.

We both laughed, and the strain between us was gone. Despite the fact that he'd lied his way into an invitation to my uncle's home, I liked him. He was smart about people. Smart about their emotions and desires.

My shoulders throbbed with tension. "Now I really have to go inside. It's late. Uncle Brett will think we're out here petting or something."

Reginald snorted. "Surely he knows—"

"He doesn't," I said. "He hasn't a clue. Carlton won't tell him because he knows it would upset me." I faced my new friend. "There is absolutely no reason to spread your private business around. Men gossip worse than women, in case you haven't figured that out. Uncle Brett is like I am. He wouldn't care. That's not true of the rest of Mobile society. New Orleans accepts sexual nature in a way that Mobile never will. If you're going to visit here, you might as well have a good time invited into the homes of the wealthy."

"I've had to hide who I am my whole life."

I could read the sadness that came over him. It wasn't fair that he couldn't be free to love whom he chose. Nor was it fair that women were treated as children or, worse, as their husband's chattel. "You're only in Mobile for a visit. The best thing to do is keep your secrets. The most pressing matter we face is this séance."

"We're going through with it, even knowing I can't channel the spirits?"

"I think we should, Reginald. I can assist you." I grinned. "Let's make Uncle Brett happy. Then what you do with the rest of your stay is up to you."

"Why would you do this for me?" he asked.

"Because you're going to help me solve what happened to Robert and what's going on here at Caoin House. If Eli and Eva need to be put to rest, you'll help me do it. You may not be a medium, but you're the closest thing I have here in Mobile."

"Thank you, Raissa."

"Hold your thanks until this is done." I wasn't certain we could pull it off, but I was game to try. I owed Robert resolution. He'd come into the house as a guest and died here—for what purpose I couldn't fathom, but I would find out. And if we could get Eli and Eva to rest in peace, it would be a double bonus. I was more than a little worried about the effect Eli had on me. He commanded my attention in a way that unnerved me, and I was compelled to find out why he couldn't rest in peace. My determination was the only thing that sustained me through hardships. I wasn't about to yield it to some ghost.

I went up to my bedroom. When I couldn't sleep, in the stillness of the beautiful summer night, I sat at my little desk and wrote my short story. I needed to mull a point of the story, and I went out the French doors to the balcony and gazed down into the oaks. I saw not the first hint of my pale soldier. Whatever Eli was up to, he wasn't showing himself to me. I went back inside and at last finished my tale. By the time I crawled into bed, dawn was only a few hours away.

CHAPTER NINETEEN

When I finally awoke the next morning, I buttonholed Uncle Brett in the library and convinced him to pull back his plans for a gala séance. The man *loved* a party. In that regard he was so different from my mother, Evangeline. Physically, they resembled each other with the dark, curly hair and large hazel eyes that I'd also inherited. If I'd had to cast my uncle as a book character, his strong jaw and stubborn chin put me in mind of Heathcliff.

My mother's kind smile made her a candidate for one of the Brontë brood, or perhaps Jo March from *Little Women*. But she was not someone who sought center stage or even a place in the chorus. Both of my parents were retiring, which made Uncle Brett even more wonderful to a little girl longing for excitement. Looking back, aside from my birthday celebrations, I couldn't remember my parents hosting a single party. Not even a bridge gathering or a small dinner get-together. They simply had no interest in entertaining others or in attending social events where the conversation tended toward the light and chatty.

My parents had been the stereotypes of the scholarly teachers. They were happiest in front of a fire, sitting side by side, reading. My great love of books came from both of them. But while my parents were more academically tilted, I loved ghost stories.

"Uncle Brett, were you close with Mother when you were growing up?" I asked.

"She was the older child, and she tried her best to boss me into doing the right thing. She succeeded. Most of the time." He grinned. "We loved each other, though our interests varied widely. She loved learning, and I loved doing. You're a nice blend of the both of us, Raissa."

"She often said you were a rascal who stayed clear of jail only because she watched over you."

Brett laughed out loud. "I enjoyed a good prank. Evangeline was earnest. She should have had more fun. Life is too short to be serious every minute." A rueful note crept into his voice. "If I could teach you one thing, it's that life is best spiced with a little fun. If I could go back in time, I would have worked harder to make Evangeline laugh. She had a beautiful laugh. Like the low notes of musical chimes."

"I miss her." Emotion clotted my throat. "And Father, too."

"Yes, I catch myself thinking what Evangeline would say or do. I felt she was around you right after Alex was killed. Probably my imagination at work, because I know how much she loved you."

"And now? Is she near?" It was curious that I'd never felt my mother's or father's presence, yet I could clearly see a ghost from the 1860s. More than anything, I wanted to believe they were at peace.

"I have no idea if they're roaming about Caoin House. I don't sense them at all. The truth is, your mother never really took to this place."

We'd visited when I was a child, but the visits had stopped. I'd asked several times, but my mother's response was always vague. Not the right time, or too long a journey, or that Uncle Brett was out of town. Eventually I'd stopped asking.

"Your mother was never one to criticize a decision I made, but she was uncomfortable here. She said the house was haunted. That unhappy times echoed in the halls. At the time, I had no idea how right she was. If we can make contact with her during the séance, perhaps she'll reveal something more. I've wished many times that I'd questioned her more closely."

"Did she *see* something?"

"She never said, but you did. You became hysterical, and I never understood exactly what had happened. Whatever it was upset you greatly. She never came back for another visit, no matter how many times I invited her. I chalked it up to her reclusive nature, but perhaps she really understood there was something amiss here. Maybe she knew more than she ever let on."

I wanted to dig deeper into this topic, but Winona came to the door. "Mr. Brett, I was cleaning Miss Isabelle's room, and I found this." She extended a silver locket on a chain.

The necklace pooled in my uncle's hand like quicksilver. When he snapped open the locket, he inhaled sharply. "This is not Isabelle's."

"It was on the floor beside the bed." Winona looked concerned.

With a furrowed brow, Brett asked Winona, "Did Isabelle say when she was returning?"

"No, sir." Winona shifted from foot to foot. "Miss Isabelle only said she had business meetings to attend. She mentioned something about Mr. Carlton having papers for her to sign and something about the property near the river. They're cutting timber on the off chance a big storm will blow in this summer and knock the trees over."

"I can drive into town and ask her to return," I volunteered. Her family owned timberland and cattle farms in north Mobile and Washington Counties, but chances were that Isabelle was still in Mobile. Although her title wasn't official, because a woman of her social station didn't hold a job, she was actually the bookkeeper/accountant for the family businesses. The offices were located on Conception Street not far from Carlton's law practice.

"She has her family company to run," Uncle Brett said. "Let her do her work." He wouldn't date a woman who was merely a hotsy-totsy. He liked that Isabelle had made a place for herself in her family dynasty. "When she's done with her business, she'll be in touch." He snapped the locket shut. "Thank you for finding this, Winona. Don't worry about anything. I was just . . . startled."

"Yes, sir."

When Winona left the room, I asked to see the locket. For a moment, I thought Uncle Brett would refuse, but he handed it to me. I opened it and found a miniature of Eva Whitehead on one side and a damaged likeness of a soldier on the other. The man's face had been eradicated, as if someone had taken a sharp blade and scored out his features. All that remained was the Confederate uniform. Dread crept along my neck and arms. The defacement appeared deliberate—and angry.

"Who would do such a thing?" I asked.

"A good question. I've never seen this necklace before. It isn't Isabelle's. How strange that it would appear in her room. Winona's cleaned that room a hundred times. The necklace wasn't there before. This is an expensive piece of jewelry. The weight of the silver . . ." He sounded defeated.

"Maybe one of the ghosts left it." I aimed to cheer him up.

"It was always my understanding that ghosts couldn't move objects." He was deadly serious. "I've studied telekinesis. For a spirit to have that much power . . ."

"You'll have to ask Reginald." He wasn't a medium, but he'd worked with one for years. "But I have something to ask you. Why don't you marry Isabelle?" I wasn't intent on prying, but I was curious. They were a perfect couple, and it was clear they loved each other.

Brett hesitated. "I'd like to, but I can't."

"Why not? Is she . . . married to someone else?"

"Heavens no." He motioned for me to sit across from him in one of the club chairs. "I won't marry Isabelle until we figure out what's happening here at Caoin House."

"What are you saying?" My mind whirled with dangerous possibilities—but none that would come with marriage to my uncle. Brett was fun and simple joy. He was an astute businessman, but he didn't make enemies; he wasn't a drinker like a lot of men, nor did he have a bad temper.

"While we were in New Orleans, the house was broken into again." Brett put a hand on my arm when I started to rise. "They ransacked the attic, but there's so much old stuff up there, I doubt they took anything. They pulled all the books down from the shelves here in the library. Travis and Winona put everything back in place before we got home. Nothing obvious was stolen. Travis said no vehicles came from the front drive, but he found hoofprints in the back, and evidence two horses had been tied there."

The coincidence of the house broken into and the appearance of the locket wasn't lost on me. What burglars came to *leave* jewelry? It didn't make any sense. "Nothing was taken, yet a valuable necklace has now been found. I don't think the ghosts are involved in the necklace's appearance."

Brett shook his head. "It doesn't make sense."

"What did Carlton say about the break-in?" I knew without asking that Brett had confided in the lawyer. It was the logical thing to do.

"He urged me to call the sheriff, and I did, but there's nothing the law can do. This has happened before. Whoever is responsible *knew* we'd be out of the house. That's something to be thankful for. Had we been home, someone might have been injured. I'm not a violent man, but I won't stand still and let vandals invade my home."

The break-in, which was an act of violence, a violation of the sanctity and safety of my uncle's home, made me ask, "What do you really think happened to Robert?"

"I don't think he fell from the roof, and I don't think he jumped." Uncle Brett was far more worried than I'd ever imagined. "I haven't said much, because without evidence I can't push for further investigation. The coroner ruled his death accidental, and I believe that was partly as a favor to me. To have a different ruling would have opened me and my guests up for questioning, and possible legal responsibility. A shadow would have fallen over me and Caoin House."

"But if someone killed Robert?" I tried to keep the emotion from my voice. "What if someone we know is a killer? Though why anyone would kill Robert is beyond me. I should have told you sooner that I went up on the roof to investigate. I don't see how he could have fallen, and I don't believe he jumped."

"Then we share a similar conclusion. I could twist the sheriff's arm and get him to come and look around, but what would he find? I've looked already. You were on the roof. You didn't find anything."

I wanted to tell him about the button, but I didn't. It could have been on the roof for weeks, left by some workman, except the cotton cloth came from an expensive shirt. The small, pearlescent button spoke of quality. Until I had more to go on, it was unfair to further arouse Uncle's worries. "I don't think Robert fell, and I know he didn't kill himself. That fall might have paralyzed him, and no one intent on suicide would risk becoming a cripple. Besides, Robert had no reason to end his life. He was successful and happy."

Sadness settled on Uncle Brett's features. "I wake up in the night sometimes thinking of the things I would change, if only I could go back in time. I would say no to the hunting game that Carlton set up. I would put you and Robert in the refreshment tent serving drinks and keep you there. There were so many opportunities to do things in a different way—"

"The game isn't at fault. There was no reason for Robert to be on the roof. Not a single clue would have taken him there. The party activities had nothing to do with his death. If we could figure out *why* he was on the roof, then we'd have a better chance of finding the person responsible."

"It wounds me to think someone I invited into my home is responsible. I've gone over the guest list again and again, but I come up empty-handed."

"Maybe it wasn't someone you invited! It could be the person who breaks into Caoin House. Someone could have been hiding in the attic for weeks, Uncle Brett." My skin prickled and crawled at the idea. "No one ever goes in the attic. Not even the servants."

"You're right. There could be a king's ransom hidden there and I wouldn't know. There's an air of . . . despair in the attic. Even I avoid it." His expression revealed his anxiety.

"The intruder could easily have slipped in and remained hidden." I put a hand on his knee. I wanted to relieve the guilt he felt. "Whatever happened, it wasn't your fault."

"If it wasn't a living person, I'm hoping Reginald can get to the bottom of this."

I had to bite my tongue to keep from telling him Reginald was a fraud, but I managed to keep it to myself. "When we have the séance, it would be best to limit the guest list, especially if we're probing for a murderer. Let's keep it to me, you, and Reginald."

"What about Isabelle? She'll be crushed. And Carlton, well, I'll leave it at saying we must invite him, too. He's taken with you, Raissa. He would be wounded if we left him out. And Pretta and Hubert. I've already mentioned it to them. Pretta thinks we're going straight to hell, but she can't resist participating anyway."

I wanted to argue that we could repeat the séance later with more people attending if we wished, but Uncle Brett had his heart set, and it wasn't worth an argument. "So, Carlton, Isabelle, and the Pauls will attend the séance." I turned the conversation. "What do you know about the relationship between Eva and Eli? Were they happy?"

"You're onto something, aren't you?" Uncle Brett asked with a return of his normal, quick interest.

"I don't know." I picked up the locket again as I pondered the situation. Caoin House was rife with secrets. Which ones were worth protecting? "Do you think it's possible Eva was having an affair with someone in Mobile? Someone her husband knew? A friend of the family."

Brett almost choked on his coffee. "Why do you ask?"

"Those letters are clearly from someone other than Eli. There are two possibilities. A family friend or a Union soldier. Those are the men who were in Mobile at the time."

"My word. If she had an affair with a Union officer, it would be a betrayal to the South's cause. Doubly so since her husband was away fighting for the Confederacy."

"What if someone other than deserters killed Eva?" I posed the question as gently as I could. "There has to be a reason Eli and Eva are haunting the house. The letters might be a clue. And they also might be a reason for someone to break in here and search for them."

Uncle Brett stood abruptly. "I can't fathom a sixty-year-old scandal provoking someone to break into my home."

"Think about it, Uncle Brett. Someone has been breaking into the house since before you bought it. It's not *your* belongings they want. It has to be something hidden in the house. If the love letters can prove that Eva was unfaithful, it might tarnish the Whitehead family. Are there Whitehead descendants still here in Mobile? Maybe someone from the family knows of the letters and desperately wants to retrieve them to protect the name."

"I don't think any Whiteheads survived after the 1880s. Eva and Eli had only the one daughter, Elise. And she jumped to her death from a third-floor window as family and friends gathered to see her wed."

"Oh, that's tragic." I was shocked I hadn't heard the tale before. "This is the child who was left alive beside her dead mother?"

Brett nodded. "Local lore indicated Elise was never right in the head. Her mother's death must have impacted her. Eli took her to Europe for several years, but they did return to Caoin House, where she grew up. She jumped to her death only moments before her wedding was to begin. Of course, some of the stories imply she was pushed out the window."

"By her husband-to-be?"

"There's only speculation. Elise was mentally unstable. If you're correct in assuming Eva was unfaithful, there's no telling what the child witnessed."

Or no telling what she'd seen or overheard and might repeat. "If these letters prove Eva made a cuckold of her husband, it would reflect badly on the Whiteheads. Isabelle told me that Eva's family, the Kemps, weren't wealthy, but they were well established as a Southern family of honor. If she betrayed her husband, she would be a tarnished woman, and one who would be held in contempt by the entire community. She would be viewed, even today, as a woman who cheated on a war hero— that wouldn't go over well. Her family would want to bury those facts."

"You're right. If such a thing came to light, a family could lose its social standing." Brett returned to his seat.

"And what if someone from Mobile took it upon himself to punish Eva for her infidelity? What if it wasn't deserters who killed her, but another member of Mobile society? Those letters might be the key to a lot more than a passionate love affair. Would you mind if I took them to my bedroom and studied them?"

"A good idea. I've read them all, but not with an eye toward the possible dangers they represented for Eva's reputation. I viewed them as love letters. Foolishly romantic."

I went to the shelf and began to pull the books down. When the secret panel was revealed, I pushed it open. The hidey-hole was empty. "Did you move the letters?" I asked my uncle, even though I knew he hadn't. He would have told me before I took down the books.

He rose slowly. "So the burglar took something, after all."

I felt a keen loss. "Who would do such a thing?"

"I don't know." Brett went to the library desk and opened a drawer. "I don't like what's happening here, Raissa. Let's have the séance and see if we can get to the bottom of this. If not, perhaps it would be best if you returned to Savannah."

"I'm not leaving."

His smile was haunted. "You sound exactly like Evangeline. Once she made up her mind about something, a team of wild horses couldn't change it."

"She loved you, and so do I. We'll get to the bottom of this." I spoke with more confidence than I felt, but I wasn't about to abandon my uncle at a time when he needed family more than ever.

CHAPTER TWENTY

Reginald met me under the moss-draped oaks, and we went for a stroll around the property, partly so he would be familiar with the setup but also to allow us some privacy to discuss our plans. We made our way slowly toward the cemetery, where he could make notes on some of the graves for the pending séance. While I didn't relish tricking my uncle, I wanted to give him some peace of mind. And if Reginald were revealed as a fraud, that wouldn't happen. What he did—giving information on departed loved ones—brought comfort to those he "read" for. While it might be slightly unethical, it was not cruel or mean.

I shared the information about the missing letters with Reginald, whose theories of burglars guarding family names dovetailed with mine. As we stepped under the ornate arch covered with the sweetest-smelling Confederate jasmine, we paused to inhale the slightly melancholy fragrance. The white star-shaped flower that reminded me of a pinwheel adored the warm climate of Mobile and bloomed for weeks.

"How would anyone find those letters?" Reginald asked. "They were carefully hidden for decades."

"I don't know." There were hundreds of books on the shelves in the library. It would have taken someone hours of searching. "Uncle Brett said a lot of books were pulled down. Travis and Winona cleaned up."

"Either the robber was very lucky, or he knew exactly where to look." Reginald wasn't backing down. "Who knew about the letters?"

"Uncle Brett and me. I don't think he even told Isabelle. Maybe Winona. Maybe Travis. Someone could have been hiding in the house, though." Saying the words sent a chill through me. The idea of someone creeping about, spying and eavesdropping, made my skin itch. But it was possible. Someone could actually be living in Caoin House. And I now began to wonder if that someone might not be in league with companions who enjoyed a bit of dress-up. Beautiful women in white gowns seen from a distance flitting about the grounds. An elegant soldier, saber at his side, seen outside the house on the lawn, where some trick of acoustics made it seem possible he spoke my name and called to me. "I wish the ghosts were a trick, someone manipulating my uncle and me." But I knew the truth. There were truly spirits at Caoin House.

"To what purpose?" he asked.

I shook my head, which had begun to ache. "To hide a secret from the past. Maybe Robert found something that led him to the attic and then out on the roof. He had to have a reason for going up there. He wasn't the kind of man to wander about another's house and poke into things."

"Do you believe your friend Robert was murdered?" Reginald asked the question bluntly.

The sweet scent of the jasmine had given me a pounding headache, and I felt short of breath, as if the perfume had replaced oxygen. "I think it's a definite possibility."

"We need to be careful. We can't tell anyone what we're doing," Reginald said.

As we strolled into the cemetery, a hush fell around us. The birdcalls and chatter of squirrels, which had followed us through the woods, stopped. The silence made us both glance around, and I had the sense we weren't alone.

If the soldier had followed us to the cemetery, he played hide-and-seek with me. I caught movement in my peripheral vision, but when I turned to look, no one was there, leading me to wonder if the things I'd experienced were simply tricks of my mind.

"There's a presence here now. I can't see anything, but I sense it."

"Maybe we've convinced ourselves that something is here, so we feel it."

Reginald considered my statement. "It's possible. I've seen plenty of people at séances claim to see things because Madam suggested a presence was there."

"Is she a fraud?" I asked.

Reginald hesitated. "I don't believe she is. There are those who can pierce the veil. I believe that wholeheartedly. She knew things no one could know, and I assure you she had no regiment of investigators checking out her potential clients."

"But it is possible to trick people into seeing things."

"Yes. It's possible. Just as we're about to trick your uncle."

We walked to the tomb where Eva Whitehead was buried. Reginald traced the stone rendering with his bare hands. "Even in death, she is striking," he said.

"Even in death. Take note of her. My uncle sees her, or at least he believes it to be her, so he is aware of the details of her appearance. When we have our séance, you want to present her as he envisions her."

When Reginald was familiar with her flowing curls and particulars of her dress and figure, we walked on. The morning sun filtered through a dense line of cedar trees, and beyond them I saw the vast expanse of wooden crosses. "Soldiers and slaves. Both reside in unmarked graves."

"Military cemeteries pockmark the South, but those have mostly been designated official cemeteries and are maintained by the government. A few of these graves might belong to soldiers, but I would bet these are the people who lived and died at Caoin House."

"So many." The white crosses disappeared down a slight hill and continued up the other side. There had to be at least three hundred.

"Women often died in childbirth and from infection, influenza, yellow jack. The agents of death were omnipresent."

Off to the west side of the crosses was a strange marker that caught my eye. It stood alone between the family portion and the unmarked graves. "Is that a crow? What a peculiar thing to put on a grave." The crow was so artfully executed that even though it was white marble, it looked as if it might take flight at any moment. The figure perched on a tree branch that extended from a tall white column. Grapevines climbed the column and twined around the bird's roost. Great care had been given to the monument, though it was strange and a bit disconcerting. We crossed the manicured grass to examine it.

"It's a raven," Reginald said. "Ravens are often birds of death. I grew up in a boys' home, and my best friend was a Choctaw. Raf Weaver." He brushed the dirt away from the lettering as he talked. "Raf introduced me to the idea of spirits because he could connect with the world beyond the veil of death when he went into a trance. He quickly learned to hide his ability. A home filled with abandoned boys is nowhere to display a propensity for visiting with the dead."

He didn't have to go into detail. I got the picture.

"Raf said the raven was the keeper of secrets. The raven also helps reveal secret truths that shed light on dark events. He had great reverence for the bird, which could also take on other forms. It is a shape-shifter."

His talk of death and animals capable of taking on a human form, or that of another animal, gave me the heebie-jeebies, a new phrase I'd learned that perfectly described the way my skin wanted to crawl around my body. "But why a raven here?"

"Wait a minute. There's an inscription. 'The death of love corrupts all living things,'" he read.

"What does that mean?"

"I don't know." He found a twig and brushed more dirt away. Slowly the name *Caleb* was revealed. One name only.

"A slave?" I asked.

"I'm not certain." Reginald stood and stepped back, eyeing the tombstone. "He's buried in what would be no-man's-land. Neither slave nor family member. Maybe an indentured servant or a poor relation?"

"I'll ask Uncle Brett what he knows." We'd examined the raven's base, but there was no other clue as to the occupant of the grave. "We should get back to the house." It was closing on lunchtime, and Uncle Brett would get worried if I didn't appear shortly.

"I need to prepare for the séance." He offered his arm as we walked slowly back through the cemetery. There was something about the place that defied speed. It demanded solemnity and a funereal pace.

"I'm going into town to talk with Pretta. She'll be at the candy shop," I told him. "Would you like to go?"

"No, thanks. I'm anxious as hell about the séance and failing your uncle's expectations. Madam wouldn't be pleased at all were I to disappoint."

"It will be fine." I had my own misgivings about what we were doing, but it would do no good to infect Reginald with my doubts.

We left the cemetery behind and found that our pace increased significantly. It was almost as if the land of the dead had pulled us into a world where time marched around us, never carrying us forward. Once we were free of the tombs, we found the birdsong and our laughter as we ran toward the imposing outline of Caoin House, rising white against the background of green trees and the bright-blue summer sky.

CHAPTER
TWENTY-ONE

Reginald took his notes back to his room to memorize them. I borrowed the car from Uncle Brett and headed into town. There were a few things I needed to do, and talking with Pretta was only one of them.

By the time I arrived in downtown Mobile, I'd firmed my resolve and found the offices of Dr. Langford Oyles, who served Mobile County as coroner. After a thirty-minute wait in a nicely appointed office where a young secretary cast annoyed glances at me, I was ushered into the doctor's private office. He sat behind a massive oak desk. He didn't rise when I entered and made it clear that his valuable time wasn't to be wasted on mysterious females who refused to state their business. Had I revealed my intention to the secretary, I would have been turned away without half a chance.

"I'd like to see the coroner's report on Robert Aultman," I said in a no-nonsense tone.

"Don't be absurd." He stood up quickly. "Please leave. I have no time for such things."

"Why can't I see it?"

"Women have no need to worry themselves about such matters. This has nothing to do with you, so it's best you leave before I call your"—he noted the wedding ring on my finger—"husband. I'm sure he'll be upset to discover your antics."

"My husband is dead." That took a bit of wind from his sails. "And I'm not leaving until I've read over the report. It's a public record. I'm part of the public."

"I don't know who you think you are, young woman, but such matters are not for females to dwell on. Now leave before I call the law."

"Dr. Oyles, Mr. Aultman was visiting my uncle when he died. His family has asked me to read the report." I lied with such aplomb that I surprised even myself. "Now I intend to relieve their minds about this matter. If I need to call my uncle here, I will. As I said before, coroners' reports are public documents, and I have every right to see this one." It was a huge bluff.

"I shall call your uncle myself."

"I'll wait here while you get in touch with him. The telephone lines to Caoin House are up, but not entirely reliable. Otherwise I would have called to alert you of my pending arrival." One lie fell off my tongue after the next. Phone lines had been installed and were truly unreliable, but I had never intended to warn the doctor of my visit. "I think you should know, my uncle will be upset that you doubted my word."

The doctor hesitated, a pained expression on his face and his hand over the telephone receiver. Abruptly, he pressed the buzzer on his desk. "Gladys, have you finished typing the inquest notes on Robert Aultman? Please bring them in if you have."

The door to the office opened, and the young woman I'd brazened my way past handed several typed pages to the doctor. When I reached for them, he withdrew them. "Not so fast. What is it you hope to find?"

"Nothing in particular. I'm merely reporting to the family. I want to assure them the fall was an accident. As you know, my uncle could be held responsible, and that's something we all want to avoid. Uncle Brett would be very upset if something in the report implied the tragedy was in any way his fault."

The truth was, if Dr. Oyles reported my visit—and gentle threats—to Uncle Brett, I'd be the one in trouble.

The doctor handed over the report. "You may read it here. Do not take it from this room." He left the room, shutting the door firmly behind him.

I'd never looked over a coroner's inquest before, and I was surprised at the detail. The front page was a form that listed the time and date of the accident, Robert's age and address, and the formal ruling of "accidental death."

The testimony by Sheriff Thompson was par for the course, telling of his arrival at the scene and what he found. It was difficult to read the specific details of Robert's death, and I had to remind myself several times that he no longer felt pain. The sheriff had paid attention to the angle of the body and the way Robert had fallen, with the speculation that he was peering over the roof and down at the ground watching something, which resulted in the fall. His reasoning went that something happening on the front steps and perhaps farther back on the porch caught Robert's attention. He leaned over the edifice to get a better view, overbalanced, and fell.

All of that was known to me.

It was Uncle Brett's testimony—and Carlton's—that caught me up short.

Uncle Brett had launched an investigation into Robert's past the day after the accident. Even more shocking was the revelation that Robert had been convicted of fraud in Kansas. The case involved a young widow who Robert wooed. He eventually involved himself in her financial affairs. He gradually shifted her wealth into his account and spent it. He'd served three years in the Kansas state prison, which explained why he'd managed to avoid military service.

The pages of the inquest fluttered to the floor as I tried to control my emotional response. Robert had targeted me as a possible lonely mark who was primed for the picking. He'd pretended to care for me. He'd led me on simply because I was Uncle Brett's niece, likely heir to his vast fortune.

Heat flooded my body, and I had an almost irresistible urge to break something. Instead, I picked up the pages of the report and read Carlton's statement. The lawyer had been privy to Uncle Brett's suspicions about Robert and had hired a private investigator.

Carlton and my uncle had discovered this, and no one had told me. I'd made a fool of myself, pining about Robert because I'd believed he cared for me.

Carlton went on to say that his suspicions were first aroused when he caught Robert in one of the guest bedrooms when he was supposed to be participating in the treasure hunt. Carlton had pursued him through the house but lost him. Ten minutes later, when Carlton had returned to the festivities on the front lawn, Robert had fallen to his death.

And all this had been withheld from me. Even to the point of Uncle Brett and Carlton pretending to be concerned about Robert's death and the circumstances. The truth was that Robert had been attempting to rob my uncle's guests and had fallen to his death in a cowardly attempt to evade capture.

My first reaction was anger at Uncle Brett and Carlton. I should have been told. But as I put the coroner's report on Dr. Oyles's desk and took my leave, the anger faded. No one had known about Robert's nefarious plan until after he was dead. Was there really any point in telling me then? I was safe from his clutches, so both men had chosen to spare me from the shame of my choice. How unfair to be angry at them for trying to protect me.

When I left the coolness of Dr. Oyles's office, I wandered down the street past the local peanut shop. On a whim I stopped and bought a bag of roasted peanuts and went across the street to Bienville Square, where benches had been strategically placed beneath the beautiful oaks. Absentmindedly, I fed the squirrels and pigeons as I tried to come to terms with what I'd learned about Robert. Soon I would be furious, but now I was merely wounded by his trickery. The whole thing was so calculated. And had Robert not become so greedy that he attempted to steal from the guests, he might still be in my life.

"Raissa!"

I turned to find Carlton striding toward me. I composed my expression as best I could and pasted on a smile. While I didn't want to see anyone, Carlton had gone to great lengths to protect me. "Hello." I rose and gave him a kiss on the cheek.

"What brings you to town?"

"I'm picking up supplies for the séance, and I wanted to stop and say hello to Pretta."

"Forging those female bonds of friendship, I see."

He assumed the best of me, and I was grateful for that. "Yes, you know how the weaker sex needs to gang up."

"Weaker sex, my eye. I'd match you up against any Samson."

I desperately wanted to ask him things about Robert, but I didn't. If Dr. Oyles let on to Uncle that I'd seen the report, I could ask whatever I wished. Until then, though, I would play ignorant. "You overestimate us, but perhaps that's merely wisdom."

He laughed. "May I take you to lunch?"

"Yes." I needed the diversion from my own dark thoughts. "And perhaps you can tell me a bit about the history of Caoin House."

"Seeking material on the ghosts?"

"If there are ghosts, I'd certainly like to know their history."

"I don't really believe in ghosts, but Brett has shared some of his experiences with me." The humor was gone from his expression. "I can't help but be worried about this séance. I'll have to trust that Reginald can control this, because if he can't, there could be dire results."

CHAPTER TWENTY-TWO

Lunch was delicious fresh seafood brought right into the port not three hundred yards away from where we dined. I'd never tasted such sweet white fish. Carlton explained it was red snapper caught in the saltwater just off the coast in the Gulf of Mexico. "The fish are so plentiful they almost jump in the boats," he said. "The Gulf is the nursery for seafood that feeds the world. We live in a place where God's bounty is undeniable."

I hadn't taken Carlton for a believer in a deity, but the truth was, I hardly knew him. Still shaken by the revelations I'd learned about Robert, I was twice as thankful for his solid friendship. I'd held Carlton at arm's length. Now even my sadness for Robert's untimely death had been curdled. I'd been on track to give my heart to a cad.

Dwelling on such things would only make me emotional. I lifted my chin. "Tell me about the Whiteheads," I requested. "Caoin House is remarkable. I can only imagine the people responsible for creating such an extraordinary house."

"Before and during the war, the Whiteheads were the cream of the crop of Southern gentility. While a lot of farmers came to wealth with sugarcane and cotton, Eli Whitehead was born to great wealth. His family fought for the British king in the First War of Scottish Independence. For his efforts he was rewarded with lands in Scotland, and through the centuries the Whiteheads were viewed, by the British at least, as Scottish royalty."

"To the conqueror go the spoils. War is always about greed."

My bitterness made Carlton pause, and he reached across the table and touched my hand. "It's true that old men sit home and declare war while the young men die on the field, seduced with visions of bravery and patriotism."

"And it never ends." I picked up my fork. "But let's not ruin a lovely meal with such morbid talk. Tell me more about the Whitehead family."

"In the early 1800s, Morsey Whitehead came to America. He was something of the family black sheep." Carlton leaned closer and whispered, "I hear he had a penchant for ladies of the night and gambling, so he was sent to the New World to carve out his own fortune or starve. Since he was a younger brother, he was disposable to the Whitehead dynasty."

I kept my comments about inheritance to myself. I was beginning to sound bitter and cranky, and Carlton was enjoying the spinning of a good yarn. Uncle Brett often held the floor when it came to local history, and it was pleasant to see Carlton expand into the role of raconteur.

"Morsey knew a bit about sailing, possibly because he did a stint as a pirate, or so the story goes, and he ended up in the Port of Mobile. He was a handsome rascal, and he caught the eye of a young society girl. His marriage to her sealed his fortune. To the amazement of everyone, he settled down and became a partner in her family's cotton-transport business. Morsey was quite the captain of industry and brought the first cotton gin to the Mobile area. He established a number of gins on the Alabama waterways, and had a virtual monopoly of cotton ginning and transport. Some said he was a financial genius."

"And just like that, he put aside his roving eye and love for the card table?" I kept my tone light.

"Just like that. Another man felled by the charms of a Southern girl."

He did make me laugh, and it seemed like forever since I'd had cause to. "Yes, we know how to bring a rascal to his knees. So Eli was Morsey's grandson?"

"Often it's the third generation that squanders a family's money, but Eli was the exception. He invested in the slave trade and not only gained workers to harvest his crops, but he bought and sold slaves."

"I'm all for wealth, but selling slaves was—"

"Blood money." Carlton waved the waitress over and ordered apple pie for dessert. "Brutal, shameful business. You know the McKay family. Of course we were on the losing end of the battles with England, never owned a slave. We have earned our living by our wits and intelligence."

"As I hope to with my stories." I bit my lip. "I brought my first tale to send it off today. It's really the reason I came into town." I'd vowed to tell no one I was mailing "The Unexpected Visitor" to the *Saturday Evening Post* for consideration. Yet here I was, telling Carlton my secrets.

"A celebration is in order. And soon, with the séance, you'll have material for even more stories."

"As I promised, I made a copy for you. Uncle Brett had some carbon paper." I brought the neatly stacked pages from my purse and gave them to him.

"I am deeply honored." He read the first page. "And I'm already hooked into the story. I can't wait to read it."

I took it from him and folded it. "Put it away, and please continue with your story of Morsey and Eli Whitehead." I hadn't meant to interrupt, but my ghostly tale had been burning a hole in my purse. Now I could relax and listen.

"Eli married the most beautiful girl in the South. Eva Kemp was a descendant of Southern royalty. Her great-great-uncle was Thomas Jefferson, and she had kinship with Mrs. Jefferson Davis. Eli was prouder of her than a peacock with his tail. He set out to build the most elegant house in the Southeast for her. And he did. Caoin House has a reputation that extends well beyond the South. Architects from Europe have been to tour the house to examine the details. And that's how your uncle came to know about it. A group of European investors was in Mobile looking at the modifications he'd made to the paddleboats on the river. They wanted to tour Caoin House, so Brett went with them. His decision to own it was rash." He grinned. "But the house has served your uncle well. His parties are events of state. And he loves that."

"Eli must have loved Eva very much." I thought of the ghosts haunting the property. If I were writing a fairy-tale ending, it would include two spirits so deeply in love they couldn't let go of the land that bound them together. I knew better.

"Stories in town tell how they were inseparable. He doted on her. And they were happy for a time. But then the war came, and no one in the South was happy. The devastation and destruction gutted the South for generations, Raissa. You were born into the latter part of the century, and some of the battle scars have healed. Not the racism or the bitterness. Those are still with us today."

"Yet the Negroes have the vote, and women do not."

Carlton exclaimed, "You are a sly fox, my dear! Nice way to maneuver that into the conversation. You must be taking lessons from Brett, but I will assure you that I support women's suffrage and will cast my ballot for a woman's right to vote."

"Thank you, Carlton." I was a bit ashamed of my hard push. "I feel we should work to give the Negro equal opportunity as well as women. He may have the right to vote, but he is not considered equal by most people in these parts."

"Only time will bring about that change," Carlton said. "No amount of force, whether federal or state, can legislate equality. It will happen only when the citizens wish it to."

I enjoyed Carlton's sage approach to things, but our lunch was drawing to a close, and I sought a more lighthearted tone. "So what questions will you ask Reginald at the séance?"

"Perhaps I'll ask if the ghost of Eli guards the secrets of Caoin House."

"What secrets?" I wondered if he knew of the letters.

"Surely there are secrets in that vast old place. There's been much tragedy there."

"Eva Whitehead. She was killed by Union deserters, right?" I was curious about Carlton's take on the whole murder of Eva.

"So the story goes."

"But you don't believe that?" Carlton had surprised me yet again.

"Because of Brett's interest in the house, I did a bit of research. The last year of the war, things were very hard here in Mobile. People were starving. During that final summer, fear of a yellow-fever epidemic was high, and the population was weak from a lack of food. It is probable that Union deserters butchered and killed Eva. But it is possible that the slaves revolted and killed her, or that outliers from either army or simply desperate civilians happened upon Caoin House, saw the vast wealth, and decided to take what they wanted. Eva was a fighter. She would have tried to protect the house her husband built for her."

"Are there any Whiteheads left here?"

"No, when Elise died without a child, that ended the line. Eli died in the oak grove at the age of forty-six. The death of Elise had left him deranged, to an extent. He became a recluse."

"How did he die?" I asked.

"There are no records. His death is merely reported as 'found dead.' I searched and couldn't find any details, which led me to conclude a possible suicide. A lot of paperwork was lost between the late 1800s and the present, though, so my assumption is mere speculation. There is solid evidence Eli was bereft after the death of his daughter. A depressed man, alone in an isolated house . . . it wouldn't be the first time."

"What about Eva's family? Are the Kemps still in Mobile?"

Carlton frowned. "I don't know. Isabelle may know more about that than I do. Why the sudden interest in Eva and Eli? Are you researching for the séance? Does our handsome medium need a little help?"

Carlton was shrewd, and I'd inadvertently given him a reason to suspect Reginald of being a fraud. "I'm sure Uncle Brett told you some letters were stolen in the break-in while we were in New Orleans." Though his features were schooled, I thought I saw surprise. "At any rate, it occurred to me those letters would only be of value to someone related to the people who wrote them. Why not steal the silver or something of monetary value? Those letters could only have emotional value."

"Who wrote them?"

Now I had to guard my expression. "There were no signatures, so I am operating on the assumption they were Eva's love letters." Vague was good.

He nodded. "Check with Isabelle about Kemp heirs. She's far more embedded in the social scene and blueblood lineage than I am." He called for the check. "Now, I must return to the law practice. I have a client facing serious charges, and I have to prepare for court in the morning, but it was a delight to spend some time with you."

"I enjoyed lunch very much." I didn't have to pretend. "You'll be out for the séance?"

"I'd hoped to get out before then, but my clients make even an evening off impossible. I wouldn't dream of missing the séance, though. You can count on me." He rose and assisted me from the table. We parted ways at Bienville Square as he strode down the sidewalk to work. After a moment's hesitation, I hurried to the downtown post office and mailed my story off. I was so lightheaded afterward that I almost went home. Instead, I headed down Dauphin Street to the candy store and a quick gab with Pretta.

CHAPTER
TWENTY-THREE

Pretta's face was flushed with heat as she brought a pan of cheese straws out of the big commercial oven in the back of the candy store. Two pots of key-lime custard bubbled on burners.

"Can I help?" I asked. "I'm not much of a cook, but I can help if you tell me what to do . . ."

"Could you stir that custard? It has to thicken so that I can pour it into the chocolate shells."

Stirring I could manage. I'd done plenty of that standing on a stool beside my mother. She wasn't a bad cook, but she preferred reading over cooking.

"John Henry should be here any minute," Pretta said.

"Is he a chef, too?"

"He's helped me since he was nine. Best damn candy maker in the Southeast. That boy can tell when sugar has spun by looking at it." She arranged the cheese straws on a fancy platter in an elegant pinwheel pattern. "These are for Mrs. Marcum's bridge gathering this afternoon."

Bridge gatherings were all the rage in Savannah, too, for women who had no job or career.

The back door opened, and the young man I'd met on my first visit to the shop—the one who'd knocked into me, spilling sticky soda all over me—stepped into the kitchen. He nodded a shy greeting, then washed his hands and donned an apron.

"I'll start on the pecan clusters," he said. "You've been out of those for two days, and Mr. Avery will be by this afternoon. He comes every week."

"John Henry keeps up with customers far better than I can."

I studied the young man, who was in his late teens or early twenties. He had an easy smile and a sure handle on the candy process. "I think this custard is cooked." I removed it from the heat and helped set out the delicate dark-chocolate shells that Pretta had already made. She filled the shells, and I applied a decorative curl of chocolate and a teensy slice of lime wedge. The final creation was both elegant and delicious—of course I had to sample them.

"John Henry, when you finish with the clusters, would you deliver these to Mrs. Marcum?"

"Yes, ma'am." He cleared his throat. "I don't mind the delivery, but it's a half-hour walk, and the sun is hot today. If the chocolate shells get too hot, it'll be a mess."

"I can drive him on my way home," I volunteered. "He's right. The cheese straws will be fine, but I wouldn't put my money on the custard and chocolate not melting."

"Thanks, Raissa. I may have to hire you. Need a part-time job?"

"I wouldn't mind helping you at times, but I've started my own . . . venture."

"And what might that be?"

"I submitted my first short story today." My grin spread so wide it made my cheeks hurt.

Pretta clapped her hands and jumped lightly up and down. "A ghost story?"

"Yes. I'm almost sick with anticipation." I'd held all the anxiety about submitting and probable rejection in check. With Pretta, though, I could confess my fears and misgivings.

"And how will you spend the check for the story?"

I hadn't even dared to think of such a thing. "Why, I'll take you to New Orleans for a night. We can stay at the Monteleone and go to a play or listen to music or . . . buy a painting!"

She grasped my hands. "The story will sell. I can feel it."

I didn't put a lot of stock in her feelings of success for me, but I certainly appreciated the sentiment.

We left John Henry to his chocolate making and went to the front of the store, where we began packaging the delicacies. The candy business was labor intensive. It was a relief to be out of the hot kitchen, and while I sat at the counter, Pretta made us both a Coca-Cola over crushed ice. The drink offset the humid day.

"Tell me about the story," Pretta said.

"I'd much rather *you* tell me about Elise Whitehead."

Discomfort flitted in her eyes before she covered it. "I don't think it's a good idea to tell you gossip about the place you live."

"Who told you not to tell me?" It didn't take a genius to see she'd been stampeded off this patch of grass.

"Mr. McKay. He didn't tell me not to talk or anything like that. He said you had enough unpleasantness with what happened to your new beau and all."

"Robert was hardly a beau." I sounded a bit snappy, and I modified my tone. "I didn't know him. Not really. I did like him."

"And he died at Caoin House, which was exactly Mr. McKay's point."

"But Elise Whitehead died fifty years ago, and I never knew her. Don't you think it's a lot safer to talk about her than Robert?"

Pretta spread her manicured fingertips on the cool marble of the counter. "She fell from a third-floor window on the night of her wedding." Her telling was matter-of-fact, without the pleasure of a good story.

Caoin House did have a knack for serving as the background of celebratory tragedies. "Details. How can I weave a ghost story around it if I don't have a picture? What did she look like?"

"She was as beautiful as her mother, it was said." Her features softened as she focused on the story. "Beauty doesn't guarantee happiness, I suppose."

"It's strange that there are several paintings of Eva at Caoin House, but I don't recall seeing any of Elise."

"It was said that Eli had all images of her removed from the house after she died. It broke his heart."

"So what happened? Who was she to marry? Was it a love match? Spill the beans."

Pretta rolled her eyes. "Mr. McKay will be annoyed with me."

"If he finds out." I laughed at her consternation. "He isn't my jailer or my protector. He's my uncle's lawyer."

"And he's sweet on you. Any fool can see that."

"Tell me about Elise, and then we'll discuss Carlton." I dangled that bit of gossip with great effect.

"She was engaged to Charles DeMornay, a Mobile native, who traced his ancestry back to the French settlement of Mobile. From all accounts, he was a handsome man, and it was a love match. They were to be married at Caoin House in an elaborate ceremony in the third-floor ballroom."

Pretta could pack a lot of info in when she chose. "Did she jump from the window, or did she fall, or was she—"

"She could have been pushed."

The parallels of Robert's death weren't lost on me. "By whom?"

Pretta refilled our drinks, and I wrapped my hand around the sweating glass, glad for even that small touch of coolness. "She had an argument with her father before the wedding—now this is all local legend. There's no way to document what's true and what's false."

Because Pretta wouldn't try to push me into helping, I got the candy boxes lined with waxed paper and set them on the counter. I picked up a tray of the freshly made confections and began to put them in the little wax paper shells. "Don't worry that I'll use the details exact. I'm going to turn it all into fiction anyway. I'll make up what I like, and it might be set in Mobile but not Caoin House."

That seemed to satisfy Pretta, and she picked up the story with the pleasure I'd noticed before. Together, we filled boxes as we chatted.

"We have to go back to the tragic death of Eva Whitehead," Pretta said. "No one ever really expected Eli and Elise to return from Europe. After the war, Eli left the plantation in the hands of a good friend, Able Ashford. Eli took Elise to Europe."

"London?"

"They were nomadic, from the stories I heard, living in London until they tired of that, then on to Paris and Rome and Athens and even into Turkey, Arabia, and Persia. The years passed and they continued to travel. It was almost as if they fled farther and farther away to avoid the past, both of them haunted by death and violence."

"Was the child okay?" I emptied the key-lime tray and picked up the cheese straws, which went into a different kind of box.

"She didn't speak for several years. It was in Rome, at the Temple of Antoninus and Faustina, that she spoke for the first time."

"Why there? Did something prompt her to recover her ability to speak?"

Pretta grinned with satisfaction. "The perfect questions, Raissa. That's the crazy part. That temple was built by Antoninus to honor his wife, Faustina, much as Caoin House was built to honor Eva Whitehead.

Elise fell to her knees in front of the columns and cried out her mother's name. It was the first word she'd spoken since the murder."

"Too bad she didn't cry out the names of the people who killed her mother."

Pretta shook her head in disapproval. "She was just a baby, Raissa. You have the mind of a police detective. I pity the man you decide to track down."

"I'll take that as a compliment. Now finish the story. I hear John Henry washing the pots. He'll be ready to go soon."

"While Elise didn't go to school, she received an education through her travels, and it was said she could speak five languages. Once she started to speak, she was quite good at it. When father and daughter returned to Mobile, they lived in town. Elise was frequently seen at the port translating for sea captains and her father's business associates."

I had an image of Elise now, and I felt the strings of a story tugging at me. "Why did they return to Mobile?"

"Some say Eli returned to Caoin House to sell it so that he and Elise would be free to travel for the rest of their lives. The house he'd spent so much time and money on held only sadness for him."

Perhaps that was why his ghost remained constantly outside the house, as if he didn't belong within the walls any longer. A wave of sadness swept across me, startling me with the intensity of emotion.

"Others said Eli had come home because he knew he couldn't outrun the past. Whatever his reasons, Elise met Charles DeMornay at the Mobile docks, and once they met, she no longer wanted to travel with her father."

Love had thrown a monkey wrench into their lives. "Surely her father would be happy for her?" When I married Alex, one of my biggest regrets was that my father wasn't alive to walk me down the aisle. My father would have approved of Alex, though. I knew it in my heart.

"Elise was all Eli had left to live for. And I understand Elise intended to live at Caoin House, which displeased her father."

"So was she pushed out the window?"

Pretta motioned me to take a seat on a stool beside her. She crossed her legs and leaned on one elbow on the counter. "No one knows. The story goes that there was a heated argument between Elise and Charles. The quarrel was loud, and some of the guests left the house and went for a walk on the grounds to give the young couple some privacy to sort through things."

"Did anyone say what the argument was about?"

Pretta shrugged one shoulder. "The story goes that they were arguing about where they would live in the house. Eli had suddenly decided to live with them at Caoin House, and he'd sprung the announcement just moments before Elise was to walk down the aisle. Charles was unhappy about it."

"That could put a damper on newlyweds."

"Caoin House is plenty big to accommodate several generations without folks tripping over one another." Pretta gave me a slanted look. "When you marry, surely Brett will live with you and your new spouse at Caoin House."

"That's really getting ahead of yourself. I don't even have a prospect."

"Carlton McKay fancies you," she teased.

"Time will tell that tale," I said. "Now back to the story."

"Yes, anyway, the wedding was set to take place at seven in the evening, a candlelit affair. Elise and Charles had ended the disagreement, and she was on the third floor in a small room off the ballroom that had been set up for her dressing area. From what the guests said, she was alone. The seamstress had been tucking some last-minute pearls along the train of her wedding gown, but the woman went downstairs for thread. The next thing anyone knew, Elise was dead on the front lawn, blood pooling—" She looked stricken. "I'm so sorry. I don't mean to stir painful memories."

"I asked," I reminded her. "Did she fall or was she pushed?"

"The question everyone asks. Some of the guests attending the wedding were still walking on the grounds, and a few reported that they saw a struggle in the window. Others said they watched in horror as she tumbled out the window, seemingly without provocation."

"Was it ever investigated?" I thought about Robert Aultman's coroner's inquest and the secrets it had uncovered.

"I don't know if there are records. Back then, what the rich gentry said was pretty much accepted as the facts. Still true today, too." Pretta stood up when John Henry came to the doorway and signaled her. "I can see this has upset you, Raissa. You're white as a sheet."

"No, I'm fine."

"Well, you've heard the story. There isn't much to add. Are you sure you don't mind driving John Henry?"

"Not in the least. It'll be good for me to learn my way around Mobile."

"Congratulations on finishing your story, and I'm sure you'll be published. Just don't dwell too long in the dark hallways and crypts where ghosts reside." Pretta put an arm around me. "That's for your help today. And remember, you're too pretty to become one of those women who court the darkness."

I knew what she meant. "No worries. This is all professional curiosity."

"I like the sound of that. Professional curiosity." She nodded. "Now let me get John Henry ready to go."

Within ten minutes we had the car loaded with goodies for Mrs. Marcum's party. As we drove toward West Hamilton Street, John Henry fidgeted. The closer we got to the residence, the more he laced his fingers and tapped his toes. When I pulled up in front of the stately old two-story antebellum, he hopped out of the car and began stacking the boxes.

"Let me help carry some of those." I picked up a box of the key-lime delights.

"No, ma'am, best you stay here, please." He looked up at the house as if he thought it might develop a mouth and teeth with the sole purpose of eating him.

"Nonsense. We can get all of this up to the house in one trip."

"Please." He looked at me with anguish. "Don't go up there with me. Mrs. Marcum says mean things, and you shouldn't hear them."

"Maybe she won't if I'm there."

He looked perfectly miserable. "Please, Miss Raissa. She'll be worse if you're with me."

I handed him the box of sweets and stepped back. "Okay."

He sprinted up the sidewalk and around the huge camellias that adorned the front lawn of the two-story Victorian, freshly painted a pristine white. When I heard John Henry's knock on the front door, I slipped closer, yet remained out of sight. What things could a Southern lady say to a delivery boy that would be so upsetting?

The door opened to a lovely woman dressed in a lavender silk organza that clung to her narrow waist. The swan corset was still alive and well in the Marcum house. She wore pearls at her throat and ears, and her beautiful chestnut hair was pulled up in a Gibson-girl style. Her thin lips were flattened in a line.

"Ms. Pretta sent me to deliver your order, ma'am." John Henry kept his gaze on the boxes as he spoke.

"I hope your black hands didn't touch the candies."

He didn't say a word or look up.

"Well, tell me, did you touch my confections? I won't have them if you did. I don't pay good money for a darkie to make my desserts."

"I got the key limes and the chocolate cashews you wanted. Miss Pretta got the nuts fresh from Brazil this week. She said it was the best crop she'd tasted."

"You still haven't answered my question, but here's another. What's your last name, John Henry? I hear you're going by the name Marcum."

At last he looked up and met her gaze. "That's my daddy's name. And mine."

"You're no more a Marcum than you are a monkey. You'd do well not to use that name in Mobile, pretending to be a relation to my husband. He has no Negro blood in his line." She snatched the boxes from his hand and slammed the front door.

For a long moment John Henry stood at the stoop, and then he turned slowly toward the car. I rushed out of my hiding place and climbed into the front seat. I didn't look at him because I felt his shame.

"You heard her?"

I couldn't lie. "Yes. She's an evil old bitch." Cursing wasn't the norm for me, but there was no other word that served.

"She's my aunt."

"She's still a bitch."

"That day when I ran into you and spilled the Coca-Colas, it was her brother who came after me. They look for a reason, because I use my daddy's name."

Understanding came as a bolt. I didn't know what to say. I started the car and drove John Henry back to the candy shop. When I parked in front, I'd recovered some of my wits. "She has no cause to treat you that way."

"I make her life hard. The rich ladies talk down to her because of me and my mama. Her husband's brother laid with a Negro. It isn't done here. Or at least if it is, folks keep it quiet."

"Well, it's done everywhere, and the burr under her saddle is that he got caught, and your mama has taken his name."

John Henry's grin was slow, but in the end a thing of beauty. "She is on the feisty side. Mama won't lie. Not for anyone. She said I was owed the name, and I had to take it."

I agreed with John Henry's mother, in principle. But the reality was that Mobile would always be a hard town for him and his children. I parked in front of the candy shop. "I'm sorry for the way she spoke to you."

"Not your place to send off apologies." He got out of the car. "Thank you kindly for the ride."

"Does Pretta know how Mrs. Marcum treats you?"

He considered a moment, his gaze moving down the street. "I never told her. I don't know what Mrs. Marcum might have said."

"She's a coward. She wouldn't say a word to Pretta. I'm willing to take that to the bank."

He stepped back from the car, and I headed back to Caoin House, filled with ideas for another ghost story involving the tragic Elise Whitehead.

CHAPTER
TWENTY-FOUR

The next days passed in a blur of activity, and I could only say thanks that Uncle Brett allowed us to postpone the séance for a few days. A business complication sent my uncle to town every day. Winona handled most of the household details, which left me free to pursue my writing and secretly tutor Reginald on Caoin House and the former residents. We explored the beautiful grounds and the cemetery and begged Winona for stories about the days when Caoin House was a working plantation. As the date for the séance drew near, we laid plans for quite a spectacle.

Reginald knew a multitude of tricks used by fake mediums, and we settled on some automatic writing, a series of knocks and thumps that had made the Fox sisters famous for their "abilities," and Reginald's fabricated vision of Eva Whitehead. He knew enough about her physical description and behavior now that he would be convincing. We'd agreed to leave the mystery of Robert Aultman's death alone. Reginald shot me a curious glance when I proposed this solution, but he agreed. I had no intention of telling anyone what I'd discovered in the coroner's report—that Robert had been a con man intending to use me to fleece my uncle. I didn't want that information coming out at a séance.

Friday evening had been set for the gathering. Carlton and Isabelle would stay over at Caoin House, and Uncle Brett had Saturday plans for an exploration of the wetlands that bordered part of his acreage. We'd embark from a point on Bayou Sara, exploring the exotic and wild wetlands, and eventually dock at the port in Mobile. The Tensaw River delta was a vast aquatic expanse where the Tombigbee, Alabama, and Mobile Rivers drew close together in their rush to join other waterways and pour into Mobile Bay. Locals said the area was a hunting-and-fishing paradise, though I found both activities distressful.

Before the Civil War, the area was the last stronghold for the Choctaw tribes who refused to abandon their land as thousands of Indians were forced onto the Trail of Tears and removed to Oklahoma. Many of the Indians died during the roundup and imprisonment. Others died on the journey. It was a long and brutal trek filled with starvation, harsh conditions, and cruelty. My reading on the subject had left me with lingering sadness when I thought of how this had once been the land of an entire people who were almost eradicated in the name of Manifest Destiny, another word for thievery.

The delta, though, often extracted its own price. It would never be owned by anyone. To prove the point, it changed with the seasons. Hunters and fishermen who went into the Tensaw Waterway sometimes didn't come out. The rivers shifted course, and what once had been land was no longer dry. Alligators sunned silently on the banks until they lured their prey close. Uncle Brett had told me, with great glee, that an alligator could run sixty miles an hour for a short distance. I wasn't certain I believed him, but I wasn't going to put it to the test.

The idea of a boat ride into this wilderness excited me. We would launch and demonstrate Uncle Brett's latest paddleboat technology. Before the boat ride, though, we had to get through the séance.

Reginald might not see spirits, but he had a keen eye for reading emotions from a person's expression and posture. He had long been a student of physiognomy and quoted the famous British philosopher Sir Thomas Browne to me: "And the countenance proclaims the heart and inclinations" of a man. I wasn't sure I agreed, but Reginald made some startling assertions that I knew to be true, all based on studying portraits and daguerreotypes of Eva. I was still desperately hunting a likeness of Elise for him. All in all, by Thursday evening, we were ready for the performance of our lives.

After a wonderful meal prepared by Winona, we sipped cognac and chatted, finalizing our plans. Everything was prepared with the exception of an image of Elise. I'd never been able to find one in the house. I was afraid I'd arouse suspicions if I asked Uncle Brett, and I didn't want to draw Winona into our deception. There was nothing to do but retire for the evening.

The day had been extremely hot, and I opened the balcony doors. I sat in front of my green Corona and wrote another four pages on my latest story, "The Haunting of Millicent Dupree," loosely based on the story of Elise Whitehead. In my version, Millicent had been pushed out the window by her fiancé, who'd discovered a terrible secret about her past. The rush of the story was like water falling off a cliff, and so caught up in my imaginary world was I that it was well past midnight before I realized it.

I was already in my nightgown when it occurred to me that the one place I'd failed to look for images of Elise was in the attic. The attic trapped heat, and if there were any paintings of the young woman there, chances were they were completely ruined. Still, it wouldn't hurt to check.

Hot, musty, and filled with discarded items from a multitude of households, the attic now enticed me. I'd reached a point in my story where Elise had retreated from her husband to the attic. Now, that space begged for exploration.

Uncle Brett hadn't wired the attic for electric light—fear of fire—but he had flashlights in the library. I tiptoed down the staircase, seeking one of the electric torches, but indistinct conversation stopped me. Uncle Brett was up and talking with someone. I couldn't risk detection. I returned to my room and took an old lantern from the washstand.

The third floor of the house held a wonderful ballroom, and it was here Reginald and I would set up the table for the séance. Now, though, the large, open room with the moonlight filtering through full-length windows held a touch of creepiness. My active imagination was in high gear.

I found myself holding my breath as I tiptoed through the third floor—as if I might disturb the ghosts that slumbered in the dark corners of the ballroom. On my last trip to the ballroom, I'd been intent on finding the path to the roof. Now I took note of the enormous space. What an incredible venue for a ball. It didn't take much to envision elegant couples floating around the room to a waltz. In my mind, the women wore the hoopskirts of the 1860s.

A flicker of movement behind a column pulled me up short, but it was a tree branch outside the window casting a shadow. Since Reginald's arrival, I'd seen the Confederate soldier only once, and Uncle Brett had not mentioned Eva's ghost. The idea of a séance—where these phantoms of the dead were invited to appear and communicate—had obviously driven them away. I had no problem with that outcome. Caoin House would be a much more restful place if the dead stayed in the cemetery, where they belonged. Of course, I might lose a source of inspiration for my dark tales, but I could manage with only my imagination.

I crossed the ballroom and entered the narrow hallway that led to the attic stairs. When Caoin House was originally built, the attic had been used as servants' quarters for the house slaves who were kept at the beck and call of their masters twenty-four hours a day. A system of bells and ropes, following the style of the large British estates, had been created. The bell would ring beside the servant's bed, and he or she would hurriedly dress and rush downstairs to answer the summons.

The attic space would have been broiling hot in summer and cold in winter. I pushed open the attic door and was greeted with a number of different scents. A lemony sachet reminded me of the magnolias that bloomed all about the grounds. There was also a hint of cherry pipe tobacco that seemed out of place. Uncle Brett didn't smoke, but perhaps it was caught in the fabric of some of the older furniture stored beneath drop cloths.

The partitions that had once created various bedrooms had been torn down. The attic was wide-open, stretching into darkness. In the dim moonlight, the draped furniture took on fanciful forms and almost killed my nerve to search. The magnitude of the contents was over-whelming. A covered chifforobe in the middle of the room looked like a huge man with a deformed and humped back. For a split second, he appeared to advance toward me, but yet again the oak branches dancing in the wind were at fault.

My breath expelled on a loud sigh, and I forced myself forward to a series of trunks that lined the west wall.

Something scuttled around the trunks. My own gasp startled me. I was tempted to give up my search, but I was far too hardheaded. I didn't know if the Whitehead family had taken photographs, but those might have survived the heat. And they would be here. I needed to get over the heebie-jeebies and look.

I'd come armed with a stout screwdriver, my lamp, and a book of matches. When I'd been in the attic on my way to examine the roof-top, I'd noted the dormer windows and a series of shuttered vents that allowed light and air into the room. At night, though, the moon gave little assistance.

I lit the lantern and put it on top of a flat trunk as I began the process of opening one of the large round-topped chests. The latch was rusted, but the screwdriver gave me enough leverage to pry it open.

Again, a citrusy scent filled the air, and I inhaled, thinking suddenly of my mother. I felt her near me, and the idea that she was watching over me brought an ease I hadn't felt in a long time. With my mother close, no revenant would dare to tamper with me.

The scent faded, and I returned to my task. The top of the crate was filled with elegant gloves, silk corsets, stockings, milky-white lingerie, and a lovely evening bag stitched with white pearls. These were quality clothes, still beautiful even after decades in storage. I picked up the white clutch to examine the exquisite design of a dove created by the stitched pearls. Out of curiosity I opened the bag and found a piece of paper, a list, dated April 3, 1881. The handwriting was small and tidy, as if the owner feared taking up too much space. Even in the lantern light, the cursive was easy to read. The items included were familiar to any bride—the last-minute details of lingerie, bridesmaids' gifts, safekeeping of the rings, floral arrangements, and seating at the dinner. I'd done many of those same things for my wedding, the little decisions that should have fallen to the mother of the bride. Like Elise, I'd had no mother to handle the details, and I felt a sense of sympathy for this young bride who'd attended to everything herself.

I put the list back in the purse and tucked it away. My fingers found the edge of another document. Lifting out the corset, stockings, and gloves, I discovered a yellowed envelope with Elise's name scrawled across it in fading black ink. When I picked it up, I knew, by the weight and feel, that it contained a daguerreotype. Since I assumed the wedding list and finery belonged to Elise, I was hopeful this might be a likeness of her.

Before I could open the envelope, a breeze snuffed out the lantern. The hot and humid air grew charged, and the hair at the nape of my neck prickled in warning. The attic had no means for the wind to enter, yet it had. The heat of the day had accumulated in the area, and sweat slid down my spine and covered my forehead. Someone, or something, had blown out my light.

I found myself in the deep gloom, aware I was no longer alone. Scarier than a ghost was the idea that an intruder shared the attic with me. Someone alive or someone dead. I couldn't say which I feared more.

"Raissa."

My name floated toward me, the genderless voice loaded with melancholy. I whipped my head in both directions. I couldn't discern where the speaker stood, but he, or she, was near. My eyes gave me nothing. As far as I could tell, the room was empty.

"Eli?" I asked.

A picture leaning against the wall fell forward, the glass shattering into a hundred pieces. The room dimmed further, as if some entity inhaled the feeble light from the vents. The impossible breeze kicked up, fluttering the cloths draped over the furniture, creating a flapping noise that reminded me of a dying bird's wings beating the ground.

Something dark and very quick darted behind a tall sideboard. It moved so fast I doubted I'd actually seen it. In the thickening gloom, it could have been a trick of the shadows.

Before I could think or move, something scuttled under the furniture and along the floor and struck my bare foot. I picked up a sterling-silver baby brush. Unless someone had shoved it at me, it had moved across the floor on its own. My fingers fumbled as I traced lettering engraved on the back, but I couldn't read in the dim room. An ornate cherub design embellished the handle, and the soft bristles spoke of luxury and expense. This brush might have belonged to baby Elise. Maybe she was trying to contact me.

"Who is with me?" I asked, hoping my disquiet didn't register in my voice.

"Get out!"

My ears rang with the volume of the shout, though I knew no one else in the house could have heard it. I reeled back, putting my hands over my ears to block further pain.

The quick figure I'd seen earlier darted closer, hiding behind a sofa. The creature was humped, it's body twisted in a way that no bones should ever form.

"Get out before you die." The voice was raspy, old, something ancient and aggrieved. This was not the handsome soldier I'd watched on the lawn. This entity came from darkness and relished the shadows. It hid by deliberate design.

"Who are you?" I asked again.

The trunk lid slammed shut with such force that I couldn't stop myself from falling back. I gripped the brush and the envelope I'd pulled from the trunk. If I could move, I'd willingly retreat from the attic. The entity harbored here meant to make me leave, one way or the other, and by my own volition seemed the superior choice.

"I'm going." I spoke calmly.

At the New Orleans séance, Madam had spoken briefly of powerful negative spirits, how they were dangerous, poisonous. Once incarnate, they could exert tremendous influence. Contact could offer them a portal to our world, and I hoped my visit to the attic had not provided that opportunity. The thought that this creature, this angry spirit, might follow me down the stairs and to the rest of the house made me physically sick. I couldn't help but wonder if it was this creature that Robert had encountered in the attic. I wanted to ask if it had pushed him from the roof, but I dared not speak with it again.

A strange clacking came from beneath a shrouded piece of furniture, a divan or possibly a dainty fainting sofa. I could see only the clawed feet, which had the talons of an eagle. I'd never liked furniture with legs that ended in claws, and this piece sounded alive.

I took a step toward the door, and the clacking advanced under the furniture. The menacing sound inched toward me. When I stepped to the right, it followed. I backed up, and it drew closer, hiding just at the edge of the cloth and out of sight.

Clack-clack-clack-clack-clack. The noise was relentless. Whatever it was seemed determined to burst out from under the drop cloth and find me. The clack-clack reminded me of wooden jaws snapping together, wooden teeth seeking tender flesh. I wasn't prone to such dark fancies, and I had no idea where those images came from, but they were frightening.

"Stay away," I said, unable to raise my voice above a whisper. "I'm leaving."

"Give it back."

I had no doubt what the creature spoke of. It demanded that I return the envelope. My fingers itched to pull it from my pocket and drop it to the floor, but I wouldn't. This was a clue. It had to be important. This was the thing that had brought this dark spirit out in an attempt to take it from me. The attic had been a hot, calm place until I'd found the envelope.

I forced my body to turn toward the door and take steps. It was almost as if a physical power held me in place, unyielding. I fought to free myself, to gain the stairs and the use of my voice to scream. The best I could accomplish was to take several steps toward the door.

The clack-clack-clack followed just out of sight. At last the mechanism broke free of the drop cloth and showed itself. The visage of a horrid monkey, mouth wide, sharpened teeth, eyes bulging, came out from under the sofa. It danced upright, tail spinning. The joints were mobile, like a marionette, and I recognized it as a dancing jigger, which was normally manipulated with a wooden stick in the back. The stick was there, but no hand held it. The vile toy dated from the Victorian era, but I couldn't believe it once had been the plaything of a child.

It came toward me on buckling legs, upright though it shouldn't be possible. And then I saw the grisly arm that darted from beneath the sofa. It reached for the stick that controlled the toy, but it didn't touch it. Filthy and emaciated, the arm belonged to a child.

My scream lodged in my throat. It refused to come out, to release, to serve as a cry for help to those on the lower floors of Caoin House. I thought my throat would explode.

The door of the attic opened, and a tall form with broad shoulders stood at the threshold. "Raissa, what are you doing here in the dark?" Reginald asked. "I thought I heard a struggle up here."

"Thank God you're here!" I could have kissed him, so profound was my relief.

"What is that?" His gaze had fallen on the jigger, and in the dim light it looked like a dead, rabid monkey.

"Don't touch it!" I brushed his hand away as he reached down.

Reginald had brought a flashlight, a far smarter move than my lantern. He turned it on, and the circle of light illuminated the jigger, which was even more gruesome than I'd thought.

"That's a real monkey head," Reginald said, fascinated in the way a small boy might be with something disgusting. He reached for it again.

"Don't touch it. The damn thing danced out from under that divan, and no one was manipulating it." A hand and arm had been there, but not attached to the toy. There was no way I'd be able to explain this to Reginald, much less Uncle Brett.

"Let's get out of here." I pressed him toward the door. The oppressive sensation that prevented me from moving was gone, but the attic was not a safe place. Not for me and not for Reginald. "Something bad is up here."

"Like a ghost?" Reginald wasn't amused, but he was curious.

"Like something bad. We're leaving." I grabbed the wrist that controlled the flashlight, and the beam bounced around the room. As the light passed across the alley between big pieces of furniture, I saw someone standing in the shadows.

I cried out and fell against Reginald, who luckily caught me. "What is it?"

"Someone is here." I was almost panting with fear.

"You're too sensitive, Raissa," Reginald said, stepping in front of me as if to protect me. "Something is here. I can sense it, but not like you. It's vaguely disquieting to me. It must be awful to you."

Something flitted past in my peripheral vision. "Eli?" I stood slowly away from Reginald. Dread brushed along my skin, a sensation I'd never felt before from the soldier. "Eli, what's wrong?"

The area in the center of my forehead, the place Madam had called the third eye, felt as if a great pressure was being exerted against my skull. For the first time in my life, concerns for my health overrode every other thought. A terrible vise gripped my head. I had to get out of the attic and away from the pressure.

"Raissa, what is it?" Reginald held my shoulders to keep me from falling as I put my hands to my head, pressing back against the internal pressure. Almost blinded by the pain, I stumbled toward the attic door and the stairway to the ballroom. The only thought I could hold on to was getting out of the attic before my head exploded.

"Raissa!"

The sharp command came from behind me, and it was a feminine voice. My control over my body was minimal. Someone else manipulated me, and Reginald was frozen in place beside me. I turned without conscious will. Shadows flitted about the attic, and the wind flapped the drop cloths. The scent of a heavy perfume, something lush with an undertone of sex, moved over me. The light, citrusy scent that had occupied the attic when I'd first entered was overwhelmed by this stronger, more powerful scent.

"Who's here?" Reginald asked. "There's a woman up here. I've helped Madam with her wealthy female clients, and I know this musky perfume is expensive."

"Who are you?" I managed to ask.

One flickering shadow moved closer to us. I could discern the vague outline of a feminine form that grew more and more solid as it approached.

She was beautiful. A dark-haired woman in a white gown that trailed the floor. The gown was tied at her slender waist with a red sash that matched the red of her lips. Her skin was a pale ivory, flawless, and her dark hair fell in curls about her shoulders.

"Eva." I knew her. I knew her in my bones.

"Give it back," she said. Her voice was soft and melodious, filled with the manners and charm of a time long past, but there was also something beneath the request. A threat.

"What do you see?" Reginald asked.

I ignored him, concentrating on the spirit not ten feet from me. "We want to help you," I said. "To help you find peace."

"Give it back." The demand was clearer. The edges of her voice sounded frayed. Beneath the lilt, anger hid.

She wanted the envelope, and that made me more determined than ever not to give it up. "Reginald, we have to go."

"Who's with us?" he asked. "I know there's a female entity here, but I can't get more than that." He was excited that he'd begun to pick up on spirits. I wanted only to escape.

"We have to get out of here." I grabbed his hand and dashed for the doorway, pulling Reginald hard behind me. He was almost deadweight until we reached the door, and then he seemed to snap out of the trance that held him.

I pushed him through the door, slammed it, and forced him down the stairs into the ballroom.

"That was . . . intense," he said, looking back longingly as if he wished to return to the attic. "The perfume . . . who was she?"

"Eva Whitehead." I had no doubt. I pulled the envelope from the pocket of my skirt, realizing that I'd also put the baby brush there.

"What's that?"

I turned the brush over and traced the elegant scroll of letters. "Baby Whitehead" was etched in the silver. So it was Elise's brush.

"This is a terrific find, Raissa," Reginald said. "I can make it appear at the séance. "What's in the envelope?"

In response, I slowly slid the picture out and stopped.

A young man dressed as a pirate stared out of the picture with a stoic expression. He wore the trademark pirate head scarf, a short jacket or fearnought. Nude from his waist to his boots, his erect penis was of remarkable proportions. I gasped and almost dropped the picture as I stumbled. The one thing I hadn't anticipated finding in the trunk was pornography.

"My good Lord," Reginald said. He was well and truly shocked.

Curiosity drove me to look further. The envelope contained a note. I slipped it free and opened it.

"Caleb is unable to visit Friday evening, but I am sending Carlos in his stead. I believe you'll find his attributes equal to Caleb. This is, of course, my gift to you. Your opinion will be of great value to the other ladies."

The note was unsigned. The potential repercussions dove at me like angry mockingbirds. If this was what I assumed, and if other Mobile society women were involved, the scandal might rock the foundation of polite society. It might also account for the past deaths of Eva Whitehead and for the current burglaries of Caoin House. An 1860s male prostitution ring linked to Mobile society would account for many things.

My first thought was to rush downstairs and wake Uncle Brett, but I resisted. The entity's powerful demand to give the picture back still had me upset. The spirits in Caoin House had taken issue with my possession of the image. I knew very well this scandal would impact the lives of some very powerful people in Mobile and cast a shadow over genteel society.

"This could cause a lot of trouble," Reginald said, echoing my thoughts.

"I know."

"What are you doing to do?"

I slid the picture back in the envelope and returned it to my pocket. "For the moment, nothing. Let's get through this séance before we do anything else."

Reginald nodded and took my elbow to escort me back to my bedroom. Dawn wasn't far away. Perhaps I could catch an hour or two of sleep, because I knew I would need my strength to get through Friday and the séance.

CHAPTER
TWENTY-FIVE

The day passed in a blur of activity, which allowed me to sidestep my fatigue and anxiety. I chopped onions with Winona, harvested and prepared the fresh herbs she needed for the light dinner menu she was preparing, arranged flowers for the front entrance and the guest bedrooms, and helped set up the table and chairs in the ballroom. On this last chore, Reginald had given me explicit instructions on where and how.

Once lunch was done, I borrowed the car and went to the local newspaper under the guise of looking up material for my ghost stories. My uncle's name gave me access to the newspaper morgue, where clippings of past stories were organized into topics. I focused on searching out records of a child's death at Caoin House only to discover that several families who'd owned the house had suffered tragic losses. One young boy in 1892 had disappeared into the swamp to the south of the house. The body was never found. Another was accidentally shot hunting in 1898. And just before Uncle Brett bought the house, a ten-year-old boy fell from the roof and broke his neck. Three families, three accidental deaths of children. Male children. The unhappy news added another level of dread to the night's proceedings.

Sitting in the dusty filing room, I was consumed with guilt. I hadn't come clean to my uncle about the photograph of the half-naked pirate I'd found among Elise's things. Caleb had been mentioned in the note. I had to wonder if it was the same Caleb buried in the Whitehead cemetery. Who was he? Uncle Brett might know, but Reginald had extracted a promise that I wouldn't reveal the photograph until after the séance. He was right that the scandal would be too much for Uncle Brett to keep to himself. My uncle didn't have a malicious bone in his body, but the half-naked pirate, standing proud, was not something he would be able to keep quiet about. I had no choice but to honor my word to Reginald, but I felt deceptive, which made me uncomfortable.

Armed with a notepad half-filled with facts, I returned to Caoin House by four. The small break had given me renewed energy. I kept reminding myself we had only to get through the night.

Isabelle arrived not five minutes behind me, pulling into the front drive with a happy toot of her horn. Since Travis was busy in the cemetery—on the off chance our séance resulted in a tour—I helped carry Isabelle's bags to her room. While I tried not to probe into Uncle Brett's romantic life, I was amused to notice that she continued the subterfuge of staying in her own room in the south wing where Brett had his quarters. I couldn't help but wonder if the guest-room cover was for me or Winona. Propriety was still alive and well at Caoin House.

Uncle had gone to the docks with the ship captain for the last-minute preparation of our boat ride early Saturday morning. He was determined to herd us out of the house and to the Bayou Sara dock at daybreak so we could enjoy the awakening of the natural world. Eighty years ago, the variety and beauty of the bird population in the delta area had attracted painters, John James Audubon among them. Isabelle had collected dozens of the exquisite works and decorated her room at

Caoin House with the delicate and detailed pictures of the beautiful winged residents of the area.

Isabelle noticed my interest. "I love the Audubons." She opened her suitcase. "Before I claimed this room as my own, it was filled with paintings of dead people on every wall. It had a disturbing feel."

"Family portraits?"

"I can only assume the subjects were former residents. I know Brett reveres all things Caoin House and the past, but I found it too depressing, and when I asked him to remove the artwork and the wallpaper, he had painters here the next day. I much prefer the light walls and the birds for company."

"Were the portraits of the Whitehead family?"

Isabelle shrugged. "Not Eva, that's for sure. The best portrait was of a young boy, and there were no male Whitehead heirs, so obviously not a member of that family." Her brow furrowed lightly. "It was a troubling painting. I got it into my head that something tragic happened to the child, and I simply couldn't have it in the room. You know how an idea can plant itself and the roots dig in. I couldn't look at the boy without thinking of the tragic ways he might have died."

The image of that dirty, twisted, childlike arm darting out from beneath the drop cloths made me rub my skin as if I felt a chill. I knew exactly what Isabelle described, and in talking with Reginald, I'd come to see this, too, as a type of awareness to spirits. Isabelle wasn't a medium, but she was a sensitive. Based on my afternoon studies at the newspaper, I suspected the young boy had died a tragic death. I didn't want to spill the beans about the three young boys who'd died here at Caoin House, in case Reginald needed to use it for his routine, so I said nothing. The art of flimflam, when it came to a deceptive medium, involved a lot of research and expert delivery of all visions and facts. Reginald and I both would have to act convincingly.

"Perhaps it was someone close to the family," I suggested, hoping she would divulge more.

"Maybe. But I'm glad the portrait is gone. The room is so much cheerier." She went to the windows that opened like doors and stepped out onto a small porch that ran down the south wing. "I love this house, but there are times I've been uncomfortable here. I have reservations about this séance."

"Me, too." I joined her at the wooden balustrade. In the distance I could hear the sweet trill of birds that preferred the more aquatic regions of the swamps not too distant from the house. One child had drowned there. When I gazed into the green distance, I half expected to see him, but the vista was uninhabited by human or haint.

"I love the drone of insects at dusk, as long as they're outside the window screen." A soft breeze lifted Isabelle's hair and made her look much younger than her forty years. "They're very soothing, the night sounds. But sometimes I've heard things that weren't part of the natural world."

"I know. Caoin House is haunted. But maybe after tonight, the spirits will be at rest." I hoped I wouldn't be punished for my lies.

"What if we stir up something that's better left at rest?" she asked.

I could have told her something was already stirred. Something distinctly unpleasant. But there was no point predisposing her to a bad evening. If Reginald's and my plan was effective, we'd entertain Uncle's guests and have an enjoyable drink afterward. Reginald's reputation would remain intact, and he could return to New Orleans and whatever path he chose to pursue from there. He could make a good living holding sessions for those desperate to make contact with dead loved ones—and he could bring them peace and release at the same time.

"If you're settled in comfortably, I'll check with Winona. Dinner is at seven, and the séance will begin at nine."

"We're not waiting until midnight?" she asked with a smile.

"Not since Uncle will have us up at five in the morning. Reginald said the spirits aren't aware of time. They only appear more frequently at night because our barriers are down. We're more inclined to see them when darkness rules than when they appear in the daytime and we humans are caught up in the hurly-burly of everyday life."

"Reginald is quite the authority, isn't he?" Isabelle was amused. "And, yes, Brett is determined we see dawn in the delta. Sleepy alligators and all."

"And why not? It'll be extraordinary." I gave her a light hug. "The other guests are due to arrive, so I should greet them. See you at dinner."

On the way to the front of the house, I met Reginald, who filled me in on his afternoon activities while I told him of the three dead boys I'd discovered in my newspaper digging. I gave him the list of their names and ages to use as he needed.

To my dismay, Reginald had retrieved the monkey jigger from the attic. His trip had been swift and to the point, but he said he didn't see or feel anything out of the ordinary. He'd placed the jigger at the top of one of the columns with a thread running to the back of my chair so that when I shifted my weight in the chair, the jigger would fall to the floor. This would be strategically staged for the most dramatic effect. When the jigger fell, I was to rush, pick it up, snap the thread, and toss it on the table to shock all in attendance. Then I was to say I'd been directed to do so by an angry spirit, presumably Eva. Reginald would then communicate with the spirit, determine that she wanted to be reunited with her daughter, Elise, who had *not* been buried in the cemetery, as far as I could tell from researching the plots and burial records.

Reginald would "communicate" with Eva and Elise, arranging their reunion in the spirit world, which no one could prove or disprove. This would supposedly put an end to the haunting of Caoin House. When we'd first conceived the idea, I'd been more enthusiastic. After my encounter with the female entity in the attic last night, I wasn't sure this was a productive path. I consoled myself with the notion that Reginald would ultimately bring peace to my uncle. The part that troubled me was the idea that Eva wasn't so easily placated. More disturbing than that was the other entity in the attic. The child. I couldn't get the dirty gray arm out of my head. The jigger belonged to that child. And I had a terrible feeling he, or she, might come calling to claim it.

A knock at the front door alerted me that more guests had arrived. A reluctant Pretta and an eager Hubert stood on the porch with overnight bags. I showed them to the guest rooms Winona had indicated, all on the same wing and floor as my room. A sense of anticipation hung in the air, and I felt the thrill of stage fright as I mentally rehearsed my role. Reginald and I might not resolve the haunting of Caoin House, but we would put on a damn good show. The more I worked with Reginald, the more I liked him and respected his intelligence.

And he was very good at weaseling information from people, particularly women. His matinee good looks put women at ease, and his attention to them often made them talkative. Winona, who was a paragon of housekeeper virtues, had fallen victim to Reginald's charms and told him which bedroom Elise Whitehead had once used, the room she'd grown up in.

Pretending to be put out, I said, "I've asked her several times to tell me about Elise, but she refuses. You could charm your way into Cleopatra's inner circle."

His eyebrows jumped up and down. "It's a talent."

"It's a crime," I said. Reginald's powers of "persuasion" should have been classified illegal. "Where is the bedroom?"

"Second floor, north wing of the house," Reginald told me. "I'll entertain the guests if you can look for anything of Elise's. You have a better excuse for being in the bedroom than I can come up with. Remember, I can get information from objects, but a picture would be the most helpful."

"I'll take care of it," I promised.

It was six thirty before I finally got around to my detective work. I'd never been in the second-floor room that had been Elise Whitehead's. I'd never had a need. It was a beautifully proportioned room with delicate crown molding, a small marble fireplace, and a canopied bed that reminded me of a younger person. The walls were painted a soothing green. The morning sun would brighten the color, but now dusk had settled over Caoin House.

I had to hurry. If I found anything of value, Reginald needed time to incorporate it into the evening's plans.

I searched through the drawers of an antique marble-topped dresser with an inset marble slab, where a washbasin had once rested. The drawers were empty, save for the sachet bundles someone, likely Winona, had left to keep the furniture from smelling musty. The room held no traces of Elise, and I wasn't surprised. This had been a long shot. Several families had owned and lived in Caoin House since the Whiteheads sold it. To think a remnant of Elise would remain was a vain hope. In a last-ditch effort, I checked under the bed. The space was empty, except for a thin layer of dust. Winona gave the unused rooms of the house perfunctory cleaning on a regular basis, but Caoin House was huge, and she had more to do than clean rooms no one slept in.

I swept my hand over the wood floor and stopped. One of the planks didn't fit into the flooring properly. The craftsmanship of Caoin House was superb. This flaw was out of character, and Uncle Brett had said there were often numerous hidey-holes in old houses. To check this properly, I had to move the bed.

With a bit of grunting and effort, I shifted the bed so I had access to the floor. The work was cleverly done, but someone had cut out a section of the flooring and replaced it. I had to make a flying trip to the library for Uncle Brett's heavy letter opener, but when I returned I was able to pry up the section. Holding my breath, I removed the flooring and peered into a shallow hole that held an ornately carved box some two-by-three feet with a depth of at least ten inches.

I pulled it out and worked the latch. When it opened, a citrusy magnolia scent wafted out. In the attic, I'd thought the scent might be my mother, but now I believed otherwise. This was Elise's scent.

The box was neatly packed. Beneath a layer of tissue paper was a pile of silky undergarments. I couldn't be certain, but I felt this might be a part of Elise's wedding trousseau. The once-pristine white silk had an ivory tint now, the purity dulled by age. This would have been the small traveling case Elise intended to carry on her honeymoon. I removed a beautiful white nightgown with crocheted inserts at the shoulders and a plunging neckline. If Elise took after her mother and father, she had been a beautiful young woman. Wearing the nightgown, she would have been any groom's dream.

As I lifted the gown free of the trunk, an envelope slipped to the floor. I picked it up. There was no name, no address.

Footsteps outside the door panicked me, and I pushed the letter into the pocket of my skirt. Reginald sauntered into the room, taking in the lingerie spread on the bed that was catawampus to the wall. "Searching for a costume?"

"Actually, I was looking for a likeness of Elise."

"Then let me help."

"I may have it." I pulled the envelope from my pocket and dumped the contents on the bed. A dark-haired woman with clear eyes looked up at me from a photograph. She bore a resemblance to Eva, but there were traces of her father in her olive skin tone. She wore a wedding dress designed for a princess, and she held a bouquet of anemones. The portrait's sepia tones made me guess at the color of the flowers, but I believed them to be red, a beautiful but strange choice for a bride.

"Are you familiar with the legend of Aphrodite and Adonis?" I asked Reginald. I had no doubt that Elise had been familiar. She was a student of mythology. She'd uttered her first words on the steps of a temple for a goddess.

"What are you getting at?"

I pointed to the flowers the bride held. "When Adonis was gored to death by a wild boar, which was jealous Aries in disguise, Aphrodite sprinkled nectar on her lover's wounds. Wherever his blood and the nectar fell to the earth, red anemones sprang up. These aren't flowers I'd select for a bridal bouquet."

"Perhaps the Whiteheads aren't students of ancient mythology." Reginald lifted the portrait from my hand. "She's a beauty," he said as he studied the photograph. "Why isn't she buried in the cemetery?" He sat on the side of the bed. His casual pose belied the way he was taking in the room, remembering the small details he would use in the séance. I could almost hear the cogs of his brain spinning.

"We didn't find her grave, but she has to be buried here." There were a number of graves without markers. It was possible her stone had broken and been removed. "She would be near her mother."

"I searched for her this afternoon while you were in town. Travis even helped me. There's no evidence of her grave. Travis says she isn't buried there."

His point was well made, but I couldn't very well ask Uncle Brett any questions about her if we intended to use Elise in the séance. It would be a dead giveaway that I was priming the pump. We had the nightgown, the photograph, and the jigger. It would have to be enough.

CHAPTER
TWENTY-SIX

The ambience of the room was perfect. Although Uncle Brett had wired the house for electric lights, Reginald and I chose candles and lamps. We needed the room dark to perform our magic. The seating had been carefully arranged so that Pretta and Hubert were on either side of me. Brett, Isabelle, and Carlton, the three most likely to try to spot our chicanery, were on the other side of the table. Late additions to the evening, something I hadn't anticipated, were Dr. and Mrs. Lister Martin. He was my uncle's physician and had a keen interest in the occult.

Carlton had arrived late, just as we sat down to eat. He'd been tied up in court all day, and then had preparatory work for his client for the trial that would continue on Monday. As Reginald and I had explained the evening's agenda, he'd been quiet and watchful.

Winona's delicious dinner was filling but light, and Uncle Brett shut the spigot on the wine and gin after everyone was relaxed but not drunk. As Reginald explained, alcohol didn't mix well with spirits from the other side. He followed the rules Madam had taught him.

Now it was time. The open floor-length windows that went all around the ballroom offered a delicious cross breeze that brought the sounds and scents of a summer evening into Caoin House. We sat in our appointed chairs and put our hands on the surface of the round table, our pinkies touching.

I'd drawn the pattern of a pentagram on the table, per Reginald's request. He sat at the apex. "Breathe deeply, in and out," he said in a rhythmic voice that could easily hypnotize. "In and out. Visualize a party here at Caoin House. Hear the laughter of the guests, the sound of the musicians. It's a dance. Caoin House is ablaze with candles and the glitter of jewels. The young men are loud and excited, the women determined to push away the dark rumblings of war talk. We're celebrating the last days of the old South, a time of graciousness and beauty before the beginning of the Civil War. The young Southerners can't wait to prove themselves on the field of battle. They all know they'll whip the Yankees in a matter of days, and victory will be theirs."

Even though I knew what he was doing, I felt myself pulled along, creating the fantasy of a jubilant South, ready to show the North what for. There were those who could foresee the tragedy coming headfirst at the Confederacy, but their voices were shouted down. War is an aphrodisiac for young males. The battlefield is viewed as a proving ground, not a place to die. War is a ticket to make money for older men, who have no qualms about sending children to their deaths.

I had begged Alex not to join up, but in truth, he had little choice. He would have been branded a coward had he not. And he felt it was his duty. *Duty, honor*—those were empty words to a widow.

"Raissa."

I knew Alex's voice immediately. He stood in a far corner of the room. Everyone else at the table sat with their eyes closed, their chests moving slowly in and out as Reginald led them in the relaxation exercise. No one else was aware of Alex's presence.

I didn't have to speak aloud to communicate. I thought Alex's name, and he came closer. I couldn't help myself. I checked his body, making sure he was intact and not torn by the bullets that had ripped through him. He smiled, because he knew exactly what I was doing.

"I'm okay."

"And I am not. You left me." Pain and anger filled me to the brim, seeping out of my eyes in the form of tears. I'd thought I'd dealt with all this, but I'd deceived myself. "You promised to love me, and you left me. Just like my parents."

He came so close that the paleness of his skin was illuminated by the candles. "It wasn't my choice. I didn't want this."

He spoke the truth, and I felt my anger leave so suddenly I thought I might tilt sideways off my chair. "I miss you."

"I'm here to say good-bye, again." He waited for my response. "I'll wait for you, Raissa. In another time and place, we'll be together again."

His image flickered, and I knew his visit was a final good-bye. "I'll always love you."

He heard me as clearly as if I'd spoken aloud. "I would stay and protect you, but I can't. Be careful, Raissa. There is darkness around you."

"From the spirits at Caoin House?"

"And from those who walk among the living."

I wanted to ask him more. He could tell me things, but he was gone as suddenly as he'd arrived.

I fought down the wave of sorrow that slammed into me. Swallowing the lump in my throat, I finally regained control. Alex was gone. He had been for nearly two years. I'd adjusted to his death in the same way I'd adjusted to his departure when he went overseas. Now I would accept the idea that his spirit had moved on. I wanted that for him. I didn't want him trapped or waiting. I didn't want him haunting a time and location where there was no room for him. My wish for him to move toward a new future had come true.

I felt someone staring at me. Carlton watched me with the acuity of an eagle. He'd registered my emotions, and I suspected he knew I'd sensed or seen something he couldn't see. Carlton's quick intelligence was a challenge at the best of times, and tonight I had to be careful. He wouldn't disrupt the evening's program, but he would quickly smell a charlatan. I wanted to protect Reginald. I didn't want Carlton to know the truth about my friend.

"I feel someone is here with us," Reginald said.

First would come the automatic writing where the name of the boy would be revealed.

"Who is here?" I asked in a low, throaty voice as Reginald had taught me. Reginald had slipped into what appeared to be a trance. I got up and put a pencil in his hand and then lightly held his hand to the page. Head thrown back, and the whites of his eyes showing, he began to move his hand in a very erratic way. He made bold swoops and scrolls on the page. When a page was covered, I quickly changed sheets. As his hand became less frenetic, he formed letters, and I read them aloud.

Our audience was enthralled. The doctor's wife was writing the letters down as I called them out.

"F."

Reginald's hand looped and scrawled. I moved the page.

"R."

"E."

"D."

"D."

"I."

"E."

"It's Freddie," Mrs. Martin gasped.

"A child," Reginald intoned in a flat, emotionless voice. "A child dripping water. He has drowned. He wants his toy."

The pencil snapped in Reginald's hand, a crack that brought an audible gasp from our audience. Reginald was very good at this. His dramatic timing was honed.

"Freddie," Reginald whispered. "Freddie." His body shuddered. "He is here with a beautiful woman."

I returned to my seat, carefully watching the people at the table. For this to succeed, they needed to be rapt on Reginald, not me. To that end, he jerked and quivered, his throat muscles working convulsively.

"Can you communicate with us?" Reginald asked.

I used a wooden knocker that I'd attached to my thigh to strike the table, making a loud thump. Both of my hands were on top of the table for all to see.

"Thump once for no and two for yes."

I thumped twice.

"Are you Freddie's mother?" he asked.

One thump.

And on it went, the questions we'd worked out, until we'd established that Eva Whitehead was in the room, and she was protecting Freddie. They both wanted to move on, to be done with lingering in Caoin House. Reginald gave a few more details of noble Eva as protector of the poor drowned boy, of her love for Caoin House, how she appreciated my uncle's efforts to care for the house and grounds, and, finally, Reginald spoke to the boy again.

"Freddie, are you feeling safe enough now to leave Caoin House and join your family? They're waiting for you, you know."

I thumped the table for a yes.

"I'm going to help you, okay?"

I thumped the affirmative again. The timing was perfect. Everyone watched Reginald intently. All I had to do, as soon as Reginald said something about the boy wanting his toy, was scoot my chair forward an inch or two, pull the jigger down from the column, and then toss it onto the table with a scream—proof beyond a shadow of a doubt that a young boy had been with us.

"Freddie, is there anything you want to tell us?"

I slipped to the edge of my chair, ready for my cue. The one thing I hadn't prepared for was the young boy stepping out from behind one of the columns. Water dripped from his hair and clothes. He was sodden and blue-gray with cold. I inhaled sharply, causing Reginald and everyone else to look at me.

The boy didn't walk, but he floated closer to us, a moth to the flames of our living warmth.

"I'm so cold," he moaned. "So cold. She pushed me, you know. She hated that I was alive and she was dead. She said so."

I couldn't look away from him. Reginald struggled to regain control of the table, but it was too late. The boy came to stand not two feet from me. "She'll hurt you, too. She's cruel. She doesn't want me to go."

"Who will hurt you?" I asked the question, even though I knew it would split the table's focus from Reginald.

"She owns this house." He looked over his shoulder. When he turned back, he put a finger to his lips. "She doesn't like laughter, and she knows secrets. She knows all the secrets."

"Tell me a secret," I said.

"Raissa is communicating with the boy," Reginald explained to the table, doing the best he could to keep up with what was happening. "Keep your hands joined, breathe, stay quiet."

"She saw the man fall from the roof."

"She saw Robert fall? Was he alone on the roof? Did he stumble?" I was as stunned by the turn in the conversation as others at the table, especially Uncle Brett, who pushed back in his chair.

Carlton started to rise, but Isabelle stopped him. "Be still," she whispered fiercely.

"He didn't fall," the boy said. "I didn't slip into the swamp either."

"Tell me," I said.

He looked over his shoulder, and fear crossed his pale features. "She's coming. She's coming." He put a finger to his lips. "She's coming."

Before I could move, the jigger flew ten feet across the room and landed in the center of the table. It slid to a stop in front of Carlton, the horrid monkey head glaring up at him.

Mrs. Martin screamed and fainted dead away, toppling out of her chair to the floor. The men jumped up, breaking the circle. I couldn't move. I watched as Eva came out of the shadow. She wore the white gown with the red sash, but her beautiful face was contorted with rage. She roared toward the table in a rush of wind. The candles guttered and then went out. The room was plunged into darkness.

CHAPTER TWENTY-SEVEN

Pandemonium reigned for five or ten minutes before Uncle Brett found his way to the light switch and flooded the room with electric light. Mrs. Martin was in a dead faint but otherwise unharmed. Isabelle was shaken but was helping calm the other guests, as was Reginald. Carlton had stepped away from the table and stood by a window, his expression grim.

The horrid monkey-head jigger remained on the table, and I went to remove it. No point in upsetting anyone further, and it was a gruesome little thing.

"What did the boy tell you?" Carlton asked. He was at my side, his hand offering support on my shoulder, before I was aware he'd moved.

I shook my head. I needed time to sort through what the boy had said. He'd implied that Robert was pushed off the roof, as Freddie had been pushed into the swamp. But by a ghost? By Eva, because she was angry at being cheated out of her life?

"That's a dreadful bit of work," Carlton said, indicating the jigger. "What kind of child would play with that?"

"A dead child," I said without thinking. "He was so forlorn. So . . . alone."

"You saw him?" Carlton's voice held no inflection.

"It was probably my imagination. You know—Reginald set the stage, and my imagination did the rest."

"You certainly have an imagination. I read your story, Raissa. I had to sleep with the lights on. You have a true gift."

Oh, the lure of literary praise. I basked in it, even when the room around me was still in turmoil. "Did it really scare you?"

"I am reluctant to admit it, but yes. When the ghost appears on the lawn and the wind is buffeting the oak limbs, I could see her clearly." His hand moved lower on my back, a reassuring pressure. "This story will sell. Your career is launched. And tonight should certainly give you grist for your creative mill."

"Most certainly." Across the room, Reginald spoke with Uncle Brett. Isabelle was helping Mrs. Martin out of the ballroom and down to the parlor. Now it was truly time for a drink.

"I'll take care of the monkey thing," Carlton offered.

"No, I'll return it to the attic. If it's the boy's possession, we shouldn't destroy it." I spoke too quickly.

Carlton's look was speculative. "No child should play with something that ghoulish."

He was probably right, but I reached for the jigger. I wanted the boy to have it. He had so little else. Halfway there, my hand stopped. "Impossible." The word slipped from me as my fingers reached into the monkey's toothy mouth to retrieve the piece of fine cotton fabric and a button from a man's dress shirt. It was the button I'd found on the roof where Robert had fallen.

"What is that?" Carlton asked.

"A clue," I said, tucking it away in my pocket.

"To what?"

"I don't know, but I promise you—I intend to find out." The young boy, Freddie, had indicated Robert was pushed. No matter that Robert was a con man and a liar—he didn't deserve to die. *If* someone pushed him, I would get to the bottom of it. There were many secrets at Caoin House, tragedy upon tragedy. Robert was only the latest. I suspected Eva was behind the bloody actions, and she had to be stopped. The ghosts bound to Caoin House and the grounds would never rest in peace until the light of justice was shone upon them, and the tragic circumstances that kept them trapped were revealed.

Reginald loaded the Martins' bags into their car, and we both stood on the steps and waved them good-bye, smiling and pretending that they were not fleeing a house they now viewed with horror. Mrs. Martin's pale countenance told me of her distress. She stared straight ahead, unwilling to even look at Caoin House. The flying jigger, coupled with the candles going out, was more than poor Mrs. Martin could sustain. Her husband had yielded to her pleas to leave the property immediately.

After the taillights disappeared down the drive, Uncle Brett gathered everyone in the parlor. Uncle Brett, Carlton, and even Isabelle downed gin and bourbon as if the supply might disappear before they could get their fill. I wanted only to go to bed. Exhaustion tugged at my muscles and bones, but Uncle needed my presence. There were questions to be answered about the ghost boy I'd seen.

First, though, I needed a moment with Reginald to make sure our stories corroborated each other's. Things had not gone exactly as planned, and while it was clear to all that I'd seen the ghost of the boy, Freddie, I wanted everyone to believe Reginald had seen him, too. Therefore, we needed to share the same imagery.

I pulled my coconspirator aside in the kitchen, and we ducked into the boot room, amid the winter boots and jackets that waited for the change of season. I gave him a brief description of the boy, and Eva's presence.

"Raissa, the female ghost is dangerous." He put his hands on my shoulders to force me to settle and pay attention.

I took a deep breath. "I know. She's so angry."

"She isn't gone. You know that."

I nodded.

"We need to make her leave, before someone else is harmed. It's going to take a lot to send her away from here."

"I know, and it scares me. Right now, though, let's discuss Freddie. He drowned in the swamp." I confirmed his suspicions. "He said he was pushed, like Robert. He didn't say Robert's name, but I'm certain that's who he meant."

"How did the cloth and button end up in the monkey's mouth?"

"I don't know." I'd tucked the bit of evidence into the corner of my dresser drawer for safekeeping. I had no way of knowing how to use it to find answers, but now I was positive it was a significant clue.

"We have a lot of work to do." Reginald sounded determined, and that made me feel better. He wasn't going to jump ship and leave me.

"Raissa?" My uncle's voice came through the solid door of the boot room. He was calling from the dining room.

"Here, Uncle Brett." I slipped out the door before he could find me huddled with Reginald. "I'm in the kitchen."

"Come to the parlor. Our guests have questions. And where is Reginald?"

"I thought he went upstairs," I lied. "I'm sure he'll be right down. The evening has taken a toll on him."

"It was quite a success!" Uncle Brett's spirits were hardly dampened by the macabre turn of events. I took his arm, and we left the kitchen. Reginald would be right behind me.

I entered the parlor, where the guests looked a bit more relaxed. Only Carlton was absent, and I knew instantly he was in the ballroom, possibly the attic, looking for the tricks of the trade he believed Reginald had used. He wouldn't be far off, but he was sadly mistaken if he thought we'd made up everything. Carlton was smart, though, and I wasn't certain Reginald and I had cleared away the evidence of our chicanery.

"Let me retrieve Carlton," I said. Before Uncle could protest, I slipped from the library. Reluctant though I was to return to the ball-room, I hurried there. As I suspected, Carlton was under the table, looking for trickery. Thank goodness I'd put the knee knocker in my dresser drawer, along with the button.

"Find anything interesting?" I asked.

Carlton rose from the floor. "Where did this come from?" He held the wedding portrait of Elise.

"I don't know. Where did you find it?"

"In my chair. Did Reginald put it there?"

I could answer that honestly. "No. I had the picture in my room. Reginald had no way to acquire it."

"Then you put it here."

His tone angered me. "I did not. But what if I had? What is this portrait to you?"

"I'm sorry," he said. "I thought you might be trying to scare me. To play with my emotions." He handed the picture to me. "I had no cause to sound so accusatory."

"It's okay." My relief was great. "I do love it that my stories give you a chill, but I wouldn't manipulate you in such a way."

"I know. I shouldn't have snapped at you. I'm concerned for you and your uncle. I don't think we should dabble in these dark realms anymore."

I thought of my uncle's refusal to marry Isabelle—because he was afraid for her here. Reginald, too, understood that we had to banish the spirits at Caoin House for true happiness to prevail. "I wish we could close this door and never open it. There is something here at Caoin

House." I held his gaze. "There are secrets. Strange things happening that can't be accounted for."

"And all harmless until tonight," Carlton pointed out. "I feared Mrs. Martin would suffer a heart episode. She was terrified." A rueful grin crossed his face. "This will be all over Mobile by eight in the morning."

Mrs. Martin was probably on the phone now. I matched his sheepish grin. "Caoin House will be painted a den of satanic spirits. Uncle will adore it."

"Brett is happy as a pig in mud." He offered his arm. "Let's rejoin the others. Your uncle will think we're up to mischief."

As we descended the stairs, I took the opportunity to ask questions I didn't want my uncle to hear. "Why isn't Elise Whitehead buried in the family cemetery?"

"She isn't?" Carlton was as surprised as I had been by the news.

"We could find no evidence of her grave. If she's there, her burial plot was left unmarked."

"That doesn't make sense." Carlton rubbed his chin, and I was struck again by the dimple, which only added to his handsome visage. "Elise was Eli's beloved daughter. After Eva's death, father and daughter were inseparable. Some people think she jumped to her death. That would have prevented her from being buried in hallowed ground, but not a family cemetery."

"Unless Eli was so angry at her that he cast her out."

"I hadn't considered that aspect," Carlton said. "There's something very strange here, and it goes all the way back to the Whiteheads." He escorted me down the stairs.

I was sorely tempted to tell him about the pornographic picture of the pirate. Somehow everything was linked together. It was a matter of unraveling the ball of string. If I told him, he might be able to shed light on the situation, but Carlton's blood ran bluer and truer than anyone else's in the region. His ties to blood and land were strong.

The McKays, the Browns, and a few other families were the foundation of Mobile society. Revealing the pirate daguerreotype might upset
Carlton unnecessarily. To him and Mobile society, Eva was a victim of
deserters or vagabonds. She was a fallen flower of the South. The truth
would upset that image and much of the fantasy of the lonely and long-
suffering Southern woman. I didn't want to visit trouble on Carlton
until I had proof.

Carlton opened the library door, and we rejoined my uncle, Isabelle,
Pretta and Hubert Paul, and Reginald.

My uncle clapped his hands to get our attention. "Thank you all
for coming. Tonight has been . . . unsettling, I know. Rest assured that
the spirit high jinks are complete for the evening. I've spoken with
Reginald, and he's assured me the spirits are gone."

"Yes, Freddie and his lovely companion have been banished,"
Reginald said. "The house is free of all paranormal entities." He came
to stand beside me. "Raissa and I will make a final sweep of the third
floor to be sure all is tucked away."

"I'll accompany them," Carlton offered.

"If you don't come back, we aren't coming to save you," Uncle
Brett teased. "Now, we'll finish our libations and then be off to bed.
Remember, we're leaving Caoin House at five in the morning. I want
to be in the delta when the sun comes up."

"And with that, I propose we check the house tomorrow after we
return from our adventure on the water. When it's daylight." I didn't
relish a final sweep of the ballroom—and I certainly wasn't going into
the attic. Like everyone else in the house, my nerves were on edge. I
would welcome the sun.

"I concede to the wishes of the lady." Reginald gave a low bow. "I'm
going to bed then. I want to be fresh to wrestle with the giant alligators
that I've heard inhabit the swamps of the delta. Tomorrow we'll face
real danger. Tonight was just a bit of spirit drama. Those alligators have
teeth and jaws with the power to snap steel."

Uncle Brett slapped his thigh. "Don't give away all my surprises, Reginald." He was delighted with Reginald's teasing. He'd completely recovered from the evening scare, and it was as if it never happened. Uncle *was* the sun. An occasional cloud might drift across him, but it never lingered.

"Off to bed, my fellow scamps," Uncle Brett said. "Winona will be here at five in the morning to prepare breakfast. Be dressed and at the table. We leave at five thirty."

A groan came from Isabelle and Pretta before they filed out of the library and to their respective rooms. Hubert gave the gentlemen a nod and cast a smile at me before he departed with his wife.

CHAPTER
TWENTY-EIGHT

I'd fallen into a light and restless sleep when I became aware of a chill wind blowing through the open French doors from the balcony. A storm must have blown up, because the breeze was at least twenty degrees cooler than when I'd gone to bed. I considered getting up and closing the doors, but instead I snuggled beneath the sheet and cotton spread, pulling the pillows into a hug for warmth. Such a cool evening was a gift in summer.

"Raissa."

Someone called my name, dragging me from sleep to wakefulness.

"Raissa, come to me."

The developments in the attic made me wary of heeding his call. This ability to connect with me was unsettling, especially in light of the drama with Eva and the child who haunted the attic. I'd never considered ghosts physically dangerous before.

I threw back the covers and rose from the bed. The cold wind had disappeared, and the night was warm and rich, spiced with the scent of gardenias. When I stepped out on the balcony, I realized the doors to the unoccupied bedroom that adjoined mine were also open.

"Raissa, come down."

The soldier stepped out of the shadows of a tree trunk. He stood proud, his uniform perfectly cut, the silver handle of the sword quick in the moonlight. He removed his hat, and the wind ruffled his dark hair. He was so handsome. Wide shoulders, tapered waist, strong legs encased in boots that came to his knees.

"Eli." I whispered his name. What had possessed Eva to betray the man she'd married and who'd built a mansion for her? He'd gone to war and left her alone, but most of the women of the South had endured similar separations. I wondered how many others had fallen victim to carnal needs. I understood loneliness, but I didn't comprehend breaking a vow.

And Eli was so handsome. He had a dark charm all his own.

He held a hand out to me—an invitation, but to what?

I wondered again that he didn't come inside. He was, after all, the master of Caoin House. Instead of lurking about the premises, he should be inside, in the library or the parlor, seeking my presence there.

"No," I replied. I had to be up at five, and my watch showed it was 3:00 a.m. I would be a walking corpse if I didn't get back to sleep.

"Raissa." His tone carried more command. "Come down. Secrets. There are secrets. Danger."

After the encounter with Eva in the attic, I was wary. But if Eli wanted a confrontation and had secrets to share, I would meet him halfway.

"Hurry!" He faded slightly, the moonlight penetrating him.

Afraid that he would leave without sharing his confidences, I ran barefoot in my nightgown, the flimsy material floating behind me as I descended the stairs. It was possible Eli had the answers I sought, if he would only share.

A moment later I'd unlocked the front door and stepped into the embrace of the night. The cry of a hoot owl told me the night predators were out. The smaller songbirds fell silent, aware that a hunter was among them. Leaving the safety of the house, I stepped onto the dew-soaked grass that was like a soft carpet and went to the oak grove, the trees now blackened silhouettes in the moonlight.

The lawn was empty, and I stumbled to a stop, uncertain where to go. Then I saw him. He was only twenty-five feet away. My imagination hadn't magnified his good looks. He was a handsome man in the prime of his years. His dark hair, straight and black, fell over one golden-brown eye. His smooth olive complexion was marred by a scar on one cheek in the shape of a scythe. Instead of detracting, it added to his good looks.

The strangely cool breeze fluttered the fabric of my gown. I crossed the front lawn and moved deep into the oak grove. Grass blades and twigs clung to my bare feet. Eli remained slightly ahead of me. He moved without effort, as if nothing held him truly connected to the ground. No gravity or law of physics could contain him.

Moonlight paled his gray uniform to silver, and his dark hair caught and reflected Luna's light. He turned back to see that I followed and moved more swiftly.

"Eli!" I was out of the house in my nightgown. I'd meant to go only to the steps, but I was halfway through the oak grove. "Eli, stop!"

He turned back to face me and looked toward the house. "Hurry! Now."

I looked toward Caoin House. The doors to both rooms that shared my balcony were open. Something moved in the room beside mine, as if someone, or something, stepped back into the shadows to avoid detection.

Fear shot through me. Ghost or human, the intruder had no business in those rooms. "Eli, wait! What is it? What's in that room?"

But he didn't wait. He steadily drew away.

I chased after him, determined to uncover the promised secrets, to find the source of the danger that stalked Caoin House.

We left the more manicured lawn near the house. Sharp sticks and roots in the path stung my feet, yet I couldn't stop. He was fifty yards ahead, but when he looked at me, I heard his voice like a whisper in my ear.

"Hurry, Raissa. You are in danger."

He took the path to the cemetery. When we came to the lych-gate covered in blooming Confederate jasmine, the sweet scent cloying around me, at last I balked. My body came to a standstill as I fought the unexpected desire to follow him into the land of the dead.

"Stop!" I cried. "Stop! I won't go farther." He knew things, and I wanted to make him tell me, but I wouldn't go into the cemetery with him. Eva had turned on me, and I had no reason to believe Eli was any different. Perhaps the betrayal of his wife, her death, his daughter's peculiar fall had driven him insane. He could be as wickedly deceitful as Eva had been.

"The grave." He drew closer. "I am tiring. Come now. Danger."

"No. Tell me here."

"Beware of those who lie." He left, disappearing into the night.

"Raissa!" Another voice called my name. Running down the path toward me, flashlight in hand, was Carlton. "Who were you with?" he asked. "I heard you talking to someone."

Carlton and I were alone at the edge of the cemetery. My body shivered, not from cold but from shock. "I'm alone."

"Who was out here?" Carlton asked again.

How to explain that I'd followed a ghost across the lawn and almost into the cemetery? "It was a dream," I whispered.

"And who was in your dream?" Carlton put his arm around me and pulled me close against him, offered his strength as support as he began to walk me back to the house.

"Eli."

"Eli Whitehead?" He was surprised.

"He had something to tell me."

Carlton faced me, brushing the tangled curls from my face. "I worry for you, Raissa. I worry that your big imagination will put you in danger."

Still struggling to free myself of the night's strange events, I didn't want to argue with Carlton. "It upsets me, too."

He tilted my chin up with his finger so that I gazed into his eyes. "I'm falling in love with you, Raissa. The idea that someone, or something, might mean harm to you is more than I can endure. I want to take care of you, to be sure you're safe."

His words were seductive, because I now felt the need for a protector, but I couldn't lead Carlton on. "I don't know what I feel," I said. "You're a generous, kind man. I—"

I didn't finish. He kissed me—a long, searing kiss that caught me by surprise. My brief marriage had given me a taste of what it meant to have "the other" in my life. Someone to count on for companionship and affection. Someone to hold in the long hours of the night when bad dreams sent me on a walkabout. And someone for me to pour my love on, because I had so much I wanted to share.

Carlton's arms tightened around me, and I gave myself to the kiss. This was not the exploratory kiss of a young man. Carlton had, no doubt, experienced numerous lovers. He was not a libertine, but he was an attractive, wealthy man with no encumbrances. He was free to take as many lovers as he wished.

"I've restrained myself as long as I could," Carlton whispered into my ear. "I want you, Raissa."

And in that moment, I wanted him. I was a widow, not a callow young girl. The pleasures of intimacy were known to me, but I didn't have the freedom to take a lover. Not openly. And certainly not on my uncle's front lawn, which was where this encounter was headed.

Regard for my reputation, and for Uncle Brett, made me push Carlton away. For a moment I thought he might resist, but he stepped back, breathing heavily, as was I.

"I'm sorry," he said. "I've thought about this moment for so long. I let my need overrule my sense. I didn't mean to take advantage of you."

I struggled to regain my breath. "You don't owe me an apology. I wanted it, too." I'd never been so direct in speaking of my desires. "This isn't the place. Anyone could be awake and watching." Pretta and her husband were on a front-facing room on the second floor. Travis was always up before the sun.

Carlton looked around, and slowly a grin replaced his determined need. "No, it isn't the place I would choose to make love to you. I want our first time to be silk sheets, champagne, and strawberries, a place with soft music and candles." He nodded toward the house. "We don't have an audience . . . yet. But it could happen."

The thought of all the houseguests gathered on the porch watching us act out our passion broke the tension. It was too easy to imagine pretty Pretta's face, eyes and mouth wide in a mien of lustful disapproval. She thought Carlton was handsome. Isabelle would only arch an eyebrow, acknowledging that we'd given in to our human nature. And Uncle Brett? I wondered if he would approve of my growing intimacy with Carlton. "Now that would be a delicious scandal."

"We could blame it on the ghosts of Caoin House."

And in some regards, we wouldn't be that far off. It was Eli who'd lured me into the front yard with promises of secrets to be shared, who'd left me vulnerable to Carlton's advances. But no one other than Reginald would understand that explanation.

"Let's go back inside." The hands of my watch were inching toward four thirty. It was pointless to go back to sleep, but I could wash, dress, and tidy myself up for our aquatic adventure. As I took my first step, I cried out in pain.

"What's wrong?"

I looked down at my poor bruised and scraped feet.

"You've hurt yourself," Carlton said as he knelt to examine the damage. "You didn't feel anything?"

I shook my head. "The dream was so intense."

He scooped me into his arms and began the journey back to the house. "Tomorrow, when all of the guests have gone, I want to hear about this dream that's so powerful you cut your feet and don't feel anything."

By the time that happened, I would have a story ready to tell. For the moment, though, I enjoyed the sense of being carried in a man's arms. Maybe it did play to the damsel-in-distress syndrome that I disdained, but for these few minutes, I allowed myself to enjoy it.

CHAPTER
TWENTY-NINE

The *Caleuche* was a beautiful vessel with spacious accommodations. Uncle Brett had designed it for a floating business office, and as such, it had all the amenities. The name came from Chilean mythology—a ghost ship. While most of the party remained inside sitting comfortably in plush chairs, I took a position on the bow of the paddleboat. We were headed into the heart of darkness, a wonderful term coined by Joseph Conrad in his novel of the same name. The Tensaw delta was a place of great mystery, and only those who'd grown up in the area could successfully navigate the intricate and winding waterways that curled and doubled back upon themselves, leading the unfamiliar into watery cul-de-sacs and dead ends.

"Raissa, you're very quiet this morning." Pretta came to stand beside me. The morning sun peeked over the tree line.

"Last night took the wind out of my sails." I didn't mind admitting that much, and I was glad Carlton had told no one about my nocturnal adventure. "The séance was intense."

"What did you really see?"

I wasn't about to tell her the truth. "Reginald would be the one to ask. I was merely his assistant."

"That horrid little toy that flew across the room. How did you do it?"

I smiled. "I promise you—I didn't. Nor did Reginald. That was spirit phenomena, like the tapping. It's how spirits communicate."

"Reginald says that spirits with the power to move objects are dangerous."

He'd told me the same thing. "Yes, Madam warned us of such things. But the spirits are gone now. Reginald helped them move on."

"Move on to where?" Pretta's pink cheeks were paler than normal.

"I don't know."

"Do you think spirits can be evil?"

It was a question that nagged at me, too. "If humans can be evil, then I suppose spirits can, also." Logic might not be the best approach to supernatural laws, but I wasn't certain anyone could answer this with absolute fact. The pantheon of beliefs covered a lot of ground about what happened after death.

"Do you think the ghosts at Caoin House are evil?" Pretta asked.

"Evil or not, they're gone. At least Reginald thinks they are. We'll know in a week or two." But I already knew. Eli was there. And at least one other—the one who'd been in the room beside mine watching us.

"I'd love to see a ghost," Pretta said. "You know these swamps are haunted by the Indians who died here while hiding from the federal troops trying to push them to Oklahoma. Folks say it's the ghosts of the Indians who kill hunters and trappers who go off into the swamps."

"Really? They believe the ghosts literally kill people?"

"They do. Or at least a lot of the locals do. They see the moving lights in the swamp and believe it's torches carried by raiding parties of Indians as they prepare to attack."

"You know the area well, Pretta. This is fascinating."

"I wasn't always a candy maker. When I was a child, I traveled with my grandfather, who was a physician. He treated a lot of the Native Americans and those without the resources to come to town for care. While he was busy with treatments, I talked with the family members. I loved stories, and they were happy to share with me."

I pulled a tiny notebook and pen from my purse and took down her tale. "What else do people say?" This thrilling story would make the foundation for another creepy tale by the chilling Mr. James.

She thought a minute. "There was a tiny shred of gossip attached to Caoin House. The property stretches all the way to the Chickasabogue Creek, which feeds into the delta."

"What gossip?"

"I've heard the rumor that Eli Whitehead often stole Choctaw children and worked them as slaves."

"Are you serious?" The Indians were free people. To enslave a man, woman, or child, whether black or red, was despicable.

"That's the rumor."

"Is it true?"

She laughed. "I don't know. People can say anything they want. Proving it is another matter."

"I never viewed Eli Whitehead as the kind of man who would do such a thing." But he owned and worked slaves. Children were frequently taken from their parents and sold far away. Husbands and wives were split apart and sold separately. Was it such a big step to steal a child—a free asset?

"Eli is hard to pin down," Pretta said. "Hubert's family knew the Whitehead family back in the 1850s and 1860s. Eli loved beauty and beautiful things, but he had a dark streak, according to the Paul family stories."

"Such as?" I wanted to ask why she'd failed to mention this earlier, but to do so might sound like an accusation.

"The stories I heard most often involved his jealousy. Eva was beautiful, and men were drawn to her, which he loved. He enjoyed being envied. But at a certain point, he would grow angry. He was the same way about Elise. He ran off a number of suitors, some of them from prominent Mobile families, so you can see that left a bad taste. He settled on Charles Todd DeMornay. He made certain Elise's future husband met all of his demands."

"Poor Elise. A dead mother and a controlling father." I wondered what role this played in her tragic death. While I might never know the truth, it was certainly fodder for a tale.

"There were other stories, too. That Eli acquired more than one Indian child, for himself and for his friends. Most of the children were sold away from Mobile because he feared they would escape and return to the swamps where he'd never be able to retrieve them."

Movement in my peripheral vision made me jerk to the north. Standing among the trees and fronds was the silhouette of a man. He walked to the edge of the water and stood motionless, as if he watched us passing by. Not ten yards away, an eight-foot alligator sunned in the mud.

As we drew abreast of the figure, I caught the flash of something shiny where the sun struck it. I used my hand to shade the sun from my eyes and froze. I recognized the uniform. Eli Whitehead had left the grounds of Caoin House and was spying on us from the swamps.

The truth struck me like a fist to the heart. The child in the attic. The poor child clinging to a gruesome toy. Was he the unhappy spirit of a child stolen and sold into slavery who had died at Caoin House? I felt myself sway, and I grabbed the railing.

"Raissa, you should sit down. I think the ride is making you seasick."

"Yes." I let Pretta lead me into the cabin and to a chair. "I haven't acquired my sea legs," I said by way of explanation.

Carolyn Haines

"Let me make you a seltzer," Uncle Brett said.

Isabelle came to sit beside me. "Last night was a strain for you, Raissa. Are you okay?"

"I am." I hugged her. "I'm tired, and I did get a little queasy. I'm right as rain now."

I sipped the refreshing beverage Uncle Brett gave me and returned to the deck with Pretta, Isabelle, and the men. Carlton came to stand beside me. When the others had drifted away, his fingers found my hand and gave a squeeze.

"This is some of the loveliest scenery in the world." He pointed to an inlet where five beautiful white cranes stood in the shallows fishing. The birds saw us and took flight, their wings spanning at least five feet, and their long skinny legs trailing behind.

I told him of my sense of journeying into Conrad's literary terrain. And then I asked about the story Pretta had mentioned.

"I've heard the same rumors," he said, "but I've never seen any solid proof. Caoin House estate was once part of the Choctaw nation. The land was taken from the Indians. The methods used were brutal and unjust. Eli Whitehead was no different from any other white man at the time. He took advantage of every situation to build his fortune."

"Even stealing the children of free people." It made me sad.

"I don't know that it's true, but it's certainly possible."

"Do we ever know the truth?"

Carlton slipped his arm around my waist and pulled me against him while the others were busy talking and laughing. "My truth is that I want you more than anything I've ever wanted."

His words thrilled me, but they also made me shy. "I'm not ready for this, Carlton. I found out things about Robert."

"What things?"

I couldn't tell him that I knew Robert was a con man. I would never tell anyone. "He wasn't the man I thought he was. Let's just leave it at that."

"So you liked someone you didn't know well. That's no reason to lose faith in your judgment. You're a smart, talented young woman. Never lose faith in yourself. Besides, Brett can vouch for me. I am what you see." His palm stroked my cheek, and his grin was devilish. "And one day, when you're a famous writer, you can support me and we'll travel to exotic places."

"Like Eli and Elise?"

He looked a bit shocked. "Not as father and daughter."

It was my turn to be shocked. "I didn't mean that."

"Thank goodness! I intend to have you, Raissa James. I will win your heart and make you mine."

He was succeeding with the heart-winning part, or at least convincing me to open to the possibility. But I wouldn't be rushed. This was too important. "Look," I said, pointing to a small cove filled with the jutting stumps of cypress knees. It was an eerie and enchanted vista.

The rest of the crew came out to the deck as we moved slowly around the secret pathways of the delta. Uncle Brett had hired a boat captain whose lovely golden skin tone and high cheekbones spoke of possible Choctaw heritage. He certainly knew the byways of the delta, and there were many intersections of canals and streams. It would be easy to get lost.

Reginald was deep in conversation with Pretta and Isabelle, and Hubert had joined Brett. When Carlton went to refresh my seltzer, I listened to Reginald put the finishing touches on last night's performance. He had to make the women believe the spirits of Caoin House were gone. Judging from their expressions, he was making a success of it.

As the sun rose higher, we found alligators lazing in the shallows. At first I thought they were logs bobbing in the muddy brown water. More than one moccasin zigzagged through the river. We were safe in the boat, but the sense of nearby danger held an edge of excitement. Uncle Brett was the perfect showman, telling of the history of the area, the place where the last slave ship to enter the United States—illegally—had gone down. A host of stories that I filed away for future use as rich texture for my supernatural tales.

Uncle Brett's invention, a more powerful mechanism that propelled the wheel of the paddleboat, appeared to be a huge success. The boat easily maneuvered upriver without strain, and under the expert command of the captain, moved about the delta with great agility. It was everything Uncle had hoped. He was on the way to making another fortune.

We returned to the Mobile dock famished and excited by the beauty of the Tensaw area. At last the *Caleuche* was securely moored. A member of the boat crew came forward to hand me off the boat, but Carlton stepped to my side and took over. To my surprise, a young man in gray slacks and a starched white shirt standing on the dock called out to Carlton. At Carlton's signal, he ran to us and delivered an envelope to him.

Carlton read the address and tapped the envelope against his hand, watching me before he extended it. "It's a telegram. For you."

"For me?" Curious, I tore into it. When I read the three sentences, I didn't believe them. I looked up at Carlton; his face creased with pleasure.

"Congratulations!" he shouted. "Everyone! Raissa has sold her first story. She will be a published author in a few short months!" He whispered in my ear. "I took the liberty of asking the editor to send a telegram if he accepted your story. Waiting is too hard."

"Thank you." I floated on a sensation that was impossible to describe. My story would be published in the *Saturday Evening Post*. People across America would be able to read the tale I'd made up. It was thrilling.

"Raissa! I knew you would be published! I told you, didn't I?" Pretta kissed my cheek. "This is wonderful."

Uncle Brett clapped his hands. "Well, then, we should celebrate. It's not every day a budding literary genius is in our company. My favorite downtown establishment, the Dockery, is open. Why don't we adjourn there? Drinks are on me." Uncle Brett swept me into a hug and kissed my cheek. "My niece, soon to be the literary light of Mobile."

Questions came at me from all sides as we made the short walk to the restaurant, which served delicious Gulf seafood and also the beverages no one seemed to believe were illegal. Prohibition might be the law, but my uncle and his friends ran their alcohol consumption wide-open.

Uncle Brett, Isabelle, and the Pauls entered the club while I stood on the sidewalk to catch a minute with Reginald. He grabbed my hand and kissed it with all the aplomb of a French royal. "You did it." He spun me around. "You achieved your dream, Raissa. I'm so happy for you."

"I can hardly believe it."

"Now you must write another. One day your stories will be known by an entire country. You'll be spoken of in the same breath as Mr. Poe."

I had to laugh at that. "It's one story. I believe we're getting ahead of ourselves. And we have more serious matters to discuss. What about Caoin House?"

"I've convinced Brett and Isabelle the house is free of all negative spirits," he said, "but that's a dangerous lie. Raissa, you need to be careful. They know you can see them." The skin beneath his eyes was white with tension.

"Can't you send them on their way?"

"I did what Madam taught me. Sometimes a spirit won't leave until an injustice has been righted." He pulled a cigarette from his jacket and lit it. "I might take the train to New Orleans and consult Madam about Caoin House. Maybe there's additional action, something I haven't thought of. Maybe a priest . . ."

I didn't like the idea of a priest. The gossip would be all over Mobile. It was bad enough that the Martins had been so badly frightened. If a priest was called to the house, the reputation of Caoin House would be lost. "The ghosts aren't only in Caoin House. I saw Eli in the swamps just after Pretta told me how he supposedly stole Choctaw children and worked and sold them as slaves."

Reginald's face went stony. "That isn't good. The spirits aren't confined, then."

"And they're growing stronger. Last night Eli called me out of the house. I was all the way to the cemetery with him before Carlton pulled me from the dream state."

"Dammit, Raissa. You shouldn't go back to Caoin House. It's dangerous there for you."

Harsh lines at the corner of his mouth told me how concerned he was. "I'm not taking it lightly—I promise."

"The entities in Caoin House are very strong. They're able to move matter. For most spirits, summoning the energy to knock or tap drains them. These ghosts manifest, and they are able to move objects. They have physical powers, which is extraordinary."

"I am concerned, and I promise to be careful. He promised to tell me secrets. I thought he could help me figure out how to rid Caoin House of the ghosts."

"I'll sleep in the hallway outside your room from now on. You can't go out into the night with Eli again."

Isabelle came to the door and opened it to speak to us. "Brett is waiting to make a toast in your honor, Raissa. He's so proud of you." She didn't wait for an answer but closed the door.

"We have to go inside," Reginald said. "The celebration is to honor you and your story. You can't stand out here with me." He crushed his cigarette underfoot and lightened the mood with a devilish grin. "People will talk."

"Let them." But I noticed Carlton and Uncle Brett coming toward the open door. I stepped inside with an apology on my lips. In a moment I was swallowed in the raucous toast Uncle Brett offered.

I let my worries about Caoin House slip away as I basked in the pleasure of hearing praise for my accomplishment. Carlton, that devil, had a copy of the story with him. At the urging of my friends, I read a few pages, to give them a taste. They were suitably chilled, and I relished the sensation.

For the first time in my life, I knew what it felt like to be special, to be admired, to have earned the applause of my friends. It was something that could be highly addictive.

We'd settled at a table in the corner to eat gumbo and the delicious po'boy sandwiches composed of the best fresh French bread and fried shrimp or oysters. We were a merry group, and I realized how much I wanted to live in Mobile. I had friends; I now had a career; I had the beginning of a rich and fulfilling life. Uncle Brett was the total opposite of my mother, but they shared enough quirks and characteristics that I could allow myself to let him be my guardian. I could go to him for advice, and that was something I'd sorely lacked since Alex's death.

I didn't believe that women were incapable of making big decisions—not at all. I was equal to any man. But even the smartest men needed advisers and friends and those who could give a valid opinion. Uncle Brett offered those things to me, yet he never pushed to control the outcome.

I was a lucky woman. I hadn't felt that way in a long time, but looking around at Pretta's laughing face and Isabelle's glow of love as she looked at Uncle Brett, I counted myself among the luckiest of people.

Carlton caught my eye and held up his glass in a salute to me. My answering grin hurt my face. We clicked glasses. This was a perfect evening. Life could not get better than this.

CHAPTER THIRTY

A commotion in the back of the club made me look up as the bartender left his post. He returned a moment later, his face strained. Though he looked at Pretta and Hubert, he spoke in Carlton's ear.

The change of expression warned me that tragedy had struck our happy group. I didn't know who or how, but I had no doubt. Something awful had happened.

Carlton took Hubert's arm and led him away from the group. A moment later, Hubert exploded. "I will find who did this and make them pay. That boy never hurt a fly. He worked; he helped his mother. He saved his money to have a better life."

Pretta rose slowly as all conversation at our table stopped. "What's happened?"

Impulse sent Isabelle and me to either side of her.

"What is it?" she demanded of her husband. "What's wrong?"

Hubert struggled to contain his emotions. "It's John Henry. Someone lynched him in Bienville Square. He's dead."

Pretta's knees caved, and she would have gone down had it not been for Isabelle and me catching her. We eased her into a chair, trying to control our own reactions. For the longest moment, Pretta merely sat and stared into her husband's eyes. Her mouth opened, and a piercing scream brought tears to my eyes. "No! No! No!"

Hubert came to her and held her tight as she sobbed against him.

Uncle Brett went to the bar and discreetly covered the bill for the evening. He signaled Reginald over, and they conferred for a moment. Next, he went to Carlton. The lawyer wanted to argue, but at last he conceded.

Finally, Uncle Brett came to me, and I understood that my immediate future had been decided. "Reginald and I are going to Bienville Square. I want a word with the sheriff. This can't be swept under the rug. Someone will pay for this, but it has to be handled with some delicacy."

"Will someone be held accountable for this?" Images of John Henry's careful preparation of candies, his ready smile, and his easygoing nature came to me. "Someone should pay."

"John Henry laid claim to someone else's name," Uncle Brett said softly. "He challenged a white family. His claim to the Marcum name casts a shadow on their heritage. Their standing in society. There are many people in this city who couldn't let that pass. I know Pretta and Hubert talked to him about the consequences, but he refused to stop calling himself a Marcum."

"It was *his* name. Why shouldn't he claim it?"

"Because it cost him his life. Is a name really that important?" Brett put a gentle hand on my shoulder. "I don't like the way things are, but flying in the face of people with power is never smart. I want things to change, but it will have to be a gradual process. When you back people into a corner, when you confront them with a truth they aren't ready to hear, they can become aggressive and brutal."

I'd heard the same arguments about women and the vote. "You can't color this any way but wrong." To my horror, I started crying.

My uncle hated tears because he felt helpless. He put an arm around me and looked immensely relieved when Carlton stepped up and offered his handkerchief. "Can you look after Raissa? I want to have a word with the sheriff and to see to the body."

"Yes," Carlton said. "I'll take her to my club, where she can find some quiet. Pretta and Isabelle can join us. The streets are going to be explosive, I'm afraid."

"I'll return for her later."

Carlton took my hand. "Raissa, will you spend some time with me? After things settle, I'll drive you back to Caoin House. Your uncle has things he must do, and worry for you will only make it harder on him."

Uncle Brett didn't give me a chance to respond. This had already been decided between the men. Gracious acceptance was the only card I could play. "Thank you, Carlton."

"That's my girl," Uncle Brett said. He motioned to Reginald, and they rushed out the door, their leather soles slapping the sidewalk until they faded in the distance.

Hubert eased Pretta into a chair. He whispered to her, and she cried out again and reached up to detain him, but he grasped her hands and removed them from his shirt. "I have to go. Someone has to speak for John Henry and his mother. I don't want them to defile the body."

"Pretta will be safe with me and Raissa and Isabelle. We'll go to my offices, and once things are calm, I'll see the ladies home."

"Thank you, Carlton." Hubert kept glancing at the door, but he was reluctant to leave Pretta.

"Go," she finally said, and he shot through the door without a backward glance.

"Ladies?" Carlton took Pretta's elbow and helped her stand. "We should move along. A mob is capable of any violence. Pretta, you and Hubert employed John Henry. Let's not give them another target."

Those worlds galvanized Pretta, and we set off down the dark city street. In the distance I heard the rising and falling roar of a crowd of angry people. I turned back to look toward the square and saw flames. I could only hope the mob wasn't burning John Henry's body.

Carlton's law offices were a few blocks down Dauphin Street, and he ushered us there, a shepherd moving a flock along a sidewalk that was quickly filling with vehicles and men. The lynching news spread like a contagion.

To avoid Bienville Square, the site of the lynching, Carlton turned us down a narrow alley that ran between the three-story brick department stores that sold the latest fashions. We were halfway along when someone at the other end swung a flashlight beam into our faces.

"That's the bitch who gave that boy a job. Get her!"

I grasped Pretta's arm and tugged her back the way we'd come. Isabelle ran beside me.

"Run!" Carlton remained behind, standing his ground to give us time to escape.

I looked back as the mob descended on him, but Pretta's hysterical sobs kept me moving away. Leaving Carlton to fight alone tore at me, but I had no choice.

Pretta, Isabelle, and I were swept into the mob that surged toward Bienville Square. The smell of alcohol was strong as the men pushed past us, not even really seeing us. The bloodlust of the mob had been aroused.

We were at the park before I knew it, and the wall of moving people stopped. Voices yelled angrily, calling for others to be lynched. The language was profane and disgusting. Packed in with men taller than I was, I couldn't see anything.

Isabelle signaled toward a break in the crowd. Pretta cried and sniffled, but there was nothing we could do except keep moving. We pushed and squeezed to the edge of the crowd, pulling Pretta with us.

At last, we made it to the curb on the opposite street. I looked at the square and froze with dread. Uncle Brett was climbing a ladder that Hubert and Reginald guarded, punching anyone who tried to get near. John Henry swung from a rope looped over the limb of one of the beautiful old oaks.

"Come on!" Isabelle pushed me down the sidewalk. "If they see Pretta, they may hang her, too."

I grasped my friend's hand, and we ran. Most of the crowd had made it to the square, and now the streets were almost empty. We ran and ran until we came to the alley where we'd left Carlton. There was no sign of him.

"Do you think—" I couldn't utter the words.

"Carlton is too smart to die on the end of a rope." Isabelle frowned. "We have to get her inside, but that could be trouble."

A lone figure stood beneath a streetlight two blocks down the street. I noticed a piece of a wooden pallet in the alley, and I picked it up. It wasn't much of a weapon, but better than none. "Let's go. If he does anything, give me enough room to swing at him."

We led Pretta, who had given up any attempt to take charge of herself. She drifted as if in a nightmare, and I knew she was in shock.

The figure came toward us at a run, and I rushed forward, club ready.

"Raissa!"

I dropped the stick and ran into Carlton's arms. I'd never been gladder to see anyone.

"Oh, thank God you're okay," Isabelle said as she joined us. "Hurry—we need to get Pretta to safety."

At last we reached the cool dark-paneled offices, and Carlton had us seated in the semigloom of the shuttered interior. The quiet was a blessing. Pretta's ragged breathing was the only noise as Carlton bustled around with glasses of water and a damp cloth to cool Pretta's hot eyes and face.

Isabelle was as distraught as I was, but she managed to keep her composure, an incentive for me to hold myself together. We had pressing duties—first and foremost to comfort Pretta.

"I can't believe this," Pretta said again and again when at last she could speak. "Maybe it's a mistake?" She lifted her tearstained face to us, hoping we would agree.

"Tomorrow we'll take food to his mother," Isabelle said, her tone level and devoid of any emotion. "I've been meaning to find someone to help me with my herb garden and to do some ironing. His mother may have some time to help me out. Carlton, do you have any domestic work?"

"I do, and several of my clients have also mentioned the need for child care or cleaning. I'll be sure and impress upon them the importance of taking on additional help."

Isabelle was thinking of the future and John Henry's mother. What would she do without her son to help her? I simply couldn't believe that the young man I'd met, a gentle young man who took pride in his work, had been murdered in such a brutal way.

I was like a dog with a bone. "Why would someone kill a young man, little more than a boy, because he took his father's name?"

Carlton sighed, but Isabelle patted his arm. "Let me answer. Name is everything, Raissa. In society, it's heritage, bond, calling card, history, accomplishments. Mobile is a city where social standing is more important than ever. This is a closed society. Old money and old family. A man can go to the bank and borrow enormous sums on his family name alone. No collateral. For a black man to take an honored name and to use it, the affront was bound to result in tragedy."

"Then the whole society is wrong." I grew only angrier at her logic. "It is *all* wrong."

"Many things are wrong," Carlton said, coming to sit beside me on the leather sofa. He drew me against him. "Women who can't vote or own property is wrong, and that *is* changing. Change will come for the Negro, too. It will. But it must come at a pace that doesn't threaten those who hold the reins of power. John Henry pushed too hard. The Marcum family has a lot of power."

I hated it that anyone could twist the facts to make an innocent young man look guilty. "I don't think he pushed too hard. The name was his at conception. Mr. Marcum didn't deny that John Henry was his son. He simply ignored the situation. He's as much to blame as the person who hanged him. And Mrs. Marcum, too. You have no idea how she spoke to John Henry when he made deliveries. She's an evil bitch." My grip on the sofa whitened my knuckles.

"None of us disagrees with you, Raissa. If only the rest of the world could catch up to you, we would live in a better country."

"Will they find the person who did this?" Pretta asked.

"I can promise you that Brett, Hubert, and I will stay after the sheriff. I suspect he'll try to shirk his duty, but I won't let it drop. You ladies must not engage in this matter."

I heard what Carlton said, and I also heard his promise. He would work for change, but only in a way that kept the status quo balanced. Nothing sudden. Nothing unpleasant. It wasn't enough, but it was more than I would get from most men.

"Pretta, is there anyone at your home?" Carlton asked.

"I can call my sister-in-law. I'm sure everyone has heard by now. I should do that. She'll be worried."

Carlton showed her to a desk with a telephone in another room, and we all sat silently, listening to her weep as she arranged to meet her sister-in-law.

"Isabelle, are you okay?" Carlton asked. "Do you want to go home or stay for dinner in town?"

"Home," she said. "Between the séance and the boat ride and this terrible thing, I'm exhausted. I want nothing more than a hot bath and a cool bed." She rose. "And we should get Pretta to her house. She's going to collapse any minute."

"I'll bring the car around." Carlton rose. At the door he paused. "You'll stay here?"

I nodded. When he was gone, Isabelle turned to me.

"The men won't let this go, Raissa. There are those who view this as a crime, though many will not. This is dangerous, for all of us. Watch your tongue. You don't want to bring trouble to your uncle."

I took her meaning immediately. If I blathered on about how wrong this was, I could draw the ire of those who believed hanging a man barely out of his teen years was what he deserved. I would not necessarily suffer, but my uncle could. "Thank you, Isabelle."

"Mobile society is graciousness and mannered, but that's only the surface. There are many layers, some stuffed with money and privilege. Beneath that is something much darker. Beware of it."

"I will."

Pretta joined us, and we escorted her to the sidewalk, where Carlton waited in the car. We took her home and saw her inside, where she fell into tears in her sister-in-law's arms. Isabelle was almost gray with tension, and we took her to a lovely home not far from downtown. The gracious pillars supported the second floor, and the grounds bloomed with summer flowers.

"I will be in touch," she said as she kissed my cheek. "Remember, bide your time. This will be redressed, but with caution for the people we love."

I kissed her cheek and settled back in the car as she went up the steps and disappeared into the front door.

"She loves your uncle," Carlton said.

"He's a lucky man."

"Let's go to my club. I want the rest of the evening to pass and the city to settle down. If there's going to be trouble, it will be soon. Once we're beyond that threshold, I'll drive you home."

"Wouldn't it be better to go home now?" I asked.

"I want to be here, in case I'm needed."

Unspoken were the words that there might be more violence. "Of course. I'm happy to stay in town."

"Good. Then we'll try to spend the time in a way that brings you pleasure. I regret this terrible thing has marred an evening when you should celebrate your future publication."

That he'd remembered my story in all the events made me smile. I would never forget the grotesque scene of John Henry dangling from the tree limb, but it would do no good to tell Carlton. Focus on the present—that would be my mantra for the rest of the evening. "There'll be many days to celebrate, but I thank you. You're a good friend to support my career dreams. How thoughtful of you to have the editor send a telegram."

"I knew the story would sell, and I wanted the news to come as quickly as possible. You have talent, Raissa."

"Thank you. Now let's put aside everything else. Tell me about your law practice. Where did you go to school? We've spent so much time talking about Caoin House. I want to know more about you."

We went first to his club, a private men's club whose members were lawyers, bankers, judges, timber barons, railroad men—those who controlled the money. Women were allowed only on the arm of a member, and only in the bar and dining room. It was an elegant three-story building of dark paneling and masculine antiques. The club lounge and dining area was on the second floor. I could easily imagine what went on in the upper floors.

A few young women were there, and not wives or daughters. They were beautiful and elegantly dressed in the drop-waisted flapper style that revealed plenty of cleavage and leg. Their heavily kohled eyes gave them an exotic look. I'd never, to my knowledge, been in a room with mistresses.

"Are you amused?" Carlton asked.

"Maybe." I wasn't certain. I'd learned the McKay law firm had served the prominent families of Mobile for decades. He was the secret keeper of high society. I knew about his business but very little about the man. I decided to resort to direct questions. "Do you have a mistress?"

"No." His expression indicated amusement as he tipped the waiter who brought our drinks.

"Why not? It would surely be easier than a girlfriend, and if you aren't inclined to marry, it's the perfect solution." I wasn't a sophisticate, but I also wasn't a rube.

"Who says I'm not inclined to marry?"

I sipped my drink and thought. "I'm certain you can have the pick of women in Mobile, yet you haven't taken a wife. I assumed you preferred bachelorhood."

"I want a wife and family. I just haven't found the right woman. I wouldn't want to marry unless I was in love. I see that future with you."

"You hardly know me." Talk of love was flattering, but I'd been in Mobile only a short time. "With all the things that have happened, I don't know who I am any longer. And I don't know what I feel, about anything or anyone. I'm not certain I want to stay in Mobile. Tonight has . . . changed things."

"I know more of you than you realize," he said. "I've heard about you for years from Brett. He's very proud of you, in case you aren't aware. I've heard all about how you survived the loss of your husband and parents and took up teaching. How strong you are. How you refuse to let life get the better of you. I've heard all about you, Raissa. But it's been spending time with you these past few weeks that's convinced me I feel more for you than warm regards." He held up a hand. "Don't say anything. Just think about it. Think seriously."

"Carlton, I like you. I admire you, but I can't say more than that now, and I need to be certain of what I truly feel. I would never want to play you false."

"Will you consider my affections for you?"

"I will."

"And that is enough." He picked up my hand and kissed the palm. "And I fully expect you to become a famous writer." He squeezed my fingers. "I want that for you. I want to support you in your career. I find it exciting to watch you grow into your own person, an independent woman."

He couldn't have wooed me with better words.

CHAPTER
THIRTY-ONE

The rush of the wind off the Mobile River was cooler than the still air trapped between the buildings of downtown Mobile. It also bore the aroma of fruits and spices, different cultures. The city had grown quiet, and police officers walked the beat, batons in hand, a reminder that order would be restored or punishment would be swift.

After leaving the club, Carlton and I walked south. He was killing time, making sure that Brett and Reginald were safely home and waiting before he delivered me. Carlton studiously avoided the area around Bienville Square as he escorted me along the gaslit sidewalks. The street had emptied of most cars, and the loud voices in Bienville Square had been quelled. Now the night was soft and gentle.

"We could head home," I suggested. My feet were dragging, and I feared I would fall asleep in the car. Tumultuous emotions, from fear to rage to sorrow, made me feel hollow and sluggish. I longed for the comfort of my room.

"Another little bit," Carlton said.

I appreciated that he didn't want me to be alone at Caoin House, so I didn't argue. I focused on walking with some degree of decorum.

"Will you tell me the truth about what happened at the séance?" he asked as we walked beside the railroad tracks. Up ahead, the train station blazed with light, even though it appeared empty.

"There's nothing to tell. Reginald connected with some entities, and he believes he's released them to find peace." I had to be careful. Carlton was smart, and he already sniffed a bit of subterfuge about Reginald.

"When is Reginald returning to New Orleans?"

"I don't know. I enjoy his company, so I will be sad to see him depart. Uncle is very generous with the car to allow me to drive whenever I wish, but it's nice to have a friend close at hand."

"Especially one who shares your interest in ghosts." Carlton patted my hand that rested on his arm.

Up ahead, a crew unloaded a cargo ship. I wondered if it was fruit from Central America or something more pedestrian. We slowed our pace as we watched the men moving the cargo boxes. They worked with precision and rhythm.

"Most people never think how produce arrives at their table," Carlton said. "A lot of people have lost that connection between where an egg or banana or bowl of peas actually comes from and the number of hands necessary to get it onto the dinner table."

He was right about that. The war had seen a sweeping change in America as more and more people left farms to move to cities and work in factories. Although I'd had a small garden in Savannah, I'd grown mostly herbs and tomatoes and peppers. Everything else I purchased at the grocer, never really thinking how far a potato might have traveled to reach me.

"You have an interesting way of thinking." I enjoyed the strange turns our conversation took. I stifled a yawn, and Carlton instantly swung me around to walk back to the place he'd parked his car. "Time to head home. I'm sure Brett is at Caoin House waiting for you. If he'd needed me, he'd have sent a runner to find me. He knew where we were."

"Carlton, can you find out if the sheriff has arrested anyone for John Henry's murder?"

"No."

"Why not?"

"They won't arrest anyone, Raissa. Your uncle and I will fight to have someone charged, but the truth is, nothing will happen. There's tacit agreement among the people who control things that this needed to happen. An example has been set. No other Negro will dare try to attach himself to a society family."

"And for wanting what was rightfully his, he will die and no one will avenge him?"

He swung me around to face him. "That's how it works, Raissa. I'm sorry. It isn't just or fair. Promise me you won't involve yourself in this. I know Isabelle warned you. Rash actions will impact Brett as well as you. These are hateful people, and they won't hold back just because you're a female."

I didn't want to argue. I was tired, and Carlton wasn't the enemy. He didn't agree with how things went, but he couldn't single-handedly change a country's behavior. "I am tired. I don't know that I'll come back to town for a long while. There's really no need. I have everything I require at Caoin House."

"Except me."

"You have an open invitation to visit at Caoin House whenever you can."

"Then I will visit you. Frequently." We'd arrived at the car, and he opened the door and seated me. He stopped at his law office, promising he'd only be a minute. He wanted to check to be sure no messages had been left there for him. I chose to wait in the car. I was almost dozing when a young man ran up the steps to the office and pounded on the door. He was frantic.

Carlton came outside, and for a long, tense moment he spoke with the young man, who gestured wildly, pointing north. A terrible feeling dropped over me. Dread. Something else awful had happened. There'd been another incident, more violence.

The young man hurried away, his shadow growing shorter and shorter as he neared a street lamp, and then growing long again. Carlton got in the car and drove without saying a word. The clock on the Bank of Mobile showed 11:45 when we passed. For once I was too afraid to ask questions. Carlton's expression was grim, but finally I had to know.

"What's wrong? Something terrible has happened. What?"

He pulled the car over and stopped, then grasped my hands. "There's been an accident."

"What kind of accident?" I couldn't see that anything was amiss downtown. The streets were truly empty. "Is it Pretta?" I wondered if the Pauls would be targeted for hiring John Henry. "Are they okay?"

His grip on my hands tightened, and the call of a mockingbird came from one of the few remaining downtown trees. Most had been cut to make way for the power lines.

"It's Brett and Reginald."

The bird cried again.

"What happened?" The lights on the street seemed to flare into brightness.

"There was a wreck. Brett's car went off the road. They've taken Reginald to Caoin House, and the doctor is on his way."

"And Uncle Brett?"

When he didn't speak, I couldn't stop the sob that broke from me. "Tell me, dammit. What about my uncle?"

"Brett has disappeared." Carlton wiped a sheen of sweat from his brow. "They've searched all along the road. There's no sign of him."

"That's impossible. He has to be there."

"They're still searching with torches and lights. I'll take you there now."

I motioned frantically. "Hurry!" My uncle might be missing, but he hadn't disappeared. He couldn't just vanish. He had to be near the accident. "How far from Caoin House?"

"About a mile. They were almost home. It seems they hit a patch of sand in the road, and it grabbed the car's front wheels and flipped it."

"Flipped it?" I could visualize the wreckage. "Uncle Brett was a very good driver. He knew the sand patches. He wouldn't have been going fast enough to flip a car."

Carlton turned north toward Caoin House and pressed the gas. "I don't know."

"Who found them?"

"The groundskeeper."

"Travis? Why was he awake and on the main road?"

"Someone had attempted to break into Caoin House, and Travis was on the way to get the sheriff." Carlton focused on the road, his hands gripping the wheel, white-knuckled.

"Who was trying to break in?"

"Travis didn't catch them, but he said two men. Many things need an explanation."

"How badly is Reginald hurt?"

"He was unconscious. He has a head injury."

I refused to cry. Crying did no good, and it weakened my resolve to fight.

"We'll find Brett. He has to be in the vicinity." Carlton hesitated. "Unless someone came by and picked him up."

"Why would they take Uncle Brett and leave Reginald?"

"I don't know, Raissa. There's evil loose tonight. The hanging of that unfortunate young man, and now this."

"Has the sheriff been called?"

"I sent the messenger to the sheriff's office and asked that officers be sent to help with the search."

Thank God for Carlton's level head and his affection for my uncle. Another question occurred to me. "Who sent the messenger to your office?" If both Uncle Brett and Reginald were unable to speak . . . it made sense to notify Carlton because he would best know what to do. But who had been at Caoin House to think to notify the lawyer?

"Travis called for a doctor and asked the hospital to send a messenger to find me. There was great concern you were in the car with the men and had also disappeared."

And would I be gone, had I been in the car?

I thought of Eli, standing among the palmettos in the Tensaw delta. He was not confined to Caoin House, as I'd first assumed. The ghosts of Caoin House were powerful. This I was learning with each passing day.

My uncle was a careful driver. For him to flip his car, something had to have startled him. Made him swerve. And now he was gone. Without a trace.

"Raissa!" Carlton called my name sharply.

"Yes, sorry. I was thinking."

"Thank goodness. I was afraid you'd slipped into a trance or something."

I took a few deep breaths and turned in the seat to face him. "I'm sorry. It's just that Uncle Brett would never have left Reginald unconscious in the road. So I can only assume that someone took my uncle. Someone who may have caused the wreck."

"Why would anyone deliberately wreck your uncle?"

"I don't know, but I intend to find out."

"Do you have any suspects?" Carlton asked.

I did, but I wasn't going to tell him about them. He would think I'd lost my mind if I said I suspected Eli and Eva. "Who are my uncle's enemies?"

Carlton hit a straightaway on the narrow road. We drove in a tunnel of darkness, able to see only as far as the car's headlamps revealed.

It would be easy for someone to plunge out of the darkness and cause an accident.

"Raissa, your uncle has been outspoken about certain social matters. I can only think that he must have aggravated someone at Bienville Square when he went there. I'll find out more tomorrow, but I suspect Brett insisted that the body be cut down and taken to the Negro mortuary. That would upset those who meant to make a spectacle of the hanging."

"Upset them enough to ambush him, possibly kill him, or kidnap him? What kind of people are these?"

When he answered, Carlton's voice was harsh. "These are people who would kill a woman for sleeping with a Negro or someone who isn't white. They would kill a child of such a couple. There is growing unrest, Raissa. These men are threatened. Women are demanding the vote and equality. Negroes are demanding fair treatment. These white men feel their manhood is challenged, and that is dangerous. They can and do lash out."

A million angry retorts spun in my head, but none should have been aimed at Carlton. He was the messenger, not the message. He wasn't the one hanging young men or causing wrecks. *If* the wreck were deliberately caused. I'd jumped to a conclusion, and now my thoughts were running away from me.

"I'm sorry," I said softly. Carlton's hand grasped mine and held it until he needed to shift gears when we saw the lights of the sheriff's cars on the side of the road. We'd made it to the wreck site.

CHAPTER
THIRTY-TWO

The sheriff and four deputies searched the area around the wrecked car with flashlights and drawn guns. There was no sign of Uncle Brett. I rushed to the car, which lay on its side in a patch of deep sand. Thick woods encroached on either side of the road, and the black night made it difficult to see. The beam of a flashlight illuminated blood covering the steering wheel and front seat. Whether it belonged to Uncle Brett or Reginald, I couldn't say.

Insects buzzed and stung as I made my way around the car, hoping to find something that would lead to Uncle Brett's recovery. Mosquitoes and yellow flies were the bane of the summer, and a swarm soon hummed around my head and bare legs, stinging any piece of exposed flesh. I tried to ignore them as I searched the ground for clues, but I couldn't help but worry that my only living relative lay injured somewhere, a feast for bloodsucking pests.

Sheriff Thompson made no attempt to speak with me—rather, he acted as if I were not even there—but he pulled Carlton aside. Brett was my uncle, but because I was a woman, I was excluded from hearing the details of my uncle's strange disappearance. Anger propelled me forward into the middle of the conversation. I introduced myself, though the sheriff knew exactly who I was

"Is there any sign of my uncle?" I spoke pleasantly but with firmness. Carlton attempted to catch my eye, but I refused to look at him.

"Miss Raissa, it's best to let the men handle this. Mr. McKay can speak with you when we have more information." The sheriff puffed up like an adder. "It's best you go home. That psychic fellow needs your attention."

Thank goodness he couldn't see the color that mounted in my cheeks. I was dismissed like a child, and Reginald was reduced to "that psychic fellow." I wasn't so easily brushed aside. Somewhere along the path of life, I'd found my backbone. "Were there any indications someone stopped to help my uncle? Perhaps he's been taken to the hospital."

"Miss, I don't have anything to tell you. My men are searching the area. The best thing you can do is go home."

"How many men do you have investigating the hanging of John Henry Marcum? My uncle may have been abducted by the same people who killed that young man." I couldn't stop myself, and this time Carlton physically intervened. He put an arm around my shoulders, turned me away, and propelled me to his car.

"You can't do that," he whispered fiercely in my ear. "For Brett's sake, you must control yourself." He opened the door and assisted me into the passenger seat. "Stay in the car. I'll find out what I can."

"If I were a man, *I* could find out for myself."

"But you aren't, and I thank God for that." He slammed the door. He was back in ten minutes, and we drove into the black night toward Caoin House.

"Does he have any clues? Did he say anything?"

"You can't challenge authority that way, Raissa. It won't help your uncle's case. It only makes the sheriff and his men angry. And trust me—we want them on our side in this."

"Why? Sheriff Thompson couldn't investigate himself out of a blind alley."

Carlton sighed. "Sheriff is an elected position. The man who wears the badge is . . . approved by those who run the town. Be wary. This is deep water, and you'd better be able to swim if you rush to jump off the bank."

"I believe Brett must be alive. No one would steal a corpse." He had to be alive. And the accident wasn't an accident. Someone had caused my uncle to flip his car. Two possible reasons came to mind—either he had angered someone about John Henry Marcum and this was payback, or someone had taken him because he was valuable to them. "We'll likely get a ransom request."

"Excellent point," Carlton said. The edge in his voice caught my attention.

"You suspect someone!" I twisted so I could watch his profile. "Who?"

"Casting suspicion won't do any good right now. Let me just say, if Brett is still alive, we'll find him and bring him back."

When we turned down the driveway to Caoin House, I choked on a sob. When my tears had settled to a slow drizzle, Carlton spoke with great tenderness. "Brett is a tough old bird. I think you're correct. He's alive, and someone has taken him. Perhaps as a Good Samaritan or maybe for ransom. We'll know soon enough."

The rise and fall of his voice was comforting, and his reasonable tone and words helped me gather my raw emotions.

"Pray that we receive a ransom request. If they've taken him for another reason—"

"Because he stood up for a young man who happened to be a Negro?"

"Whatever their ulterior motives might be—it doesn't matter. The only thing that matters is getting Brett back safely."

"Yes." My voice was raspy and worn.

"You're tough, too, Raissa. More than you know. Now buck up. We have to face what awaits us at Caoin House. While our attention is on finding Brett, we have to assess how serious Reginald's injuries are and how we're going to deal with them."

We'd take care of Reginald until he was well, and for as long as he chose to stay. I didn't say it, but there was no other option. He was now a part of Caoin House, and I would nurse him back to health.

Travis stood at the top of the steps when we pulled up. He trotted down, moving with grace and agility, and opened my door. "Thank goodness you're home. Mr. Reginald is in a bad way. I have to find Mr. Brett, but I couldn't leave a wounded man alone."

"How badly is Reginald hurt?" Carlton asked.

"He's unconscious. Dr. Martin checked him over. We owe the doctor for his conscientiousness because he truly didn't want to be in Caoin House. He said his wife had a terrible experience here."

I ignored the comment. "Why didn't he take Reginald to the hospital?"

"He's better off here. There's nothing else they can do for him in the hospital." He cleared his throat. "Dr. Martin said if there was swelling on the brain, he might be permanently . . . injured. We were instructed to keep him quiet and calm."

"Did the doctor give any indication of time? When he might wake up?" I was desperate to talk to him.

"If he doesn't wake up in the next twelve hours, it won't be good." Travis looked everywhere but at me. "It's serious. When the brain swells, it can be . . . bad."

"I can't believe he survived with those injuries," Carlton said. He got out of the car and put the key in my hand. "I'll head back to the accident scene with Travis. You stay here and take care of Reginald."

"You can't leave me here alone with a man who might be dying. What if he gets worse? What if—" I broke it off before I humiliated myself. Now wasn't the time to be a coward.

"I'll leave you the car. If you need help, drive to the accident scene. The sheriff or his deputies will find me. Someone will help you."

I doubted that. Sheriff Thompson had made it more than clear that he viewed me as an intrusion. A woman who didn't know her place. If I were lynched, he wouldn't hunt for my killer either.

The key dug into my palm, I gripped it so hard. "Thank you, Carlton. Please, find Uncle Brett."

"Winona is on the way," Travis said. "She's bringing her son to help. I didn't know if we'd need a strong back, but if something should happen, he can get Reginald into the car."

"Go." I stepped back, unwilling to detain them but afraid to enter the house alone.

I wasn't trained in medicine, but Alex had written me more than once about friends who'd suffered concussions from shells and grenades. If the bleeding filled the brain cavity, even if it was drained off, there was always damage and most often death. If the pressure in Reginald's head became too great . . . I wished Alex had never included such vivid details.

Travis stared directly into my eyes. "Mr. Brett wouldn't concede defeat. Ever. That's why we'll find him, and Mr. Reginald will wake up soon. He'll wake up and be his old self."

"Don't lose hope," Carlton said. "Now, let us go. The more people looking, the better our odds. We'll be back as soon as we can."

The sun would be breaking in a few hours. Searching would be a lot more productive, but it might also be too late if Uncle Brett was severely injured. I watched them drive away with a sense of dread. The night sounds of birds and small animals scurrying were suddenly magnified. It made me ashamed to admit it, but I was afraid. Afraid of Caoin House and afraid for my friend and uncle.

The taillights of Travis's car had barely disappeared when Eli shifted from behind a tree in the oak grove. He wore the cavalry uniform, forever crisp and fitted to emphasize his physique. While I might have sympathy for him, I had no time for his games. He made no effort to come closer or to communicate. He merely watched.

"Go away!" I shouted. "Go away now!" I whirled and ran into the house, slamming and locking the door. The foyer echoed with emptiness. I was alone in the house with a seriously injured man and spirits I knew to be malevolent.

Reginald's room was on the same wing as Uncle Brett's, and I went there with great trepidation. I didn't want to see my friend helpless and possibly dying. I wondered why the doctor hadn't insisted on taking him to the hospital, but it was true that he would receive the best care here at Caoin House. Winona would help me organize professional nurses, and he would be given all that we could provide.

I tapped on the door out of habit and entered his room. A lamp burned on the bedside table. He looked so at peace, I feared he was dead. I rushed forward to find a pulse and stopped a foot from the bed. To my utter horror, the jigger had been placed in a rocking chair pulled close to my injured friend. The evil little monkey head, teeth bared, stared at me. Travis hadn't put the toy there. I didn't want to think who, or what, might have done so.

Ignoring the toy, I forced myself to the bedside. Reginald's olive complexion was ashen. A lump on the side of his head made me flinch. My mother had always said, though, that if the lump developed outward, then it was the best outcome of a blow to the head. That was surely little consolation to Reginald in his limbo state between life and death. The terrifying thought that the spirits in Caoin House might come to take him tormented me. I controlled myself. A pulse beat in his neck. The flow of his blood was steady and rhythmic. It was a good sign, and I would take whatever I could get.

"Reginald." I smoothed his hair back from his forehead and then picked up the cloth in a bowl of cool water Travis had left at the bedside. I stroked his face with the damp cloth, then put it on his forehead. Maybe cooling his brain would be helpful.

"You're going to be fine." I spoke with determination. "You'll wake up and be just like new, except for a terrible headache. The pain of the headache will be so severe it will nauseate you, but that will pass. You'll tell me what happened and how we can find Uncle Brett. I'm sure he's okay. We just have to figure out where he is." I hesitated. "And who has him. No one can help us but you, so you have to wake up soon."

I immersed the cloth in the cool water, wrung it out again, and reapplied it to his head. The swelling was just above his temple. In my mind's eye I could see the accident happen—the car traveling along in the dark tunnel of trees, the sand grabbing the front wheels and twisting them so that the forward impulsion of the car and the trapped wheels resulted in the car flipping over. Reginald's head must have struck the dash so hard it rendered him unconscious. Uncle Brett may have been thrown from the car.

Reginald's wound showed broken skin in a peculiar shape—rectangular. To pass the time as I cooled his forehead, I tried to think what along a car's dashboard could make such a mark. I'd examine the car closely when I got a chance.

I pushed the horrid little jigger out of the chair and kicked it under the bed.

Holding Reginald's hand, I talked to him. I spoke of New Orleans and Madam and the future. At last his regular breathing lulled me to near sleep. Still holding his hand, I leaned forward and let my upper body rest on the bed beside him. I wanted to stay awake, but I couldn't. I felt as if I were falling into total blackness, and I let go.

A clicking sound brought me to wakefulness. Reginald lay rigid in the bed, his eyes wide-open and unseeing. For a moment I thought he'd died, but the clicking came again. It took me a moment to realize his right hand was tapping on the bed frame. A distinctive pattern, one that was repeated over and over. Short staccato taps followed by longer ones.

Reginald was as still as death, except for his right hand, and it moved with a frenetic energy that terrified me, tap-tapping against the bed frame. It was as if Reginald had died, but his hand remained alive. His wide-open eyes stared blankly, and the tapping fingers communicated desperate need.

I wanted to push back from the bed, from the frantic fingers. My only thought was escape, but I couldn't move. Reginald's dancing fingers cast a spell on me. They wanted to communicate, those long and slender fingers so well manicured.

At last, the fear receded. As my logic took control, I recognized the possibility of Reginald's tapping fingers. The pattern was rhythmic, repetitive. In his military training, Alex had learned Morse code. He'd signed his letters to me with the dots and dashes that spelled out "I love you." Was it possible Reginald was trying to communicate in that manner?

I grabbed a pencil and pad from the desk near the bed and began to jot down the series of dashes and dots that were repeated over and over and over at an ever-increasing pace. I had no clue what the series might mean, but Uncle Brett kept a codebook in the library. At one point, before the telephone lines had been connected to Caoin House, he'd communicated with his business in town with a key and the code.

The more Reginald tapped, the more I believed he was communicating with me. He was giving me a clue or a direction or something. I had to figure out what his taps and silences meant. Before I lost my nerve, I ran out of the room and to the library. It took me long moments to find the book on the fourth shelf, but I grabbed it and ran back to Reginald's room. His hand had stilled. In the lamplight, he looked dead.

I checked his pulse and discovered that the steady beat remained calm and measured. For all the hand activity, his breathing and pulse were unperturbed. How was that possible? It was almost as if his hand had acted of its own volition. I could easily remember the sequence of sounds.

I opened the codebook, found the key, and translated. I, N, E, M, I, N, E, M, I, N, E. It was the same four letters over and over again. Inem, inem. It didn't make sense. I moved down the list of letters until I hit upon the right combination. Mine. *Mine.*

My heart grew to a thrumming lump that pushed the air from my lungs. Reginald's sightless eyes stared into nothing. His pale profile never changed, but I knew the person in the bed was no longer Reginald. Not now. Not any longer. Reginald was gone. He belonged to them now. To her. Mine. Eva had him in her grip, and she wanted me to know it.

If I was ever to find my uncle, I had to save Reginald. He had to be released from the hold Eva had on him. If he could awaken, he'd tell me what had caused the wreck.

CHAPTER
THIRTY-THREE

I'd never felt more alone and less competent to handle the task before me, but self-doubt had to be mastered. There was no one else to turn to. Winona would soon arrive. She would watch over Reginald, but it was up to me to solve the puzzle of Caoin House. If I wanted to save Reginald and find my uncle, the mystery about the past and what had happened to Eva, Elise, and the three young boys who'd died at Caoin House, as well as Robert, had to be solved. While Robert hadn't been the man I'd thought him to be, he still hadn't deserved to be murdered.

I had four clues—the button torn from a white shirt, the locket left behind with Eli's photograph scratched out, the daguerreotype of the semiclad young pirate, and the gruesome child's toy, the jigger that appeared in places it should not.

All but one of those items had come from the attic. Answers would be found in that dreaded place. I couldn't wait for Winona. I had to take action. If Eva was capable of manipulating Reginald's hand—and I had no doubt that she was behind the Morse code message—she was capable of doing much more to his unconscious body. She could possibly kill him. And would, without hesitation, if it suited her needs.

I kissed Reginald's cheek, urging him to hang on, and retrieved the jigger from under the bed. Fear and revulsion mixed as my fingers grasped the toy, but I fought back my qualms. Uncle Brett kept flashlights in the guest bedrooms, and I found one and strode through the silent house toward the third floor and the entrance to the attic. As I crossed the darkened ballroom, lit only by the stars and moon, my nerve faltered. Approaching the door at the top of the narrow stairwell, I wanted to wait for Winona to arrive and ask her to come with me. Too much was at stake for cowardly delay. I climbed the narrow steps.

A low, rasping sound came from behind the attic door, as if someone were moving furniture. My fingers clutched the doorknob, which was freezing on a hot summer night. I turned it slowly, pushed the door open, and stepped inside. The beam of light I swept across the room revealed strange and dangerous shapes. I fought to remember it was only furniture beneath the dustcovers. But it was more than chifforobes and trunks there. The room contained another entity. Something furious and deadly.

I walked farther into the room, and a hunched body scurried over the bare floor behind the furniture. The bony arm of the poor child reached to me from my imagination, but the flashlight beam revealed nothing but the ordinary clutter of an attic. I walked toward the trunks I'd been exploring when I'd found the photograph.

I put the jigger on the floor. "I've brought your toy back." If there was an entity in the attic who might help me, it was the boy.

"Child?" I asked. "I know you're angry, but I need your help. I don't know what happened to you or why you're here, but I need you. Unless you want to spend eternity in this attic, help me."

Silence. The attic held only heat and the smell of old things. The boy wasn't interested in finding the answers that might free him. My understanding of lingering spirits and whether they could be good, evil, or both came from my reading, and conversations with Reginald, who'd passed on what he'd learned from Madam Petalungro. The famed medium contended there were malevolent spirits who couldn't be helped and didn't want help. They fed off their power to terrify mortals and to wreak mayhem in the lives of those they'd targeted.

The entities at Caoin House wielded great power. They could move physical items. The necklace Winona had found in Isabelle's room and the jigger placed on the chair beside Reginald's bed were only two benign examples. Children had died in the house. And so had Robert. Were ghosts responsible? I didn't know.

The entity I identified as Eva left no doubt that she was malevolent. Whatever happened to her at Caoin House had left her furious, and her fury manifested in dangerous ways. She'd rendered me immobile on my last visit to the attic. And Eli, my gallant Confederate ghost, had powers of his own, appearing on the lawn and promising secrets that might be a trick.

The young boy, though, I hoped to reach. By nature, children were innocents. No child should spend eternity in a hot and dirty attic, hiding behind furniture and playing with a monkey head.

"I don't know if your name is Freddie or not, but I want to help you. Reginald and I both want to help. I know you visited him."

Something scuttled near the back wall. He was listening.

"I'm not sure I can change anything for you, but I will try. I believe if I can understand what happened in the past, I can bring justice. If it's true that injustice binds some spirits to this plane, then maybe I can set you free."

Movement and noise came from my right. I swung the flashlight and watched as the heavy cloth covering a small mountain of furniture slipped to the floor. I walked across the attic and shifted the beam across several dressers. Hatboxes, stacks of newspapers flaking and molding, and the smell of something dead and decomposing made me reluctant to step closer. But I did. I'd been through too much to back away now.

I pushed the newspapers aside, inciting an attack of sneezes, and burrowed beneath the heavy furniture. Tucked far back was a flat-topped trunk bound with leather straps. The monkey jigger sat atop the trunk, a key in its wretched mouth.

"Thank you," I whispered as I unlocked the trunk. It was possibly a trap. I'd investigate the trunk only to find something horrible or nothing at all. My actions were taken on faith, a belief that at least one spirit haunting the attic wanted me to find the truth.

I knelt beside the dusty trunk and opened the lid. A musky scent filled the air around me. An age-stained bit of white silk peeked from beneath the rough wool of a cheap, heavy coat. I removed the mud-crusted coat and several layers of newspaper and revealed a baby girl's heirloom silk christening gown. I pulled it out, and two incredible silk booties and a matching bonnet fell to the floor, along with a lace-edged handkerchief. EKW. Eva Kemp Whitehead.

I'd found a trunk with her things. Perhaps an answer would be there, also.

As I went through the old clothing, riding gloves, and boots, I tried to sense the woman Eva had been before her brutal murder. She'd demanded food for the starving women and children of Mobile. She'd been the jewel in the crown of Mobile society. A lover other than her husband had written her passionate letters. And she'd kept a photograph of a half-naked male prostitute. But who had she really been?

As I dug through the items of female and child clothing, I realized the trunk had been packed with an eye toward a trip. The items chosen were necessities, not luxuries, with the exception of the child's christening gown.

At the very bottom of the trunk, my fingers found the binding of a thick and heavy book. I removed the layers of clothes and trinkets and at last retrieved the book. I recognized the cover instantly. This was the big book Eva held on the tree branch in her magnificent portrait that hung in Uncle Brett's morning room.

The Book of Beloved was stamped in gold lettering on the front. The weight of the book told me it was more than printed pages, and when I opened the cover, I inhaled sharply. The first page revealed a daguerreotype of an Indian in a buckskin shirt and headdress. His lower body was naked, his penis on display. "Running Wolf, full-blooded Choctaw Indian, without blemish, attentive to the needs of any woman" was written below the photo. And then the price. Two dollars for the night.

If there had been any doubt about the pirate and his profession, *The Book of Beloved* made the truth clear. Though I knew I should hurry, I flipped the next page to find a cowboy. The young man took a swaggering stance, but his eyes were completely dead. "Cowboy Pete, horse wrangler, small scar on shoulder, can ride hard and gentle any mare. Two dollars for the night."

How many of these men had visited Eva while her husband was on the battlefield? And not only Eva, but many of the matrons of Mobile high society. The note I'd found included with the pirate's photograph had puzzled me, but no longer. It had referenced a substitution for the evening—at no charge. And Eva's endorsement of the pirate had been requested, something of value for the other ladies to know.

The Book of Beloved was a dirty secret Mobile society would want to keep hidden. At any cost. Possibly even the murder of a woman who may have threatened that secrecy. Eva Whitehead might never have been the victim of deserters, but of someone who meant to silence her. I understood now. She'd packed her trunk with the things she'd need to run with her child, to escape Caoin House and Mobile. She'd intended to take the book with her.

I flipped another page and stopped. My Confederate soldier stared up at me, dark eyes expressionless. His hair caught the flash of the camera's powder. One hand rested on the hilt of his saber, and the other held his hat. He stood in his tunic and boots and nothing else. "Caleb the Rebel, scars on back and face, a champion on the field of love. Two-fifty a night."

I sat back on the floor as if my joints had melted, dragging the book with me. Nothing I'd presumed was correct. This wasn't Eli. This was Eva's lover, no doubt the man who'd written her the stolen love letters.

Holding the book in my lap and the flashlight with one hand, I flipped through the pages. There were thirty-six men, all dressed as iconic figures from Roman gods to court jesters and even slaves. All half-nude with erect penises. All available—for a price—for an evening's entertainment. The flesh trade had flourished in Mobile, but this was directed at lonely women, not the more typical brothel for men. Whores and mistresses, kept under the very noses of their wives, were an acceptable way for a man to exercise his carnal pleasures. Women had never been allowed such freedom.

As I flipped the pages, I wondered at the boldness of this book. The photographs were minor works of art, the men posed to display their assets. The exquisite costume detail told of time and attention taken to create the fantasy that must have lessened the matrons' qualms about their activities.

Even the brief description of the men and their talents worked toward the high-society sensibility with wit and playfulness, a bit randy but conveyed with taste. The idea was rather genius. It wasn't hard to imagine how the book had been passed from house to house. The women made their selections, let the proprietor know, and the male prostitutes would appear at their homes at the appointed hour. Very discreet.

I turned back to the picture of Caleb, doing my best not to stare at what was so artfully exposed.

"Why are you here at Caoin House?" I asked him. "Why you and not Eli?"

A cold breeze drifted through the attic, forcing me instantly to my feet. I clutched the book in my arms. She was here. I couldn't see her, but I sensed her. My body reacted before my brain engaged. I put the book back in the trunk and piled the lingerie on top before I shut the lid. Moving slowly, I edged toward the stairs. Being trapped in the attic with Eva was more than I could handle.

I was ten feet from the door when it slammed shut. The sound reverberated in the room, and I wondered if it might wake Reginald from his unnatural sleep. Frozen on the spot, I forced my feet to move. The door might be shut, but I could open it and escape.

I focused the flashlight beam on the brass doorknob. I had only to step forward ten steps, grasp it, open the door, and ease down the stairs. Left foot, right foot. My concentration actually moved my feet. Tiny steps, but steps nonetheless. I reached out for the knob.

The bony arm of the child came from beneath a chest of drawers pushed against the wall beside my escape route. He tugged at the wide leg of my trousers with enough force to pull me off balance. I tried to right myself, but my feet caught in something, and I went down hard, knocking the wind from my lungs when I hit.

Gasping on the floor like a fish pulled from water, I had no idea if I was injured because the need for oxygen superseded everything else. When the bony arm of the little boy reached toward me, my survival instinct kicked in.

I scrabbled, crablike, ramming my body into a stack of wooden crates. The top one tumbled down, striking my shoulder on the way to the floor, where it exploded. The wooden cars of a toy train set, birds and turtles carved from cedar, and a *McGuffey's Eclectic Primer* struck my body. I snatched up the book as I hurtled to my feet and grabbed the doorknob. The door flew open with such ease that I almost fell backward again, but I righted myself and rushed down the stairs so fast I could easily have broken my neck.

When I cleared the ballroom and stairs to the main floor, I paused to catch my breath. Footsteps echoed in the hallway as someone approached. I whirled to face Winona, who had a tray in her hand. Her expression registered shock at my appearance.

"Miss Raissa, are you okay?"

"Yes," I said too quickly. "Yes, I think I am."

"Mr. Reginald is moving about. I think he'll awaken soon."

"Really?" I was afraid to believe something good might happen.

Winona stepped around me. "I'm going to prepare some broth for him. It would be good if you were with him when he opened his eyes. He'll likely be disoriented."

"Of course. Thank you, Winona."

"I'll make some coffee for you," she said. "I suspect you'll not be sleeping tonight, so you might as well drink some. Steady your nerves." She had begun to walk away when she paused. "Is there any word on Mr. Brett?"

"Carlton and Travis are searching with deputies and volunteers. They'll find him, and he'll be perfectly fine." Repetition might make it come true.

"He's a strong man, and he loves you and Miss Isabelle. Whoever has harmed him will come to a bad end. I feel it." Winona's look was fierce. "Mr. Brett won't leave this life. He'll come home to you."

"Thank you," I said, and I meant it. Winona kept her own counsel, but she was nobody's fool.

I hurried to Reginald's room to find my friend, his color much improved, stirring restlessly in the bed. The lump on his head had swollen even more, giving him a lopsided appearance, but I was glad to see color in his skin. His hand twitched on the coverlet, but there was no attempt to tap out Morse code. Did he even know the code? I'd have to ask when he regained his wits.

I took a seat in the chair beside the bed and realized I was still holding the primer. Out of habit I opened the cover. In a ragged scrawl, the words *Property of Horace Whitehead* centered the page. Then the date *1869*.

But Eva and Eli hadn't had a son. They'd had only Elise. And Eva had died in 1865 only weeks before the South conceded defeat.

Horace Whitehead. I knew the boy in the attic now. I'd assumed him to be the boy drowned in the swamp, but I'd been wrong. This was Eva's blood. I had to find out how he'd lived and died. The mortality rate for children in the 1800s was high, but Horace was a child left out of the Whitehead lineage. A bastard.

Eva had done a lot more than have an affair with the male prostitute. She'd conceived a child and passed it off as Eli's. But what had happened to the boy? No one had spoken of him. There was no record of his birth or childhood that I'd read or heard referenced. Elise was always noted as an only child.

The thin arm in the attic. The attachment to the gruesome jigger. My gut tightened as my worst fears scampered about my brain. With the example of John Henry Marcum so fresh in my mind, I dreaded to ask what Eli Whitehead had done to a bastard child who took his name.

CHAPTER THIRTY-FOUR

"Raissa?"

I looked up to see Reginald staring at me. He seemed to lose focus, his eyes rolling loosely about and finally closing.

I dropped the book and grasped his hand. "Reginald, thank God you're awake." The dire warnings by the doctor had hidden deep in the recesses of my mind. If he didn't wake, if his brain bled and filled the cavity, if the damage was internal . . . he could have so easily died.

He fidgeted in the bed and struggled to sit up.

"Don't!" I tried to pin him to the bed, but he was strong. Even in his weakened state, he had more power than I did.

The bedroom door opened, and a strapping young man stepped into the room and gently held Reginald to the bed. "Stop fighting," he said softly. "You'll hurt yourself worse." The young man's diction had the hint of Europe or some exotic location I couldn't pinpoint.

The sheer size of the young man must have registered with Reginald. He relaxed into the pillows.

"Who are you?" Reginald asked.

"I'm Framon, Winona's son."

I recalled Carlton's mentioning something about Winona's son being available to help, but no one had told me Framon was home from Paris. My old friend was a man now, an educated man wearing the latest fashion. And I was glad to see him. "Thank God you're here," I said as I grasped his hand.

"Mother told me what had happened. I'll do whatever I can," Framon said.

Introductions were polite, but I had urgent questions. "Reginald, what happened to Uncle Brett?" I didn't want to upset my friend again, but I had to find out what, if anything, he knew.

"They took him."

His words shook me to my very core. "Who?"

"Men. In white sheets. They jumped in front of the car. Brett swerved to avoid hitting two of them. The car went over." He tried to sit up again, but Framon gently pressed him back to the pillows. Reginald closed his eyes. Sweat popped out on his brow. I used the cool cloth to remove it, forcing myself to halt the questions.

"Steady," I whispered. "Be steady, Reginald. I need answers, but if you get upset, you won't be able to help Uncle Brett."

He nodded, and Framon relaxed his hold on Reginald's shoulders.

"Tell me from the beginning. What happened at Bienville Square?" I wanted to squeeze the facts from him, but I had to be thorough and hear it all. Every detail might be important.

"Bienville Square was a scene from hell. It was awful. That poor young man, hanging like that from an oak, his face distorted . . ." He took a deep breath. "There was an argument. Brett started to climb a ladder to cut John Henry down to take the body to the Negro funeral parlor, and these men tried to stop him. They were angry. They said the body should hang as an example to other uppity coloreds, to show them their place."

Beside me, I could feel the sudden tension in Framon's body, but he remained completely quiet at the bedside.

"Carlton warned me the situation was explosive," I said. "I saw Uncle Brett on the ladder, and you and Hubert fighting the riffraff away."

"Carlton was to keep you away from that scene." Reginald swallowed drily, and I held a spoon of water to his lips. He nodded. "The sound of the body hitting the ground is something I'll never forget."

My sympathies for John Henry had been pushed behind my worry for my uncle. "Did you recognize any of the men?"

"I don't know Mobile, so I didn't, but they knew Brett. They called him by name. And he did speak to one of them . . . Vernal. And there was a doctor, too. Not the one who came for the séance, but a different one. Brett called him Langdon or Langson or something."

"Langford. Langford Oyles." The coroner, like the sheriff, would have no real interest in finding the people responsible for John Henry's death.

"That's him."

"What did he say?"

"He said something like the Airlie family thought they could run over people in town, but they couldn't. Something about being rich didn't mean anything in the long run, and that the family members should learn their place."

That was directed at me. He'd not forgotten my demands to see the coroner's report. "He's not a pleasant man."

"They ganged up like they were going to hurt Brett, but for some reason they didn't." He coughed and went into a spasm that scared me badly enough to signal Framon to help me pull Reginald to a sitting position.

My friend took another sip of water, and when he was settled again, I picked up my questioning.

"Did anyone follow you and Uncle Brett home?"

"No. We were the only car on the road. It was late. We were driving slowly, so they must have gotten ahead of us and set up the ambush. I think Brett took his time driving because he needed to let the events of the evening settle. He told me a lot, Raissa. He's thinking of selling Caoin House, and based on what he explained, I can't say I disagree. There are lovely homes in New Orleans or along the Florida Gulf Coast with ports and river systems. You and he could live anywhere and build a life. Isabelle would go wherever he asked."

Thank God Isabelle hadn't been in the car with the two men, and I now understood Uncle Brett's reluctance to marry her. Still, the idea of selling Caoin House hit me hard. My uncle loved Caoin House, and it had become my home. But those were decisions to be made once Uncle Brett was safely home.

"What about the accident? The men stepped out of the brush on the side of the road—was there another car?"

"No."

"They were wearing white robes?"

"And strange pointed hoods that covered their faces." His eyes widened. "Brett hit the brakes and turned the wheel, intending to go onto the verge to miss running them down. The sand trapped the front wheels. The car bucked and flipped on its side. I was stunned and couldn't move, but I heard them come up to the car. One of them kicked me hard, and when I didn't react, they assumed I was unconscious or maybe dead. They came and pulled Brett from the car, and I heard them say something peculiar."

"What?" My heart fluttered.

"War means fighting, and fighting means killing."

Framon's hand tightened on the foot of the bed until his knuckles whitened.

"I don't understand." The quote was familiar but only vaguely. The men who caused a wreck and took my uncle didn't seem the type to be scholars.

"I tried to stop them from taking Brett, and they realized I wasn't dead. One of them came up and struck me in the head with the butt of his rifle. I'll remember his boots for the rest of my life." Reginald touched the huge lump on his temple. "He meant to kill me, and I was helpless to defend myself."

"They probably believed you were dead or so mortally wounded that you would never wake up. They could have shot you, but a gunshot might have alerted someone."

"*I* thought I was dead." Reginald wasn't being humorous.

"They got what they wanted." They had my uncle. Reginald was merely an inconvenience and not worth a bullet.

"Who's behind this?" Reginald looked up as the door opened and Winona brought the broth, some toast, and a cup of coffee for me.

"I'll find out. Things are not as we assumed here." I wanted desperately to tell him about *The Book of Beloved* I'd found and the secrets revealed, but the information was dangerous. Winona and Framon might be targeted if they knew, and I would not have that on my head. I would tell only Reginald and Uncle Brett. We were the inner circle. We would protect those who relied on us, and we would right the present and reveal the past.

While Winona assisted Reginald with the broth, I went to the library. What a luxury it was to have such a fine collection of books. The problem with finding the quote, though, was that I had no idea where to begin. It sounded vaguely military. I pulled down several historical military volumes, scanning as quickly as I could. My shoulders ached, and my eyes felt as if sandpaper had been rubbed across the corneas.

The library door opened, and Framon entered. He shut the door behind him. For the first time, I really looked at him. He was handsome, with golden skin with red tones, and the same strange green-gold eyes that Winona had. The boy I'd tagged after was still there.

"I know those words," he said. "War means fighting, and fighting means killing."

"What do they mean?"

"Before and after the Civil War, Indian children were stolen from the local tribes and sold as slaves. They may not have been called slaves, but that's what they were. The tribes that hid in the Tensaw swamps lost dozens of children. Boys and girls. Night riders wearing white sheets would come into the settlement, herd the people into the center of the village, and pick the children they wanted."

I couldn't follow what his story had to do with a quote about war, but I didn't interrupt.

"My grandfather told me the stories of how the night riders would repeat that quote as they made their selections, tearing children from the arms of their mothers and fathers. 'War means fighting, and fighting means killing.' It was a threat to the Indians to be quiet and not report the kidnappings. It meant the white men would come and kill us all."

"Where does the quote come from?"

"Nathan Bedford Forrest."

Forrest was a revered Confederate general. Eli Whitehead had ridden into battle with him in Tennessee. Eli had been campaigning with Forrest when Eva was so brutally murdered. Forrest was also linked with an organization known for terrorizing nonwhite people, the Ku Klux Klan.

"What do you know about Eva Whitehead?" I asked Framon.

He shook his head. "The Native people didn't kill her, though we feared we would be blamed. My grandfather said the whole tribe moved deeper into the swamps after Eva's murder."

"Did he say what happened?"

Framon looked past me to the library window. I turned, and Caleb, the man I'd mistaken for Eva's husband, stood framed in the window. Behind him, the first light of dawn could be seen graying the summer horizon.

I faced Framon again, only to find his gaze had wandered to the shelves of books. Had he seen Caleb? I didn't think so.

"Who was the man called Caleb? You know him, don't you?"

His smile was slow. "My great-uncle."

His answer took me completely by surprise. "He was a . . ."

"Slave who was forced to be a prostitute. He was one of the stolen children."

"Do you know who stole him?"

"Morsey Whitehead, Eli's grandfather."

The web of connection with this young man and his mother, Winona, the Whitehead family, and Caoin House made me feel like a sea turtle trapped in the strangle nets of the fishermen that trolled the Gulf of Mexico. I'd seen the wounded turtles, so ancient and magnificent, washed up on the shores, dying of the wounds from the nets, some still trapped and unable to free themselves. I owned that feeling now.

"Eva and Caleb had a son, didn't they?"

Now it was his turn to be surprised. "Few people know this. He was held here, in this house, a child prisoner. Eva tried to keep him safe here at Caoin House. She successfully hid her pregnancy until she gave birth and then pretended he was the child of a distant relative. When Eli returned and she was murdered, the boy disappeared. Some said that Eli built a special room for him and never allowed him out of it. It's told that he grew to be a man in that room and died, surrounded by the toys of his childhood. Some of my people believe he was starved to death."

The bony arm of the child shooting out from the furniture. The hiding and cringing. Was that spirit in the attic all that was left of a child so horribly abused that he slunk around like an animal? What had Eli Whitehead done? I wasn't certain I wanted to find out.

"How did Caleb die? You know he's buried in the cemetery, in neither the family nor the slave section. In a place alone."

"I know why, too."

I looked outside to find Caleb still at the window. He wore the Confederate tunic, and now his uniform was torn and tattered, covered in mud and blood. I thought I heard the vaguest whisper: "Secrets." I couldn't be certain, though. "What happened?"

"Caleb ran away from his master in Mobile and stole the book of photographs, a book showing all the male prostitutes who serviced the society women of Mobile. He brought it here to Eva. As insurance for their safety. As long as they had the book, they wouldn't be killed because Mobile society had to keep the secret of the book hidden. Caleb and Eva planned to take their son and daughter and flee Caoin House and the South. Caleb was at last a free man. Horace and Elise were also free. They had only to escape."

"Wait!" I stopped him. "Elise was also Caleb's child?"

He nodded. "But Eli didn't know. He'd been home at the time she was conceived. She could have been his, and she looked so like Eva that he accepted her as his daughter. The boy, Horace, had golden skin and the green-gold eyes of the Mobile Choctaws."

"Eli found out the truth about Elise's lineage on the night of her wedding, didn't he?"

"Elise knew all along who her real father was, and she intended to announce her heritage *after* vows were exchanged with Charles DeMornay. Once she was wed, the revelation that she came from impure blood and wasn't a Whitehead was punishment for her father and her husband. Elise might have been born the daughter of a slave, but at the time of her wedding, she was supposedly a free woman. Eli had kept her chained to him her entire life. He'd selected her husband, and he meant to force her to marry DeMornay, a man well known in the region for his peculiar appetites. It was rumored the city's prostitutes feared him."

"Eli would marry his daughter to a libertine or, even worse, a sadist?"

"Money, power, social standing. Eli would, and did, many terrible things to acquire and maintain all three. He'd raised a daughter bitter and angry at his unyielding control. He wasn't aware she'd learned the black secrets of the Whitehead past. She'd found *The Book of Beloved*, and once she was wed, she intended to wreck the future of both households."

"So that's why there are no photographs of Elise in the house."

"Yes, Eli had every likeness of Elise destroyed. He murdered her by throwing her out the third-floor window, and then he set to erase all evidence of her. There is no grave for her in the cemetery."

Reginald and I had both noticed that, but we'd assumed, wrongly, that her marker might have, over the years, been destroyed and never replaced. The truth was far more difficult to grasp. "Eli murdered his entire family."

"They were not *his* family."

"That's not exactly true. Eva was his wife. He believed Elise to be his daughter and raised her. Surely he once loved her. And the innocent boy . . ." The bony arm, the darkened skin indicating bruising. Eli had tortured an innocent child because of his bloodline. It was monstrous.

"My people believe Eli came home unexpectedly and found Caleb with Eva, planning their escape. They were able to hide *The Book of Beloved* before Eli killed them both. Eli's alibi was tight—he was fighting the Yankees in Tennessee with General Forrest. He took the boy and left Elise to sit beside the body of her mother. Eli played the role of the grieving husband to the hilt. Elise was too young to tell anything different. Caleb's body was never found, and the young boy, Horace, was never seen again by anyone. The presumption was that he'd been returned to his relatives by Eva. In those days, people disappeared frequently, so no questions were asked."

"There's a marker for Caleb in the Whitehead cemetery."

"Caleb's grave is empty."

"But the headstone?"

"My grandfather commissioned it, and we placed it there during one of the times when the house was up for sale. We wanted a reminder of Caleb at Caoin House. He loved Eva, and he fathered two children here. All died tragically."

Now I understood the destruction of Eli's image in the locket Winona had found. Someone, perhaps Horace, had attempted to give us a clue, but we hadn't interpreted it correctly. I needed to sit down. "Why didn't Winona tell me any of this?"

"There are those who listen, but most do not. We had to *know* you would listen. My mother doesn't waste her breath."

"Why are you telling me now?" I asked.

"You're in danger. And your uncle, too. Reginald as well."

I couldn't deny that. Reginald had narrowly escaped death, and Uncle Brett was missing still. "Do you know who abducted my uncle?"

He shook his head. "But I'll help you find out."

"How?"

"With great care. Your uncle's life depends on our discretion and the speed with which we find the head of the snake. We must strike hard and fast. Remember"—his expression held anger and sadness— "war means fighting, and fighting means killing. The past has come full circle."

I glanced out the window to find that Caleb had begun to retreat into the haze of a hot summer dawn. He floated backward, then paused beneath an oak limb. He lifted his hand as if he meant to signal me, but the sun broke the horizon with a golden sliver of light, and he was gone.

CHAPTER
THIRTY-FIVE

Winona fried three skillets of bacon, preparing a huge breakfast for the volunteers who'd searched all night for Uncle Brett. Before I had a chance to talk to her, the house was flooded with men. Carlton and Travis had returned, bringing a dozen members of a cobbled-together search party with them. Winona had known this, and I didn't ask how.

As the men ate rashers of bacon, sausage, dozens of eggs, biscuits, sawmill and red gravy, and grits, I paced on the front porch. I couldn't eat while Uncle Brett might be suffering.

Carlton came out the door with a cup of coffee in one hand and a biscuit wrapped in a clean linen cloth for me. "You have to eat something. If you collapse, how will that help Brett?"

I took the biscuit and, after the first bite, realized I was starving. I wolfed it down and accepted the sweet, light coffee Carlton had made for me. He'd taken the trouble to learn what ingredients I liked.

"Did you find anything to indicate what happened to my uncle?" I dreaded asking. If he knew, he would have already told me.

"Searchers are fanning out through the underbrush," he said. "Now that the sun is up, the search will speed up considerably. We'll find him."

"Was he dragged from the car? Surely there were tracks, something the sheriff could follow. A two-hundred-pound man can't disappear, leaving no evidence."

Carlton maneuvered me away from the doors and windows. "The sheriff's men mucked up the scene so badly we couldn't track anything. Don't worry, though—I believe your uncle was taken for ransom or to achieve some goal. He won't be harmed unless we fail to deliver what the kidnappers want. And we won't fail in that. No matter what it is, we will give it to them."

Carlton's assurance took the sharpest edge off my anxiety, but I was far from reassured. People who would cause a wreck and callously slam an injured man in the head with a rifle butt would take other nefarious actions. If murdering my uncle served their purposes, that's what would happen. Wealth didn't protect us, because we were outsiders and had proven ourselves as such.

"How will we find him?" I so wanted to believe Carlton had some magic. "Reginald can't remember anything useful."

"He's lucky to be alive."

"They believed he was either dead or dying or they would have cut his throat."

"These are obviously not criminal geniuses at work," Carlton said. "There will be evidence we can find."

"Carlton, there's something I should—"

The glint of a car passing among the trees caught my eye. As the vehicle came clearly into view, I realized it was the sheriff's car. He drove at a high rate of speed. As soon as the car stopped, Sheriff Thompson stepped out of the vehicle and Carlton bolted down the steps to meet him. Thompson clutched something in his fist.

Carlton took the piece of red material from the sheriff's hand and looked up at me. I knew what it was then—Uncle Brett's pocket square. He'd tucked it in his jacket yesterday morning as we left for the boating adventure. I ran down the steps and took it from Carlton, checking for and finding the initials *BA* embroidered onto a corner of the silk. "Was there a note?" I asked the sheriff.

He took Carlton's elbow and moved him away. Clearly Sheriff Thompson had no intention of speaking with me about Uncle Brett. I wanted to fight for my right, but I stepped back. Uncle Brett's life hung in the balance.

Sheriff Thompson looked at me and blanched. It was then I felt another presence. Framon stood at my elbow. He'd come up so silently, I hadn't heard him. He spoke softly so Thompson couldn't hear. "It's a ransom request, isn't it?" Framon watched the sheriff with studied contempt. "He probably wrote it himself."

His suspicions might not be far from the truth, but I couldn't afford to say so. "Carlton will find out. I'm just a woman, and no one speaks to me."

"You share that honor with the Indians who live here. They're not considered to be fully human, like a woman."

Carlton shook the sheriff's hand and strode quickly to me. "It's exactly as I anticipated. They have Brett."

"Who has my uncle?"

"The men who hanged John Henry. Right now, identity doesn't matter. All that matters is getting Brett back unharmed."

"How much do they want?" I asked. My uncle was wealthy, and Carlton would have access to the funds. We would pay and be done with this.

"That's a problem," Carlton said, and the worry was evident on his face. "There was no request for money. The note merely said Brett was alive." Carlton gripped my upper arm. "I'm afraid this is not good. They should have asked for something, and then we would have asked for proof of life. This pocket square is definitely Brett's, but it is not a guarantee that he's alive."

For a moment I felt the earth tilt, but Carlton supported me until I regained my balance. "Brett is alive. I'm certain of it. If he were dead, I'd know."

The pity on Carlton's face made me angry, but it was Framon who spoke to the lawyer. "These men who hold Mr. Brett, do you know them?"

"I have suspicions but no proof."

"They're the men who lynched the colored man?"

"Yes, I believe that to be true," Carlton said. "Without proof, though, there's no legal recourse. And let me warn you, slander isn't tolerated in Mobile. The courts have dealt with such things harshly."

"The law has never been a friend to my people—no disrespect, Mr. McKay," Framon said. "The courts have no interest in justice where the Choctaw are concerned. We have our own methods." He pivoted and crossed the front lawn, disappearing into the oaks now filled with the shadows of the morning sun.

"So Framon has returned from Paris," Carlton said. "I'm sure Winona is delighted to have him back. I'd hoped Europe would take the edge off his anger."

Framon's anger wasn't my concern. "Carlton, if you know the people who have Brett, could you talk to them? He isn't dead."

Carlton took my elbow and maneuvered me up the stairs and into the cool front hall of Caoin House.

"There is something very wrong here, Raissa." Carlton's voice was a low whisper. He glanced in all directions to be certain we were alone. "None of this makes sense. It isn't about money. Has your uncle found anything here at Caoin House that might anger highly placed people in Mobile?"

"Like what?" I knew exactly what Carlton was referring to, but for my uncle's safety, I would never admit that I'd found *The Book of Beloved* and the host of secrets that would rock Mobile society. I'd known the information was dangerous, but I hadn't anticipated the lengths to which someone would go to protect those secrets. If Uncle Brett was not already dead, he would be instantly killed. And I would likely be the next target.

"The sheriff said there was a note with the pocket square."

"Where is the damn note?" My fury eclipsed my common sense, and I jerked open the front door and went to the porch. "I have a right to see it."

Carlton followed, equally angry. "And what right would that be?" He maneuvered me to the far corner of the porch and kept glancing back, as if someone he distrusted might be spying on us. "The note was delivered to the sheriff, Raissa. I'll try to make him show it to me, but that's not a given. Sheriff Thompson is angry with Brett and with you." He stared unflinchingly at me. "He won't say why, but he has a real burr under his saddle about you."

I had no intention of confessing my actions to Carlton. I'd done nothing wrong, except question the authority of the coroner, a man I now knew to be involved in illegal activities, including murder. "Let Thompson be angry. We've broken no laws."

"Oh, laws have nothing to do with how things operate here, and you know it. Now put aside all of that foolishness, and let's concentrate on what will save Brett." His face softened. "I don't want to be harsh, but this is serious. Brett's life depends on what we do next and how we do it. If there's anything you found or heard about, please tell me."

"I've found nothing except that horrid jigger and some old lingerie."

"What did Reginald learn at the séance that he failed to tell the rest of us?"

"Sheriff Thompson and the men who are holding Uncle Brett are afraid of what a ghost said at a séance?" My voice was laced with ridicule. "Invite them to Caoin House, and let them see for themselves."

Carlton's hands grasped my upper arm. I feared he might shake me, he was so intense.

"This isn't a joke. The word is out that Brett engaged with some spirits. It was ill advised for him to have Dr. Martin and his wife and the Pauls in attendance, but Brett is too hardheaded to listen to me. Now the hornet's nest is stirred. Someone out there thinks Brett is onto a secret, and it is one they're willing to kill for. What did Reginald learn during the séance?"

The look in Carlton's eyes, the desperation of his hold on my arms, spoke of his deep worries for Uncle Brett. "The ghost of the young boy from the séance isn't one of the children of former owners who died here at Caoin House."

"Then who is it?"

I forced calm through me. "He is Eva Whitehead's son, Horace. Eli murdered him, perhaps here in this house. Just as Eli murdered Eva and, ultimately, Elise. The big secret is that Eli Whitehead was a murderer who killed anyone who came between him and what he viewed as the honor of his name." That much I could tell Carlton, without revealing anything about the book. While this accusation might prove shocking to Mobile society, it began and ended with Eli Whitehead and involved no one alive today. This was speculation derived from a séance. People would likely scoff at it. They might even whisper behind my back. I didn't care.

"How do you know this?" Carlton asked. "Is there proof?"

"Absolutely none. The ghosts told Reginald, and he told me."

"If there was just a bit of evidence to back this up, I might have something to take to Brett's abductors that would satisfy them."

"I'm sorry. There's nothing except the word of a ghost."

"I'll speak with our resident medium when he's feeling better. Do you think the ghosts will reveal more to Reginald when he's up to another séance?"

I hated lying to Carlton, but if he was the messenger to the men holding Uncle Brett, he had to believe what he was selling. "The ghosts are gone. Reginald heard their complaints and sent them on their way. There's no way to contact them now."

"The men holding Brett will want something more substantial."

"Then we have nothing to offer them, except money. Reginald can't undo what's been done. He'll get no more information from any of the ghosts. They're banished. Caoin House is free of the past."

"I'll speak with Thompson. I hope this is enough to satisfy the kidnappers."

"I do, too. Thank you, Carlton." I hoped with all my heart he could convince Thompson, who I had no doubt could speak with the kidnappers whenever he chose.

And as soon as Uncle Brett was home safely, I intended to find out who in Mobile had so much to lose by the secrets in this old house. Uncle Brett's abductors would pay. There was obviously something in Eva's murder and *The Book of Beloved* that was acutely important, and knowing the bloodline obsession in Mobile, I suspected what it might be. Birthright in Mobile might not be as clear as some families wanted to claim.

Duty pulled me into smoothing out the running of the house. A private nurse arrived to tend to Reginald, and the hall clock struck two o'clock before I had time to return to his room. I'd packed lunches for the searchers, drawn maps of the property, consulted with Carlton and Winona, and finally escaped the hive of activity in the kitchen to check on my friend.

As I went down the empty corridor to his room, I had the unsettling sense that someone was watching me. The ghosts were not banished from Caoin House—but I hoped they would remain hidden for the time being. I'd been up for nearly thirty-two hours without sleep, and my nerves were taut. If Reginald continued to improve, that would be a huge load off my shoulders.

I tapped lightly on the door and stepped into the room. "Reginald—" The bed was empty. There was no trace of my friend. Even the dirty clothes he'd been wearing were gone. Only the rumpled sheets and an empty tray containing the remnants of a sandwich and coffee indicated he'd been in the room.

"Damn!" Too late, I knew where he was. Off with Framon. And they'd deliberately slipped away from me. "Damn, damn, damn!"

CHAPTER
THIRTY-SIX

Winona was in the kitchen washing the mountain of dishes, the result of feeding numerous search volunteers. She looked as exhausted as I felt. "Did Framon say where he was going?" I tried to sound casual, though my heart was pounding.

She shook her head. "He knows what he's about. I don't question him."

"I believe he and Reginald left together." My panic was contained.

"He has my car."

Her lack of worry grated on my nerves. "Reginald just came out of unconsciousness. He shouldn't be out of bed."

"They may save Mr. Brett," she said. "Framon thought it was urgent. I trust him."

She was right. If anyone could find Brett, I believed it would be Framon. The young man knew both the history and topography of the region. He was acutely aware of the forces at work. And Reginald had a talent for watching people's reactions. He caught the twitches, aversions, and tells that frequently gave away the truth. He would help

Framon. But I wanted to be with them, to help find my uncle. "Did they say where they were going?"

She shook her head. "I didn't ask. Mr. Reginald took sandwiches and vacuum flasks of coffee." She hesitated. "Mr. Reginald sounded . . . okay. He was lucid and clear. Framon will watch over him."

"Did they say when they would be back?"

"No."

It miffed me that they'd left me behind, but the logical part of my brain understood they'd slipped out when it was opportune. I'd been busy. As much as I wanted to go to the search site, it was best I stayed at Caoin House.

"Can I help prepare food?" I asked.

Winona looked around the kitchen. "You should rest. You've been up too long."

My eyes were dry, and a throb of pain had moved from the base of my skull to my forehead. Even so, I wasn't sure I could sleep. "Will you wake me if Framon and Reginald come back? Or if Carlton shows up?"

"I will."

I dragged myself up the stairs and to my bedroom. Winona had made my bed, and I stepped out of my clothes and fell on top of the soft comforter. The balcony doors were open, and the light murmur of conversation, the words indistinguishable, came from the oak grove where searchers took a break. At times urgency lifted the voices more clearly to my bedroom, but not long after I stretched out, a heavy lethargy came over me. Sleep took me with a swirl and tug as constant as the tidal pull of the ocean.

In my dreams, I went back to Wassaw Island, a wilderness paradise off the Georgia coast. The summer sunshine and the tang of salt on the air filled me with awareness of the preciousness of each minute. I time-traveled in my dream to the days I'd been invited as a guest of the George Parson family to vacation on the island, which was littered with cannonballs from Union shelling.

The Parsons were friends of Uncle Brett, and as his niece, I'd received many invitations to visit the primitive barrier islands with the sand dunes, palmettos, and sea oats. I'd loved those trips, especially after Alex had been called up to serve and was sent overseas. The sandy island beach was as close as I could get to Europe, to the battlefields where Alex hunkered in foxholes or charged toward the enemy. I stood on the beach and stared beyond the Atlantic horizon and imagined what my husband did so far from home.

In my dream, and I knew I was dreaming, Alex walked barefoot in the sand toward me. The wind whipped his white shirt, and his slacks were rolled up to his calves to avoid the surf. A strand of his fine, dark hair hung in his eyes, but the wind lifted it. He was whole and perfect and happy as he came to me.

"Be happy, Raissa," he said when he'd stopped a few feet from me. He approached no closer.

"I miss you." Time had sealed my misery and grief into a cyst, but it ruptured, and the longing for Alex almost brought me to my knees. "Please, don't leave me."

"Life is only a transition. And it is brief."

"Take me with you." I would go with him. I would leave my body on the bed and take his hand and never look back.

"It's not your time."

"I don't want to stay without you."

He looked toward the ocean and the sound of the surf. "It's not your time, Raissa. You have much to do. My work was finished, and now I must go on to the next episode."

I thought I'd let Alex go. Little by little, I'd allowed life to creep back over me, to pull me into the small joys of each day, the pleasures of my uncle's company, my writing, the fresh strawberries from the garden Travis tended. Little by little my body had awakened from grief to joy. Those pleasures were nothing compared to the loss of Alex and the life we'd planned.

"I could kill myself and meet you."

He laughed, and the sun fanned the small wrinkles at the corners of his eyes. "No, you won't."

"But I want to."

"The pain grows easier with time. You won't harm yourself because you are not done yet."

"No, I won't." It was foolish to pretend otherwise.

"Beware, Raissa. There's danger near you." He looked out to sea again, and his stance changed, as if he heard someone calling his name. He leaned toward it, but then turned back. "Love doesn't die. It changes, but it doesn't die."

He was gone, and I was left with the taste of salt on my lips, my own tears mingled with a gift from the ocean.

I woke to a penetrating silence all around me. When I went to the balcony to look over the grounds, everyone had left. The oak grove was empty. Either the men had gone back to search again, or my uncle had been found. I threw on clean clothes and hurried downstairs. Winona's kitchen was scrubbed and spotless, and it echoed with emptiness. The afternoon heat settled over the house. I felt as if a spell had been cast. The house had shunned all other guests. I was alone.

A sudden noise came from the stairwell. I knew it instantly. It was the clacking of the dreadful jigger. I wasn't alone in the house, after all. I should have known better. Caoin House was never empty. The spacious old rooms were beleaguered with secrets and unhappy spirits.

The jigger clacked, a series of pulses. *Mine.* I knew the dots and dashes, the Morse code. *Mine.*

As I forced myself up the stairs, I couldn't be certain I wasn't still asleep. Sounds came to me, but they were muffled. The clacking of the jigger, the only clear and distinct noise, moved rapidly ahead of me, now on the third floor. My destination was the attic, whether I wanted to go or not.

When I entered the ballroom, the light changed. From the warm glow of the afternoon sun, the columns and hardwood floor took on the shadings of midnight. The white sheer draperies gusted playfully at the tall windows, casting dancing moon shadows across the room. The table where we'd held the séance remained in the center of the space, and the chairs were drawn back, as if waiting for someone to arrive and be seated.

The clacking jigger had fallen silent, but the room pulsed with another entity.

I wanted nothing so much as to run back down the stairs and out the front door of Caoin House. I wanted the sunshine, the oaks. I wanted Alex and the ocean's kiss on my skin. I wanted anything except to walk up the steep flight of stairs and open the attic door.

One foot after the other, I climbed the stairs. My hand gripped the brass doorknob and twisted. The attic door opened on hushed hinges. I stepped into the space and inhaled dust and the faint traces of a lemony perfume.

"Who's here?"

The oppressive heat made me short of breath, and the stillness was like a gauzy layer of damp fabric across my mouth and nose. Dragging in air became a chore.

Movement in a dark corner of the attic made me whirl, but I found only the draped furniture and heavy air. Whoever was in the room had no intention of facing me head-on. I couldn't tell if it was the child or Eva, or perhaps someone else. Someone I might not want to meet.

"I know what happened to Elise." The room inhaled my words.

I tried again. "I want to help."

A curtain fluttered at one of the vented windows, and I looked through the slats to the oak grove three floors below me. Caleb stood between the rows of oaks, his uniform once again clean and pressed. He doffed his hat.

"I know who killed you, Caleb," I said. "Eli Whitehead. He murdered his entire family. His wife, his daughter, his son. All of them." The truth sat like a stone on my chest. "He was an evil man."

A trunk lid banged open. When I whipped around, I saw the boy. He stood by the trunk that had contained *The Book of Beloved*. "Horace, I won't hurt you." He didn't run. I could clearly see his gaunt body and painfully thin legs.

"He'll hurt you." He backed into the shadows. "Run away."

"Where are you buried?" I would find his remains and put them in the family cemetery, where he should be, beside his mother and sister.

He shook his head. "Run! Before it's too late."

He disappeared, but the trunk remained opened. I went to it and removed *The Book of Beloved* from beneath the layers of lingerie. Reginald, Framon, Carlton, and my uncle would understand the value of the book. They would agree with me that lancing the boil of the past was the only way to put the present to rights.

I would carry the book to the library, and by the time I did, my uncle would be safely returned. I negotiated with God, though I knew such efforts were wasted. I'd tried to safeguard Alex's life with such bargains. And failed miserably.

Cradling the book, I stood up to leave, but some fabric at the top of the lingerie pile stopped me. Or at least a dark stain on white cotton did. I hadn't noticed the stain when I'd previously been in the trunk. I picked up the cloth and shook it out. It was a man's white dress shirt, bloodstained on one shoulder. My brain hadn't registered the significance of the shirt, but my gut immediately did. I examined it more closely.

The placket had been torn, and a swatch of fabric and button were missing. Exactly like the piece of fabric and small pearl-white button I'd found on the roof.

Heart pounding, I closed the trunk and sat on the lid. The fresh bloodstain raised the possibility that it belonged to Robert's murderer. I folded the shirt and placed it on top of the book of photographs.

Now I had two important leads to show Uncle Brett as soon as he came home.

Winona brought tea to the library, and I sat at Uncle's desk, sipping the hot liquid, hoping to clear the fog from my thoughts. *The Book of Beloved* was safely tucked behind a stack of biographies of people so old and dull, I expected they hadn't been touched since my uncle put them on the shelf.

I'd matched the piece of cloth and button to the bloodstained shirt and placed both into a drawer in my uncle's desk. I was no detective, but I could read the evidence—there had been a fight between Robert and someone else. In the fray, the button had been torn away and the bloodstain acquired. The questions were, who did the shirt belong to, and how did it get into the trunk in the attic of Caoin House?

When I'd finished my tea, I went upstairs to my dresser drawer and picked up the locket that had been left in the house the night it was ransacked. Clicking it open, I studied the picture of Eva and the defaced image of Eli. The obliteration of Eli had been Eva's doing. Or perhaps Elise or even Horace, the child prisoner, had lashed out at the man who tortured them. So many people had hated Eli, and for good reason.

But why would any of the unhappy spirits in the house target Robert Aultman, a visitor with no connection to Caoin House or the past? Robert was lured to the rooftop—neither ghost nor man could haul a fully grown man across the slippery slate. Robert was a con man, perhaps, but he'd been in Mobile a mere few days. Not long enough to earn an enemy who wanted him dead.

Robert's death was tied, somehow, to Caoin House and the events of the past, but I couldn't make the pieces fit together, no matter how I twisted and turned them.

When I'd checked the coroner's report, I'd written down the names and address of Robert's family. I retrieved my notebook from my bedroom, making a quick tour of the house. Everything was still and quiet. Winona was busy in the kitchen, and I hurried back to the library and locked the door. I didn't know what a long-distance phone call would cost, but I'd pay Uncle Brett back from the money I received from the publication of my short story.

Hand shaking as I dialed the operator, I inhaled and steadied my voice as I asked to be connected with Robert's parents in Jacksonville, Florida. I could only hope they had phone service.

When Mrs. Aultman answered the phone, I introduced myself and expressed sympathy for the loss of her son. She was clearly puzzled at my call, and I did my best to explain how I knew Robert.

"I'm so sorry to intrude on your grief, but there are things about his death that . . . trouble me."

"None of it made sense to me." Her shaky voice was laced with anger. "Robert was excited about the future. He was a great admirer of Mr. Airlie's steam power and had high expectations of aligning himself with the inventor. The war was over, and he was beginning a new life."

I blundered into what I needed to know. "I know Robert had been in some trouble with the law—"

"What are you talking about?" Mrs. Aultman's voice was sharp through her tears. "My son was never in trouble. He was a decent man who was highly regarded by the entire community."

"But the coroner's inquest report?" I wasn't about to be diverted from my quest. "You read it?"

"My husband demanded a copy of the report, and we read it together. I don't have a clue what you're going on about. Robert had no enemies, and he'd never been in trouble with the law. He conducted himself with honor. There was no one who wished him harm, and there was nothing in the coroner's report that said otherwise."

This was more difficult than I'd anticipated. "I only want to know if someone from his past could have wished him harm."

"My son was a good man. I don't know what you're implying, but I won't hear it. What I know is that my boy went to a party at your uncle's home, and he fell to his death, without explanation. Now here you are calling and implying that he was less than an upstanding man. Shame on you. Shame on you." She slammed the phone down.

Line noise hummed in my ear.

Dr. Langford Oyles had been in charge of the inquest. One report was filed in his office, but he could have composed a different report for the Aultman family. Based on what I'd learned about how things worked in Mobile, it was possible the coroner had prepared a special report for the Aultman family. But if that were the case, the Mobile report had been written specifically for someone in Mobile to read.

I remembered how easily I'd bluffed my way into Oyles's office to read the report. He'd questioned my desire to see it, but he'd quickly given in and left the room. He could easily have dismissed my thin excuse and sent me packing. But he hadn't.

Two systems were at work in Mobile. One for the average citizen, and one for the elite. Those who pulled the strings could manipulate something as simple as a coroner's inquest report—and much more. But why? What reason would anyone have for painting Robert Aultman as unsavory? Who would benefit from such an action? Who might read the report?

Uncle Brett.

If my assumption was correct, and Robert's reputation had been distorted and maligned for my uncle's benefit, then it followed that the person behind the change in the coroner's report and Robert's death had attended the party.

I pulled the white shirt from the desk drawer and examined it in the library's sunny window. A faint pale stain that I'd missed on initial inspection was on the left cuff. I would take the shirt to Winona and ask about the stain.

My fingers reached for the door lock when half a dozen books tumbled off the library shelf and hit the floor. *The Book of Beloved* slid from its hiding place and landed on top, the page open to a photograph of a young man in a rough cotton shirt. "Tom the slave. Brand on right shoulder. He can pick a sack of cotton and still pleasure the wenches. Two dollars."

The young man in the photo was handsome, with light skin and the features of his white ancestors. He was a child of mixed race, and apparently he'd been sold into prostitution. How a father could pamper and raise one child and sell another was beyond my comprehension. Blood and race.

A breeze fluttered the curtain near me, and I looked out to see Caleb standing now four feet from the window.

The pages of *The Book of Beloved* ruffled but didn't turn. Tom looked out from the page. He was a handsome man with carefully schooled features that revealed none of his thoughts or personality. The book fluttered again, and the photograph of Tom slipped free and fell to the Oriental rug.

After picking up the photograph, I took it to the kitchen with the shirt. Winona had worked for my uncle almost since he'd bought the house. Her family and friends worked for and among the elite of Mobile. She might have more answers.

I paused at the kitchen door and watched her. She stood at the counter chopping onions and celery for a large bowl of chicken salad. She'd already deboned the boiled chicken and diced it.

My hand trembled slightly as I held out the photograph of the half-naked male prostitute named Tom. "What do you know about this man?"

The knife never missed a slice as she chopped the celery. "Tom was a legend in Mobile. I thought all evidence of him had been destroyed."

"How was he a legend?"

"He was the son of a prominent Mobile businessman, born into slavery. His father thought it amusing to sell him into prostitution when he was little more than a boy. As the war was ending, he escaped from his master, along with my ancestor, Caleb. Caleb came for Eva and the children, and Tom went north."

"What happened to him?"

Winona stopped chopping. "No one knows. He was never heard from again."

"Do you think he was killed? Like Caleb?" If he'd been at Caoin House when Eli arrived, he would likely have been killed, too.

Winona stopped her work. The knife blade rested on the cutting board. "I don't know. I hope he made it north and began a new life." She took the photograph from me and held it. "His features were white. His hair was straight. If he made it away from the South, he could have passed."

"For white?"

"Yes. A few were able to pass. Maybe he was one of the lucky ones, but I suspect his bones are somewhere in the swamp south of Caoin House. Folks around here don't care for mixed-blood boys getting out of line." She stared without blinking. "You know that well, don't you?"

"I do." I held the shirt out to her. "Can you get this stain out?" I asked.

She returned the photograph and took the shirt. "It's only champagne. Bleach will remove it." She shook the shirt out, eyeing the missing button and the bloodstain. "This shirt is ruined." She examined it more closely. "How did you come by Mr. Carlton's shirt?"

"I, uh, found it." I struggled to keep my face calm and my voice steady. "How do you know it's Carlton's?"

"Sometimes when he stays for the weekend, I launder his clothes. His shirts are made from a special cotton they grow in Egypt. I take extra care with his clothes. Mr. Brett isn't so fussy, but Mr. Carlton likes everything just so."

"Thank you, Winona. If Reginald and Framon return, please tell them I'm waiting in the library." When I walked away, I kept my posture straight, even though I felt unsteady. Winona's innocent words had shattered my world.

When I reached the library, I closed the door and leaned against it.

CHAPTER
THIRTY-SEVEN

I had to take action, and quickly. I put the shirt, photograph, and *The Book of Beloved* away, tidying the library to hide all traces of what I'd discovered. I used the simple chores to keep my panic at bay. I prayed that Framon and Reginald would return before Carlton did.

When everything had been put back in place, I took the key to Carlton's car. I would drive to town and speak with Isabelle. Now that I feared Carlton was behind Robert's murder and very likely my uncle's abduction, Isabelle was the only person who might be able to help me figure out where Uncle Brett was being held. Isabelle knew Carlton and the men who ran the city.

I'd opened the front door when Travis and Carlton braked at the front of the house. The lawyer was out of the car before it came to a full stop. He charged up the stairs, striding over the place Robert had been pushed to his death—and I had no doubt now that Carlton had pushed Robert to his death—without even looking down. I had no time to linger and ponder Carlton's cruelty or his reasons.

I dashed to the parlor and hid in the lush velvet draperies that puddled at the windows. Carlton charged through the front door.

"Raissa! Where are you?" Without waiting for an answer, he ran toward Reginald's empty room.

The minute he was out of sight, I slipped out the door. Travis slowly pulled the car away from the house, and I jumped on the running board. "Drive," I said, cowering down so that the vehicle blocked me from the view of the house.

"Miss Raissa." Travis depressed the clutch, and the car began to slow.

"Drive, Travis. Away from the house. To your cottage. Please!"

The car shot down the drive. After he'd turned down the path that curved away from the main drive and led to his cottage, he slowed to a stop.

"What's wrong?" he asked.

"Where did you look for Uncle Brett?"

"We searched the ground where the wreck happened, but we couldn't find any tracks except for a place where it looked as if a body had been dragged toward the road. Maybe put in a car. We looked around the docks in Mobile, where Mr. Brett's boats are located. We got some of the stevedores to help search, but we couldn't turn up a thing. The sheriff said he'd spoken with all of the men involved in the lynching, and none of them knew anything about Brett's accident. They all have alibis for their time."

"Did you go to Carlton's law office?"

Travis frowned. "No. Why would we?"

"Did you see Isabelle?"

"Mr. Carlton stopped by, and she came to the curb. She's sick with worry. News of the wreck and Mr. Brett's disappearance is all over the city."

"I need the vehicle," I said, jumping down and walking to the driver's side. I still had Carlton's key, which meant he didn't have access to a vehicle, except Travis's, which I meant to take. That would slow Carlton down.

"What's wrong, Miss Raissa?"

"I'm relying on you to pretend nothing is wrong, but Carlton is behind Brett's abduction."

His face reflected horror, then doubt, and finally outrage. "Why?"

"I don't know. He wants to marry me. I'm Uncle Brett's only heir. I don't know if he means to kill Brett or simply ingratiate himself with me by abducting my uncle and then somehow saving him."

"Maybe I should beat the answer out of him." Travis flexed his hands on the wheel.

"No. Act as if you know nothing. Brett's life depends on it. Now give me the car. If anyone asks, just say you left the key in it and some-one took it—you assumed one of the searchers."

"Where are you going?" Travis was rightly suspicious. "Mr. Brett would never forgive me if I let you get hurt."

"Carlton is stranded here at Caoin House." I held up the key to his car. "Keep this just in case you really need it, but do not give it to Carlton."

He nodded as he pocketed the key. "Where are you going?"

"To speak with Isabelle." She might be the one person who could help. "I'll be safe. I promise. Keep Carlton here and in your sights."

"And if I have to use force?"

"Do whatever is necessary." I signaled him out of the car. I slid behind the wheel and took a moment to study the way the car oper-ated. I'd only driven the car Brett had wrecked, but I had no choice but to learn quickly.

The car bucked a bit as I set off, but by the time I was on the main road, I'd learned to operate it. I was headed south toward Mobile, and what I hoped would be the answer to my uncle's location. I had no way to warn Reginald and Framon about Carlton's deceit. I had to trust that the two men would guard their tongues.

As the now-familiar scenery of pecan orchards, groves of oaks, and the darker forests of pine flashed by me, I finally had a moment to think. I couldn't be certain of Carlton's motives, but I had suspicions. Carlton killed Robert because I'd shown an interest in him. Carlton's plan all along had been to woo me. Robert was an unexpected inconvenience and therefore had to be dispatched. The shorts set, the typewriter, the support to become a writer and independent person were all part of Carlton's plan. He'd calculated every step, even the séance in New Orleans. I don't know what he'd hoped to accomplish, but Reginald had become an unexpected impediment, too.

I had no doubt that the men who struck him in the head presumed that he was dead or so close to it that he would die before help arrived. Carlton had orchestrated sending Uncle Brett and Reginald alone. He'd made sure I was safe in his company. If Uncle Brett had been killed, Carlton would have been the hero who stepped in to help me with the burden of Caoin House and Uncle Brett's estate. However the accident played out, he would be the person who saved the day. He would be my hero, my white knight.

The idea sickened me.

I passed the site of the wreck. Uncle Brett's car remained on its side. I wanted to get out and look around, but I didn't dare waste the time. I had to get to Isabelle and hope she could tell me a place of special significance to Carlton. One that was isolated. I drove as fast as I dared.

Mobile was a changed place. Gone were the indolent mothers pushing prams around Bienville Square. The docks were busy, but a hush had fallen over the rest of the small city. I couldn't say if it was John Henry Marcum's murder or my uncle's disappearance, but the sunny ease of a normal summer day had vanished. The park was empty, and so were most of the streets. It was almost as if the city held its breath, waiting for something to happen.

I drove to Isabelle's house, but I parked several blocks away at the end of an abandoned alley so that the car was hidden. When I hurried down the sidewalk, I had the sense I was being watched, but whether by the living or the dead, I couldn't say.

Isabelle's door knocker hammered loudly, and when she opened the door, more than a little surprised, I pushed past her into the house. "I don't want to be seen," I said.

"Why ever not?" She grabbed my upper arm. "What's wrong? Is there news about Brett?"

"No, he's still missing. No word."

"Why isn't Carlton with you? Surely he didn't send you to town by yourself."

"No, he didn't send me anywhere." I had to break the news to her in a way that allowed her to accept it. "I think Brett is alive, but Carlton is handling all the details. He's excluded me."

"He's trying to protect you. Don't be so touchy about these things. Carlton believes in equal rights for women—I assure you."

"How do you know?" What I really wanted to ask was how anyone truly knew the heart of another.

"He's spoken up for women many times." She frowned. "Come and sit down. I'll get Mara to make some coffee or tea."

I shook my head. "Does Carlton own any property, like a hunting club? Something away from downtown?"

She moved me to the parlor and almost pushed me into a chair. "Why are you asking these questions?"

"Please, Isabelle. It's important. Brett's life may hang in the balance."

"Carlton has some property in the south part of the county, about ten miles from here."

"Have you ever been there? Can you draw a map?"

"There's a hunting cabin. I've been there once or twice, for breakfasts or parties. I can draw directions, but I want to know why."

"Brett may be there." I had to get word to Reginald and Framon. They would be able to find Brett if he was a prisoner in the cabin. "Is there anyone you trust to take a message to Travis?"

"Yes. Carlton has an assistant—"

"No!"

"Raissa, what's wrong with you? You're acting . . . unhinged."

I had to win Isabelle's help. "You've known Carlton a long time."

"I have, and I don't like what you're implying about him. He would never harm Brett. He's helped your uncle since Brett first moved to Caoin House. It was Carlton who mentioned that Caoin House was for sale to Brett. They've been inseparable."

I had no solid evidence and no time. "My uncle's life is in danger. I know you love him. Do this for Brett. If I'm wrong, I will do everything in my power to make it up to you and Carlton. Now I can't trust him. I need to send word to Travis where we're going. Reginald and Framon, Winona's son, can meet us. No one else can know. If you have any regard for Brett's life, please listen to me."

Isabelle read the anguish on my face and put her arms around me. "Okay, I'll trust you. I can get Rolley Mose to take a note to Travis or Framon, whomever he sees first. Rolley can't read, so there's no danger he'll interfere."

"Thank you. How do we find Rolley?"

"He makes deliveries for Littleton's Grocery. I'll drive there and loan him my car so he can make the journey. He can drop me back here on his way. You stay here. I'll get Mara to make some iced tea for you. You look like you're about to drop."

"Thank you, Isabelle." She was going against a longtime friend on my say-so. And because she loved my uncle.

"Stay here. I'll return as soon as I can." She picked up her purse and ran toward the back of the house where her car was parked.

I took a seat on a wing chair that faced the front window. From this vantage point, I could watch the traffic on Saint Francis Street. I would see Isabelle when she returned, and I would be ready for the drive to Carlton's secluded cabin, where I hoped my uncle was being held hostage.

Isabelle's housekeeper, Mara, brought a tray with a tall glass of iced sweet tea and a plate of lemon confections. Mara was a grandmotherly woman with a serene face and an easy smile. I thanked her and drank thirstily. She was almost out of the room when I thought to ask her, "Mara, do you know Carlton McKay?"

"Of course," she said. Her smile was genuine. "He's such a gentleman."

"Yes. He is."

"I hear he's sweet on you."

"Why has he never married?"

Her smile dimmed. "It's a sad story, Mrs. James. Such a shame for a man as good as Mr. McKay to live alone. He was scarred as a young man. Marked by tragedy."

"Sit for a moment," I urged her. "Help me pass the time until Isabelle returns, please." I waited until she was settled on the edge of a chair. "I always felt there was great sadness in Carlton's life, but he never talks about it. Men are so . . . stoic."

"Oh, he'd never let on about the pain he's been through. Men like him, they don't. His brother's death changed him. He was still in school when his brother drowned in the Black Warrior River up at Tuscaloosa. Mr. Carlton was never the same. Took the joy right out of his life."

"How terrible. Were Carlton and his brother close?"

Mara went to a hunt board and pulled open the big center drawer. She returned with a large photo album. "Carlton and Craig were like peas in a pod. There are some photos of Miss Isabelle and Carlton as young people." She offered the album to me.

"Thank you, Mara." I put my tea on a coaster and set the book on my lap. The first photos were of Isabelle and Uncle Brett at various social functions. The glossy black-and-whites portrayed them both as movie-star types in gowns and tuxedos. Seeing Uncle Brett with his dark, unruly hair, holding Isabelle in a dip, made me miss him with a bolt of intensity. He had to be okay. He had to return to me safe and sound.

I flipped the page, studying the sneak view of Isabelle's social life. Her work with charitable organizations, a few pictures taken at hen parties. There were also photos of happy gatherings with Pretta, Hubert, Dr. and Mrs. Martin, Carlton, and others. In each photo, Isabelle was stunning, as she was in real life.

At last I found photos of Isabelle's family, and older photographs of her when she was a young socialite. Carlton was easy to spot. He'd hardly changed.

When I flipped the page and saw a beach gathering, my breath caught. Beside Carlton was a young man who looked identical to the photo of Tom the slave in *The Book of Beloved*. I took the photo album closer to the window so I could study the picture more closely.

There was no doubt. The young man in the shade of a big umbrella on the sand could be the same person in *The Book of Beloved*. "Who is this?" I asked Mara.

"That's poor dead Mr. Craig," she said.

"Why did Carlton feel guilty about Craig's death?"

"He blamed himself, because he was supposed to be on the river expedition with all the young people."

"Why wasn't he?" I fought to keep my voice level.

"Oh, he was with that pretty young girl, Veronica Cartwright. That's her right there." She pointed to a beautiful blonde girl who sat across from Carlton, her gaze locked on him. "They were to marry, and instead of going to the river with Craig and their friends, Mr. Carlton went home with Miss Veronica to ask her father for permission to marry her."

"And Craig drowned while Carlton was away courting."

"And then Miss Veronica fell off while riding her horse. Broke her neck on the spot. After that, Mr. Carlton never let anyone get close to him. He's led a solitary life since, and that's a shame. Such a nice, handsome man living all alone."

Such a nice, handsome man who blazed a trail of tragedy everywhere he went, was what I wanted to say, but I didn't. I had only suspicions against Carlton, and a photograph that told a story that would ruin the McKay family in Mobile.

Carlton's grandfather was a slave. A black man. The lynching of John Henry Marcum told me what happened to a person of Negro descent who took the name of a white man.

"Miss Raissa, are you okay?" Mara leaned forward and touched my hand. "You're cold as ice."

"I'm fine." I closed the photo album. "Thank you for all your help." I rose and put the book back in the drawer of the hunt board. When I looked out the window, Isabelle was getting out of her car. The young man behind the wheel sped away from the curb.

"Isabelle is back. We'll return in several hours. If we don't . . ." Who would Mara contact if we didn't return? "Call Miss Pretta at the candy shop and tell her I asked her to get in touch with Travis."

Mara put a hand on my wrist. "Is something wrong?"

"Yes." It was silly to lie. "If Isabelle and I aren't back by six o'clock, call Pretta and ask her to contact Travis. He'll know what to do."

"What if Mr. Carlton calls looking for you?"

I had to trust that her love for Isabelle would override her fondness for Carlton. "Don't mention that I was here. Just say Isabelle is tending to family business in McIntosh."

"That would be a lie."

"Yes, and one that might save our necks and Uncle Brett's, too."

CHAPTER THIRTY-EIGHT

Grand Bay was a small community built around the road that led to Pascagoula, Mississippi. Isabelle explained the area as we drove as fast as the rutted road would allow toward Franklin Creek. A number of creeks and branches fed into Grand Bay and, ultimately, Mobile Bay.

"The men love the hunting camps, and most of the Mobile elite own large tracts of land." Isabelle tried hard to keep the conversation moving forward. "There's lots of game, from deer to quail, but there's a lot more than hunting goes on at these camps. The drinking and womanizing are notorious. Even though Brett is a terrific shot, I'm glad he doesn't participate in the sport."

"Me, too." I didn't care for firearms, though I wouldn't object to having one right now. "Thank goodness you know where Carlton's camp is."

"When we were younger, we would come here in the winter for parties. There wasn't a dark cloud on the horizon in those days. Now . . ." She pressed the accelerator harder. We continued in silence until we turned down a sandy path that led into a pine thicket. The ground sloped down, gradually, and the underbrush grew more thickly on either side of the car. We descended into what felt like a tropical jungle.

The unpainted house, a dark gray, blended in with the thick foliage. Isabelle stopped fifty yards from the house and killed the engine. For a moment we sat. "What will we do if someone is holding Brett hostage?" she asked.

"You knock on the front door, and I'll sneak around to the back. You can say Carlton asked you to check on Brett." I gave her a weak smile. "If there's no one there, then I'm wrong."

"I don't know what to hope for—that we find Brett and save him, or that this is a false lead and Carlton isn't involved."

I wished I could offer her the possibility that Carlton was innocent, but I knew better. Carlton was guilty of more than abducting my uncle. A lot more. Now I understood why Caoin House had been burglarized so many times. He hadn't been after the love letters between Caleb and Eva, but had been seeking something more important, *The Book of Beloved*, which contained evidence that would ruin him. The photograph of Tom the slave, were it compared with his younger brother, would have told the truth about Carlton's bloodline. The tragic events that followed Carlton led me to dark suspicions. I believed that rather than run the risk that the book might one day reappear and the secret would be freed, Carlton had killed his own brother, Craig McKay, because his resemblance to his grandfather, Tom the slave, was undeniable. The only solid piece of evidence making that link was *The Book of Beloved*.

"Carlton is a dangerous man. I believe he's killed twice now, maybe more. Robert and his brother. He won't hesitate to kill again." Carlton would do whatever was necessary to survive. "When you go to the door, be careful, Isabelle. Don't let on that—"

"That we're operating on the idea my good friend is a murderer and a kidnapper?"

"I'm sorry." And I was. More than anything I wanted Carlton to be the man he'd presented himself as.

"Be careful." I eased out the passenger door and felt a hand on my shoulder. I almost screamed, but another hand covered my mouth and pulled me against a chest like a wall.

"Reginald! Framon!" Isabelle got out of the car and ran to hug them. "Thank God you're here."

"Mose let us read the note, and then he went on to give it to Travis. Is Mr. Airlie inside?" Framon asked.

"We don't know," I said. I told them our plan, and they agreed.

Using the dense trees for cover, I slipped toward the back door with Reginald as my shadow. Framon covered Isabelle, who would employ her theatrical skills to convince whoever was in the cabin that her reason for being there was legitimate. I muttered a prayer that we would all be safe.

I'd reached the west side of the cabin when I heard her bold knock. The door opened immediately, and a gruff, male voice called out, "What are you doing here?"

"Carlton sent me to check on Brett."

"Oh yeah? He didn't say anything to me."

Isabelle laughed. "Does Carlton tell you every move he makes? How else would I know to come here? How else would I know Mr. Airlie is here? Use your noggin, man, and let me in before I have to tell Carlton you were rude to me."

"I don't like this." The door creaked open wider.

"Too damn bad," Isabelle said. "I'll check on Brett, and then I have to meet Carlton at the docks. Now move out of my way. I can't be late."

I didn't wait to hear more but pushed through the thick underbrush, ignoring the sharp thorns and limbs that tore at my skin and clothes. Reginald was right beside me, and when I looked back, he nodded once as if to say, "We can do this." At last I positioned myself so I could watch the back door. One man guarded Brett, and I hoped he was the only man on watch. I found a thick limb, solid and light enough that I could wield it. Reginald nodded again and slipped past me to maneuver to the side of the cabin. He'd enter a window and be ready to come to Isabelle's and my assistance while Framon would crash through the front door.

I climbed the back steps and turned the knob. The door opened, and I stepped into the kitchen.

Isabelle murmured to someone, a sound of comfort and relief. She'd found Brett.

I eased forward, sliding across the threshold into a larger room that held a table and chairs. The voices came from the room beyond. Praying I wouldn't hit a creaky board, I continued. When I arrived at the door, I peeked around the jamb to find Isabelle kneeling beside Brett.

"Bring me water and a cloth. Now!" Isabelle snapped at the guard. "This man needs attention." In a moment, Reginald nodded from the dark interior of a bedroom. He was inside the house, and he, too, carried a big stick.

I couldn't tell if Brett was able to communicate or not. He was sitting up, his hands tied behind the chair. That gave me hope.

The guard grumbled, but he came toward me to fetch the things Isabelle required. I was ready for him. With the limb high above my head, I waited from him to cross into the dining area. When he did, I brought the limb down on his head with all my might.

The blow should have stunned him, but it didn't. It only made him angry, and he turned to me with a roar. He took one step, and Reginald brought the limb down across his shoulders with great force. The man fell to his knees, and I swung again, the limb catching his head like a baseball.

He toppled to the floor, unconscious.

Framon and Reginald checked the rest of the cabin to be sure no one else was on the premises. I rushed to Uncle Brett's side as Isabelle untied the rope that bound him.

"Are you hurt?" Isabelle asked, kneeling at his side. "Can you speak?"

He beckoned me into his arms and hugged me close. "Quite a swing, young lady. And I see Reginald isn't dead, as I feared. Framon, you picked the perfect time to come home from Paris."

Isabelle put her arms around him and began to weep. "I was afraid you were dead," she said.

"Too mean to kill, too tough to eat," Brett said, standing and bringing her to her feet. He swayed a moment but regained his balance and refused Framon's hand.

Reginald used the rope to confine the unconscious guard, a man no one recognized. He'd be hog-tied until someone came to release him and take him to jail.

"Where is Carlton?" Uncle Brett asked.

"At Caoin House. He was behind all of it." The words rushed out.

"I know," Uncle Brett said. "There's no time to lose."

Though I thought it was a poor plan, Uncle Brett insisted that Isabelle and I drive him to Caoin House. Framon and Reginald would follow, leaving their vehicle at Travis's place and sneaking into Caoin House through the south wing.

Uncle Brett was weak but perfectly able to take command of the situation. He couldn't identify the men who'd caused the wreck, nor did he know who'd brought him to the cabin. The fact that it was Carlton's cabin told him all he needed to know.

Isabelle drove, and Uncle Brett reclined in the backseat. Pale and shaken by the incidents of the past twenty-four hours, he listened as I told him what I'd learned and what my suspicions were. To her credit, Isabelle no longer attempted to defend Carlton. Finding Brett at his cabin was the final push for her.

"So all along, Carlton was after the book of photographs of the male prostitutes," Uncle Brett said. "He could have asked me for it. I would have given it to him, if I'd known where it was. He should have known I wouldn't care about bloodlines or such foolishness."

"Carlton never trusted anyone. He couldn't imagine life without his place in society. He's done terrible things to preserve that place."

"Do you believe Caoin House is cursed?" Brett asked.

"Eli Whitehead was a terrible man. He murdered his wife, Eva, Elise, and Horace. He murdered Caleb, too, I believe. The house isn't cursed, but there are entities there who want justice."

"Perhaps we should sell the house, Raissa. My steamships will navigate all kinds of waterways. We could even go to Central or South America. We could leave all of this tragedy behind. Isabelle, would you come with us?"

"We can settle the future of Caoin House later. What are you going to do about Carlton?" Isabelle asked.

Brett sat up. We'd passed Mobile and were not far from the turn-off to Caoin House. "I will have him arrested. He murdered Robert Aultman because he viewed him as a competitor for Raissa's affections. He had me abducted and Reginald nearly killed."

"Will Sheriff Thompson actually arrest him?" I couldn't trust the lawman to do the right thing.

"He will. Carlton has friends in the power circles of Mobile, but, like it or not, I have the financial resources. If he'd married you, Raissa, and done away with me, he would have power, money, and control."

I turned away from the conversation and watched the trees whip by the car. "What is wrong with him?" I couldn't grasp Carlton's actions, his ability to plan such cruel deeds. Social standing didn't matter more than human life.

"Carlton and Eli Whitehead are much alike," Uncle Brett said. "There is something missing in their character. Their desires justify any action. There are new techniques in the treatment of mental illness. Perhaps this will be explained."

I didn't want an explanation. I wanted justice, but Carlton had been as close to a son to Uncle Brett as anyone would ever get. There was no need to grind my heel into the wound of his betrayal. "What about the ghosts?" I asked.

"Reginald is still here. Perhaps now he can truly put them to rest."

Uncle Brett was an optimist. I had to give him that. "Once Carlton is arrested, we'll plan another séance," I said.

The outline of Caoin House rose through the trees as I spoke. We were home.

Isabelle stopped short of the house, where we were still hidden from view by the trees. Uncle Brett and I got out of the car. Reginald and Framon followed our plan. We would meet at the house. Uncle Brett was steady on his feet, but I was still concerned. I offered my shoulder for support, but he stepped back.

"Raissa, excuse me for a moment." He walked around the car and leaned down to kiss Isabelle long and hard.

I should have been embarrassed, but my delight far outweighed the discomfort of being a voyeur to their passion.

"I'll have a ring tomorrow. You can either accept me as your husband or turn me down, but I won't wait any longer to ask. Will you marry me?"

"Nothing would please me more." Isabelle drew him to her for another kiss.

When they separated, Uncle Brett set out for the house, and I followed. We traveled on foot, hoping for the element of surprise. Carlton's car remained parked in front of the house, but that meant nothing since I'd given the key to Travis. We had no way of knowing if Carlton was in the house or not. Our plan was to slip inside and ascertain the circumstances. If we could take Carlton before he suspected we were onto him, it might prevent bloodshed.

Uncle Brett moved toward the south entrance with the intention of arming himself and retrieving guns for Framon and Reginald. Isabelle drove on to Caoin House, pretending that she knew nothing. She would be our diversion if Carlton was in the house. I maneuvered to the west side of Caoin House, planning on gaining access through the kitchen. If Carlton saw me, I'd hurl myself into his arms and kiss him with such passion he would be occupied until Uncle Brett apprehended him. It was a dangerous plan, but we'd been unable to devise anything safer.

As I angled through the pecan orchard, I saw Caleb, tall and athletic, in his uniform. He made no attempt to come closer or to speak to me. And I had no time. Still, I took some comfort in knowing he was at my back. He knew I was trying to right a terrible wrong.

Dashing across the open space, I made it to the side of the house and ducked low beneath the kitchen windows. The stillness that held Caoin House enthralled seemed sinister. The searchers were gone. There was no evidence of anyone alive in the house.

I peeked into the empty kitchen. Another ominous sign. Winona should have been there.

Since the room was empty, I slipped into the boot room and continued to the kitchen. The stove was hot, but nothing was cooking. Danger lurked all around me.

I heard the front-door knocker. Isabelle was right on time. She knocked again. "Raissa!" She called my name. "Raissa, are you home?"

Footsteps moved to the front door. "Miss Isabelle, no one is here. You should come back tomorrow." Winona sounded calm, but this was far from her normal behavior.

"May I come in?" Isabelle asked, even though both Brett and I had warned her not to enter the house.

"It would be best if you came back later. Mr. Brett is still missing, and everyone has gone to search for him. I'm busy in the kitchen."

"Nonsense. I'll give you a hand." I clenched my fists. Isabelle was inside the house. She'd stepped straight into danger, and there was nothing Uncle Brett or I could do to protect her.

"Has anyone heard from Carlton?" Isabelle asked. She sounded completely at ease. I could only envy her acting ability.

"No. He and my son are out searching."

"So Framon is home from Europe. I'd love to see him. I'm dry as a whistle—could I have some cold water or maybe some iced tea?"

"It would be best if you went back to Mobile, Miss Isabelle. I'll send word if we have news of Mr. Brett."

"Where's Raissa?" Isabelle walked toward the kitchen with bold assurance.

"She's out. She and Travis went to search."

So Travis was somewhere on the property still. That was good news. He would be an asset.

"I stopped by the sheriff's office, and the deputy there said they had no leads regarding Brett's disappearance. How is Reginald? Is he awake?"

Winona hesitated. "He's, uh, still unconscious."

My throat constricted. Had Carlton captured Framon and Reginald? Had he injured them? I hadn't seen Winona's car near the house, so I'd assumed the two were still following the plan, but something was definitely up with Winona. If Carlton had somehow gotten hold of Reginald and Framon, he would have hostages.

The back door creaked open, and I whirled to find Travis filling the door frame. He held two pistols. "I saw you sneaking in," he said. "Carlton's here, and he's up to something. Your uncle has rifles and guns in his suite."

"Uncle Brett is safe. He's in the south wing getting the weapons."

Travis nodded and handed me a Smith & Wesson revolver. He tucked his into the back of his trousers. "I'll see if I can talk to Carlton. If you get a shot, take it."

I'd never actually fired a pistol. I regretted not taking Travis up on the shooting lessons my uncle had offered. As if he read my mind, Travis said. "Pull the hammer back; hold it with both hands. It'll kick, so hold it out." He demonstrated. "Be sure you hit him."

"I can't kill someone." It simply wasn't something I could do.

"Then shoot his leg. Just don't miss."

He didn't give me time to disagree. He moved out of the kitchen and toward the main part of the house. "Miss Isabelle, it's good to see you, but I regret the circumstances."

Peaking around the doorjamb into the foyer, I could almost feel the waves of fear and frustration that rose off Winona.

"Invite Isabelle into the library." At the sound of Carlton's voice, everyone froze. Thank goodness Isabelle snapped out of it.

"Carlton, is there any word?" She met him and hugged him. "I'm sick with worry. I couldn't stay home a moment longer."

Travis cast a glance in my direction, but he, too, picked up his cue. "Mr. Carlton, is there anywhere I could look?"

"The searchers are out in force. The best we can do is wait."

"Is Reginald awake?" Isabelle tempted fate with her question.

"Unfortunately, no," Carlton said. He took her arm, blocking my shot. "Step into the library with me, and we'll wait together. Travis, do you think you might drive into town? I have a message for the sheriff, and it seems the phone service is out here."

I wanted to scream to her to run. To get away. If I could fire a shot and throw everyone into pandemonium, Travis could use his weapon.

"Of course." Travis shifted his weight from foot to foot.

"Come with me to the library," Carlton said.

The look of horror that swept over Winona's face told me that Carlton would soon have Isabelle and Travis as hostages if I didn't act.

I edged out of my hiding place, the gun in my hand. I pulled the hammer back. Before I could aim and take a shot, the horrific monkey-head jigger slid across the polished foyer floor and stopped at Carlton's feet.

"What the hell?" Carlton glared at the toy, then turned his attention to the empty parlor. "Who's there?" Carlton drew a revolver from the waistband of his slacks. He pointed it toward the direction the jigger had come from. "Come out now."

"Carlton, really?" Isabelle put a hand on his arm that held the gun. "We—"

He backhanded her. "Shut up."

Travis started forward, but Carlton's gun stopped him. "I don't need any of you. No one except Brett, who will tell me what I want to know."

I was ready to step forward and tell Carlton that only I knew the location of *The Book of Beloved*. That was the thing he sought. The documentation of his bloodline that he would destroy.

Before I could move an inch, though, the jigger retreated across the floor. It moved of its own volition. If Horace was at the helm, I couldn't see him.

Carlton loosened his hold on Isabelle's arm and backed away. "That thing is possessed."

The moment he was clear of Isabelle, I aimed the gun at his leg and pulled the trigger. The shot echoed in the house, deafening me. Winona and Isabelle ran. Carlton ran after them. I'd missed. After four steps, though, Carlton stumbled, unable to keep his balance. I'd missed his leg, but somehow the bullet had found his foot. He went down in a heap, a furious glare pinning me.

"Don't make another move." Travis pointed his revolver at Carlton. For a moment, Carlton considered his options, and I feared Travis would kill him on the spot. At last he dropped his weapon.

Uncle Brett, Framon, and Reginald stepped out of the parlor. Reginald reeled the jigger toward him with the fishing line he'd tied to it. His grin said it all. Framon and Uncle Brett were equally jubilant.

"Travis, I think you should get the sheriff," Uncle Brett said, taking control. "Perhaps the phone lines are up at the Gunderson house. You can try there so you don't have to drive all the way to town."

"Yes, sir," Travis said.

"And call Dr. Martin." Brett looked down at the lawyer with more pity than anger. "Carlton doesn't deserve our tender mercies, but I don't want him to bleed to death on the foyer floor."

Uncle Brett hugged Isabelle, then came to me. "An excellent job of saving the day, Raissa." He took the gun from my shaking hands. "I think Travis will have his hands full with shooting lessons in the future. I believe you have a natural talent, but it needs a bit of honing."

Because it was over, at last, I looked at Uncle Brett and burst into tears.

A week passed before Reginald and I found ourselves in the ballroom gathered around the table. Once again, we were hosting a séance. Uncle Brett and Isabelle sat side by side. The four-carat diamond on her left hand caught and refracted the candlelight. The wedding was set for October, when the crisper air would allow Uncle Brett to plan the party of all parties on the grounds of Caoin House. If tonight went as planned, the unhappy spirits of Caoin House would be set to rest. Mr. and Mrs. Brett Airlie would live in peace at Caoin House.

Joining us for the séance were Winona, Framon, and Travis. Without their help, Carlton would never have been arrested for his crimes. Uncle Brett had invited the three of them, and to my surprise, all had agreed to participate.

Reginald signaled that he was ready to start. This time there would be no tricks. None were necessary. At the far corner of the room, Caleb stood with his hand on Horace's shoulder. Beside him were Elise and Eva. There was no sign of Eli. Whatever the fate of his spirit, he was not at Caoin House. There were others, though—the drowned boy and two others, and a host of less distinct entities—and perhaps some slaves who'd never made their peace. Reginald and I intended to release them all.

Reginald explained to our ghostly audience that Carlton had been punished, and Eli Whitehead's sins had been revealed. As Reginald spoke, the darkness that surrounded Eva dissipated. Light seemed to fill her, and she pulled Elise to her side. Horace, too, joined his mother. At last, Caleb joined them. "Thank you," he whispered, and I knew it would be our last communication.

"The secrets have been revealed. The truth is known," Reginald said. "You are free to move on."

The ceremony was simple, but it was enough. Even as I watched, they disappeared.

"Are they gone?" Reginald asked.

"They are."

"Then it's time for a drink," Uncle Brett said.

We left the ballroom, traipsing down to the library, where Winona served canapés and even agreed to sip a glass of crisp white wine. When everyone was engaged, I took a glass of wine and slipped out to the front porch. The sun was setting, the end of another long summer day, and I watched the shadows gather beneath the oaks. Caleb was truly gone. I felt his absence more than I would have imagined.

Carlton had been revealed as a murderer. He'd confessed to pushing Robert Aultman off the roof to clear the way for his romantic pursuits. He'd lured him there by telling him I'd sprained my ankle and needed help. He'd also convinced Dr. Oyles to falsify the inquest report.

Carlton had known me well enough to believe I'd pursue the matter of Robert's death. And I had. I'd played into his hands, doubting Robert and myself. It had left me vulnerable to his lies and manipulations.

Behind me the door opened, and Reginald sat down beside me on the steps. He put an arm around my shoulders. "It's been quite an adventure," he said.

"A painful one," I agreed.

"Who's that coming down the drive?" Reginald asked.

I didn't recognize the car or the driver. When the young man jumped out, he held an envelope in his hand. "Special delivery for Miss Raissa James."

"That's me." I took the letter. Reginald tipped the young man, who drove away.

"There's no name or postmark." It had come by special carrier. I ripped open the letter. A single sheet unfolded in my hand.

Dear Mrs. James,

Madam Madelyn Petalungro has informed me of your extraordinary work with Mr. Reginald Proctor in the realm of spirits. In fact, I hear you've become something of a gumshoe in the realm of the dead. Pluto's snitches, I would call you. And just in time I have learned of your work in solving the mysteries of the dead.

I invite you to Montgomery, Alabama, to help me save my friend from a terrible fate. It is a story I believe you'll find fascinating, especially since I understand you are soon to be a published author, as is my husband. If you and Mr. Proctor consider coming to Montgomery for a visit, I promise you will be well rewarded for your efforts.

Camilla Granger is—or was—a delightful young woman who is soon to be married to David Simpson. Camilla's dragon of a mother is pressing for the marriage. Camilla longs for a period of independence, yet she loves David. And he loves her. So she has consented to the wedding.

David has renovated a property, Roswell House, for their home. It is a stupendous property, but something is not right there. The first time Camilla visited, our gentle friend became a frenzied assassin and attempted to cut her intended's throat. She is currently at Bryce Hospital, a mental institution, and her mother is pressing for a lobotomy.

Camilla is in desperate need of the services Madam Petalungro assures me you and Mr. Proctor can provide. Madam would come herself, but she is unwell and cannot travel. I am begging you to drop all you are engaged in and come to help my friend before it is too late. I believe a dark spirit has taken possession of my friend, and there is no help for her if you don't come.

I will provide payment, as well as room and board, while you are in Montgomery. My husband, Scott, has a keen interest in this matter and hopes to use the entire experience as a basis for one of his stories. I believe he would be helpful *in your writing career, Mrs. James. Please call Juniper 45640 with your answer. Reverse the charges, please. I await your decision. Please make haste. My friend is on the edge of losing her mind—and very possibly her life.*

The highest regards,
Zelda Sayre Fitzgerald

Reginald read the letter with an expanding grin. "She's quite the flapper," he said. "And a case of potential possession. Are we going?"

"How can we not?" I answered. It was the perfect solution, allowing Uncle Brett and Isabelle a chance to enjoy Caoin House alone. Truly alone. And Reginald and I could expand our knowledge of the dead. It was certainly an intriguing case. "Pluto's Snitch. I like that. How can we say no?"

ACKNOWLEDGMENTS

Writing is a solitary profession, but within the ranks of writers and readers, I've found my family of choice. I want to thank my wonderful friends and readers for giving the manuscript a careful vetting. When I asked for volunteers to see if the book resonated, I was overwhelmed with the generous response of dozens of volunteers who read astutely and gave me valuable input. A special thanks to Claire Matturro, Thomi Sharpe, Mahala Church, Stephanie Marks, and Rebecca Barrett. Between where I started and where I ended up, it was a long and sometimes very dark journey.

Thanks to my editors, JoVon Sotak, Bryon Quertermous, Sarah Shaw, Robin O'Dell, Jill Kramer, and the entire Amazon team. Always, many thanks to my agent, Marian Young.

A special thanks to Rick Fortenberry. Writing is a crazy business, but you help me keep it in perspective.

ABOUT THE AUTHOR

 Carolyn Haines is the *USA Today* bestselling author of more than seventy books, including the popular Sarah Booth Delaney Mississippi Delta mystery series. A native of Mississippi, Haines writes in multiple genres. She's a recipient of the 2010 Harper Lee Award for Distinguished Writing and the 2009 Richard Wright Award for Literary Excellence. She has also been honored by *Suspense Magazine* and *Romantic Times* for best mystery series. *The Book of Beloved* is the first book in her new series, Pluto's Snitch. An animal advocate, Haines founded a small 501c3 rescue, Good Fortune Farm Refuge. She cares for nine dogs, nine cats, and six horses.